Mrs de Winter

SUSAN HILL

Mrs de Winter

SINCLAIR-STEVENSON

First published in Great Britain in 1993
by Sinclair-Stevenson
an imprint of Reed Consumer Books Ltd
Michelin House, 81 Fulham Road, London SW3 6RB
and Auckland, Melbourne, Singapore and Toronto

Reprinted 1993

A CIP catalogue record for this book
is available at the British Library
ISBN 1 85619 330 6

Typeset by Falcon Graphic Art Ltd
Wallington, Surrey
Printed in England by Clays Ltd, St Ives plc

Part One

CHAPTER

One

The undertaker's men were like crows, stiff and black, and the cars were black, lined up beside the path that led to the church; and we, we too were black, as we stood in our pathetic, awkward group waiting for them to lift out the coffin and shoulder it, and for the clergyman to arrange himself; and he was another black crow, in his long cloak.

And then the real crows rose suddenly from the trees and from the fields, whirled up like scraps of blackened paper from a bonfire, and circled, caw-caw-ing above our heads. I should have found it an eerie, melancholy sound on such a day. But I did not, their cry brought a lift of joy to my heart, as the cry of the owl the previous night and the distant rawk of the seagulls at dawn had done, and the tears rose up at the same time to choke me. It is real, I said. It is now. We are here. Home.

Now, looking up, I saw the coffin. Remembered.

But the coffin was not black, that dreadful shape was pale – plain, pale oak, and the handles and ornate corners glinted as the sun caught them, and the flowers they were placing on

3

top of it now were golden, a great cross of chrysanthemums, all the colours of the afternoon light and of the October countryside around us, bronze and copper and lemon and greenish white, but most of all, that incomparable gold. The day was gold too, the day was not black. It was a perfect day. In the hanger that lay along the rise, the beeches were on fire, they flashed orange, and the sycamores were crimson, though the oaks were only just turning and still showed green at the heart.

There were dark yews beside the lychgate, tall obelisks. But above them, a walnut, quite bare, spread out its elaborate, delicate tracery of branches. This place, to which I had scarcely been, was in a mild, sheltered dip of the wider, bleaker landscape; the high moors, the crags and cliffs and open sea, were far away. Here, we were near to the soft blur of woods that sloped down to the hidden river.

Even without turning my head, and being careful not to gaze and gawp about me in a way that would have been unseemly, I noticed so much, so many different trees, and tried to name them all, for these were the very things I had thought of and dreamed about and remembered, in such detail, almost every day for so many years, these were the secret recollections that I had kept close to me, the inexpressible comforts. Trees such as these, places, days such as this. Ash, elm, chestnut, lime. Ilex. The sturdy, stubbly little hedgerows studded about with blood red berries, like currants in a cake.

Then, I remembered how the bracken would be now, what a glorious mesh of gold and exactly how the fronds would curl. I imagined it brushing against my legs and against the silken bodies of the dogs as we walked, heard in my head the dry swish and rustle it made and the cracking of the twigs underfoot. The thought almost made me faint, I was overcome again by one of the great surges of emotion that had been rising within me, disorientating and confusing me, for the past week, ever since the call had come, and most of all, overwhelmingly, since the previous night. I did not know how to deal with them or control them, they were so unfamiliar, it was so long since I had experienced any such feelings. We had been so careful to live an even, steady, unemotional life, we who had been through such storms and at the mercy of so many battering emotions, and then thrown up on that calm, dull, distant shore at last, so relieved, so grateful. After that, what emotions we experienced had been sure and steady and deep, like some underground river which flowed through us, and upon whose strength we could utterly rely, which never varied its pace, and never pitched us to and fro, did not let us down, but above all, had no control over us.

But now, I was no longer calm or strong, now I was at the mercy of these new feelings, this great wave that had gathered pace and force until this morning it had overwhelmed me, knocking the breath out of my body, scattering my wits; the feelings I knew on returning home, on being here again, in this English countryside, after the years of exile. I gripped my fingers together tightly in the palms of my hands, felt the bones hard inside the black gloves.

On the slope that rose behind the church, they were ploughing, turning the last of the earth over to a deep, ruddy brown. I could see the tractor chugging along its slow, careful furrow, and the man who sat on it turn his body to look back, and the birds, like a cloud of gnats streaming behind.

It was October. But the sun shone and it was warm on our faces, and the light lay so beautifully upon the land, I wanted to turn towards it, not to shelter from it and shade my eyes, as I had grown used to doing against that other, harsh, bright sun under which we had been living. This was the sun I would have embraced, not shrunk from, this the light I had so longed for, so missed and so often, often remembered.

The crows caw-cawed again, and then, abruptly, fell down, plummeting into the trees, and were still, the blue sky was empty.

The men had shouldered the coffin, and were turning, and we turned and arranged ourselves, took our places behind them. Beside me, Maxim held himself stiffly, and when we shuffled off, moved oddly, jerkily, as if he were a jointed thing, made of wood. His shoulder was as close to mine as it could be without quite brushing against me, and I looked at him and saw the muscles taut around his mouth and the fine lines at the corners of his eyes, saw that he was deathly white; and I was a thousand miles away and could not reach him, he had gone from me into the past and into his own, private, closed up world, the one he had re-entered the day the news had come to us and into which I could never follow him.

I wondered if he remembered that other slow, terrible walk behind a coffin, that last funeral. I did not know. It is a mistake to believe that we can always share another's thoughts, however close they may be to us, however much we may feel that we are a part of their innermost selves. We are not. For twelve years, in so many ways we had been as one, everything had been shared, there had been no secrets.

Yet the past still held secrets, the past threw its shadows, and the shadows sometimes separated us.

I looked away from him, and up and around me, and it came again, that wild surge of emotion, and the sense of unreality too, so that once more, I was made giddy and had to grip myself. This could not be, I was not here. Surely we could not have come back.

We had come back, and it was as though I had been starving for years and suddenly set down at a banquet, a table laid with the most succulent and tempting of foods: or else parched, desiccated with thirst, and having had only rust and sand and ashes in my mouth, and was lying now, level with a cold, clear stream and able to cup the water into my hands and lift it to my face and drink, drink. I was greedy and I fed, thirsty and I drank, I had been blind and now I saw.

I could not take in enough or ever have my fill of what was around me, the fields, slopes, hedges, trees, the rise of the ground ahead, the ploughed earth, the hanger of golden trees, the smell of the soil and the rustle of the late leaves, the sense of the distant sea; the narrow lanes, the small houses, the distant sound of shooting, the bark of a dog at a cottage gate as we passed in our grave procession; threads of blue smoke coiling out of chimneys, into the golden, sunlit air. A man on horseback, the great, gleaming rump of the mare rounded like a chestnut. The man had slowed for us, then stopped and taken off his hat as the cortège crept by and I had peered at him from the car window, half smiled, but he had sat at attention and not glanced at me. I wondered if he had been a friend, a neighbour, had turned to Maxim to ask.

But Maxim had not seen, I thought he was quite unaware of me, or of the day, the point we had reached on our journey, of the rider standing there. Maxim stared ahead, seeing, or else trying desperately not to see, other places, other scenes. But I could no more have stopped myself from looking about me, and drowning in everything I saw, than I could have caused my own heart not to beat. However tragic the reason for our being here, I could still only be glad, light headed with joy at the beauty, the glory of this world outside the black car's window, only weak with disbelief and gratitude – though my joy made me guilty, too, and I must keep it to me, and could not have admitted it, to him, to anyone.

The previous night, sleeping fitfully, uneasily, in the strange, cold bed, my mind and body still unsettled by the discomfort and tedium of the journey we had made, I had woken out of some confused, troubled half dream of train wheels and flat, grey, dull French fields, to perfect stillness, perfect silence, and for a few seconds, been bewildered, uncertain where I was or why. Then, at the moment I had remembered, I had felt that first shock of excitement and happiness. To be here, to be in England, after the years of exile and homesickness and longing – the joy of it had blotted out all other reality.

The room had been filled with a wonderful soft moonlight, it touched the white painted dressing table, gave a sheen to the pale walls, lay across the surface of the mirror and the glass of a picture and the silver backs of my brushes, and turned them to water. I had gone quietly across the room, afraid to make any sound that would awaken him, fearing even to glance at the long hunched shape, folded into itself like a foetus in the bed, knowing how exhausted he had been, drained by the physical and emotional turmoil, and that he needed the refuge of sleep. I had packed for us so quickly, uncertain which clothes to bring – for there were no servants to see to these things now, everything fell to me – and had to riffle for a few minutes through my case until I felt the soft cotton of my dressing gown against my fingers.

Then, wrapping it around me, I went back to the window-seat and pulled the curtain open a little. Maxim had not been disturbed and after another moment I had unlatched the window and slid it open.

To me, then, looking out over it, that garden was a magic place, a scene from some fairy-tale and I sitting at the casement. What I saw was a landscape of such tremulous beauty, such wonder, and as I looked, I knew, as one sometimes can know absolutely, that I should never forget these moments, whatever happened in the rest of our lives, they would be memories I should feed off, as I fed sometimes, secretly, off memories of the view of the rose garden, from our old window at Manderley.

There was a great round holly tree in the centre of the lawn, that cast its shadow in perfect circle, like a dropped skirt on the pale grass; through a gap in the yew hedge at the far end, I could see the silver coin of the pond in its hollow stone basin. The last of the dahlia and chrysanthemum heads hung stiff and black, but their stalks were brushed by the moonlight, and the slates of the old lean-to roof gleamed silver grey. Beyond the garden, the orchard, hung with the last few apples, silver here and there among the dark branches, and beyond the orchard, the paddock, rising slightly, and in the paddock two of the horses, the greys, stood, pale as ghosts.

I looked and looked and thought I could never have my fill, and as I looked, some lines came into my head, poetry I supposed I must have learned as a school child, and had never thought of again until now.

> Slowly, silently now, the moon
> Walks the night in her silver shoon.
> This way and that she peers and sees
> Silver fruit upon silver trees.

But I could not remember any more.

It was not only the sight of the garden that so moved, so deeply pleased and satisfied me; the smell of the night air, coming through the open window, was indescribably sweet, quite unlike the hot, heady smell of the night air we had grown used to in what I now automatically thought of as our exile. That had been sometimes exotic, often intoxicating, stifling, occasionally foetid. But always strange, foreign. This night smell was that of my childhood and my growing up, it smelled of home. I smelled the cold, and the frost touched grass, and tree bark, a faint smokiness, smelled turned earth, and damp iron, clay and bracken and horse, I smelled all of these, and yet none of them precisely, I smelled the garden and the countryside that lay beyond and all around it, in the air of an October night, under the riding moon.

It had been late and quite dark when we had arrived the previous evening. We had eaten dinner without tasting the food on our plates, as we had eaten all the lumpen, dreary meals on the journey, and we had felt stunned, exhausted with the disorientation of travel, and grimy and uncomfortable in our clothes. My face had felt stiff, my mouth seemed difficult to move, and my tongue somehow peculiarly swollen. I had looked down the table and seen that Maxim's skin was transparent, and that there were smears of tiredness beneath his eyes, and the eyes themselves were dulled. He had smiled slightly, wearily, wanting reassurance, and I had tried to send it to him, for all he seemed by now quite distant from me, and oddly unfamiliar, as I remembered him seeming long ago, during that other time.

The coffee had tasted queer, bitter and muddy, the dining room was cold, and too barely lit by an overhead fitting. I had noticed that there was a tear in the ugly yellow parchment of one of its shades, and that the beautiful furniture had a bloom to its surfaces, the carpet was slightly stained. Everything seemed to lack love, lack care. We had struggled to pick over the meal and had said very little once we had come upstairs, only murmured this and that, nothing of consequence, remarks about the journey, the dreary, tedious miles across a sad, grey Europe. We had endured it, staring out of the windows of the train, seeing such ugliness and damage everywhere, so much dereliction, and so many sad, sallow faces, staring without animation at ours as the heavy train passed. Once, I had waved at a little file of children, waiting at a crossing, somewhere in the central plain of France. None of them had waved back – perhaps because they had not even seen me – they had only stared too. But because of my tiredness and emotion, the anxiety like a sickness in the pit of my stomach, after the shock and sudden upheaval, I had felt oddly rebuffed and saddened by the incident, so that I had

11

begun to brood upon other things and been unable to redirect my thoughts.

Now though, looking steadily out over the moonlit garden, I was quite calm, quite steady. I sat on and on, and somewhere in the depths of the house heard a clock strike three, and was still wide awake and only glad to be so, grateful for the tranquillity around me, and the coolness of that silent garden, the sweetness of the air. I knew, even though I was ashamed of it, deep contentment, great peace.

I had not moved for almost another hour, not until Maxim turned suddenly, flailing his arms about abruptly and muttering something incoherent, and then I had closed the window against the chill that had crept into the room, and slipped back to my bed. Though first I had straightened the covers around him and smoothed his face, settled him as one would settle a restless child.

He did not wake, and just before dawn, I too, had slept.

In the morning, the instant I awoke, it was the light I was so aware of, how very different it was and how welcome and familiar. I had gone again to the window and looked out at the pale sky, blue slightly filmed over, and the dawn that was strengthening over the frost touched garden. I could have been nowhere else in the world but here and I had almost wept then at that early light, at its clarity and subtlety and softness.

As we had set off for the church there had been skeins of mist weaving in and out of the trees, dissolved by the sun even as we watched, as the frost was melted by it, and I had instinctively looked over to where I knew that, miles away, the sea lay. When we had arrived at Dover on the previous evening it had already been dark, and coming across the channel the sea had simply been dull, grey and heaving about outside the ship's windows, so that in a curious way, I had no real sense of its being the sea at all: and then the car had sped us away, and on to the long road.

In spite of all that it had meant to us for ill, all the harm it had caused, I had missed the sea while we had been abroad, missed the slow drag of it up the beach, the hiss and suck over the pebbles, the crash of it, smacking down on to the shore of the cove – the fact that it was always there, sensed even through the densest fog that muffled every sound, and that whenever I wanted to I had been able to go down and simply look at it, watch its movement, the play of the light upon it, see it change, the shadows shift, the surface roughen. I had often dreamed of it, dreamed that I had gone there at night when it was calm and still and gazed from some place above down upon the moonlit water. The sea we had lived close to and walked beside at times during our exile was a tideless, glittering sea, translucent, brilliantly blue, violet, emerald green, a seductive, painted sea, quite unreal.

Climbing into the black car that morning, I had paused, turned and strained my eyes and ears, willing myself to have some greater sense of it. But there was nothing, it was too far away, and even if it had been there, at the end of the garden, Maxim would have shrunk from any awareness of it.

I had turned and climbed into the car beside him.

The men in black had reached the church porch and paused there to shift their burden slightly, settling its weight between them. We stood uncertainly behind, and suddenly a robin flitted into the dark hollow of the porch and out again, and the sight of it lifted my heart. I felt that we were people in a play, waiting in the wings to go on to a stage, the lighted open space ahead of us. We were very few. But as we began to move under the arch I saw that the church itself was full. They rose as they heard us. I supposed they were all old neighbours, old friends – though I did not think that by now I would recognise many of them.

'I am the Resurrection and the Life saith the Lord. Whosoever believeth in me, though he should die, yet shall he live . . .'

We stepped inside and the heavy wooden door was closed behind us, shutting out the autumn day, the sunlight and the turned fields, the man ploughing and the larks spiralling upwards and the robin singing from the holly branch, the ragged, black crows.

The congregation stirred like standing corn as we passed on our way to the front pew, I felt their eyes burning into our backs, felt their curiosity and fascination with us, and all the unspoken questions, hanging in the air.

The church was beautiful, and the beauty of it made me catch my breath. I had never let myself think very much of how I missed such places as this. It was an ordinary, unremarkable English country church and yet to me, as rare and precious as the greatest cathedral. Sometimes I had slipped into a church in some foreign village or town, and knelt in the darkness among the black-shawled old women mumbling over their beads, and the smell of incense and guttering candles had been as strange as everything else to me, they had seemed to belong to some exotic religion, far removed from the austere stone church of home. I had needed to be there, and valued the quietness and the atmosphere of reverence, been half attracted, half repelled by the statues, the confessional boxes. I had never managed to put any prayer into words, never formed actual phrases, either on my lips or in my mind, of confession or petition. Only a sort of incoherent but immensely powerful emotion had sometimes surged up, as though forced by some pressure deep within me, and it had come close to the surface without ever erupting. It could never be properly expressed, and I supposed it was like a desperate touching of wood, for . . . For what? Our protection? Salvation? Or merely that we should continue to be left alone in our safe, dull haven for the rest of our lives, untroubled by ghosts.

I dared not admit to myself how much I had missed and longed for an English church, but sometimes in reading and re-reading the newspapers, when they managed to reach us from home, I came upon the public notices for the services on the following Sunday, and reading slowly down them the words filled me with great longing. Sung Eucharist. Mattins, Choral Evensong. Stanford in C. Darke in E. Byrd. Boyce. Lead Kindly Light (Stainer). Thou wilt keep him . . . Like as the Hart . . .

Preacher. The Dean . . . the Precentor . . . the Bishop.

I had spoken the words silently to myself.

Glancing surreptitiously to either side of us now, and then up to the altar ahead, I saw the grey stone arches and ledges and steps, and the austerely carved memorial tablets to local squires long dead, and the Biblical texts lettered in the clear windows.

Come to me all ye that are heavy laden.

I am the vine, ye are the branches.

Blessed are the peacemakers.

I read the grave, measured words as our steps fell, like the steps of soldiers treading the dead march, down the stone flagged aisle to where the trestles stood. There were flowers, golden and white as the sun and stars, in great jugs and urns on the table beside the font. I had thought that we were shut in from the countryside beyond the church, but we were not. The sun came striking through the side windows, on to the wood of the pews and the pale stone, the beautiful, limpid English autumn sunlight that filled me with such joy and recollection and sense of homecoming, it fell on the backs of heads and of raised prayer books, set the silver cross momentarily on fire, fell softly, gently, on to the plain, good oak of Beatrice's coffin as the men set it down.

CHAPTER

Two

Maxim had brought out the letter. He had left me sitting at our usual table overlooking the little square of which we had grown so fond, and gone back to the hotel for cigarettes.

It was not so warm, I remember, clouds kept slipping in front of the sun and a sudden gust of wind had rushed down one of the narrow side alleys between the high houses, swirling a few scraps of paper and leaves. I had pulled my jacket up round my shoulders. The summer was over. Perhaps, later this afternoon, we would have one of the storms which had begun to break up the weather in the past week. The clouds came again, and the square was in shadow, featureless, oddly melancholy. Some small dark haired children were playing in a bowl of mud they had made among the cobbles, stirring it with sticks, fetching more dust in little wooden ice cream scoops, their voices, bright as birds, chattered across towards me. I always did watch them, always listened and smiled. I tried not to let children upset me.

The waiter passed by and half glanced at my empty cup but I shook my head. I would wait for Maxim. Then, the church bell began to sound the hour, a thin, high, tinny note, and the sun came flooding out again, sharpening the edges of the long shadows, warming me, lifting my mood. The small boys all clapped and let out a cheer at something that delighted them, in their mud. Then, I looked up and saw him coming towards me, his shoulders hunched, his face the mask behind which he always, automatically, tried to hide any distress. He was holding a letter, and as he sat down in the flimsy, metal café chair he threw it on to the table, before swinging round and snapping his fingers to the waiter in a way he so rarely did now, the old, arrogant way.

I did not recognise the handwriting at all. But I saw the postmark and put out my hand to cover his.

It was from Giles. Maxim did not look at me as I read quickly through it. '. . . found her on the floor in the bedroom . . . heard a heavy thump . . . managed to get her up . . . Maidment came . . . some movement back in the left side almost at once . . . speech poor but clearing a bit . . . she knows me all right . . . nursing home and medical people don't say much . . . awful . . . live in hope . . .' I glanced back at the envelope. It was dated three weeks before. Our mail took so wretchedly long sometimes, communications seem to have deteriorated since the end of the war.

I said, 'She's sure to be much better, Maxim. Perhaps even recovered completely. We would have heard by now otherwise.'

He shrugged, lit a cigarette. 'Poor Bea. She won't be able to bray across four counties. No hunting for her.'

'Well if they make her give it up altogether that will be nothing but a good thing. I never think it can be sensible for a woman turned sixty.'

'She has held everything together. I've been no use to her. She doesn't deserve this.' He got up abruptly. 'Come on,' took out some coins and dropped them on the table, and began to walk away across the square. I looked back to smile apologetically at the waiter, but he was inside, talking to someone, his back to us. I don't know why it had seemed to matter, to make some slight contact with him. I stumbled, almost slipping over on the cobbles, to catch Maxim up. In their huddle, squatting, the little boys bent their heads close together and were quiet.

He was walking out towards the path that ran around the lake.

'Maxim . . .' I reached him, touched his arm. The wind blew, rippling the water. 'She will be all right now . . . fine . . . I'm sure of it. We can try and telephone Giles this evening can't we? But we would have heard . . . he wanted to let you know, and it's wretched that the letter was so delayed . . . he might even have written again, though you know he isn't one for letters, they neither of them are.'

It was true. For all these years, we had received occasional, short, dutiful letters in Beatrice's enormous, girl like hand, telling us very little, mentioning neighbours sometimes, trips to London, the war, the blackout, the evacuees, the shortages, the hens, the horses, and carefully, tactfully, nothing of very personal importance, family matters, the past. We might have been distant cousins, long out of touch. Because we had moved about, and then come here, after the war, the letters had often been addressed to a poste restante, and for a long time had come only once or twice a year and been hopelessly delayed. I was the one who replied, in the same, cautious, stilted fashion, my own handwriting as unformed as Beatrice's, ashamed of the triviality of our little bits of news. As Beatrice simply never referred to them, I had no idea at all whether they arrived.

'Please don't look so worried. I know a stroke is a dreadful thing and it will have been so frustrating for her, she longs to be active, can't bear to sit still, stay indoors. She won't have changed.' I saw the flicker of a smile flit across his mouth, knew that he was remembering. 'But plenty of people have strokes, quite minor ones, and recover completely.'

We were standing watching the empty, steely water that lay, ringed around by trees, and the gravelled path. I heard myself chattering pointlessly on, trying to reassure him. Not doing so. For of course it was not only of Beatrice that he was thinking. The letter, the postmark, Giles's handwriting, the address at the top of the paper, all of it, as ever, dragged his mind back, obliged him to remember. I had wished to spare him all of it, but it would have been wrong, I knew, to hide the letters, even could I have done so successfully, it would have been a deceit and we had no deceits, or none that counted, and besides, I would not have had us pretend that he had no sister, no family anywhere but me.

It was Beatrice who had handled all the affairs from the day we left, signed things, taken decisions, Beatrice and, for the first year or two, Frank Crawley. Maxim had not wanted to be told anything of that, anything at all. Well, I thought now, perhaps it had all been too great a strain on her, we had taken her strength and good, open nature too much for granted. And then, there had been the war.

'I have scarcely been a support to her.'

'She has never expected it, she has never once said anything, you know that.'

He turned to me then, his eyes desperate. 'I am afraid.'

'Maxim, of what? Beatrice will be fine, I know it, she . . .'

'No. Whether she is or is not . . . not that.'

'Then . . . ?'

'Something has changed, can't you see? I am afraid of anything changing. I want every day to be as today was when we awoke. Things that are there are there, and if they do not change, I can pretend, I don't have to think of any of it.'

There was nothing to be said to him, no platitude that could help, I knew that. I stopped burbling uselessly about how good a recovery Beatrice was sure to make. I simply walked slowly beside him along the shore of the lake and then, after a mile or so, back again in the direction of our hotel. We stopped to look at some geese on the water. Fed a pair of sparrows some crumbs I found in the bottom of my pocket. We met hardly anyone. The holiday season was all but over. When we got back there would be the papers, and a little, precious time with them, before our single glass of vermouth, a punctual, simple lunch.

All the way, in our silence, I thought of Beatrice. Poor Beatrice. But there was some movement already back in her side, the letter said, she knew Giles, had speech. We would telephone, wire flowers if it were possible, assuage our guilt that way.

Just for a moment, as we went up the hotel steps, I had a vision of her, clear as day, striding towards me over the lawn at Manderley, dogs barking around her feet joyously, her voice ringing out. Dear, good, loyal Beatrice, who had kept her thoughts to herself and never asked a question, had loved us and accepted what we had done absolutely. My eyes had welled with tears. But by now, she would be striding out again. I even began to plan out my letter that would tell her to slow down, take more care of herself. Give up hunting.

Maxim turned as we went through the doors, and I saw from his face that he, too, had convinced himself, and so could relax the mask, turn back to our own, frail, comfortable existence with relief again.

I am ashamed now, and it is a shame I shall always live with, that we became so happy, so light hearted that evening, turning our minds away from everything outside our own selves and the comfortable bubble in which we were cocooned. How smug it seems that we were, how self-centred and unfeeling, deliberately persuading ourselves, because it suited us to do so, that Beatrice's stroke must have been slight and that by now, surely, she would be up and about and fully herself again.

I did a little shopping in the afternoon and even bought some cologne, of a kind that was new to me, and a precious packet of bitter chocolate which was once again occasionally available; it was as though I were one of the rich, bored, frivolous women we had so often observed, passing her time in buying this and that, indulging herself. It was not like me, and I do not know why I behaved in such a way that day. We had tea and then dinner, and after dinner we walked again, as we usually did, beside the lake and went to drink our coffee in one of the last of the hotels to have its terrace still open in the evening and tables out under the awnings. The fairy lights were lit above our heads, shining midnight blue and crimson and an ugly orange on to the tables and our hands and arms as we stretched them out to our cups. It was milder again, the wind had dropped. One or two other couples were about, strolling past us, coming in for drinks and coffee and the tiny, cherry and frangipane tarts that were a speciality. If Maxim was sometimes unable to prevent himself from thinking of things that were far away from here, he concealed it very well from me and lounged back in his chair, smoking, the same figure, only a little more lined and grey haired, that I had sat beside in the open car driving up the mountain roads at Monte, a lifetime ago, the same man who had ordered me, gauche and red with embarrassment, to his own table, when I had been lunching alone and knocked over my glass of water. 'You can't sit at a wet tablecloth, it will put you off your food. Get out of the way,' and to the waiter, 'Leave that and lay another place at my table. Mademoiselle will have luncheon with me.'

He was rarely so imperious now, or so impulsive, and his temper was generally so much more even, he was more accepting of things, and of tedium most of all. He had changed. Yet as I looked across at him now, it was the old Maxim that I saw, the one I had first known. It should have been like so many other evenings as I sat beside him, talking of little, knowing that he needed only the reassurance of my presence to be content, and quite used by now to being strong, to have him dependent upon me. And if, at the very back of my mind, today as on a few other days during the past year or two, I was conscious of some faint restlessness within myself, a faint struggling, new voice, something that I could not have explained or defined but was only like 'a cloud no bigger than a man's hand' I was as careful as ever to turn myself away and refuse to face or to acknowledge it.

They brought more coffee, thick and black, in tiny, glazed cups, and Maxim ordered cognac.

I said, 'There goes the chemist,' and caught Maxim's eye as always in gentle, mutual amusement, as we both turned slightly to look at the man walking past us along the waterfront, a peculiarly erect and thin man, who was the local pharmacist and spent all day immaculate as a priest in a long white coat, and each evening, punctually at this time, walked the length of the lake path and back, wearing a long, black coat, and holding a small, fat, wheezing pug dog on the far end of a lead. He made us laugh, he was so solemn, so humourless, everything about him, the cut of his clothes and of his hair, the set of his head, the way he wore his collar carefully turned up, even the type of lead the dog had, was unmistakably foreign. Such small, regular sights, such harmless shared amusement, marked our days.

I remember we began to talk of him to speculate about his status – for we had never seen him with a wife, or indeed, with any other person at all, and to match make for him with various ladies in other shops, or else in the hotel lounges and at café tables of the little town, eyeing other dog-walkers as likely prospects and later, as it grew chilly again and the fairy lights on the terrace were wholly extinguished, walked back hand in hand, beside the dark, silent water, and pretended, though without speaking a word of it, that all was as it had been. We did not mention the letter.

It is strange that, when we recall the dramas of life, the moments of crisis and tragedy, the times when we have suffered and when dreadful news has come to us, it is not only the event itself that impresses itself forever upon the memory, but even more, the small, inconsequential details. Those may remain clear and fresh, attached to the incident like a permanent marker label, for the rest of our lives, even though it might seem that panic and shock and acute distress have caused our sense of awareness to falter and our minds to go quite blank.

There are some things that I do not remember at all about that night, but others stand out like scenes of a tableau, vividly illuminated.

We had come, laughing about something together, into the hotel, and unusually, because he seemed in such a determinedly gay mood, Maxim had suggested that we have a liqueur. Our hotel had no pretensions, but, perhaps years ago, someone had decided to try and attract outsiders and made a bar out of one of the dim little lounges next to the dining room, shading the lamps and adding fringes to them, setting a few stools about here and there. In daylight it was unenticing, dull and shabby, and we saw through it, we would never have dreamed of coming in. But in the evenings, sometimes, you could catch a fleeting mood and pretend it had sophistication, and because we no longer had taste for that, for the sort of smartness as we would have found in the bars and restaurants of the grander hotels, we came in here just occasionally, and it pleased us, we had grown quite fond of it, and felt indulgent towards it, as one might to a plain child dressed up in grown up party clothes. Once or twice, a couple of well dressed middle aged women had sat together at the bar gossiping; once, a fat matron and her goose necked daughter had perched side by side on stools, smoking, looking greedily around. We had huddled in the corner, our backs to them, heads bent a little, for we still had a fear that one day we would come upon someone who had known us, or merely recognised our faces, we were forever in unspoken dread of a sudden dawning look, as our story began to come back to them. But we had enjoyed speculating about the women, glancing at their hands, their shoes, their jewellery surreptitiously, trying to place and assess them, wondering about them, as we wondered about the life of the lugubrious pharmacist.

This evening there was no one else in the room and we took, I remember, not our usual back table but one slightly better lit and nearer to the bar itself. But as we sat down, before the boy could take our order, the manager came in, looking round for us.

'The gentleman has telephoned, but you were out. He says that he will try to speak to you again soon.'

We sat like dumb things. My heart was pounding very hard, very fast, and when I reached out my hand for Maxim's it felt strangely heavy to lift, like a dead hand that did not belong to my body. It was then that for some bizarre reason I noticed the green beads that ran round the bottom of the lamp fringes, a horrid, glassy frog green and saw that several were missing, leaving gaps, breaking the pattern they had been designed to make with some other, pinkish beads. I think they should have resembled the upturned leaves of tulips. I can see them now, ugly, cheap things that someone had chosen because they thought they were chic. Yet I do not remember much of what we said. Perhaps we did not speak. Our drinks came, two large cognacs, but I scarcely touched mine. The clock chimed. There were footsteps once or twice across the floor of the room above, a murmur of voices. Then silence. Outside, in the season, there would have been the sound of guests coming in, on warm evenings we would have sat out for a while on the terrace, and the fairy lights that were strung around the lake shore would not have been switched off until midnight, there would have been so many strollers, locals, visitors. It had just enough pleasant life for us, this place, just enough activity and diversion and even a sober sort of gaiety. Looking back, I am astonished at how very little we asked of life then, those years give off such a staid, contented air, like a period of calm between storms.

We sat for almost an hour but there was no telephone call, so that in the end, because it was clear that they were waiting politely to put out the lights and close, we began to gather ourselves to go upstairs. Maxim finished my drink as well as his own. The mask was back over his face, his eyes were dull as he looked at me occasionally for reassurance.

We were in our room. It was fairly small but in the summer we were able to open two doors that led out on to a tiny balcony. It overlooked the back of the hotel, the garden not the lake, but we preferred that, we would not have wanted it to be too public.

We had scarcely closed the door behind us when we heard footsteps, and then the sharp rapping on the door. Maxim turned to me. 'You go.'

I opened the door.

'Madam, the telephone again, for Mr de Winter, but I could not make the connection to your room, the line is too bad. Will you please come down?'

I glanced at Maxim, but he nodded, gesturing me to go, as I had known that he would. 'I will take it,' I said, 'my husband is rather tired.' And I went quickly, apologising to the manager as I did so, along the corridor and down the stairs.

It is the detail that one remembers.

The manager led me to the telephone in his own office, where a lamp shone on to the desk. Otherwise, the hotel was in darkness. Silent. I remember the sound of my own footsteps on the black and white tiles of the lobby floor. I remember a little wooden carving of a dancing bear on the ledge beside the telephone. An ashtray full of small cigar stubs.

'Hello . . . hello . . .'

Silence. Then a faint voice, a lot of crackling, as if the words were alight. Silence again. I spoke frantically into the mouthpiece, trying to be heard, to make contact. And then he was shouting in my ear. 'Maxim? Maxim, are you there? Is that you?'

'Giles,' I said. 'Giles, it's me . . .'

'Hello . . . hello . . .'

'Maxim is upstairs. He . . . Giles . . .'

'Oh.' His voice receded again, and when it returned

sounded as if it were coming from beneath the sea, there was an odd, booming echo.

'Giles, can you hear me? Giles, how is Beatrice? We only got your letter this afternoon, it was terribly delayed.'

There was an odd noise that at first I took to be some new interruption or interference on the line. Then I realised that it was not. It was the sound of Giles crying. I remember that I picked up the little carved wooden bear and began to roll it over and over in the palm of my hand, smoothing it, turning it.

'This morning . . . early this morning.' His voice came out in odd gulps, and kept tailing away into tears. Once he paused for several seconds to overcome them, but did not succeed. 'She was still in the nursing home, we didn't get her home . . . she wanted to come home . . . I was trying to work things out, do you see? I meant her to be at home . . .' He sobbed again, and I did not know what to say to him, how to cope with it at all, it made me sorry for him, but embarrassed too, I wanted to drop the receiver, to run away.

'Giles . . .'

'She is dead. She died this morning. Early this morning. I wasn't even there. I'd gone home, do you see, I'd no idea . . . they didn't tell me.' He took a deep, deep breath, and then said, very loudly and slowly, as if I might not have heard or understood, was deaf, or a small child. 'I am ringing to tell Maxim that his sister is dead.'

He had opened the balcony windows and was standing

29

there, staring out into the dark garden. Only one lamp, beside the bed, was lit. He said nothing when I told him, nothing at all, he did not move, or look at me.

I said, 'I didn't know what to say. I felt awful. He cried. Giles was crying.'

I remembered the sound of his voice again, as it had come to me over the bad line, the great sobs and the heaving of his breath as he tried to control them and could not, and then I realised that all the time I had been standing there, in the hotel manager's stuffy office, clutching the receiver so tightly, I had had in my mind a terrible picture not of Giles sitting somewhere on a chair in their house, perhaps, in his study, or the hall, but of him dressed as an Arab Sheikh, flowing white robes covering his huge frame and some sort of teacloth tied around his head, as he had been on the dreadful night of the Manderley fancy dress ball. I had imagined the tears coursing down his spaniel's cheeks, staining rivulets in the brown make up he had taken such trouble over. But the tears that night had not been his, he had been awkward and embarrassed; the tears, of shock and bewilderment and shame, had only been mine.

I wished I did not think of it so much now, I wanted that time wiped clean from my memory, but instead, it only seemed to grow more vivid and I had no power to hold back the memories, the pictures that came quite unbidden, at all sorts of odd times, into my mind.

A cold breeze blew in through the open window.

Then Maxim said, 'Poor Beatrice,' and again, after a moment, 'poor Beatrice,' but in an oddly dead, toneless voice, as if he had no feeling about her at all. I knew that he did, must. Beatrice, more than three years older, and very different, had been loved when nobody else at all had been able to arouse any feeling within him. They had spent little time together since childhood, but she had supported him, sided with him unquestioningly, loved him naturally and loyally, for all her bluff, undemonstrative manner, and Maxim, forever impatient and peremptory with her, he had loved her, and relied upon her and been dumbly grateful to her, too, so many times in the past.

I moved away from the window and began to go restlessly about the room, opening drawers and looking into them, wondering about packing, unable to clear my mind or to focus, tired but too tense, I knew, to sleep.

At last, Maxim came inside, and latched the windows.

I said, 'It will be far too late tonight to find out anything about tickets – which will be the best way to go. We don't even know what day the funeral is, I didn't ask. How stupid, I should have asked, I'll try and telephone Giles tomorrow, and make the arrangements then.'

I glanced across at him, a confusion of thoughts and questions and half plans bubbling about inside my head. 'Maxim?' He was staring at me, his face appalled, disbelieving. 'Maxim, *of course* we shall have to go. You see that, surely. However could we not go to Beatrice's funeral?'

He was white as paper, his lips bloodless. 'You go. I can't.'

'Maxim, you *must*.'

I went to him then, held him without speaking more than murmured reassurances, and we clung to one another as it began to creep over us both, the terrible realisation. We had said that we could never go back, and now we must. What else could possibly have made us? We did not dare begin to speak of what it meant, the enormity of what was to happen lay between us, and there was nothing, nothing to be said.

In the end we went to bed, though we did not sleep and I knew that we would not. At two o'clock, three, four, we heard the chimes of the bell tower from the square.

We had fled from England more than ten years ago, had begun our flight on the night of the fire. Maxim had simply turned the car and driven away from the flames of Manderley, and from the past and all its ghosts. We had taken almost nothing with us, made no plans, left no explanations, though in the end, we had sent an address. I had written to Beatrice, and there had been a formal letter and two sets of legal documents, from Frank Crawley and the solicitor and then from the bank in London. Maxim had not read them, scarcely even glanced at the paper, had scrawled his signature and pushed them back to me as if they, too, were burning. I had dealt with everything else, what little came to us, after that, and then there had been our fragile year or so of peace, before the war had sent us in search of another place, and then another, and after the war, at last, we had come to this country, and finally, this little lakeside resort, and found relief again, become settled, resumed our precious, dull, uneventful life, completely closed in upon ourselves, needing and wanting no one; and if I had begun recently to be restless, to remember again, and known that it had been there, the cloud no bigger than a man's hand, I had never spoken of it to him, and would have cut out my tongue before doing so.

I think that I was not only too tense to sleep that night, I was afraid too, in case I had nightmares, images I could not bear and could not control, of things I wanted to forget forever. But instead, when I did fall into a half sleep, a little before dawn, the images that slid before my eyes were entirely tranquil and happy ones, of places we had visited and loved together, views of the blue mediterranean, the lagoon in Venice with the churches rising and floating out of a pearly mist in the early morning, so that when I came awake again I was quite calm and rested, and lay quietly beside Maxim in the darkness, willing for him to catch my mood.

I had not yet fully faced what else was with me in the dream, the curious excitement and joy that were fluttering there. I had been too ashamed of them. But now, I admitted them quite calmly.

Beatrice was dead. I was very sorry. I had loved her dearly and I think that she had loved me. In time, I knew that I would weep for her, and miss her and feel very great distress. And I must face Maxim's anguish, too, not only at her loss but at what it meant we had to do.

We had to go back. And lying there in our hotel bedroom in that foreign town beside the lake, I allowed myself to feel, secretly, guiltily, a wonderful anticipation, although it was mingled with dread – for I could not imagine what we would find, how things would look to us, and above all, how Maxim would be and what anguish our return would cause him.

It was clear in the morning that it was very great but that he had instinctively begun to deal with it in the old way, by shutting things out and refusing to think or feel, concealing everything behind a mask and acting like an automaton, going through movements in the detached, mechanical way he had mastered long ago. He scarcely spoke, except of trivial things to do with the preparations, but stood at the window or on the balcony staring out at the garden, silent, pale, distant. It was I who made the arrangements, organised our travel, telephoned, telegraphed, booked tickets, worked out connections, I who packed for us both, as I usually did now, and it was when I stood looking at the row of clothes in the wardrobe that I felt the old feeling of inadequacy creeping back. For I was still not a smart woman, I still did not care to waste much time in choosing clothes, though goodness knows I had enough time to pass. I had gone from being a gauche, badly dressed girl, to being an uninterestingly, dully dressed married woman, and indeed, looking at them now, I saw that my clothes were those of someone entirely middle aged, in unadventurous background colours, and it suddenly struck me that in this way too, I had never been young, never been at all frivolous and gay, let alone fashionable or smart. At the beginning, it had been through a combination of ignorance and poverty; later, untutored, in awe of my new life and position, and in the shadow of Rebecca, the immortally beautiful and impeccably, extravagantly dressed, I had chosen safe, uninteresting things, not daring to experiment. Besides, Maxim had not wanted it, he had married me because of, not in spite of, my ill chosen, unbecoming clothes, they were all part of the innocent unworldly person I had been.

So, I had taken out the plain, tailored, cream blouses, the sensible beige- and grey- and mole-coloured skirts, the dark cardigans and neat, self-effacing shoes and packed them carefully, and was oddly unable to imagine whether it would be warm or cold in England, and afraid to ask Maxim for his opinion, for I knew that he would have closed his mind to it completely. But it was all done quite quickly, and the rest of our belongings locked away in the wardrobes and drawers. We would return, of course, though I did not know when. I went down to reassure the hotel manager that we were keeping on the room. He had tried to make us pay a deposit and, confused, anxious to get everything over with, I had been about to agree, thinking that it must be usual and was only fair. But when Maxim had heard he had suddenly sprung to life, like a dog that has been sleeping and is roused to temper, and snarled at the man in his old, thin lipped, imperious way, told him we had no intention of paying more money than we would owe in the normal course of events, he must accept our word that we would return. 'He hasn't a chance of letting the rooms to anyone else at this end of the season and he knows it perfectly well. The place is emptying now. He's lucky to get us. There are plenty of other hotels.'

I bit my lip and could not meet the manager's eye, as he watched us climb into the taxi. But Maxim's spurt of temper had died and for the rest of the journey, all that day and night and for the whole of the following day, he was shrunken into himself, silent for the most part, though gentle with me, taking food and drink when I proffered it, like a child.

'It will be all right,' I said, once or twice. 'Maxim, it will not be as bad as you expect.' He smiled wanly, and turned his head to look out of the train window at the endless, grey plains of Europe. Here, there was no autumn sunshine, no glorious, sifting light, here there were only rain sodden fields and ragged trees and dull, huddled villages, bleak little towns.

There was just one other thing. It was fleeting, momentary, but it terrified me, it came so unexpectedly and with such force, and for a second it froze my heart.

We were at a railway station on one of the borders, and because they were changing engines we had half an hour to wait, enough time to get out and walk up and down the long platform to stretch our legs. There had been a stall selling cooked sausages, good hot coffee and schnapps, and sweet, spicy cakes which we dipped in and soaked, before eating greedily. Maxim was watching some pantomime to do with a man and a great heap of luggage piled on to a rickety trolley. Amused, standing beside him, I was thinking at that moment of nothing, nothing in particular at all, neither past nor future, simply enjoying the break from the motion of the train, the taste of the cake and coffee. Then Maxim had turned and glanced at me, caught my eye and smiled, and as I looked into his face I heard, falling into my head as clearly as drops of water falling on to stone, 'That man is a murderer. He shot Rebecca. That is the man who killed his wife,' and for one terrible moment, staring at Maxim, I saw a stranger, a man who had nothing to do with me, a man I did not know.

And then the guard had blown the warning whistle to summon us back on to the train.

CHAPTER

Three

'Man that is born of woman hath but a short time to live.'

The crows were whirling in the sky again, rising, scattering, falling; on the hillside, the man still ploughed. The sun still shone. The world was quite unchanged.

'In the midst of life we are in death; of whom may we seek for succour but of thee, O Lord, who for our sins art justly displeased?'

I was holding my breath, as if waiting for something to happen. And soon, of course, it did; they moved forward and began to slip the ropes. I looked up. Maxim was standing a few paces away from me, stock still, a black shadow. We were all black, in that golden sunshine. But it was Giles whose face I watched, as I looked at him across the open grave, Giles, heavy jowled, sunken eyed, weeping and doing nothing to try and restrain his tears. Giles, with Roger beside him. But I could not look at Roger's face, I slid my eyes away in embarrassment. Now, they were stepping forward.

'For as much as it hath pleased Almighty God of his great mercy to take unto himself the soul of our dear sister here departed, we therefore commit her body to the ground.'

Now they were leaning down and scattering their handful of earth. I reached for Maxim's hand. His fingers were unresponsive and cold, and as I touched them I saw Beatrice again, vividly before me, as I saw her all the time now, Beatrice in her tweed suit and brogues striding towards me across the lawns, her plain, open face curious, interested, full of friendliness. Beatrice, from whom I had never had an unkind or unfair word.

'I heard a voice from heaven say unto me write, from henceforth, blessed be the dead which die in the Lord.'

I wished that I could weep then. I should have wept, it was not for want of feeling that my eyes were dry. Instead, I thought how glorious the day was and how much she would have revelled in it, riding out somewhere on one of her hunters, or walking the dogs – she had scarcely ever seemed to be indoors during the day, and then I thought again how wrong it had been, how unfair. Beatrice ought to have fallen off a horse in a ripe old age, hunting to the end, and happy, careless on such a day as this, not been enfeebled and humiliated after a stroke when she was not even sixty. Or else it should have been Giles, fat, unhealthy looking Giles, crumpled now, his moon face creased and wet, a great white handkerchief held to his mouth. Or Roger. I glanced at him quickly again as he stood beside his father, and had the appalling thought that death would surely have been preferable to such disfigurement, but knew that that was for our sakes, to spare ourselves the unpleasantness of having to look at him, not for his.

There was a silence. We stood around the grave, looking

down on the pale oak coffin and its dark crumblings of earth. They had taken off the golden flowers and laid them on the grass, and now I saw how many others there were, lining the graveside, heaped beside the path, wreaths and crosses and cushions of gold and white and bronze and purple set like jewels in their green setting, and as we turned I saw how many people there were, standing back a little, respectfully, to let us pass, perhaps fifty or sixty of them. How many friends Beatrice had had, how loved she had been, how well known and liked and respected.

Now, as we went uncertainly forward, back to the cars, the play over, Maxim gripped my own hand very hard. They were staring at us and trying not to stare, they were thinking, wondering, speculating, I felt their eyes, though I cast mine down, I wondered how we would get through it, or how we could face them afterwards, at the house, whether Maxim would be able to cope at all.

But as my thoughts were swirling in panic, at the worst moment, when we were surrounded by the people like a black forest of trees crowding in upon us, I half stumbled, moving from the grass to the gravelled path, and as I did so, felt a hand steadying me on the other side, away from Maxim, so that I did not fall, but looked directly up and into the concerned, unassuming, wonderfully familiar face of Frank Crawley.

Long afterwards, I was to recall how his presence there changed everything for us, changed the rest of the day and how we managed to get through it, gave us support and reassurance and strength, and remember all over again how much it had always done so, how very much we owed to him. He had been Maxim's agent, hardworking, loyal, efficient, and his staunchest, truest friend, he had suffered with him in so many ways, almost as much a victim of Rebecca as Maxim had been. He had known the truth of things and remained silent.

But to me he had been more, a rock when I had believed that all around me was swirling, raging sea and I about to drown in it. He had been there from my first day as a young bride at Manderley, sensitive, unobtrusive, anticipating my anxieties, smoothing my path, relieved that I was as I was, young, gauche, inexperienced, nervous, plain, and seeing through it all to the real person underneath. I would probably never know exactly how great a debt I owed to Frank Crawley, in how many thousands of small, vital ways he had come to my aid, but I had many times thought of him during our years abroad, and with affection, and had given thanks for him too, on those odd moments I had spent briefly kneeling at the back of some foreign church. I thought that I had perhaps only known two people in my life who were so wholly, unconditionally good. Frank, and Beatrice. And today, they were both here; only Frank was alive and little changed and Beatrice was dead, and the past came flooding back to me, like a river overflowing the bare, dry land of the present.

When the funeral was over, and we were standing on the path beyond the graveyard, formally, stiffly, shaking hands with so many people, most of whom we did not know, and when we had finally turned away and walked back towards the black, waiting cars behind Giles and Roger, at that moment Maxim would have run away if it had been possible, I knew, without his need to speak, that it was what he wanted. He would simply have got into one of the cars and ordered them to take us, we would not even have said goodbye, we would have sped fast and far, to the trains and the boat, and our exile again. We had come, done our duty. Beatrice was dead and properly buried. There was nothing to keep us here.

But of course, we were obliged to stay and no mention was made of an alternative.

'It was so good to see Frank,' I said. The funeral car was lumbering out of the gateway, turning into the lane. 'He looks so much the same, though his hair has gone grey – but then, he is older.'

'Yes.'

'We all are. I expect we looked quite changed to everyone. Older, I mean.'

'Yes.'

'It is more than ten years.'

Why did I say it? Why did I go on talking in that way, when I knew that it would only make us think of the past? It was in shadow, unacknowledged for all that it lay between us. Why did I drag it forwards into the full, glaring light, so that we were forced to look at it?

Maxim turned. 'For God's sake, what's the matter with you, do you think I don't know how long? Do you think there is anything else at all in my mind? Do you not know that it's all I have been able to think of for three days? What are you trying to do?'

'I'm sorry. I didn't mean . . . it was only something to say . . .'

'Why must you say anything? Do we need small talk?'

'No, no. I'm sorry . . . Maxim, I didn't mean . . .'

'You didn't *think*.'

'I'm sorry.'

'Or perhaps you did.'

'Maxim, please . . . it was foolish of me, stupid, a stupid remark. We mustn't quarrel. Not now. Not at all. We never quarrel.'

It was true. We had not quarrelled since the day of the inquest into Rebecca's death and the nightmare journey with Colonel Julyan to London to see her doctor, since the night of the fire. We had had too close a brush with mortal danger, there had been too much misunderstanding, we had almost lost one another as a result of it. We knew our own luck, knew the value of what we had too well to dare to take any risk, even of the slightest angry word over something trivial. When people have been through what we had, they do not tempt fate.

I held his hand. 'It will soon be over,' I said. 'We will have to be polite to people, say the right things, for Giles's sake. For Beatrice. But then they will be gone.'

'And we can go. First thing tomorrow. Perhaps even tonight.'

'But surely . . . we will have to stay and support Giles a bit longer? A day or two. He looks so awful, poor man, so broken.'

'He has Roger.'

We were silent. Roger. There was nothing to be said.

'He has plenty of friends. They always did. We would be no use to him.'

I did not reply, did not press it, not yet, did not dare to say that I wanted to stay, not because of Giles or Roger or Beatrice, but because we were here, home, back at last and my heart was full. I felt released, new born, desperate with a sort of sickness at the sight of the autumn fields, the trees and hedgerows, the sky and the sunlight, even the black flocks of swirling, flapping crows. I was guilty and ashamed, as if I were betraying Maxim and my loyalty to him as his wife, so that then, in a small, pathetic gesture that only I could understand I deliberately turned my head away from the window and refused to look at what I saw and loved, and instead kept my eyes only on Maxim's pale, ill looking face, and on my own hand holding his and on the black leather of the car seat and the shoulders of the driver's black coat.

We were slowing down, the house was there, we could see Roger helping his father out of the other car.

Maxim said, 'I can't face it. I can't stand what they will say and how they will look at us. Julyan was there. Did you see him?'

I had not.

'On two sticks. And the Cartwrights and the Tredints.'

'It doesn't matter, Maxim. I'll talk to them, I'll deal with them all, you will only have to shake hands. Besides, they will want to talk about Beatrice. No one will mention anything else at all.'

'They won't have to. It will be written all over their faces and I shall see it. I shall know what they are thinking.'

As I paused, as the door opened, in that split second before I began to get out of the car then, I heard what Maxim had just said being played and replayed over and over again in my mind, so that the second seemed to last for an eternity, I was standing there, frozen, forever, there was all time and no time in which I heard it. 'It will be written all over their faces. I shall know what they are thinking.' And my own small, secret, poisonous voice supplied the answer. 'He is a murderer. He shot Rebecca. That is Maxim de Winter who killed his wife.'

'There's Frank now. Hell.'

'Maxim, Frank of all people will be careful not to say anything. Frank will help us, you know that. Frank will understand.'

'It's the understanding I don't think I can cope with.'

And then he left the car, turning away from me, I saw him cross the drive, saw Frank Crawley step forward, offer his hand, saw him touch Maxim's arm for a moment, drawing him into his protective circle. Sympathetic. Understanding.

And the golden October sun shone down on us, all the black crows, gathering for the feast.

People were very kind to us. I felt their kindness like a blanket wrapping us round, warm, suffocating, and they were tactful, too, they tried not to stare. I could see them trying. Wives had said to husbands before setting out, Now remember, if the de Winters are by any chance there – and I've heard that they may be coming – don't ask . . . don't mention . . . don't stare, and so they did not, they avoided us, skirting the far side of the room, or else they did the opposite, strode up to us heartily, to get it over with, looked us straight in the eye, wrung our hands and at once turned back to the table and busied themselves over the sherry and whisky and sandwiches and cold pie, cramming their mouths full so that they might be excused from speaking.

It did not matter, I did not care, I felt cocooned from them. I went around the room with a plate, offering savouries, and all the time speaking of Beatrice, remembering her, agreeing that her illness and death had been so hard, so unfair, and missing her, too, needing her there to help me, longing to hear her make some booming remark that would set everybody laughing. I could not believe that at any moment she would not come in through the door.

They were all so very kind. It was only when I turned my back on this or that one, that I felt my face had been scalded by the things thought and left unsaid, to hover in the air. I met their eyes and saw questions, questions, questions. As often as I could I went to Maxim and stood close to him, touched his hand or his arm to reassure him while he had to listen to someone else reminisce about his sister or else drone on interminably about how it had been here during the war. He rarely spoke himself, but only smiled thinly and moved on every few minutes, afraid to stay too long with anyone in case, in case . . . Once, I heard the word 'Manderley' drop like the tolling of a bell into a sudden silence at the heart of the room, and spun round, panic stricken, almost dropping a dish, knowing that I must reach him, protect him, that it must not be said again. But then the voices rose and closed over it and the word was drowned, and when I next caught

45

sight of him, he had moved on again, I saw his stiff back on the far side of the room.

Not long afterwards I found myself standing beside the french windows looking out on to the garden and the countryside beyond, and then I could shut the people out, pretend they were none of them here at all, I could gaze and gaze, at the light and the trees, the brown and the green and the blazing of the berries that studded the holly.

'I'm sure it would be quite all right for you to go outside. I think you could do with a break couldn't you?'

Frank Crawley, dear, reliable, predictable, thoughtful Frank, the same Frank, full of concern, as sensitive as he had always been, to how I felt. I glanced quickly over my shoulder, back into the room. He said, 'Maxim is fine. I've just been with him. Lady Tredint is boring him about evacuees. The war has been over for almost four years but you'll find it is still the main topic of conversation down here. Not the wider aspects, of course, but things like who under declared the number of eggs their hens laid so as to keep more back for themselves – a matter not easily forgiven or forgotten.'

We began to walk slowly up the garden away from the house and as we did so, I felt the strain and worry of it all slip from my shoulders, I could turn my face to the sun.

I said, 'I'm afraid we knew so little of what was going on here. Letters went astray. We only heard the worst news, about the bombings, and what was happening in other countries.' I stopped. 'I suppose we ran away from those things, too. Is that what people say?'

'I think,' he replied carefully, 'that people became very

inward-looking and preoccupied with their own affairs.'

'Oh, Frank, thank you. How good you are. You even put me in my place in the nicest possible way. You mean, out of sight, out of mind. We were really far too unimportant to be thought of or gossiped about at all. People just forgot us.'

Frank shrugged his shoulders non-committally, always polite.

'You see, we have lost our sense of perspective, Maxim and I. In . . . in the old days . . . we were, or rather Manderley was at the centre of things down here, you know that, everyone was interested, everyone talked . . . but the world has moved on, hasn't it? It has had much greater concerns. We're of no importance now.'

'Of course you are remembered, of course . . . it's only . . .'

'Frank, don't mind, don't be sorry . . . God knows, it is what I've wanted for us both, to be small and insignificant, part of the past, and all but forgotten. You must know that.'

'Yes indeed.'

We had reached the old orchard, from where we could look back to the sturdy, white house, or up, to the horses in the meadow.

'Poor things,' I said, seeing them eye us and lift their heads and begin to move. 'Shall we take them some apples?'

We began to pick up a few windfalls from the grass and then make our way slowly towards the fence, and the horses saw us and came trotting down, sleek and handsome, the chestnut and the grey.

'Who will ride them now? Does Giles still ride? Or Roger? I don't know what has been happening – what will happen.'

'And I'm afraid nor do I. I've only kept in touch very irregularly these past few years.'

I knew that Frank had gone to live in Scotland, where he managed a huge estate, knew that as soon as the war was over, he had married and had two sons straight away, and I knew too, looking at him now, that he was entirely happy, settled, and almost completely detached from the past, and I felt a strange pang, I did not know precisely of what – grief? Loss? He was the only other person who had cared for Manderley almost as much as Maxim, our last link with it. Now, like Beatrice, though in a different way, I felt that Maxim knew Frank had gone.

We were standing beside the fence, the horses were munching the apples, picking them gently from the palms of our hands, their lips curled back. I stroked the warm mossy muzzle of the grey. Then I said, 'Frank, I want to stay in England so much, I wish I could tell you how I have longed to come home. How I have dreamed about it. I never speak of it to Maxim – how can I? I wasn't sure how it would be. But never mind about the people, never mind what they think or whether they care at all. It isn't the people.'

'I understand.'

'It's the places – this place, here, these fields . . . the sky . . . the countryside. I know Maxim feels it too, I'm absolutely certain, only he daren't acknowledge it. He has been as homesick as I have, but with him . . .' My voice tailed off. There was only the sound of the horses quietly chomping, and of a lark somewhere, spiralling up into the clear sky. The word Manderley lay between us, unspoken, we felt it, everything it had been and meant charged the air like electricity. At last I said, 'I feel so disloyal. It is wrong for me to be saying any of this.'

'I don't see that,' Frank said carefully. He had taken his pipe out of his pocket and was beginning to pack the bowl with tobacco from the old leather pouch I remembered that he had always used, and the sight of it brought back another scene like this, when I had poured out my anxieties to him and received sound support and reassurance. 'It's perfectly natural, surely. You are English. Very English. This is home, for all the years you have spent living abroad. As you say, it is the same for Maxim and I'm sure he knows it.'

'Could we come back? Would . . . ' I hesitated, choosing my words. 'Frank, would there be . . . anything at all to prevent us?'

He pulled on his pipe for several minutes and I watched the first, thin blue smoke plume up into the air. I was stroking and stroking the horse, rubbing its muzzle, my heart pounding, and the horse, delighted at this rush of attention and affection after perhaps too much neglect, pawed at the ground and pushed hard into my hand.

'You mean to do with . . . what happened?'

'Yes.'

And then the inquest and the verdict were there with us, too, taking their ghostly places beside the spirit of Manderley, and we did not refer to them, either.

'I really don't see why there should be anything to prevent your coming back if you both want to,' Frank said.

My heart leaped. Stopped. Pounded again. And then I said, 'Frank, did you go back there?'

He looked at me, his eyes steady, full of concern. He said, 'Yes, of course. I had to.'

I held my breath. Then he put his hand under my elbow, and began to guide me gently, away from the paddock and the horses, out of the orchard, back towards the house.

'It is over,' he said.

I did not reply. But the ghost crept after us across the grass, newly awakened. The people were gone, it was not of them that I thought. Rebecca was dead, and her spirit could not haunt me any more, I did not think of her at all that sunlit October morning. Only of the place, the house, the garden, the Happy Valley, slipping down to the hidden cove, the beach. The sea. And, secretly hugging it close and quiet to myself, I welcomed it.

Curiously, it was not seeing Frank Crawley that made things hard, for Maxim most of all, I could tell by the expression on his face, the way that his eyes seemed to have sunk, inwards, so that the sockets looked half hollow. Frank was nothing but a comfort, we were both easy with him. We sat later, listening to his talk of Inverness-shire, the mountains, the lochs, the deer, the glories of that wild countryside he had so clearly grown to love, and of his wife Janet, and the two little boys. He had snapshots, and we admired them, and now, only the present filled the room, there seemed to be no shadows at all lying between us – except a very different kind of shadow, which I could scarcely acknowledge. But at the sight and talk of the two boys, Hamish and Fergus, I felt the hollowness I had grown so accustomed to, followed by a spurt of wild hope. We never spoke, now, about our having children. It had been different then, with the bright future before us and Manderley for them to inherit. I was not even sure that Maxim would want any children now, there did not seem to be any place for them in our exile. But if we were to come home . . .

I looked up, and into the eyes of old Colonel Julyan, and felt an ice form about my hopes and small, secret, gleeful plans.

There were just a few of us left, Giles and Roger, Maxim and I, an elderly cousin, and Julyan and his daughter. His wife was dead, and she, a plump, plain, cheerful young woman, lived with him now and devoted herself, apparently quite contentedly, to looking after him. We had been speaking beforehand, haltingly, of Europe, the countries we had stayed in, the place where we lived now. Then Julyan said, 'I remember advising Switzerland. The night after all that business in London.' A silence fell like a sword into the room. I saw Frank glance urgently at Maxim, heard him clear his throat. But Julyan was going on, he seemed to have no sense whatsoever of the atmosphere, no idea of what he was saying. 'Of course, it was a holiday I had thought of, just until it all blew over and the gossip died down. But then there was that shocking business of Manderley, and then the war of course. One forgets. Never expected you to leave altogether though . . . and be away for, what is it, ten years or more? Must be ten years.'

Then, as we were stock still, frozen with horror and embarrassment, quite unable to speak, he began to struggle to his feet, fumbling with his sticks, knocking one on to the floor and waiting for Frank to retrieve it for him – because no one quite knew what he was intending to do, no one did anything to stop him. Only his daughter put her hand on his arm, as he reached for his glass, lifted it and began to speak again.

'Father, do you think . . .'

But he shook her off, and she subsided, flushed, giving me one, desperate glance.

Julyan cleared his throat. 'It calls for a few words, I think. In spite of the sadness of the occasion . . . the reason we are all here . . . ' He looked at Maxim, and then at me. 'You've been missed and that's the plain truth. I've often been over here – Giles will vouch for that, and we've sat in this room and spoken about you.' He paused. I looked at Giles, bent slightly forward, staring at the table, the jowls of his face plum coloured. Looked at Roger, and as quickly, away. 'It's up to me to say it. The past is dead and buried . . .'

I squirmed, not daring to meet Maxim's eye. The old man seemed to have no idea what he had just said.

'Done with. Well, let it be so.'

He shifted his weight on the sticks, balanced awkwardly. The hall clock struck three. 'All I meant to say is that it's damned good to see you both again and . . . and welcome home.' And he raised his glass to us and then, alone, slowly and solemnly, drank his toast.

For a moment, I thought that I might die, or scream, cry out or faint, or simply get up and run away. I felt sick with embarrassment and disbelief, desperate with anxiety for Maxim and what he felt, and what he might be about to do.

Even Frank seemed paralysed, and tongue tied, even he had found no way of coming to our aid.

But to my surprise, Maxim sat, very still, very composed and then, after a moment, took a sip from his own glass, his eyes on Julyan. 'Thank you,' he said quietly. That was all, but it meant that somehow I could breathe again, though there was a tight pain in my chest and my face felt hot. But it was all right, nothing terrible had happened, we were still here at the lunch table, all of us as we had been, and it was today, October, the day of Beatrice's funeral, and the past was the past and had no power over us.

In the end they went, Julyan's daughter taking an eternity to get him to the door, for he insisted on walking without any help at all and it was an awkward, painful business over the gravel and then he had to be settled and the car cranked and warmed up and backed to and fro, under the old man's direction.

But at last they were gone, and then there was only another hour or so before Frank, too, had to leave, a car was coming to take him to the station, from where he would go to London and then, on the night sleeper, home to Scotland.

The afternoon light lay softly over the fields, lemon coloured, with the leaves spinning and sifting down through it, the last of the apples falling. It was quite warm. I wanted to be out there because it was so beautiful, I could not bear to miss a moment of it after so long away, and could not face being shut up in the house either, hearing the clock and the creak of the stairs and the patter of the dogs' feet as they went

53

in and out of every room, looking for Beatrice, and Giles's great, heaving sighs. But Maxim would not come out, he had gone suddenly ashen, with tiredness and strain. 'I'll lie down,' he said, 'sleep a bit perhaps. Then there is only the rest of the day to get through.'

I did not reply. We were standing in the hall, the doors open on to the garden. It smelled faintly of apples. Somewhere in the shadows Frank Crawley hovered tactfully, waiting to be of use – his habitual way which had always so irritated Beatrice. 'What a dull creature he is,' she had said to me on that first day, 'never has anything interesting to say.' I had known then that she had been wrong to dismiss Frank's dullness and steadiness, his lack of excitement, wrong to be impatient with him, and I wondered now if she had come to understand his value in the end, seen through to his true worth.

'Go out,' Maxim said now, 'it's what you want. Go out there while you can.' And looking into his face, I saw that he knew, knew to my heart, what I felt and longed for and had tried so hard to conceal. He smiled, a wan, tired smile, and bent to kiss my forehead lightly. 'Go on.' Then he turned and began to go, dismissively, away from me, up the stairs.

I went out.

CHAPTER

Four

The previous night I had woken because of my own disorientation, after the long journey and shock of arriving here.

Now, it was a sound that awakened me from the deepest of dreamless sleeps, and for a few seconds, as I sat up in my bed, I was confused again, thinking somehow that I was back in our hotel room, and wondering vaguely why the window seemed to be in the wrong place.

Maxim was absolutely still; we were both exhausted, emotionally, with the strain of it all, I felt slow and stupid with tiredness. What had I heard? Nothing. It was perfectly quiet and the room dark, there was no moon tonight.

Then it came again, the sound that must have awoken me, an odd, muffled noise I could not place – it might have been animal or human.

I lay down again, but as soon as I put my head on to the pillow it was louder, and closer, seeming to come up to me through the floorboards, or down the walls of the house, so that in the end I got up and went quietly to the door.

Standing in the dark corridor, I thought at first that it was one of the dogs, still distressed by Beatrice's absence, perhaps, and confused by the changes in the household routine, whimpering and pacing about. But the dogs were shut away in the kitchen quarters below. This sound was coming from a bedroom.

And then, I realised that what I was hearing was the sound of sobbing, a man's sobbing, interspersed with mutterings and sudden, little cries.

I did not want to go to him, I felt a dreadful sort of horror and shame of it. I wanted to return quickly to bed and stuff my fingers in my ears, pull the pillow over me to shut it out, too many long hidden emotions threatened to sneak to the surface as a result of my hearing the crying voice.

But then, out of my guilt sprang pity, and the natural desire to comfort, to help, and so I stumbled along the corridor, and round to the front of the house, feeling my way with my hand along the wall, my feet cold on the worn old carpet that ran down the centre of the polished boards – for Giles and Beatrice did not seem to have bothered about too much luxury, they lived in the house as they had first come to it thirty-odd years before, not bothering to replace or repair very much, probably not even noticing how things were or if they got worn, always preferring to be outside, and giving their attention to the horses, the dogs, the garden, as well as to their friends. It was one of the things that had endeared them to me. I had felt so comfortable in this house, the few times I had visited, after the grandeur and formality of Manderley, which had been so terrifying to me, and far more than I could ever have lived up to.

At the far end of the corridor I stopped outside Beatrice's bedroom; the sound of crying was quite clear, only a little muffled by the closed door.

I hesitated, trying to be calm, trying to compose myself, hating it. And then I went in.

'Giles.'

For quite a long time he did not see or hear me, did not look up, so that I coughed, and made a little rattling noise with the handle, and then, at last, spoke his name gently again.

'Giles – I heard you – I couldn't bear it. Is there anything I can get for you, anything I can do?'

The bedside lamps were on, and he was sitting beside Beatrice's funny old-fashioned dressing-table. I could see the reflection of his thick neck above his navy-blue dressing-gown, in the triple mirror. The wardrobe doors were hanging open, and one or two drawers of the chest, too, and some of her clothes had been pulled out and were strewn on the floor, across the bed, over the back of the chair, her tweed skirts and sensible woollen jumpers, a purple frock, a maroon cardigan, scarves, underclothes, a camel coat, her stole with the fox's head hanging down, its small beady eyes gleaming up at me horribly.

Giles was clutching an old peach-coloured satin wrap to his face – I remembered seeing Beatrice in it once, years ago, and I stood, staring stupidly, just inside the door, not knowing what else I might do or say. And after a while, though without any start or surprise, he looked up. His eyes were swollen and reddened and welling over with tears. There were tears on his face, streaking through the blue shadows of beard, I could not only see and hear, I could almost smell and feel his misery, the depth of his helpless grief.

He did not say anything, only stared at me, like a child, and then began to sob again, his shoulders heaving, not making any effort at all to stop, he held the peach wrap to his face and cried into it, and wiped his eyes with it, and took in occasional great gulps of air like someone drowning. It was horrible. I was appalled at him, and appalled at myself, too, for the way his abandoned grief repelled me. I was so used to Maxim, he was the only man I had ever known at all, and Maxim had never cried, never once, it was unimaginable. I did not think he could have cried since the age of three or four. When he felt deeply, it showed in his face, he became very pale and his skin tightened, his eyes went hard, or else a shadow would somehow fall, but his self control was otherwise absolute. I did not dare think how he would have responded to Giles now.

In the end, I closed the door and went and sat on the edge of the bed, nearer to him, and for a long time was simply there, silent, miserable, huddled into my dressing-gown, as Giles sobbed, and after a while something inside me, some pride or reserve, simply broke down and I did not mind any more, instead it seemed right that he should be allowed to give way to his feelings like this, and that I should simply be there, to let him, and for company.

'What am I going to do?' he said once, and then again, looking up at me and yet, I thought, not really speaking to me or wanting an answer. 'What am I going to do without her? She has been my whole life for thirty-seven years. Do you know where we met? Did she ever tell you? I fell off my horse and she came up and got me back on again, and led us home – I'd broken my wrist – she simply took off a belt or a scarf or some such and led my horse with hers and it was a difficult beggar, and it went as quiet as a little child's pony, had it eating out of her hand. I ought to have felt such a bloody fool – I'm damned sure I looked one, but somehow I didn't, I didn't mind at all, she had that effect on me straight off – I never cared less about anything at all with Bea, relied on her, you know, totally, for everything. I mean, she was boss, she saw to things – well, of course, you knew that. I'd never amounted to much, never would have done, though I was quite all right, only somehow or other Bea made it all work and set me on my feet and after that, I was right as rain, not a care in the world, happy as Larry – it's very hard to explain.'

He was looking at me now, his eyes searching my face, for – what? Reassurance? Approval? I did not know. He was like an old lap-dog, rheumy-eyed.

'I know,' I said. 'I always saw how happy you were – how well you were suited. It was – well, everyone saw it.'

'Did they?' His face lit up suddenly, with a pathetic, sloppy sort of eagerness.

'Of course,' I said uselessly. 'Of course they did.'

'Everyone loved her, they all admired her, she never made an enemy, for all her sharp tongue – but she could say what she thought, give someone a piece of her mind, and then that would be that, forgiven and forgotten – she

59

had so many friends, you know – all those people today, all those people at the funeral – did you see them all?'

'Yes, yes, Giles, I saw them – I was very touched – it must have been such a help to you.'

'A help?' He looked round the room suddenly, desperately, almost as though he had forgotten for a moment where he was, and then at me, and his eyes did not take me in either.

'A help,' he said dully.

'Yes, that so many people who had been fond of Beatrice were there.'

'Yes, but there is no help,' he said, quite simply, almost as if he were explaining something to a stupid child, 'You see she is dead and she died when I was not there. She died in a hospital, she wasn't at home, I wasn't with her, I failed her, I let her down. She never ever failed me, never once.'

'No Giles, no, you shouldn't blame yourself.' Useless words.

'But *I am to blame.*'

I did not say 'no' again, I did not speak at all. There was no point in it – nothing to say.

'She is dead and I don't know how I can go on with things, you see. I'm nothing now, nothing without her. I never amounted to anything, I don't know what to do. What am I going to do? I can't be without her, you see, I can't be without Beatrice at all.' And the tears sprang from his eyes and poured unchecked down his face again and he sobbed, great, raucous, ugly sobs, as unrestrained as a baby. And I went clumsily over to him and sat beside him, and held him, a burbling, helpless, lonely, grieving, fat old man, and then, at last, I wept with him, and wept for him, and for Beatrice, too, because I had loved her . . . but they were not only tears for Beatrice, they were in some strange way, for so much else, other losses, other griefs, and when there were no more tears, we sat, quietly, I holding poor Giles, not minding him at all, only glad to be there, some small comfort for him in that silent, grieving house.

He began to talk again, after a while, and once he had begun, could not stop – he told me so much, about Beatrice, their years together, little happy stories, private memories, family jokes, it was a whole innocent lifetime he laid before me; I heard of their wedding, their buying this house, Roger's birth and growing up, their friends, their neighbours and so many horses, dogs, bridge parties, dinners, picnics, trips to London, Christmases, birthdays, and as he talked, and I listened, it dawned on me that he scarcely mentioned Maxim, or Manderley, or anything to do with that part of life, not out of tact – he was too far gone, too deeply immersed in himself and the past to think of that, scarcely even aware of my presence, let alone what I stood for – but it was as though Manderley and Beatrice's early years there, her family, had scarcely impinged upon his own life and consciousness at all.

I remembered the first time I had met Beatrice and Giles, that hot day at Manderley, a lifetime ago and in another life – and I another person, a child, and I had watched him as he lay on his back in the sun after lunch, snoring, and I had wondered with genuine bewilderment why ever Beatrice had married him, and thought that because Giles had already been fat and unattractive, and apparently well into middle age, they could not conceivably have been in love. What a very childish thing – how very naive and stupid and lacking in all knowledge I had been, to believe that one had to be handsome and smart and debonair and sophisticated in manner, seductive as Maxim had been, to be fallen in love with and loved and happily married. I had known nothing, nothing at all, I blushed with shame now to think of it. I had known only a little of being swept off my feet, and of first, passionate, blinkered love, a love that I now saw had been as much like a schoolgirl crush as anything else. I had known nothing of the love that came only with time and age and everyday life together, or of love that had endured misery and grief and suffering, and things which just as easily break apart, sour and destroy love as nurture it.

I felt strangely old that night, infinitely older than poor helpless Giles, stronger, more capable, wiser. I felt so sorry for him; I knew that after all, he would come through, somehow, stumble on and make the best of things, but that it would never be the same for him, and that the best of his life was over, with Beatrice dead, and Roger so maimed and disfigured after his flying accident. Though perhaps the fact that his son was likely to remain at home with him always, because of his disability, might give him a reason for going on and pulling through and eventually enjoying life again. I did not know. He did not mention Roger at all, it was only Beatrice he thought of and wanted tonight.

I have no idea how long we sat there together; I cried a little but Giles did not stop, even when he was talking, he cried, and did not try to restrain or control it, and although at first it had so embarrassed me, after a while, I came to respect him for it and to be moved, because of the depth of his devotion to Beatrice and his grief, and also because he felt close enough to me to be able to weep so, in front of me.

Twice, at least, I asked if he wanted me to get him tea, or brandy, but he refused and so we just sat on, among the mess of clothes, in the bedroom that grew cold, as the night drew on.

And then, as though he were coming to out of some sort of fit or trance over which he had had no control, he looked round the room, almost in bewilderment, as if uncertain how we both came to be there, and found a handkerchief from somewhere, and blew his nose several times with great, trumpeting noises.

'Sorry,' he said. 'Sorry, old thing, only I needed to be here – couldn't have done without it.'

'I know Giles. It's perfectly all right. I understand.' I stood up, and said, rather lamely, 'I was very fond of Beatrice too, you know.'

'Everybody was. Everybody. All those people, those friends.' He wiped his eyes, and then, looking up, said, 'She never had an enemy in the world you know. Apart from Rebecca . . .'

I stared at him stupidly, for somehow I had never expected to hear the name again, it sounded odd, like a word in another language. Rebecca. A word from another life. We never spoke it. I do not think it had crossed either of our lips since that terrible night.

For a few seconds in the quiet room, it was as though some beast I had thought long, long dead, had stirred faintly, warningly, and growled, and the sound struck fear in me, but then it was silent and still again and the fear was only the faintest echo of an old fear, like the memory of a pain long past, I did not so much feel it as recall that I had once done so.

'Sorry,' Giles said again, 'sorry, old thing.'

But whether it was for mentioning Rebecca's name, or his keeping me up with him while he was so distressed, I could not tell.

'Giles, I think I should go back to bed, I'm really dreadfully tired, and Maxim may have woken and wondered where I am.'

'Yes, of course, you go. Good Lord, it's half past four. Sorry . . . I'm sorry . . .'

'No, it's fine, don't be sorry. Really.'

When I reached the door, he said, 'I wish you'd come back now.'

I hesitated.

'Old Julyan was right, and Beatrice was always saying so. Damn silly, she said, them staying away this long, when there's no need.'

'But we had – have to – Giles, I don't think Maxim could have borne to come home – when – when – there wasn't Manderley any longer – and oh, everything . . .'

'You could buy another place – come here – there's enough room here – no, no, but you wouldn't want that. I wish she'd seen old Maxim before – she wasn't one to talk about feelings, but she missed him – all through the war – didn't often say it but I knew. I wish she'd seen him again.'

'Yes,' I said. 'Yes. I'm very sorry.'

He was staring down at the peach satin robe that he still had clutched in his hand. I said, 'Giles, I'll come and help put all this away in the morning – just leave it now. I think you ought to try and get some sleep.'

He looked at me vaguely, then down again at the robe. 'It wasn't her usual thing, she didn't go in for silks and satins and that sort of stuff, more for sensible sort of things.' He was staring and staring at the shiny, slippery material. 'I think Rebecca must have given it to her.'

And, as he spoke, a terrible, vivid picture came into my mind, a picture so clear I might have been there, of Rebecca, whom I had never seen in my life, tall, slender, black-haired Rebecca, spectacularly beautiful, standing at the top of the great staircase at Manderley, a hand resting on the rail, her lips curled in a faint, sardonic smile, looking directly at me, summing me up, scornful, amused, wearing the peach satin robe that now lay crumpled in Giles's fat, stubby hands.

I ran out, and down the corridor, almost tripping over and banging my shoulder painfully against the corner of the wall as I saved myself, and found our room, and burst into it, trembling now, terrified because she had come back to me, she was haunting me again, when I had believed that she was quite, quite forgotten. But in our room, in the first, thin light of day, seeping through the worn old cotton curtains, I saw that Maxim was sound asleep, still huddled in the same position as when I had left him, he had not stirred at all, and I stopped dead, and then closed the door with infinite care, for I must not wake him, and could not speak, nor ever tell him anything of this. I must deal with it myself, lay the ghost, send the beast back to its lair, entirely on my own. Maxim must not be troubled or disturbed by it, Maxim must never know.

I did not get into bed, I sat on the dressing stool by the window, looking out through a chink in the curtains at the shapes of the garden, the orchard and the paddock beyond, everything turning from night into grey pre-dawn, colourless, insubstantial, and it was beautiful as ever to me, the sight of it filled me again with longing, and then I was not frightened, I was angry, angry with memory, angry with myself, angry with the past, for its power to spoil and sour this for me, but most of all, angry, in a hard, cold, bitter way with her, for what she had been and done to us that could never be undone, the way she could reach out to us over so many years, as strongly in death as in life. Rebecca.

But as the light strengthened, and I saw the trees and shrubs and then the horses take on distinction and shape, and then the pale, pearly mist of dawn began to rise and weave about them like silk being spun out by some invisible hand, and draped in and out restlessly, silently, a strange exultation began to well up in me, a joy and a glory in the morning, the new day, with this place, home, England, the life ahead of us, so that I wanted to fling open the window and shout across the countryside, all those miles, to where she lay in that dark, silent crypt alone.

'I am alive!' I wanted to shout. 'Do you hear? I am alive and so is he, and we are together. And you are dead, and will never harm us again. You are dead, Rebecca.'

Five

We breakfasted by ourselves in the dining room. Giles slept in, and I had seen Roger go up to the horses when I was dressing, plodding slowly and heavily, from behind the same shape as his father, the same thick neck set low down on to broad shoulders, so ordinary a man, rising thirty, dull, pleasant, his head full of little other than horses and dogs. I scarcely knew him, he had never impinged much upon our lives.

But he had flown and fought in the war with nerve, with distinction, earned a DFC and finally, been shot down and burned almost beyond recognition, so that if he had turned round now, I should have seen not the old, round and fresh, open faced Roger, but a hideous mask of stretched, shining, flaking skin, alternately white and with vivid staining, and eyes narrowed, looking out of scarred, lashless lids, so that I had to brace myself each time not to flinch, not to look in revulsion too quickly away. The damage to the rest of his body was unimaginable.

Roger, calling softly and waiting, as the grey and then

the chestnut horse came trotting down, his future irreparable. The picture of him came to me again now as I sat, sipping my coffee, watching Maxim peel an apple, and the sight of his hands on the fruit bringing back to me, as they did every day, the memory of that first breakfast I had seen him eat, the morning in Monte Carlo when I had gone, sick with love, with misery, to tell him I had to leave for New York that day with Mrs van Hopper. Every detail of what he wore, ate, drank, every word of what he said, was immortal to me, no detail would, could, ever fade or be confused or forgotten.

He glanced up at me, and whatever the expression on my face was, read it, and through it to what I felt and thought, unerringly, I have still not learned to conceal things, my hopes and fears, every nuance of passing emotion, still show as clearly on my face as on that of a child, I know. I am still not a grown woman in that way. I think he would not want it.

Now, in that dining room full of old fashioned oak furniture, with the chill of the night still on it because the heater did not work very well, and the dreadful memory of yesterday's luncheon when old Colonel Julyan had struggled to his feet to toast our return, now, Maxim laid down his apple and the knife neatly by his plate, and reached out across the table and took my hand.

'Oh, my darling girl, how very badly you want to stay longer, don't you? How much you are dreading my getting up and telling you we should pack, now, at once, and have the car come as soon as possible. You have changed since we got back, do you know that? You look different, something has happened to your eyes – your face – '

I was ashamed then, deeply ashamed, I felt guilty that I had failed to conceal anything at all from him, have my own secrets. Clinging to my own joy at being home, afraid that he did not share it, terrified, as he said, of having to leave too soon.

'Listen.' He had got up and gone to stand by the window and now he gestured for me and I went at once to stand beside him. The top gate stood open, Roger had led the horses out.

'I can't go there – you know that.'

'Of course – oh, Maxim, I would never dream of asking – it would be out of the question – I couldn't bear to go back to Manderley either.'

Though as I said it, glibly, reassuringly, I knew that I lied, and a little snake of guilt stirred and began to uncoil slightly, guilt and its constant companion deceit. For I thought of it night and day, it was always in my mind somewhere, just out of sight, waiting for me, I dreamed of it, Manderley. Not far. Just across the county, away from this low, lovely, gentle inland village, across the high, bare back of the moors and so down, slipping between hills, following the cleft in the land along the river, to the sea, and belonging to another life, years ago, to the past, and yet as close as my next breath. Empty? Derelict? Razed completely? Built upon? Wilderness? Or restored, alive again? Who knew? I wanted to find out. Dared not.

Manderley.

I scarcely faltered, all of it came into my mind and before my eye, in a single encompassing second. I said, 'I wasn't thinking of – of Manderley.' It was still hard to say the name, I felt Maxim tense at once. 'But, oh, Maxim, it is good to be in England. You feel it too, don't you? The way it looks – the light – the trees – everything. Couldn't we have a while longer? Go to a few places perhaps – out of the way places, I mean – not anywhere from – from before. New places. No one will know us or see us – and then we can go back again and take it with us – it will see us through until – whenever. Besides, I don't think we should leave Giles just yet, it would seem so cruel.' I had told him a little, very briefly, about the night before. 'Just a few days more here – to help him begin to sort things out and then – well, Frank invited us up to Scotland. Couldn't we go there? I'd love to see it – I've never been – and meet his family – it was good to see him so happy and settled, wasn't it?'

I babbled on, and he indulged me in the old way, and all was light and easy between us, the secrets I held close to me remained concealed. And what pathetically small things they were, I thought suddenly, going back up to our room, little enough, God knows, to suffer such guilt about.

It was agreed very easily. We would stay here with Giles and Roger until the end of the week, and then go at once to Scotland, to stay with the Crawleys. Maxim seemed quite happy, and I knew that my reassurance about not returning to any of the old familiar places, or anywhere with family connections, but most of all, any places in which we would be remembered and recognised, had meant a great deal and, I thought, quietened his most serious fears. He wanted to see nothing, go nowhere, meet no one, who had the slightest connection with his past and the old life, with Manderley, and most of all, with Rebecca, and Rebecca's death.

This house, Beatrice's house, he could cope with now, I thought, and he might even enjoy ambling gently about the lanes and fields within a short distance. That was what I told myself.

And I – I was wonderfully, gloriously happy, that we could be here longer, and then go to Scotland, and, after that, perhaps, though I scarcely dared to make my ideas coherent, to spell it out even to myself – after that, when Maxim was more relaxed and unafraid, when he had discovered how easy it was to be here and that there was no threat – after that, might we not stay even longer, go elsewhere, spend the last golden autumn days gently exploring this or that quiet corner of England that was unknown to us? Would that not be every bit as good, as restful and unthreatening to him, as being abroad? So long as we kept far, far away from the old places – from Manderley.

I sang as I went upstairs to change, and realised, when I caught myself, that it was 'On Richmond Hill', and that I had not sung or heard it for years, not since I had learned it at school, and yet it came into my head now, fresh and clear. I found that I remembered every word of it.

I could not persuade Maxim to come out. He would wait for Giles to get up, he said, he must try and talk business matters to him, in case there was anything he had to know or attend to concerning Beatrice's affairs. I was surprised. I thought he would have avoided anything that might bring him close to learning about how things had been disposed over Manderley, but he was curt, took *The Times* into the morning room and closed the door, and when I glanced there, from the garden on my way out, I saw that he had his back to the window, and the paper held high, and knew then how much it hurt him to be here, and that he could not bear to look out even at Beatrice's and Giles's old garden and orchard, which were nothing, nothing like any of the gardens at Manderley.

He is doing it for me, I thought. He is doing it out of love. And within me rose, as well as love in return, a flicker of the old insecurity, the disbelief that I could be loved – by any man, and this man, above all, for I still saw him in some sort, as a God, and in spite of the way things had been between us for all of our time in exile, how much stronger I had tried to become, how dependent he had grown on me, in spite of it all, deep down, I had no real confidence, no belief in myself as a woman who was loved in that way. Occasionally, still, I caught myself staring down at my wedding ring as though it were on some stranger's hand, and could not possibly belong to me, turning it round and round, as I had done the whole time on our honeymoon in Italy, as if to convince myself of its reality, heard my own voice on that sunlit Monte Carlo morning, 'You don't understand, I'm not the sort of person men marry.'

But I smiled to myself, hearing it faintly again, as I walked up through the thick dew drenched grass of the paddock, towards the slope and the trees and the hedgerows of the open, glorious, golden countryside beyond.

I walked for more than an hour, following a path, and then leaving it and striding off across the fields, and at first I wished that Maxim had come with me, I wanted so much for him to see it all, hoping, I suppose, that he would fall in love with it again, that the pull of this country, of England, the light and the land, would be so strong that he would be quite unable to resist. I pictured him stopping, here or there, on this little rise, beside this gate that overlooked a small copse, turning to me, 'We must come back, of course,' he would say. 'I see now how much I have missed England – I couldn't bear to go back abroad now, we must stay, and never leave again, whatever that may mean.' And I would reassure him that all would be well, and no one would trouble us, that the past would never rear its head. And if it did – 'Maxim, whatever there is to face, we face it together.'

Catching myself, weaving my fantasies, even feeling my lips move in the imagined conversation, I smiled, for it was an old habit. I had dreamed all the usual schoolgirl dreams this way once, before reality overtook me, though I had indulged it very little in recent years, been too busy growing up, looking after Maxim, protecting him, being his only companion, learning tricks to keep memory from springing up, harsh and powerful, and seizing him, defenceless as he now was.

Only in my private, secret, solitary thoughts about home had I allowed fantasy free rein, only on those imaginary walks over the bare winter uplands, or through the carpet of wild flowers in the woods of spring, only in the way I could, whenever I chose, turn aside and hear in my head the songs of larks, the barking of a fox, deep in the night, the ceaseless craaw of gulls.

Now, walking towards the beech hanger on the opposite slope, putting out my hand to brush it against hawthorn and high wild rose hedge, I let my imagination run wild, saw us both walking like this every day, the dogs running ahead – or even the boys perhaps, after all.

I made up simple, innocent little exchanges with Maxim about what damage that last gale had done, or how well the corn was ripening, whether the dry spell would end soon, might we, just once, have snow at Christmas – I saw him striding a pace or two ahead of me, as he had always done, pointing to this or that, stopping to pull a thorn out of a dog's pad, turning to smile at me in the old way, happy and free. We would be as close as we had been, as dependent upon one another as we had become during our years of exile, yet it would not be so constrained, so claustrophobic, there would be others in our life again, new friends, children, we would have the best of both worlds, we would have come through and out into the sunlight, there would be no further need to hide ourselves away.

So I fancied, so I dreamed and planned and spun my hopes into a bright cloak in which to wrap myself, coming down the long grassy, sloping track that I realised led me at last towards the back of the little grey stone church, in which yesterday there had been Beatrice's funeral. I stopped. Just ahead, stood the gate in the low wall that ran around the churchyard, where the old graves leaned gently towards the grass, their inscriptions blotched and blurred by moss, or worn almost away, and where, as I stood, I could see the new grave, Beatrice's, the turf still loose, the mound quite covered in the fresh, bright flowers.

For a few moments, I stayed there, resting my arms on the gate. No one was about, but suddenly, from a holly tree, a blackbird sang, a few notes, before flying wildly out, low across the grass, sensing my presence, crying a warning. Then, it was quiet again, and I felt a great peace and calm there, sad, still, missing Beatrice, picturing her, wishing I had seen her again, thinking of all the times we might have spoken of; but the sadness had no edge to it, it was not keen, it was only poignant, in that tranquil place. I remembered poor Giles, sobbing in raw grief, the previous night, poor inarticulate Giles, bereft, vulnerable, and suddenly old, and wondered how Beatrice would have dealt with him, whatever brisk words she might have used to pull him round.

Looking back, I can see myself there, in the morning sun, that had dispersed every trace of early mist and was so warm on my face that it might have been a summer's day instead of one well into October. I can stand, as it were, outside myself, as if frozen in time and space, and it is as though most of my life consists of photographs of myself, and in between there is nothing but indeterminate grey. For in those moments, I was calm, I was content, I was, I suppose, happy. I liked being alone, I had quickly accepted that Maxim was not ready yet to walk the countryside and feel free, and told myself that it would come, he would do so, if I did not push him too quickly. I was entirely confident.

So that I was enjoying my own company, the day, these places I had so longed for, my sadness about the death of Beatrice was a muted, melancholy emotion, autumnal, I accepted it and it could not spoil or take away my joy, nor did I feel that it should. For once, I was not ashamed or guilty, for once, I revelled in my own self confidence.

But I thought that I would like to go and stand beside the grave, quietly, alone, and think of Beatrice, with love and thankfulness, and it would be easier to do so today than at the funeral, with so many others surrounding us, and pressing in upon us, all the black crows.

I slipped through the wicket gate, latched it behind me and went across the grass to the path. Beatrice, I thought. Dear Beatrice. And could half imagine her there, but not clearly, it felt too solemn, too quiet a place for her. I saw her better out in the open country, striding, sturdy, never still.

There had been so many people at the funeral, so many friends, and it seemed that everyone had sent flowers. They were piled up and lined the path and spread over on to the grass around the new grave, elaborate crosses and stiff wreaths, and simple home made bunches. Some were too stiffly done, the blooms artificial and waxy looking, as though made out of card or glossy paper, unlike flowers that ever grew in any garden; others were more modest and simple. I bent down to read the cards, found familiar names and those I did not recognise. In fond memory . . . Loving remembrance . . . With sympathy . . . With respect . . . With love . . . Ours, 'Dearest Beatrice . . . ' Giles's 'To my darling wife.' Roger's 'Fondest Love.' Some had had their cards torn off, others were quite concealed, I did not like to peer at every one, it seemed an intrusion, prying into private notes that were somehow meant – and yet not meant – to be read by Beatrice alone.

Then, as I stood up and took a pace back, I saw it. A circle of lilies, pure creamy white, set in a bed of dark, dark green leaves. It was far and away the most striking of them all, it was expensive yet not ostentatious, it was elegant, restrained, and yet it stood alone, impeccably tasteful. I can see it now,

76

apart from the rest, as if quite separately, and most carefully, placed. When I close my eyes, it is there, and I cannot tear my gaze away.

I bent down. Touched the cool, delicate, creamy, beautiful petals, the faintly ribbed, heavy leaves, and a sweet scent came into my nostrils from the flowers, intoxicating and yet faintly alarming, seductive, dangerous. There was a card, thick, cream inlaid, with a black edge, and the lettering 'In deepest sympathy' engraved also in fine black. But it was not the flowers at which I stared, in horror, not the printed words that chilled me, and froze the world and me, splintered the sky and fractured the song of the blackbird, darkened the sun.

It was the single handwritten letter, black and strong, tall and sloping.

R.

CHAPTER

Six

The very worst thing, and it came to me at once, even before my head filled up with a jumble of questions, like water pouring into a rocky hollow when the storm tide rushes in, even before the real fear, the worst was that I knew I had to bear it entirely alone, there was no one at all, no one in the world that I could tell.

But then, following hard upon the first stab of shock, there did come fear, terror, so that I felt faint and giddy, and had to sit down, there on the path beside Beatrice's grave and the piled up flowers, and put my head down on to my knees. It saved me, I felt my heart beating hard again, and the blood rush to my head, and I scrambled up quickly, in case anyone had come and seen me, I felt confused and foolish; but there was no one, the churchyard was as quiet and empty in the morning sunshine as it had been when I first came through the gate. Only the blackbird pinked its warning once or twice from a laurel bush.

The wreath of white flowers mesmerised me, I did not want to look at it again, and I could not help myself, it was as much its beauty as anything that forced me to look at it, it was so very perfect, so pale, so flawless. I stared down at it, but, probably in kneeling so hastily, I had turned the card face downwards, so that I could no longer see the writing.

Then I began to back away, I recoiled from it, as if it were poisonous, like some plant in a fairy-story, so toxic that were I merely to brush against it, I should fall down dead. I turned my back on it, and on the grave and all the other bright, useless flowers, and went quickly round the gravel path, and into the church.

It was open. No one was there. It was cold, and rather dark – the sun had not yet struck through the clear upper windows. I sat in a pew at the very back, feeling sick, and then I began to tremble, my hands shook in my lap, and I could not still them, my legs felt weak.

I felt as I knew one must feel when one has seen a ghost, shaken, disbelieving, confused, with all one's certainties and reasoning undermined, and thrown about like toys by a malevolent, gleeful child.

The wreath was ghostly, white, strange, unreal, though I had seen and touched it, and if I went back to the graveside I was certain, or almost certain, that it would still be there, but most terrifying of all was the writing, the single, black, elegantly sloping letter R. R for Rebecca, in that old, long familiar hand that was bitten with acid into my memory. It was the same. Her letter. Her hand.

It could not be the same. How could it? And then the tide did rush in, and all the rotten debris, disturbed after lying quiet for so many years, surfaced and floated up and filled my mind, jostling, bumping together, claiming my attention.

Rebecca was dead. Buried. Long ago. There was nothing more to be said about it. I *knew*.

Then who had sent the wreath? Who had chosen it with such care, perfect, as it was, to be exactly the wreath that she herself would have ordered, who had written the letter upon the card? Someone playing a foul, cruel joke, a trick, a mean, cunning, secretive action. Someone clever and knowing, someone who hated us. But why? Why? After all these years? What had we done? For I knew instinctively that although the wreath was beside Beatrice's grave, it was meant for our eyes to see, mine and Maxim's. No one wished Beatrice, or Giles and Roger, any harm.

And I must keep this to myself, no one could know, I could spill out my fear and distress to no husband, and I must pretend, too, from the moment I got back I would have to compose myself and be bright and cheerful, calm and reassuring, supportive, loving, strong. Maxim must see nothing, guess nothing, not by any flicker in my eyes, or my voice, or my face.

I wished to God that Frank Crawley had not gone. I might have told him. He was the only person in the world, but he had gone home to Scotland and his new life, no longer really a part of us.

My emotions changed and shifted, as I sat in the church, from fear and horror. I felt anger at whoever had set out to hurt us and succeeded so easily, and then I was bewildered again, then I asked, why, why? What was the point?

We had been so undemanding, only wanted each other

and a quiet, dull, married happiness, we had wanted the past to lie dead and on the whole, we had got what we had asked for and been grateful beyond words.

Now, I was in the midst of it again, the memories rose and wreathed about me like the ghosts they were, scenes, people, voices, emotions, Rebecca, the ghost of a ghost. Manderley. Yet strangely, they did not overwhelm me, they seemed poor, faded things, they in themselves had no power, they were dead, gone, had left scarcely a trace. It was the present that frightened me, this thing that had happened, the white wreath and the black edged card. R.

Yet when I went at last, slowly, hesitantly back, outside into the pale sunshine, I half expected it to have vanished, never to have been, a trick my own unconscious had somehow played, my own deep, deep fears somehow materialised for a few moments. I had heard of such things, although only half believed.

But the wreath was there, as I had known really that it would be, I saw it at once, my eyes were drawn to it and I could not look away. White against the dark, a perfect circle, on the grass.

'I won't think of Manderley.' That was what I had said. I heard my own voice, clear, convincing, false, as I had spoken the words to Maxim. 'I won't think of Manderley.'

But it was all I thought of, more than Maxim could ever be, I thought, and even though I had known it for such a short time and in such wild, desperate circumstances, I was obsessed by it now, it came again and again to me, as I walked back, it lay before me, it was on the other side of every rise, and every next bend in the lane, so that I ceased to see anything that lay around me, the trees, the fields, the slopes and woods and gentle inland sky, everything, and saw only Manderley.

Yet I had hated it, it had oppressed and terrified me, I had been crushed by it, I had found it cold and strange and bewildering, and it had sneered at me, I had never belonged there, never even known my way with complete confidence, about its staircases and corridors, among so many closed doors.

Manderley. It was not the people who came so vividly back to life now to mock me, Frith, Robert, Clarice, the little maid, Jack Favell, Mrs Danvers, Rebecca – where were they? I did not know. Rebecca was dead, that was all I was certain of. For the others, I scarcely spared a thought for the others, I did not care. I would never see them again and they did not matter.

But the house. That I longed for, and feared, and was drawn back to. Manderley. I hated myself. I must not, must not think of it, I must put it from me, or it would damage us. I had to think of Maxim, only Maxim. We had saved each other, I must not tempt fate.

I was very fierce with myself, coming slowly down the last slope, towards the paddock, seeing Beatrice and Giles's pleasant, comfortable, undistinctive house lying below, the smoke rising in a thin spear from its chimney. That would be the morning room then, he would be in there, reading the paper still, looking at his watch now and then, impatient for me to return.

I wished that I had a mirror, so that I could see my face, compose it, put on a mask, as he could. I must pretend.

What I had seen, I had not seen, what had happened had not happened. I put Manderley out of my mind, and if I could not do the same with the wreath of white flowers, I turned away from them, and would not look, and left the card lying where it was, face down to the ground.

From the house, I heard the ringing of the telephone, and the dogs begin to bark. The horses were back, heads bent to graze contentedly after their exercise. And so I went down, towards them all, and with every step, I forced myself to look forward, and to compose my face, so that it was open, and cheerful . . . it was with a huge effort of will that I blotted out the wreath and the card and its signed initial, and everything it might mean, from my conscious mind – though I knew that of course they would only sink deep down, and embed themselves forever, they would join all those other things that could never be undone or unknown or forgotten.

I wanted Maxim. I wanted to sit quietly with him in a corner of the house somewhere, with the morning sun slanting through the windows and the fire beginning to pull in the hearth, wanted the trappings of the everyday, and the ordinary around me, for protection and reassurance.

I began to make up an account of where I had been, what birds and animals and trees I had noticed, what good mornings and odd words about the season and the weather I had exchanged, with some old man working on the land – I saw his greasy peaked cap, now, I invented the string tied round the legs of his ancient trousers, just above the boots, so that by the time I went across the garden, he was quite a friend. There had been a woman with a couple of retrievers, too, I had admired them, patted them. I was trying to make up names, but all that would come into my head was Jasper, Jasper. I turned my mind hastily away.

I wanted him to comfort me but I could not ask that, I must appear totally calm and unruffled, must be all concern for him. I must pretend, pretend. But the wreath was everywhere I looked, on the path, in the shrubbery, beside the gate, upon the door, cool, and white and perfect, it stood between me and everything else I saw, and the card fluttered and turned over, so that its black letter danced insolently before me. R. R. R.

I stopped in the hall. From the study, I could hear the rumble of Giles's voice on the telephone. There was a sweet smell of fresh woodsmoke. I closed my eyes, clenched my hands and released them, took a breath.

He was sitting beside the fire in the morning room, his face in profile, the paper discarded beside him on the floor. He was very still, and, I saw at once, miles away from here, unconscious for a moment of my coming into the room.

I looked at him, saw the familiar face, lined now, his hair still thick but grey, saw his hand with the long fingers resting on the arm of the chair, but in the split second, before reaching out to him in relief and in a rush of love, heard the voice drop its syllables cold and clear and emotionless, like stones into a pool, 'That man is a murderer. He shot Rebecca. That is the man who killed his wife,' and I wondered wildly if it were a real, malevolent thing, sent deliberately to drive me mad, before, with a tremendous effort of will I shoved it aside and broke through, to reach Maxim, in time to see him look up, come to and then smile with such love and joy and gratefulness, welcoming me back.

There was coffee, brought in a homely pot by the woman who came in, not served grandly and all the better for that, and the sunshine did come through the tall windows and one of the dogs had found it and was lying along the shaft, while the other hugged the fire, which kept smoking a little, so that first Maxim and then I had to keep fiddling with it, and I was grateful for that. I was still restless and unnerved, I needed the cover of something to do.

I said, 'I heard Giles on the telephone.'

'Yes.'

'Have you seen him?'

'He came in and wandered out again – he kept apologising, and blowing his nose.'

'Poor Giles.'

'He began to irritate me, I'm afraid, I can't cope with it. He seems to be crumbling to pieces.'

He sounded harsh, and impatient. He had never felt easy with any displays of emotion, but I wanted him to be gentle with Giles, to understand him. This cold, dismissive side of him reminded me too much of how he sometimes used to be, before I had known the truth and he had allowed me to come close to him.

I knelt back on my heels from the fire.

Maxim said, 'It's hopeless. The wood's too damp.'

'Yes.' But I continued to watch the weak little thread of smoke, willing it to blaze out.

'I tried to sort out some of the business affairs with him. He doesn't know much – it's all a muddle.'

I knew that when we had been abroad and any papers had come, Maxim had signed them after barely a glance.

'I had a talk with the solicitors. They need to see me. I can't get out of it, damn it.'

My heart lurched. I had never known anything at all about Maxim's financial or business affairs, but there had been a solicitor once in Kerrith. Perhaps we would have to go over there, perhaps –

'It's not the local man,' he said, as if reading my thoughts. 'They're in London.'

'London?' I was not able to stop myself sounding eager, quickly excited at the thought.

London.

We might have to go there then, not just hurriedly, furtively, scurrying, heads down, to change trains and leave at once, but to visit, to stay for a day, perhaps even a night, too, on proper business, with time, and a little leisure. London, oh, just once, please. I had never truly liked it, never been a city person in the least, I would not feel relaxed or at home there. But in our exile, I had just occasionally thought of it, daydreamed about it after reading something in an old news-paper from home – a name would catch my eye at random. Lords. The Old Bailey, Parliament Hill Fields, East India Dock, the Mall, St. James's, the Mansion House, Kensington Gardens . . . and then I had spent a happy hour walking about, looking in grand shop windows, taking tea, listening to the band in the park on a spring morning, exploring some dark little Dickensian alley, where the houses leaned across to one another and the gutters smelled of printer's ink, an innocent, pleasant, romantic little pastime, another reminder of home.

I knew the war had dealt harshly with London, accepted that things would not look the same, would be shabbier, damaged, scarred, and I turned away from all thoughts of that last terrible visit, with Maxim and Favell and Colonel Julyan, to see Rebecca's doctor, and all that it meant, all that had come after. Well, that had been separate, we would never need to see that particular street again, it would be perfectly easy to keep well away.

London. I was a country person, I knew that it was the green fields and lanes and rises, the smell of ploughed earth and the soft calling of the wood pigeons deep in the cool woods, that I needed to live quietly among for the rest of my days. I would never be happy for long among traffic and sights, on hard city pavements, with buildings looming over me.

But London, again, just once, for a day, no more. Oh, please. I half turned to look at Maxim, and almost asked.

He said, 'He will come down here to see Giles and me the day after tomorrow.' His face was closed, his voice tight, I was warned off at once, closed my mouth and did not utter. 'It will take a few hours, I'm afraid. I want to get it all over and done and sorted out in one day. I don't want it hanging over me. You'll have to amuse yourself for half a day – but you want to do that, don't you? You want to be out.'

If he minded, he did not give a hint of it, he smiled, indulgent, again, talking in that way he had as if to a child. It was coming back, now that we were here. He had told me that I had changed, since our return, but so had he, there were flashes here and there of the old, the other Maxim.

I smiled, and turned back to the fire again, took up the

bellows and began to press them, my head down, away from him. London faded. We would not go.

'I hope all this isn't going to upset you too much,' I said.

'I shan't let it. It's got to be done, we'll just get on with it. A lot of Beatrice's affairs are – are quite separate from mine and the rest of the family's of course, and have been since her marriage. But whatever loose ends there are can all be tied up together once and for all and then we can be off.' He stood up, and came over to me, he was standing, very tall and steady, just behind me. I felt him close to my back. 'Give me those things, let me see if I can lick this fire into shape.'

I handed him the bellows, and stood up. 'But – we can go to Scotland?'

He smiled, and I saw that he looked tired, exhausted, the skin was fine and like a faint bruise beneath his eyes, and he was vulnerable again to me, and I wondered why I had been in some odd way afraid. 'Of course,' he said wearily. 'You shall have your holiday,' and bent to kiss my forehead, before turning to tackle the withered fire.

CHAPTER

Seven

For the whole of that night and the next day, whatever I saw or heard or thought, however I answered Maxim, lightly, comfortably, he was at one remove from me, I pressed a switch and life continued, but it was not real life, it did not signify.

The only reality was the white wreath, lying on the grass beside the grave, and the black letter, elegant, graceful, deadly, on the stiff card. They accompanied me, they danced before my eyes, they breathed and watched and whispered, they hovered at my shoulder, and would not cease or let me be.

Who? I kept asking myself every time I could be alone, who had done this? How? Why? Why? Who wanted to frighten us? Who hated us? When had they come? Had they been there when I had found the wreath? No, I knew, was strangely, calmly sure that that could not have been. When I had crossed the churchyard and stood beside Beatrice's grave, when I had bent to examine the flowers, and seen the white wreath first, I had been quite alone, if I had not been I would have known it. There had been no one else, no watcher in the shadows, nothing but the wreath itself to disturb me.

I was afraid, but most of all, I was puzzled. I wanted to know, I did not understand, and the worst of it was bearing it entirely alone, keeping all hint from my face and voice, hiding the faintest sign of distraction or anxiety from Maxim.

It preoccupied me completely, even while I went through the motions of passing that night and the following day, it ran alongside me, like a tune that was playing, so that at last, I simply grew used to and accepted it and that calmed me a little.

'You will have to amuse yourself for half a day but you want to do that, don't you?'

I heard his voice again as I brushed my hair at the dressing table. I had not known that being home would do this to him, and that the Maxim I had grown used to, patient, quiet, subdued, the Maxim with whom I had lived for our years abroad, would slip away so easily, to reveal so many traces of the old Maxim, the one I had first known. But with every hour that passed in England, he changed a little, it was like watching curtains blow in the wind, to reveal more and more of what stood behind and had only been concealed, not obliterated.

'You will have to amuse yourself for half a day.'

If it had happened a year ago, a month ago even, if for some reason there had been business to attend to, he would have tried to avoid it completely, to hide, it would have distressed him unbearably to have had to face it, and without any doubt he would have insisted that I be with him, listen, read the papers, see it through with him, he could not have done it without me. I had never imagined that he might change, that his old, easy, proud independence would reassert itself, that he would show any sign of being able, and willing, to deal with things alone, or for one moment wish me to be away from him. It was a shock, like watching a helpless, dependent invalid begin to recover, regain strength, show spirit and a flicker of the old fire, stand, and then walk alone again, brushing off impatiently the loving, restraining, anxious hands.

I did not know what I felt, or how much I minded, but I was not hurt. I did not take his brisk words as a rejection. I think perhaps I was relieved. And besides, the change was not total, there was much that was the same. We spent a day together quietly in the house – for apart from pacing a few times round the garden, day and evening, he had not gone out, would not go. It had turned wet and very windy, with scudding, grey clouds and a mist that came down quite close to the house, so that we could not see even as far as the horses in the paddock.

We read beside the fire and played bezique and piquet, and did the crossword in the newspaper, and the dogs slouched between us on the hearthrug, and at lunch, and dinner, Giles sat, and was virtually silent, sunken into himself, his eyes red, with heavy stains and pouches beneath them. He looked unkempt, dishevelled, broken and crumbling to pieces, and oblivious to the fact, and I did not know what to do or to say, I only tried to be kind, to pour his tea or smile at him the few times he caught my eye. I think he was grateful, in his pathetic child-like way, but then he went back to be alone in his study for hour after hour.

There was not even Roger to lighten the atmosphere, he had gone away to see friends, and I was relieved of the distress of looking at him and the guilt my feelings caused me.

For that day, we seemed to be suspended in time, in some sort of waiting room, between places. We did not belong in this house, it was vaguely familiar and yet strange, and bleak to us. We felt less comfortable than we might have done in a hotel. Maxim spoke very little, and for much of the day seemed abstracted, brooding, though he was glad, I think, when I tried to divert him, when tea came, or I suggested another game of piquet. Yet I had also a strange sense that to some extent he was merely going along with it to indulge me, keep me happy. I felt myself reverting again to my old, inferior, child-like role.

The day passed slowly. The rain blew onto the window panes, the mist did not lift. It was early dark.

'You will have to amuse yourself for half a day, but you want to do that, don't you?'

Yes. My heart pounded suddenly as I drew the curtains that night. I had a secret, it made me catch my breath as I thought of it. I could amuse myself for half a day. I knew what I would do, but I turned on my side, away from Maxim, and could not let him see me, it felt such a betrayal, the worst kind of deceit and infidelity.

The mist had gone, and there were skeins of cloud, in a clear, pale sky, blown by the breeze. It was almost like spring, except that the ground was thick with leaves that had been blown off the trees the previous day and lay in heaps about the garden and the drive.

The lawyer would be here by eleven, a taxi was booked to fetch him from the station.

I looked across the breakfast table. Giles was not down. Maxim looked formal, in a suit and stiff shirt, distant from me.

The white wreath floated, pale, insubstantial, between us.

Who? How? When? Why? What did they want of us?

I heard my own voice speaking quite easily. I said, 'I wonder if Giles would let me take the car? I think it's market day at Hemmock. I'd rather like to go.'

I had learned to drive almost as soon as we had gone abroad, though we had not owned a car, only hired one here and there, when we felt like taking a trip for a few miles to see some church or monastery or special view we had read of. Maxim seemed to like me to drive him, it had been part of the change in him, although he would never have dreamed of suggesting it in the old life. I had done it gladly, enjoying it, and enjoying even more the feeling it gave me of being different, the one who guided and was responsible. Driving a car seemed such a grown up thing to do, I had made Maxim smile, when I had once said so.

Now, he scarcely glanced up from the paper. 'Why not? He has to be here, he isn't going to need it. You'll enjoy the market.'

So that was all right, he would let me go, he had not changed his mind, did not need me here.

But I felt a pang, as I went to get my coat. I lingered, holding his hand, waiting to be reassured that he could face the solicitor, the papers, and whatever the business talk might bring up, without me.

'It's fine,' he said. 'It's fine. There's nothing to worry about.'

Only the wreath, I thought, and saw the letter traced, suddenly, upon his face. R. Rebecca.

It had never once crossed my mind that it had stood for anyone else. I saw that Maxim was watching me, composed my face into a bright smile.

He said, 'It is all like a dream, not unpleasant. I simply go through it – and it has curiously nothing at all to do with me, and tomorrow I shall wake and real life will dawn again, and we can go on with it. Do you understand?'

'I think so.'

'Be patient with me.'

'Darling, would you rather I stayed here, just in the next room – ?'

'No.' He touched my cheek lightly with the back of his hand, and I took it, and pressed my face against it, loving him, and guilty, guilty.

'I'll telephone Frank this evening,' he said, smiling. 'We can be away from here tomorrow.'

And then Giles came out of the study, looking for Maxim, some papers in his hand, and so I could ask about the car, I could go, out of their way, out of the house, dismissed with a clear conscience, to amuse myself.

What was I thinking of? What was I planning to do? Why was I making this journey, the journey I had said and believed I could never make again? Why was I tempting fate?

I was foolish, what I wanted was wrong, and it was dangerous, too. At best, I would be made wretched and be horribly disappointed. At worst, and if Maxim were ever to find out, I might destroy everything, our fragile happiness, the love and trust we had built up with such care and patience, him, myself, the rest of our lives.

Yet I would go, I think I had known from the day I knew that we were coming back, that I would go, it was quite impossible to resist. I craved it, it was like a secret, irresistible love affair, I dreamed of it, longed for it, wanted and needed to know.

No one would speak to me of it. I did not dare to ask. The only person I had mentioned it to was Frank Crawley and even then, the name had not passed my lips . . . Manderley.

There are some temptations that cannot be resisted, some lessons we never learn. Whatever happened, whatever the outcome, I had to go there, see for myself at last. *I had to know.*

Manderley. It had me in thrall, half in love, half fear, but it had never let me go, its spell was all powerful still. I realised that, as I set the old black, bull nosed car towards where the road would bend and turn a little, before running straight on, in the direction of the sea.

It was thirty miles away, on the other side of the county, so that, at first, the villages and lanes and little market towns were unfamiliar. I saw the sign to Hemmock, where I had said I wanted to go, wander round the market, perhaps have a light lunch in a little shop overlooking the square. But I passed the turning. I was going another way.

I did not allow myself to brood upon it, did not linger over any of the scenes of the past, I enjoyed the sky and the trees and the high, open moor, I wound down the window so that I could smell the autumn earth. I felt free and happy and I liked driving the car. I was an innocent on an outing, I dared not be anyone else.

But at the end of it, what did I expect to find? What did I *want* there to be? An empty shell, amidst the tangle of the deep woods, charred, and twisted, and hollow, the ashes long, long dead and cold, the creeper strangling it now, weeds choking the drive, as in my recurring dream? But I could not be sure, no one had ever dared to tell us what there was, we had refused to let the name cross anyone's lips, no letters had come with news, during our exile.

I think I half convinced myself that it was a romantic pilgrimage, that what I would find would be a sad, poignant, melancholy place, unhaunted, fallen into a strangely beautiful decay. I was not apprehensive, not afraid. Other things frightened me, the silent cat poised in the shadows waiting to spring. The white wreath – the card, the initial. Some unknown person's carefully, cunningly directed malevolence.

Not Manderley.

I stopped once, in a village half way there, to buy myself a drink of orangeade from the small shop, and as I said goodbye to the woman and went out of the door into the sunlight, hearing the ting of the bell brought a surge of memory back like a wave, and I realised, blinking, looking around me, that I had been here before, many years ago, when I had been a girl on holiday with my parents and bought a picture postcard for my collection, because the house it showed appealed to me, and the house had been Manderley.

And, standing there, looking across at the low, white-washed thatched barn of the farm opposite, that past was with me and I within it, more vividly than anything for a long time, I could touch it, feel it, nothing here had changed at all, I thought, and nothing might have happened to me in between.

I sat in the car for a long time, sipping at my bottle of sweet, warm orangeade, and I was in a strange kind of trance, suspended, frozen there, I was not fully aware of who or what I was, and why I was here, on this October day.

After a while, I started the car and began to drive on again. I left my girlhood behind in that quiet village, and then, suddenly, the road became familiar, rounding a bend I saw a signpost.

Kerrith. 3 miles.

I stopped and switched off the car engine, and through the windows, borne on the breeze, came the faint salt smell of the sea.

My heart was beating very fast, the palms of my hands were damp. Kerrith. Kerrith. I stared at the name until the letters became meaningless marks, they jazzed together like midges and apart again, they hurt my eyes.

Kerrith. The village and its harbour and its boats, the beach and the bungalows, and the cobbles down to the quay, even the swinging inn sign and the way the church gate had leaned unevenly, I saw it, in every detail.

In another mile, I would round a bend and then I would

see the brow of the hill with its belt of trees sloping to the valley, with a faint blue line of sea just visible beyond.

I heard Maxim's voice. If I glanced round, I would see him beside me. 'That's Manderley, in there. Those are the woods.'

It was the first time I came here, that day, like so many other days, strung out separately, distinctly, like a run of beads, and each of them so perfectly remembered.

Then, quite casually, unexpectedly, I heard another voice, and remembered a woman I had seen with her little boy the day the ship had run aground in the fog, on the rocks below Manderley. They had been holiday makers come over for an outing, from Kerrith.

I saw her fat face now, blotchy after exposure to the sun, the gingham blouse she had been wearing. 'My husband says all these big estates will be chopped up in time, and bungalows built,' she had said. 'I wouldn't mind a nice little bungalow up here, facing the sea.'

I felt suddenly sick. Was that what had happened to Manderley after all then, and what I should find if I went on? The woods cleared, the house razed, dozens of bungalows, neat, with pink and green and light blue window frames, and the last ragged summer flowers fading in the gardens, and was there, perhaps, a bank of rhododendrons, tamed and trimmed back, all that was left of the banks and banks there had once been? Would there be holiday boats tied up in the cove, and a line of wooden beach huts with names painted over the doors and little verandas?

Perhaps this would be what they had thought it kinder to keep from us, this desecration, this dreadful, mundane end to it all.

There was no way of telling and so I started the car again and drove on a little further, tempting fate, risking everything, probing at the old wounds. I rounded the bend. I saw the belt of trees on the brow of the hill, the beginning of the slope down to the valley. There were no new signposts, all seemed to be the same. If there were bungalows, they were hidden.

But, then, I knew that there were not, and that it was all there, as I had dreamed it, the ruin, the house, the overgrown drive, the woods crowding in upon it all, and beyond them, somewhere, the cove, the beach, the rocks, and those would be quite unaltered.

There. I got out of the car and took a step or two forwards. Looked ahead – there, oh, there, so near, I could go. Just beyond the rise. Why did I not? Why?

Go, go, go, said the voice in my head, a seductive, whispering, cold little voice.

Come.

Manderley.

The earth was spinning, the sky above me seemed made of some transparent, brittle, fragile substance and at any moment might break open.

A breeze blew, riffling the grass, caressing my face like a soft, silken, invisible hand.

I fled.

Fled back through the lanes and across the open road that ran over the moor, driving insanely fast, though with a tremendous concentration born of panic, flinging the car round blind bends, hurling it at hills, once almost colliding with a farm wagon, catching a flash of the man's startled face, his mouth open in an O, once almost killing a dog, fled back through the villages and past the signs that had led me here. Fled, back into the open gateway, and out and across the drive, fled, into the house, and saw Maxim at once, coming out of the study, and beyond him, through the open door, the others, two men in dark suits, one standing beside the fireplace with Giles.

I did not speak, there was no need. He opened his arms, caught and stilled me, and held me until I had stopped shaking, stopped crying. He knew, I did not have to tell him anything at all. He knew and there would never be a word spoken about it, and I was forgiven, I knew that too, though would not have dared to ask it.

The lawyers stayed to lunch, but I did not have to join them. I had sandwiches on a tray, sitting peacefully beside the fire in the drawing room, though I was not at all hungry, and scarcely managed a couple, and a piece of fruit, so as not to offend the housekeeper. After that, I simply sat, looking at the garden out of the window, and the afternoon sun came shafting in, and that was another small, fierce pleasure, and I cherished it. I felt exhausted, and I felt relief. I had escaped, no thanks to myself, escaped the consequences of my own wilfulness, and the demon that had driven me, and I was safe again, nothing had disturbed me, nothing had harmed me, but more important still, nothing had *been* disturbed, the smooth surface of the past lay untroubled.

Whatever Manderley was now did not concern me. It belonged only to the past and, sometimes, to my dreams.

I would not go back again.

Later, after they had gone, we walked up to the paddock, Maxim and I, and he only spoke a few words, about Beatrice's affairs, and those were not of any consequence.

'It's done with,' he said. 'All settled. There are no problems, nothing to concern us any more.'

I stopped, beside the gate. The horses were at the top of the field and did not come to us, or even lift their heads from their grazing. I shivered.

Maxim said, 'Scotland tomorrow. I should like to go off early.'

'I'll pack after dinner. There isn't much.'

'Will you have enough warm things? Will you need to stop off anywhere? I suppose it may be rather cold.'

I shook my head. 'I just want to get there.'

'Yes.'

It was true. I wanted to be away from here, though not because of this house, or of Giles and Roger, nor even because it felt so bleak and hollow and unkempt without Beatrice. I had not dared to think of our returning abroad. I could not bear to, did not want to go. Instead, I imagined the journey, up by train through England, the hours I would be able to spend simply gazing and gazing at it through the window, towns, villages, the woods, fields, rivers, hills, land and sea and sky. I wanted great draughts of it, I could not wait.

We would borrow books from here, and buy more at the railway station. When I was not looking out of the window, we would read companionably, and eat in the dining car together, and play bezique, it would be a precious time, and everything that had happened here would recede and fade until it was quite unreal.

We walked back in silence, contentedly towards our last night in the house.

At dinner, Maxim said, looking up from his fish, speaking quite without warning, 'I should like to go across to the grave in the morning, before we leave.'

I stared at him, my face flushing suddenly hot as fire, said, 'But surely you can't – I mean, there won't be time, the car will be here at nine.'

'Then I shall go at eight.' He lifted his fork to his mouth and ate, calmly ate, while my own food went cold and leaden and sour in my mouth and my throat closed so that I could not swallow it, nor speak either.

He could not go, must not, and yet how could I possibly prevent him. What reason could I give? There was none.

I glanced across at Giles. He would go, too, I thought, he would see it, blunder up and read the card, and blurt it out, ask questions.

I saw that tears were coursing down his cheeks, quite unchecked, and that Maxim was looking at him in embarrassment and looking away again quickly, at his own plate.

'Sorry.' Giles's knife clattered onto his plate as he stumbled up, fishing about for his handkerchief. 'Sorry. Better get outside a bit.'

'For God's sake, what's the matter with him?' Maxim said furiously, the door had scarcely closed.

'His wife is dead.' I knew that my voice was harsh, and impatient, and should not be, that Maxim was simply pushing Giles's distress away, not liking to witness it, that really he understood.

'Well, the sooner we go tomorrow, and he's back to normal, the better it will be for him. This is only prolonging the agony. He'll have to get on with it then.'

'Should I see if the car can come earlier – we can stop somewhere on the way for breakfast can't we? I know how hateful it all is for you.'

I felt deceitful, sly, my eager, smooth words slipping so easily out of my mouth. But it was for his sake, to protect Maxim, spare him, it was all for him.

'No,' he said. 'Leave things as they are. Ring the bell, will you? I don't want any more of this.'

I did so, and the subject of our departure the next morning was dropped, and I sat sick with dread for the rest of dinner, pushing food about my plate uneaten, and the question sounded over and over like a relentless pulse in my head. What shall I do? What shall I do? What shall I do?

I scarcely slept, I did not let myself do so, but got up just at dawn and dressed hurriedly, stealthily, like a guilty departing lover, and slipped out of the silent house, terrified of waking the dogs or disturbing the horses; but I did not, no one heard me, nothing stirred, and so I ran, taking off my shoes until I reached the lane, keeping on the grass so as not to make a sound moving the gravel, and the early morning world was still and pale and indescribably beautiful as the light strengthened. Yet I was scarcely aware of it, I was only conscious of my own footsteps, and my anxiety not to fall, heard the pounding of my heart, saw nothing.

I remember that I was not faintly afraid, there was not room even for that, there was only secrecy and urgency, and as I ran and paused for breath several times and then set off again, walking now, very fast, I prayed that I would get there, and be able to do what I had to, and be back again, and never be found out. Once, a fox slipped through a gap in the hedge, and streaked straight across my path; once, glancing up, I looked into the wide eyed, morning face of an owl upon a branch.

It was very cold in the hollows, but I scarcely felt it as I ran. If anyone had seen me, what would they have thought? A woman, running, running, through the lanes, down the sloping fields, alone in the first light of morning, slipping at last through the gate, into the quiet churchyard.

Stopping.

I waited to catch my breath. Thought, suddenly, though still strangely without any fear, that if ever one were to see a ghost, surely it would be now, in such a place as this; but I did not.

I saw nothing.

Saw only the mound beside the gravel path.

Fresh turf had been laid over it loosely now, and on the top of the turf, was a single cross of bronze chrysanthemums. I did not need to look closely at it, I remembered that it was from Giles and Roger.

The rest of the flowers had gone. When I walked around to the far side of the church I found the wooden frame on to which they had been heaped by the gardener. Earth had been thrown on top of them and a few trimmed branches from one of the trees, so that whatever wreaths lay there, lay quite concealed.

I turned away, giddy with relief, but as I passed the holly bush that stood at the corner, I noticed something in it, a piece of card caught by a torn wisp of ribbon among the prickle of dark green leaves. I put my hand in and took it, held it, mesmerised by the cream surface with its black edging, black words, and by the black initial in that sloping hand.

R.

And the holly had pricked my finger, so that when I stuffed the card away, deep into my pocket, I marked it with my blood.

CHAPTER

Eight

It rained all the way up through England, dull, steady, relentless rain, and the sky bulged with pigeon grey clouds, and after a while, even I grew weary of it and turned away from the window to my paper or my book.

I should have been very happy, I had fully expected to be, but tiredness and the after effects of those things that had happened, the distressing and the frightening things, made me feel stale, there seemed no pleasure, no excitement, in being here, after all. I was growing used to it already, and taking it for granted. The sense of freedom I had longed for was missing too, I felt confined, and oppressed. I wished that I were a woman who embroidered or tatted, so that I would have had something to do with my hands when I grew tired of reading. It would have given me the appearance of busyness, and Maxim would have preferred that, I knew, he relied upon me to be equable, a restful companion, he did not like to sense any edge to my mood, and for so long I had tried to give him what he wanted, to reassure him.

The Midlands were slate coloured, roofs gleamed black.

The rain slanted like pins across the hills as we travelled north, there was mist on the peaks.

Home, I said, we are home, but did not feel it now.

Maxim read, newspapers, a book, and once or twice, went to stand in the corridor, leaning on his elbows against the window frame.

I had looked forward to this and it was spoilt, soured, and he seemed far away, and it was my own thoughts that divided us, for I had secrets now, and must keep them. The questions that had chanted inside my head still ran on, but in whispers. Who? How? Why? Where had the wreath come from? Who had sent it? Or had it been brought and left? What did they want? They? Who? And why? Why? Why? The words kept pace with the rhythm of the wheels of the train.

The door slid open again. Maxim came back.

'Shall we go for some coffee?' I asked.

But he shook his head and went back to the paper, the paper I was sure he had already read, and did not speak to me. Did not want to speak. It was my fault, I knew it, and I could do nothing.

The train ran towards the Borders, and the hills were bare and bleak. England was empty, and I felt nothing for it, and the rain streamed down the window, taking the place of my tears.

Once, I saw a woman pass by our compartment, down the corridor, and glance in, and I happened to look up, by chance, and catch her eye, for a split second. Nothing. But then, I saw the flicker of a question, an awareness, on her face, and she stopped, took a step back, and peered at us both more closely. I raised my book hastily and turned myself away, and when I dared to glance up again, she had gone.

It was nothing, I said, nothing at all. We have not been in England for more than ten years. It is all over and quite forgotten. There has been the war like a great ravine that has opened up between then and now.

But a little later, we went for the first sitting in the dining car, and as I unfolded my napkin and crumbled the hard bread on to my plate, I knew that she was there, at the table across the aisle, she wore a purple blouse, I could see it out of the corner of my eye.

When the waiter came with our soup it splashed a little on to the tablecloth with a sudden lurch of the train, and Maxim asked irritably for a clean cover, and I tried to soothe him, and in the midst of the small, silly fuss, looked up and straight into the woman's eyes again. I felt my face grow hot, and was furious with my own gaucheness. She had a companion, a younger woman, and now, recognition shining in her eyes, she was leaning eagerly forward. I saw her plump mouth forming the words, saw her whisper, felt what she was saying, though for the moment it was not a lot, our names, perhaps; only later, safe in their own compartment, after some more confirmatory, covert glances, she would tell. 'Well – Maxim de Winter – that's his second wife – been abroad for years – they say he had to – Manderley – Rebecca. Surely you remember . . .'

She reminded me hideously of Mrs van Hopper, putting down her fork and raising her lorgnette, in the hotel dining room at Monte. 'It's Max de Winter . . . the man who owns Manderley. You've heard of it, of course . . .'

I put my hand over Maxim's, said something quickly about the view from the window, some inane remark, I remember, about there being a lot of sheep. I was desperate for him not to notice, being recognised and pointed out was the one thing he dreaded. And besides, I wanted by some touch, some slight gesture, to bring him back to me.

He smiled thinly, and said, 'This fish is disgustingly dry.'

'Never mind,' I said, 'never mind.'

'All right. Let's just look at the sheep.'

It made me giggle and he raised an eyebrow, his face softening with his own amusement, and I took a very large gulp of my wine out of relief and a sudden upsurge of happiness, and looking out of the train window again, saw that it was growing dark.

'We're in Scotland,' Maxim said, and there was a lift in his voice, a new lightness.

Scotland was another country.

We spent that night in a small hotel in Dunaig, the nearest town to the estate Frank Crawley managed. He had made the arrangements, thinking that it would be too late when we arrived for us to want a further journey, a message was waiting to say that he would be there to collect us soon after breakfast.

The rain had petered out during the final miles north and a raw wind was blowing, we were glad to be in, welcomed with reserved friendliness by the proprietress. Only a single elderly couple were staying besides ourselves, we could relax now, in the high ceilinged, old fashioned rooms, we need not worry about being recognised up here.

It felt strange, like one of our foreign hotels, but after all, I was used to that, used to putting my clothes away in yet another great hollow wardrobe on padded hangers that other people had used, used to sitting carefully on the end of a strange bed to see whether it was hard or soft, used to anonymous bathrooms and noisy plumbing, curtains too thin or too thick, drawers that did not open smoothly. It was only for one night and then we would be staying in a house again.

But I thought, placing my slippers beside the bedside table, that I did not want that, good as it would be to spend some time with Frank and to meet his family, I had had enough of hotel rooms and other people's houses, I wanted my own. I did not want to be in exile any longer, rootless, unsettled in anything but a temporary way, I was too old for it. I had never had a house, not since childhood, and that is quite a different thing. There had been hotels and, for a brief time, there had been Manderley.

But Manderley had not been mine, I had been a visitor there, too, for all the pretence, tolerated, never belonging.

I had expected to be wakeful that night, there were too many shadows at my back. I felt tense and wary, almost afraid to speak for fear I should blurt out some word that would alert Maxim. The wreath was never out of my mind, it lay there, still and white and beautiful, a picture I was obliged to look at, and when I dug my hand down into my pocket I started, feeling the hard edge of the card, and was terrified. How stupid, stupid I had been to keep it, why had I not stuffed it into the heart of the gardener's careful heap, to be burned with the flowers?

The woman's face haunted me, too. I saw again the flash of recognition, the head bent to whisper excitedly.

Maxim had been right. We should never have come back. This was how it would be for ever, this dreadful knife edge of fear, that something would happen, someone would see us, know, speak, ask, break into our peace.

But it had been broken already, a poor, fragile, transparent thing; we had never been safe.

So I thought, in despair, sitting opposite Maxim in the dark dining room of the hotel, and later, upstairs. The wind rattled the casement, and beat wildly at the side of the house, I had not heard such a wind for years. Home, it said, but where was home? Nowhere.

'Poor darling, you're white with tiredness – it's been the most appalling strain hasn't it, and I have been no help to you at all. I left too much to you, I've been hideously selfish.'

Maxim was holding me, loving, solicitous, tender, his mood changed in an instant, as it so often did, some blackness and irritability that had distanced him lifted, dissolved. I realised that I was, as he said, exhausted, I was weak with it, confused, my head aching.

When I lay down the room seemed to rock beneath my bed, the walls and ceiling to shift and then dissolve into one another, but I was not ill, I knew, it was only tiredness – tiredness and a deep, exquisite relief.

I slept, as I had not slept for a week, and quite dreamlessly, and awoke to the ice blue sky and delicate frost of a northern morning.

It was sleep that I had needed – and I was sure that it

had helped Maxim too, his mood was lighter, the tight lines around his eyes and mouth smoothed out, my depression through the journey of the previous day had been fleeting and superficial, and lifted with the lifting of the rain clouds.

Frank arrived just before ten, in an ancient Land Rover, full of spaniel dogs and fishing tackle behind a grille, to drive us across to the estate, and his house at Inveralloch.

'I'm sorry,' he said, opening the doors, 'it's a bit rough and ready I'm afraid – we don't go in for refinements up here.'

I saw him glance uneasily at Maxim, elegant as always, and at my light camel skirt, but the back of the wagon had obviously been cleaned out, with rugs laid across the seat. 'There's such a lot of rough country to be traversed every day and in winter, of course, it's especially difficult – we're generally snowed up for a few weeks on either side of Christmas.' He sounded entirely equable and cheerful about it, and looking at him, sitting easily at the wheel of the jeep, I knew that he had found his niche for life and was completely happy, the strains of the past loosed and forgotten, his old ties to Manderley quite broken.

It was a journey of over forty miles and we scarcely saw a house, apart from the odd, isolated keeper's cottage or shooting lodge. We climbed up and over the broad backs of hills, on a narrow rutted road, as the sun rose, and all around us more hills rolled away, one behind the other, towards a distant line of mountains. The earth and the trees were a blend of colours I had never seen, only read about, the shades of tweed, heather, peaty brown and deep violet, the line of the far peaks was silver. I glanced at Maxim once or twice and saw that he was looking ahead and around him with a greater interest and eagerness than he had shown once since our return. It was new to him too, another world, there were no memories here and so he could open himself to it.

I thought, perhaps he will want to stay, perhaps we can be here then, and never have to go back, and looking around me wondered if this northern Scottish landscape could be home to us.

I think I knew at once with certainty that it could not, that we were on holiday here, to rest and be renewed and suspended somehow in time and place, and that it could not last, was not right for us. For today though, it was perfect, and we perfectly content, and that day merged into the following three, as the Scottish autumn slipped down in gold and blue and late, last sunlight, towards winter.

I had not thought ever to retrieve such happiness. Maxim was a young man again, outside for most of the day and until it was dark, fishing with Frank, going with him about the thousands of wild acres of moorland and heather hills, forest and shore, walking, riding, shooting, his face glowing with pleasure and the outdoor air, the old, gay Maxim, yet more carefree than I had ever seen him.

Their house was whitewashed and four square, on a slope opposite the great loch. From its upper windows, you could see miles over the water whose surface changed and shifted a dozen times a day, from silver to steel to troubled, thunderous grey with black at its heart. Ahead, lay the opening between the hills, where the sky lightened, and there was an island. Near to ran the silver tongue of the pebbled shore with its quay and a couple of rowing boats; behind the house the heather slopes climbed up to the open hills. The village was eight miles away and there were no near neighbours. The owner of the estate was abroad much of the time and content for Frank to oversee the place and be in charge of its scattered work force. They lived a close, frugal, family life, the little boys energetic, wiry, full of friendliness after their initial reserve with us, Janet Crawley, a surprisingly young woman with a quick wit and sharp intelligence, as well as natural warmth.

It was an idyllic time, like a bubble, containing all of us within its transparent walls. We took the boats out on the loch, rowed to the island and picnicked there, Maxim and Frank tumbling and romping with the boys, so that watching, I was light headed with my own hopes and plans. We walked for miles, Janet and I sometimes, or all of us together, the boys and the dogs tireless – outstripping the rest, and every evening Maxim and I went out alone, walking more quietly, saying little, and the ghosts shrank back into the shadows and dared not show themselves.

It was I who gave them leave, I who beckoned them, who could not let them be.

Things do not happen by chance, we make our own destiny, that was what I came to believe. If I had not spoken and not constantly been looking over my shoulder, perhaps the rest of our lives would have passed quietly, we would have been undisturbed. Yet I do not think I was to blame. I had been carrying a burden and it had seemed to grow heavier, as burdens do, until I needed to set it down or be given help to carry it. I was bewildered and troubled and afraid, yes, that above all, and it became harder to conceal.

'It is so good to see Maxim like this,' Frank Crawley said.

We had driven over the track that led up from the house, and the loch shore, towards the highest hills of the estate, and now we had left the jeep and were walking – he had to check on some deer; the others had stayed behind, but I had come out with him because I was growing to love this place, love simply going about it, looking, learning its moods, the changes of light and weather, letting its space and breadth and forbidding beauty impress itself on me.

Now, standing for a few moments to get our breath, we looked down to where the gleaming loch lay, calm and quiet under the early afternoon sun.

'It's a still beast today,' young Fergus had said at breakfast, 'It won't spring.'

I was learning that the loch was alive to them, a strange, unpredictable creature, whose moods affected every day of their lives.

'He is better than I could have imagined – so relaxed, he looks so well. Younger too -- don't you think? You should stay longer, Mrs de Winter, there's no earthly reason why you can't is there? The weather is settled for a week or so yet, we shan't feel the bite of winter until November.'

I did not answer, only looked at the beauty all around me, and longed, longed for what I could not have given name to – but I suppose it was simply ordinary, unremarkable happiness, such as Frank had found.

'When you and I talked after Mrs Lacey's funeral – you asked me if there was any reason why you could not come back now. I've thought a lot about that – asked myself. And I am sure that there is not. You *belong* here – or rather in England, I think – I'm not sure this sort of life would suit you and Maxim. You could never go back – back there, you would be happiest – find it easiest, somewhere else – but I don't think life abroad will satisfy you forever – I couldn't imagine it for myself, anyway, though I know Maxim often did go to those places – and, of course, that was where he met you.'

'Yes.'

'But seeing him these past few days has made me realise that he is a man who belongs at home – even his sadness at Mrs Lacey's death has not spoiled it for him has it? He really has come out from the past – it is behind him – behind both of you. If coming up here has helped, I feel content.'

Far below, some wild duck flew, skimming down on to the loch, the edges of the sky were grape coloured, the sun high, still with a touch of warmth. The midges rose in little clouds from the heather.

I had my hand deep in my pocket and my finger was rubbing along the edge of the card, to and fro, to and fro, like the edges of a sore tooth. I had carried it there, not taken it out, not looked at it again, I dared not leave it anywhere that Maxim might accidentally come upon it. I should have burned it, or torn it into tiny pieces and buried it in the ground. Why had I not?

Frank was looking at me. He had fallen silent.

I walked away from him, a few paces, turned my back and looked up, to where the deer stood, great, proud, burnished things, alert, on the high slope.

If I did not speak, it would not be true. If I did not tell Frank, it would be a fancy, another nightmare.

We don't have to burden others with our dreams; we wake and they dissolve.

If I did not speak.

I did not speak. I simply took the card out of my pocket, and handed it to Frank.

Then, because I could not bear to watch his face, I turned back to the deer again. That was the moment I saw the eagle. It is something I shall never forget, the blue sky and the silence, the astonishing silence, and then, out of nowhere, that magnificent, soaring bird, high over the crag, a sight the Crawleys had been promising us, 'with luck,' ever since our arrival. But it was wrong, it was spoilt, even this very rare and yet very simple joy had been tainted. I think I did not feel anything, no anger or frustration, and certainly no surprise, for was I not used to it by now?

Still, I glanced back at Frank, and saw that he had seen the bird too, and for a few seconds we watched it together as it circled lazily, easily, huge wings wide outstretched and scarcely lifting, but we did not remark on it. There was nothing, now, to say.

'Where did this come from?'

'I don't know. I went by myself to visit the grave and the wreath was lying there on the grass. It was very beautiful – just white flowers set in dark green leaves. It was – exactly *right*.'

'But it had not arrived in time for the funeral – we would all have seen it.'

'Oh no. It came later. It was sent quite separately – sent or put. Yes – put – someone had placed it there – apart from all the rest. With that card. Frank – who? *Who? Why?*'

The questions that had danced in my head like gnats ever since.

Frank's face was drawn and solemn. He turned the card over between his fingers once or twice. I shivered.

'Someone wants to frighten us – or harm us.'

'Oh, I shouldn't have thought the latter –' he said at once, the old Frank, anxious to reassure. 'What reason would there be?'

'Hatred.'

'But no one hates you, you or Maxim – it was all such a long time ago. And –' He looked at the card again.

'And Rebecca is dead.'

'Yes.'

'Frank – we have to talk. You have to tell me – things I have not been told.'

I saw a change in his expression – that it had somehow closed up, become wary.

'I need to know. I must protect Maxim, above all – but I must find out about this.'

'There is really nothing to tell – no secrets. I agree with you, Maxim is happy, happier than for years. The burden has lifted – he must never find out about what is obviously just a nasty little joke.'

'A *joke*?'

'Trick, then.'

'Mean – spiteful – hurtful – malevolent.'

'Yes, I agree. All the same, I wouldn't read too much into it. Would you like me to keep this and destroy it for you? It will be safer surely.'

I looked down at the white card in his hand. He was

right, of course, I should simply leave him to deal with it. Kind, competent, sensible Frank. But the card drew me, I stared at the black letter and it seemed like a spell, attracting me.

'Listen, I'm sure it will be that rotten apple, Jack Favell – he's around somewhere still, I came upon him once during the war, saw his name in the paper to do with some nasty piece of blackmail and so forth.   Exactly typical – he had a twisted, warped mind, and a black sense of humour. I wouldn't put this past him.'

Jack Favell – I turned back to look at the crag, to steady myself, bring myself back to what was real, what was good and beautiful and true ... but while we had been talking so intently, the eagle had gone. I would not see it again, I thought, I had lost it, and I would never be able to remember how fine it had looked without also remembering all this – the card, Frank's effort at glossing over it, and now, the other name.

Jack Favell. Rebecca's cousin, one of her men, those she had despised and amused herself with, leering, drunken Jack Favell. I remembered being alone in the morning room at Manderley with him, and the feeling he had given me when he had looked me up and down so insolently. 'I wish I'd got a bride of three months waiting for me at home!'

'Frank,' I said, carefully, 'please tell me the truth.'

'I hope I have always done that.'

'Are you keeping anything about – about Rebecca from me? Anything that I don't already know from long ago?'

'No. I can give you my word about that.'

'Will – will this–' I indicated the card, 'make any difference to what we ought to do? Will it mean we can't come home?'

I was desperate for him to make it all right, to settle our future for us, desperate to believe what he had said about the wreath being some horrible, stupid joke. Jack Favell. Yes, of course, that would be just like him. He would have laughed, spittle coming out of his mouth as he did so, at the plan, he would have got such pleasure from carrying it out. I tried to picture him writing the card, tying it on to the green circlet, getting someone to deliver it – giving them instructions, for I did not somehow think that he would have brought it to the churchyard himself.

Jack Favell. Yes, of course.

'So long as there's nothing for us to fear,' I said to Frank. The sun had gone in and a bitter little wind began to cut across the heather. We were walking back towards the jeep.

'Nothing at all. Give Maxim a little more time – stay here as long as you like and then – why don't you hire a car and drive around England a bit, get used to it all again, see places you have never visited before?'

'Oh, yes, Frank, what a marvellous idea! There's no reason why we should not, is there?'

'None that I can think of.' He smiled with friendliness and open relief, as he handed me up into the car.

'Thank you,' I said, and in a sudden rush of happiness and relief, bent forwards and kissed him on the cheek, for he had given me back my peace of mind, and the anxiety and fear had receded and grown tiny, the future was secure for us again too.

He blushed scarlet and closed the door of the jeep

hastily, making me smile. It was something I wished that I could tell Maxim, we could have laughed about it together; but of course, I could not. I was so relieved, Frank made me so sure everything would be all right, after all – Frank was always so good at taking worries off my mind – Frank made me see that it was all nothing – just a nasty practical joke.

Those things were never to be said, worries, trouble, fear, and the reason for them, had to be concealed.

'I'm so glad we saw the eagle – Maxim will be jealous.'

'Indeed –'

'I just wish it had been – at some other moment –'

'Yes.'

'And that he had been there and –'

'I understand.'

'Frank – do you think anything else will happen – ?'

'Goodness knows. Well, he won't have occasion for it will he?'

'If it was Jack Favell.'

'I'd bet money on it.'

'Yes, yes, I expect you're right.'

'Put it out of your mind. I really think you must. It's despicable but don't let it eat into you – that would suit him only too well.'

'No, no, I will try. Thank you, Frank.'

'Do you feel easier about things now?'

'Yes,' I said. 'Yes, of course.' The lie came easily because I believed it myself.

We drove down the steep road towards the loch and the long, low white house, and the clouds rolled down with us, gathering in fast, so that by the time we reached the front door it was pouring with rain and we could scarcely see across to the water. Maxim was reading *The Moonstone*, sitting beside a bright fire, the little boys were constructing a pirate hideaway in one of the old outhouses. Later, Frank would drive into Dunaig with Janet to shop. It was so quiet, so unremarkable, such a happy, secure, self-contained world. I felt safe in it, no one could reach us or touch us, I wanted to be here always.

But we could not, and besides, Frank's idea filled my head, I had pushed away all thought of the wreath and the card, as he had told me to, and done it by elaborating on the idea of spending some time after this, in exploring, driving together down through an England we did not know. Looking, yes, I knew that was what I wanted to do – wander, and look, until we found a place. I had no notion about where or what it might be, only a certainty that when we had found it I should know.

I wanted to choose the right moment to broach it to Maxim. Not yet, I thought, sitting opposite him as he read, hearing a shout from outside, footsteps, another shout, the little boys happily at play. It will be like this, we shall have this too. Maxim glanced up, smiled, but abstractedly, deep in his book. I would not be able to reach him yet. Besides, I needed to be sure – I was so afraid of the trap snapping shut on my small, frail hopes and plans, of his refusing curtly, his mood tense and troubled once more, the past creeping up to remind him of why we should not stay, why we must flee away all over again.

CHAPTER

Nine

But it did not. Not at first. We were allowed our time in the sun, the fates drew back and let us be, we had a reprieve, so that I was able to cherish my hopes and my dreams, curl them in my hands and warm them so that the flame from them stayed bright.

I was as happy that following week as I think I had ever been in my life. I made a tremendous effort of will, consciously, each morning I woke and each night before I slept, to suppress all thought of the wreath, and I found that with a little practice it was quite simple after all to turn my mind away and not allow it to be troubled by any thoughts of the past and what had happened – this, I said, is now, this is too precious to waste, this is our present happiness.

And so it was. The days drifted very slowly, lazily down towards the coming winter, like the leaves from the trees, the golden sunlight lingered, gentle over the countryside, filtering through the bare branches, softening the hard lines and edges of every building. There were mists curling up from the rivers and marshes and from the earth itself, at dawn, and sometimes fine frosts at night; there was a new moon over a holly tree and Venus glittering bright beside it; there were sunsets and quiet, still nights when we lay awake and heard owls.

Maxim was a young man again, he had a gaiety and restfulness I had rarely known in him and I was young and fearless and light hearted, with him.

We left the Crawleys after an extra night's stay, and, as Frank had suggested, drove in a hired car quickly through Scotland, which, quite suddenly, Maxim said he had had enough of – it was not what he wanted and then, by ambling stages, taking a quiet route, stopping wherever it looked pleasing. The open hills and moors of the northern counties, sheep country, then the softer, lusher fields and woods, and further south long stretches of empty country, clustered villages, little stone built market towns – all were beautiful to us and welcomed us, all lay quiet under the sun.

I was surprised how little Maxim knew of England, how little travelled he was beyond the country around Manderley – he knew many places abroad far better. And I had been almost nowhere, it was new and delightful to me, so that we explored and discovered and enjoyed together.

I did not speak of the future. I thought I need not, that Maxim knew what I wanted, and as the week passed I began to believe that he wanted it too, so that my plans became clearer, they were more than dreams now. We would come back, surely, it was all right, there was no danger, no doubt. Soon, we would come back for good.

No. I did not speak of it, but I had not expected to find the place to which I knew at once that we would come, not so surely, not so soon. I was caught by it, quite unawares, as I had been by love – for it was the same, it was a sort of falling in love.

We had come to that part of England that lies sheltered by the thin, high ridge of the Cotswold hills, a countryside of trees and chequered fields and lush pastures through which small streams run, soft, undemanding, somnolent places, where everyday life moves quietly at its own pace. Here, still, we were entirely content, nothing troubled us, the only shadows were those that lay along the land.

Maxim drove lazily, the car window usually down and his arm lying along it, and we talked of small, delightful things, shared jokes and pleasures, pointed this or that charming cottage and particular view out to one another, laughed like children. We were children, it seems to me now, making up for too many years of having to be old.

Only once, did a single remark, something that Maxim said, cause the faintest echo deep within me, like the faint, far off after-sound of a bell, reminding, disturbing. We were getting out of the car, beside the small hotel we had found, in the late afternoon sunshine and as I took my bag from Maxim, glancing around the village square at the butter coloured stone houses, the tower of the church set behind, I said, 'Oh, I love it here – I love this part of England so much.'

Maxim glanced at me, half smiling.

'You do too, don't you?' I asked

'Yes. It's because it is about as far as one can get from the sea,' and he turned abruptly, to go ahead of me into the hotel. I did not move for a moment, but was left, staring after him stupidly, not understanding why he had suddenly thought of it, and anxious that he had been brooding secretly about old things: the sea, the cove at Manderley, the boat, Rebecca's drowning.

But when I followed him into the cool, dark little hall, stone flagged and smelling of woodsmoke, when I touched his arm, and looked into his face again, it was quite untroubled, his eyes were steady on mine, he made some cheerful remark about liking the place we had chanced upon.

And indeed, how could one have failed to be happy there? When I bring it to mind now, as I can so easily – my memory for places is so much stronger than for the faces even of those who have been very close to me – when I stand again beside the polished table that served as a reception desk, with its small brass bell, and the green leather bound visitor's book, in my mind I know that, but for one, terrible, random trick of fate, the memory of it would be wholly perfect.

The village was quite large, the houses and cottages set around a sloping green, with two great, noble oaks at the centre of it, and at the far side a wide stream ran clear over stones and under a bridge that spanned the road close to the hotel.

We were such seasoned hotel dwellers by now, used to sizing up rooms, picking the one with the best or the quietest situation, or to tucking ourselves modestly away, used to asking for a table far from the door, in a corner where we would not feel exposed to stares – it had become a habit, we could not lose it and sometimes I hated it, I wanted to stride about in the middle of it all, defiant, my head up, for what were we ashamed of, what did we have to hide?

But of course I never did, for his sake, because he was so exquisitely sensitive to any look, any imagined gleam of recognition or speculation in people's eyes, I would never have drawn attention to ourselves. There were only eight rooms here, though people came in for dinner, they said; the dining room was down some steps and overlooked a garden with a small stone pool in the centre, and wonderful late roses clambering up the high walls; there were small lounges tucked away, with old, comfortable chairs and deep sofas, stone fireplaces, window seats beside tiny, leaded windows; there was a clock that chimed and another that ticked loudly and there was an old, white faced labrador at the hearth, which lumbered up and at once went to Maxim, burying its nose in his hand and leaning against him. He has missed that, too, I thought, seeing him bend to fondle and stroke it, and oh, so have I, missed a dog to roam the countryside with, a companion beside the fire, there is so much like this that we could have again. And I prayed for it, an impulsive, urgent prayer.

Let us come back. Let us come back.

I had not asked Maxim what our plans were, I had not dared. I supposed that eventually we would go back to Beatrice's house and see Giles and Roger again. I knew that we would have to return abroad, because all of our possessions were left locked in the room of our hotel by the lake. But my dream, which I allowed simply to hover at the back of my mind, was that we would go there only briefly, pack everything up and have it sent home – I did not know yet where home would be. It did not matter, I glossed over that, we could rent a house anywhere, until we knew where we wanted to settle. The only thing that mattered was that we should return.

But I was afraid to voice my dream, I only hoped, only said my occasional, secret prayers.

We spent three peaceful, contented nights in our hotel, and only the sound of the stream running softly over the stones ever disturbed us, and every day we went out, to walk, to look, to linger in the late sunshine.

On the fourth day we took the car and went further – fifteen or twenty miles – meandering through winding, quite narrow lanes, between low hedges, looking across the fields to the lines and thickets of beech trees, oak, chestnut, ash, elm, some bare, some still with the last leaves clinging, up slopes, down slopes, going nowhere in particular; stopping for bread and cheese in small village pubs, drowsing a little, going on. The hedges were still thick with glistening blackberries, and dark, dark sloes, the corn was long cut and the earth brown again, here and there a yellow hayrick stood, and in all the cottage gardens as we passed we saw the wigwams of beans that had been pinched and blackened at the tips by the previous night's frost, and men digging up potatoes and everywhere, bonfires, bonfires.

We came to a crossroads in a lane lined with great tall trees, but beyond them, between the grey trunks, we saw the open country still, blue sky and sunlight.

Maxim stopped. 'Where are we?'

'I don't know.'

'We passed a sign.'

'I'm sorry, I wasn't looking.'

He smiled. He knows, I thought, I have no need to tell him. He knows my dream.

The road rose quite steeply ahead and bent away out of

sight. To our right was an even narrower lane that climbed between mossy banks.

'That way,' I said. I did not know why, there was no sign, but it was not chance, I know that, I was led.

'We're already lost. Supposing we get more so.'

'We can't – or not seriously lost. It's no more than a couple of miles to that last village and we can easily find the way back from there, it's quite well signposted.'

'Whereas here,' Maxim said, starting the engine again, 'it is not.'

'Oh, what does it matter?' I felt suddenly carefree, and light headed. 'Let's just go on.'

We went on.

The lane dipped, narrowed between the high mossy banks out of which grey green tree trunks uncoiled, then climbed again quite steeply. The trees here were higher, towering above us; in summer, I thought, they would be dense and dark, the branches matted together to form a roof.

Then, without warning, the lane opened out into a semi-circular clearing. We stopped beside a wooden signpost whose lettering was greened over, on flaking paint. I got out of the car and crossed to it. Looked up. There was no sound, except, now and then, the slightest, silken rustling of the dry leaves as a nut or a twig broke off and fell, slipping down between them. For a moment, Maxim sat on in the car.

I think I knew then, with that curious sixth sense, that absolute yet indefinable, ungraspable awareness of the future that sometimes comes to me. I had seen nothing, I was only standing under a sign in the middle of a lane.

Yet I knew. I felt a sureness, and an excitement within

me. It is here – we have found it – just round the corner, near, near. The sign pointed down a path that was scarcely more than a muddy, leaf covered track between the trees.

To Cobbett's Brake.

I said the name to myself, mouthed it quietly, trying out the words.

Cobbett's Brake.

I knew.

Then I beckoned to Maxim.

We walked over the mulch of leaves, for a hundred yards or so. The track sloped down, so that we had to pick our way carefully, holding on to one another. At one point, a squirrel leaped across the divide between two branches ahead of us, but otherwise there was no sound, except the sound we made, no movement but our own. I wondered how far we would descend, imagined what a climb we would have back to the car.

I had my eyes on the ground, placing my feet with care, so that what I saw first was the end of the track as it opened out, and the afternoon sunlight falling through the last, thin branches of the trees, on to the ground.

I looked up.

There was a rough, short path leading to a great gateway, with delicate, high, wrought iron gates between two stone pillars. We approached them almost holding our breath. And stopped and stood in silence, looking, looking down.

Below us, at the end of a drive, set in a bowl surrounded by grassy slopes that rose all around it, was the most beautiful house I had ever seen – more beautiful at once, to me, than Manderley, because it was not so imposing, not so frighteningly large and grand, but a house that went straight to my heart. I closed my eyes quickly, opened them again, half expecting it to have vanished, to have been an illusion, born of my own wishes, but it was there, still, resting in the sun, a house of enchantment and of fairy stories; yet not some towered and turreted fantasy castle, but a rose red, many chimneyed Elizabethan manor house. It was set among lawns and rose-beds and pergolas and fountains and small ornamental ponds, but they were neglected and overgrown, not run back to nature, not quite unkempt, but as though someone who lived there could no longer cope, and had tried and failed to manage without sufficient help. The tree-dotted basin of green rose gently up around it, the barley sugar chimneys and the bricks of the walls were tinted soft ochre and geranium and shell pink, buff and apricot, and all merging and blending together like the walls and roofs of some sunlit Italian hilltop town.

There was no sign of life at all, no sound of voices or dogs, no smoke from the chimneys. Cobbett's Brake was empty now, but I did not think that it was abandoned, or unloved, it was not a lost house, and beyond recall.

We stood, hand in hand, and breathless as children in the enchanted wood, gazing half in awe, half in wonder. We had often seen grand houses on our journey of the past week, mansions and halls and manors, formidable, pompous, and I had turned my eyes from them and my back to them and fled. Those places meant nothing to me and the life lived in them was not for us. But this house was of a different kind.

It was not small, but it had no sense of importance, it drew in, beckoned, welcomed, it was quite unforbidding. In spite of being deserted now, silent and a little overgrown, it had warmth, it was of a cheerful countenance.

I dreamed, standing there, and the house enfolded us, all of us, in my dream. I saw Maxim walking down the drive, saw the children clambering up the grassy slopes to where the sheep grazed, heard their shouts, saw them wave to me where I knelt in the garden, weeding one of the flowerbeds.

I saw smoke curling from the barley sugar chimney and a little, brown shaggy pony beside the old fence, at the back.

I would be entirely happy here, of that I was calmly, quietly sure, because I would make the house mine, order it in my own way, with Maxim's blessing. I realised, standing there, that I had never had my own home, never once in my life, but this would be mine, as Manderley had never been. That had belonged to others, to Maxim, to his family, for generations before, and to everyone else, to half the county, to the servants. To Mrs Danvers. To Rebecca. It had never belonged to me.

But now, I did not regret it, I did not care, Manderley vanished that afternoon, it simply went out like a candle and was gone. This, I thought, gazing down at the beautiful house, seeing the light soften and darken, the colour of the walls change, as the afternoon slipped away. This would be mine – we would come here. I knew. It was a sort of madness, a fantasy that had a stronger grip upon me than what was real, but it was so calm, so sure, I was in thrall and I had no doubts, my confidence and trust that now I had found the house, everything would somehow, one day, fall into place, was clear eyed and absolute.

I said, 'I want to go in.'

'We can't, of course. There's a padlock on the gate.'

'The fence is broken – look there – and over there.'

'No.' But he did not pull away. He stood behind me, his hand resting on my shoulder, and I knew that he felt as I felt then. I had no doubt at all.

'Come on,' I said, and I began to make my way carefully up the bank, keeping in line with the fence, my eyes never leaving the house.

And after a moment or so, Maxim followed, and glancing back, I saw that he too could not stop looking at it. Oh, the dreams of that day, the world I had stepped into, the hopes I had. I remember them so clearly.

We made our way around the east side of the house, where the garden was most neglected. An old pergola ran on two sides, with the remnants of creeper, rose and honeysuckle hanging in strands from it, wistaria gnarled and unpruned clambered up another, and a path led through them between pillars, to a closed gate. Flowerbeds and borders were overgrown, and yet I thought it had not been so very long since someone had gardened here, it would not take too much work to get it back. I saw myself planning things out, taking this down, mending that, planting more here, working hard with perhaps one local man who knew about the place and a boy; in a couple of summers, we would make it glorious again.

At the back of the house there were stables, a stone flagged courtyard with a statue of a kneeling child in the centre, an old cart and a broken barrow stood about, there was a greenhouse with broken panes, and a robin sang to us fiercely from a branch.

I looked up and up the walls to the little leaded windows at the very top. The sun was low, slipping off the house. 'Maxim . . .'

'They are most probably just away.'

'No,' I said, 'no, they're not, they've been here quite recently I think, but they have gone now.'

But then, glancing at him, I saw the sadness on his face and that he had withdrawn into it, saw that he looked old, and that he would never truly be able to leave the past, because he did not want to.

I turned back. Cobbett's Brake stood in deep shadow now, the brick of the walls and the stone paths a soft violet darkening to grey, and not only love for it welled up within me then, but something else, a sort of steely determination. What I wanted now I wanted for me, and I was startled, frightened even, by my own defiance.

Maxim had left me and was walking slowly back, head bent, not looking at the house. He will not speak of it, I thought, we shall simply leave, get back in the car and drive away, and tomorrow or the next day be gone from here forever, I shall not have been denied or refused anything, my dream will simply not have been acknowledged, and this place will never be referred to. That will be his way of dealing with it. Resentment and bitterness and a horrible self pity began to simmer and stir about within me. I was already anticipating my disappointment and how I would mourn it. I had lost all grip on reality, I had no sense at all.

It was a hard, steep climb back up the narrow track to where we had left the car, and Maxim was ahead of me the whole time. Once, once only, I stopped to get my breath, and let myself look back through the clearing, between the trees, and there it lay, quiet, closed in upon itself, merging into the shadows, but the last light from the setting sun had caught three or four of the chimneys on the west side and was burning them like coals.

I had gone from joy and hope, to desolation. I felt suddenly cold.

The car was cold, too. I held my hands together to stop them shaking. Maxim had not spoken. He sat as if he were waiting for something. I looked at him.

'I suppose we shall be too late for tea,' I said dully. 'I should like to have a hot bath when we get back.'

Maxim took both my hands, and pressed them close together between his own. 'Poor little thing,' he said, and I saw that he was looking at me with infinite fondness, infinite tenderness, in the old way. 'You try so hard to shield me and protect me, and really, there is no need, you try so hard to hide what you want, how you feel, and of course you can't.'

'What do you mean?' I said, suddenly angry and close to tears of disappointment and frustration with myself. 'Whatever do you mean? Come on, I'm very cold.'

'I know you,' he said, still holding my hands. 'I know you so well.'

'Don't talk to me as if I were stupid, as if I were some silly little thing to be indulged and patronised.'

'Yes. Yes, I was doing that. I apologise.'

'Maxim . . .'

'No, you were perfectly right to protest.'

'It's just . . .'

'I know.'

'Do you?'

'Cobbett's Brake,' he said then, rather thoughtfully. 'Strange name. Who was Cobbett, do you suppose?'

But I did not reply, I did not want to speculate idly about the house, as if it were anywhere we had chanced upon and stared at, like people touring some foreign town in which they are half interested. We were going away, we would not see it again. That was all. It would have been kinder, I thought to God, if we had never been allowed to find it.

'You are quite right about tea,' he said.

'It doesn't matter.'

'No, though I confess I should have liked some.'

'I'm sorry, it's my fault – '

'Is it? Why?'

'We've spent so long here. You should have told me – made me leave.'

'I didn't want to. So now, as there will not be tea, we had better use the time more profitably.'

'What do you mean?'

He let go of my hands and started the car. 'We passed a farm, do you remember? About a quarter of a mile from that crossroads, just before we were apparently lost. It was called Home Farm.' He turned around expertly in the clearing. 'I daresay that if we stop at it and ask, they will be able to tell you whatever you want to know about the house.'

They offered us tea there, strong sweet tea, but out of the best china service, got from the front room, and slices of warm fruit bread and butter. We were very welcome, they said, not many visitors came by, it was quiet here, always quiet. I would like that, I almost said, we are quiet people, we are used to it. Maxim talked to the farmer, about the harvest and about sheep and the dairy herd, about how the trees needed work on them, and there wasn't the manpower after the war, and rents and the hunt, walking around the farmyard and up towards the fields. He was happy, I thought, this was what he had always liked at Manderley, going around with Frank to the tenants, the farms and the cottages, knowing instinctively how to talk to the people, easily, getting on with them, in a way I had always been too awkward and unsure of my own position to do.

I stayed with the woman, Mrs Peck, in the kitchen, eating my fruit bread, warming my hands on the teacup, light headed with happiness because it was going to be all right, I knew it. I knew. In the yard the hens pecked about and a toddler went with them, on sturdy feet. We would come here often, I thought, I would bring the children, they would learn about the animals, help to feed the pigs, go out in the fields among the first lambs. They would be our neighbours.

She poured me more tea, filling the pot from the kettle on the range, and swirling it round and round as she spoke. 'It got to the war then,' she said, 'and things came on that much harder, and then, of course, all the help went, the men had to leave and there was just boys. Then, for a while, they had some prisoners of war over from the camp. Italian men, they were, without a word of English and only one or two of them seemed to want to learn any. I suppose it was the strangeness of it and the shock, being away from their own country. You'd feel adrift.'

Yes, I thought, oh, yes – you would. You did.

'One of them put up the vine, you might have seen it, tried to make it grow, and grow it did, at the side there, in the lee of the old wall. But still the grapes were only little black bitter things you know . . . '

'Will they come back – will they try and open up the house again?'

The clock ticked in the kitchen, great loud ticks in time with the thumps of my heart.

'The old couple – ? No, no. I could see they weren't managing, a long time before they would admit it. There was nothing you could say. They had to realise it themselves. It wasn't my place.'

She was sitting opposite to me at the kitchen table, a handsome woman, with a fine halo of pale auburn hair, and a broad featured face. I liked her. I saw myself sitting here, chatting through the afternoon, confiding in her, learning things about the house and the garden and the children – for I would do as much as I could myself, with a local girl and someone to cook, I did not want teams of servants running my house, as they had run Manderley, intimidating, a dreadful hierarchy.

'No, they won't come back.'

My heart leaped.

'There's the son, though, Mr Roderick – when he finishes his commission, I expect he'll come back home and open the old place up again. He's a sister, too, but married and with her own place, I doubt if she'd be interested. No, it will be

Mr Roderick. He sends us letters now and then, wanting this or that done – and of course, Mr Tarrant, the land agent, he's in proper charge.'

From the yard I heard a cry as the toddler tripped on the flags, and she went out to him, soothing, lifting him up, and I saw that Maxim and the man had come back, and were standing chatting beside the gate. The sky was duck's egg blue, shot across with blackberry and plum and indigo skeins of cloud, the sun dropping quickly down. In the far corner of the yard, the pig was snuffling noisily into her trough. I did not want to leave, I did not want the day to be over. I looked back to where they stood, waving as we drove away, and went on looking long after we had gone too far and they were quite out of sight.

CHAPTER

Ten

Every morning, during the first weeks of our marriage, I had sat opposite to Maxim at breakfast, and every evening at dinner, in such a heightened, unreal state that I had often had to stare at my own wrist or fingers, or even to make an excuse and go out to find a mirror in some cloakroom, and gaze into my own face, searching for something long familiar to which I could anchor myself. I had not been able to accept it at all, that I was there, in these places, of right, naturally and easily, that Maxim had married me, so that now I was Mrs de Winter. I remember tables beside windows overlooking the lagoon in Venice, tables outside in small cobbled squares, candlelit tables, sunlit tables, tables dappled with the shade from overhanging trees, and the colours of individual pieces of food set upon white plates, the braid on a waiter's jacket. This cannot be true, I would think, who am I? Where am I? I can't be here, I am no longer me, it is impossible that I should be so happy. I grew used to the feeling, but it never truly left me and then, when we came home to Manderley, there was a different sense of unreality.

And now I sat at another table, not very far from a great stone hearth in which a fire burned, opposite to Maxim in our village hotel, and in the circle of light from the parchment shaded lamp, I felt the old sense of being in a dream, of desperately trying to catch up with what had happened to me. We were no longer hiding away in another country, eating indifferent food, clinging to one another for safety, fearful of how we spoke, of strangers, of the past. We were free of all that, and out into the sunlight.

We would come home, I knew that. We had no need to run away again. Maxim had been forced to face it all, there had been no other way, but the worst was quickly over, he had drawn the sting of memory, all was well.

Cobbett's Brake lay at the back of my mind, rose red, beautiful, in its grassy bowl, and again and again I turned to look at it and joy spurted within me. There was no reason why it should ever be ours, but I knew that it would, I wanted it and the force of my want would make it come about. I had never been in the grip of such simple conviction before, I believed passionately, like the convert to a religion, I would make it so.

The food was delicious that night, and unlike those first dinners, when I was too light headed and delirious to want to eat, now I ate greedily, hungry, relaxed, so sure within myself. There was grilled trout, and roast pheasant with the skin dark and crisp, the potatoes fluffed and dotted with pungent tasting parsley, and some sort of apple pudding sticky with sweetness and plumped out with raisins.

We ate slowly, and drank a good bottle of claret, we looked at the fire and the sporting prints and the two oil

141

paintings of dogs above the sideboard, and the waitress was slow and plump and had a mole beside her eye, and there was no salt in the salt cellar, we had to ask for it. I looked at my own hands, at the old white scar beside my fingernail, at my wedding ring, long familiar now, but I was not here, I thought, surely this deep, rich, settled happiness, this wonderful new beginning, could not be; I would blink and we would be back in that other small, plain, much duller dining room, in our hotel beside the foreign lake.

I looked across at Maxim. It was real, it was true. I saw it in his face – we had come through.

The blow did not fall until a little later.

We spoke from time to time about the house, not practical talk, not sensible and cautious. Would it ever be sold? Or let perhaps? Would the old couple try to come back, or the son open it up again? How would we find out about it? What was it like inside? Did it need repairs, was it cold, shabby, unattractive?

I did not need to know. It would be right, I had no doubt in my mind, did not bother about it.

It was only the surprise of it we spoke of, the way it had lain there secretly, waiting for us, the way we had been lost, and taken the lane by chance, and so come upon it.

I did not have to say what I wanted to Maxim, nor to ask him. Perhaps I did not dare, in case, in case. Sometimes he still jumped, snapped out, startling me, sometimes he could be impatient, cold, sometimes he turned abruptly away, shutting me out. I did not risk that happening now, the house mattered too much, what it meant – or what I so longed it to mean – was too important.

Was I building an elaborately balanced, ornate house of cards? A castle in the air? Yes, a small, spiteful voice whispered, yes, but I turned away and laughed at it, bold, defiant. We had been led to Cobbett's Brake, every step of our journey perhaps not merely this week, but for years, had been towards it, I believed that with a terrible, superstitious vehemence that was quite uncharacteristic.

Only once, fleetingly that night, before the worst moment came, did I have the faintest of warnings, a premonition, a reminder, though I brushed it aside at once.

I went up to our room to fetch Maxim's book and, as I opened the door, saw that the moon was shining in through the window on to my bedspread and making a clear, pale pool of light, and the sudden sight of it brought the wreath of white flowers vividly to my mind, making my stomach clench in fear; they were there, I could have reached out to touch the petals, I felt the edge of the cream card against my fingers, I stared at the beautifully shaped, black initial letter R.

'No,' I whispered urgently, aloud into the empty room. 'No,' and quickly switched on the light, so that all was ordinary again, and found Maxim's book, and ran from the room, and though I knew that I carried the image of the wreath in my mind still and perhaps it would be there always, I could never finally escape, I was stronger than it could ever be. Somehow the sight of the house had given me tremendous, almost magical power, the wreath and the card could not hurt me, they were nothing, trivial, a joke, a trick. I filled myself with thoughts of the house, and it refreshed me instantly, I turned to its calm, clear image with gratitude, investing it with so much strength and goodness, and promise.

I stopped in the doorway of the lounge, and looked with such love, such contentment, at what I saw. The coffee had arrived, the pots and cups were set out on a low table before the fire, and Maxim was leaning forward out of one of the great armchairs, stroking the labrador dog as it stretched, making low grumbling noises of pleasure. No one else was in the lounge yet, so that it might have belonged to us, been a room in our own home, instead of a hotel.

I had a book but I did not want to read, I was too happy with the present and with the world I wove out of my own fancy, to want to immerse myself in another. So for a while I simply sat, beside Maxim, drinking my coffee, basking in the warmth of the fire, hearing the clock tick and then chime, and nothing touched me, and nothing could, it seemed.

But after a while, I looked around me for something to do, wishing again that I was a woman who did crochet or a needlepoint. Well, when we were there, I would, and there would be a basket of mending, too, I saw it now, a round wicker basket lined with cotton, a china knob to its lid.

There was a cupboard in the corner, the door ajar. I went to look into it and found games, boxes of draughts and chess and children's games, too, ludo and snakes and ladders; jigsaw puzzles of the Fighting Temeraire, a bluebell wood, a hunt in full cry; an old postcard album; some local maps and a gazeteer. But there was nothing to divert me for long. I was happy simply to sit, but I knew that it irritated Maxim, he looked up sharply from his book, disturbed, wanting me to settle, so that I went across to the table in the centre of the room and brought a pile of magazines. They were country

144

picture papers from before the war, carefully set in place each day, looked after, I supposed because such things had not been obtainable more recently.

I began to look through them, at out of fashion frocks and advertisements with strange, quaint lettering, pictures of hunt balls and women riding side saddle. I read an article about St Paul's Cathedral and another about hares, and it was such nostalgic pleasure, they reminded me of the magazines I had read sometimes in our exile, old copies of *The Field*, and how I had learned pages of them almost by heart, how the descriptions and drawings, the tiny details of the English countryside, had satisfied my yearning for it a little, how I had had to keep them from Maxim, for fear of stirring up too many memories and longings within him, of hurting him.

The fire slipped down, scattering sparks. The labrador shifted, grunted, slept on, from somewhere, in the depths of the hotel, a voice, another, laughing briefly, the clatter of a plate. Silence again. The others who had been dining had left, gone upstairs or out. Once Maxim looked up from *The Moonstone* to smile, once to throw a log on the fire. This is happiness, I thought, this is happiness now. And the house, Cobbett's Brake, rode like a ship, at anchor, peaceful, expectant, under the moon.

I turned a page idly.

The shock was indescribable.

The magazine was over fifteen years old. They went in for such grandeur in those years before the war.

It was a full page photograph. She was standing at the head of the great staircase, one hand resting lightly on the banister, the other at her waist, almost as if she were a mannequin. The pose was artificial, yet it was perfectly judged, the spotlight had been placed to light her in exactly the right way. She wore an evening gown of satin, in some dark colour, without sleeves, but with a strap up from the ruched bodice over one shoulder, and a sable wrap, carelessly, precisely draped, hung from her hand. Her head was thrown back a little, revealing her long, white neck, her black hair fell in casual, impeccably brushed ripples and waves, long, shining.

'You've seen her brushes, haven't you?' I heard the voice whisper. 'Her hair came down below her waist, when she was first married. Mr de Winter used to brush it for her then.'

I could see the gallery just behind her, at the top of the staircase, the balustrade, and the corridor running away into the shadows.

I realised that I had never seen her before. Everyone had talked about her, everyone had described her, I had known what she looked like in every detail, how tall she was, and slender, how elegant, how pale skinned, I knew about her black hair. Her beauty. But there had been no photograph, or drawing, or portrait anywhere.

And so, until now, I had not seen her.

We stared at one another, and now I saw the beauty and the arrogance, the flash of defiance in her eyes, the coldness, the strength of will. She looked out at me in amusement and pity, despising me, from her great height, commanding the great stairs above the hall.

'Do you think the dead come back and watch the living?' the whispering voice of the woman said.

I looked away quickly, away from her bold, amused,

triumphant gaze, at the words printed below, ordinary, plain, black and white words, from years ago, a caption line, like so many others they printed there, week after week, beneath some society photograph.

Mrs Maxim de Winter, at Manderley.

After that, the nightmare began and perhaps it was a year before we woke from it, perhaps we never did.

Only a few seconds passed while I took in the photograph, fascinated by the sight of her at last, appalled that it should be here, should have lingered on the table of this remote little hotel, among others, waiting for me, biding its time for years until we should come.

Mrs Maxim de Winter, at Manderley.

I shut the cover, mumbling something, and fled, half falling over my handbag which was on the floor as I did so, so that Maxim looked up in surprise. I heard him begin a question, but I did not stay to answer, I could not. He must not see it, he must not know. I stumbled up the stairs, my heart pounding like the sea in my chest, in my head, and she was with me, her pale, haughty, laughing face, her faintly contemptuous expression, looking at me, looking at me, tossing her black hair off her shoulders, resting her hand so easily on the banister of the stairs. Rebecca. I had wanted to see her always, she had repelled and attracted me for years, but she was dead and I had thought myself free of her. He must never see.

In our room I began to rip out the page with her photograph, my hands shaking, the paper was stiff and glossy, firmly bound in, I could not do it, and when, at last, I did, it tore, across, so that her arm and the side of her sleek, elegant dress had a jagged rip down them, and a part was left firm inside the book. But it had not touched her face. She was still looking up at me, smiling a little, commanding, as Maxim flung open the door of the room.

Then, everything was terrible, and the world, like the glossy, fashionable photograph, was ripped in two. Then, there was only my fear and Maxim's anger and his withdrawal – for he behaved at once as if I were somehow to blame and had done this thing on purpose.

I had no time to hide the sheet of paper, he pulled it out of my hands, and I saw his face whiten, his lips press together, as he looked briefly down at her.

Mrs Maxim de Winter, at Manderley.

If I could have seen ahead before it happened and asked how he would be, I might have said, gentle, worried for me, but calm about it, tender, holding me, telling me to put it from my mind, not to let it trouble me, because it was nothing, that it was all over, she could no longer hurt us.

But he was not like that, so that I knew she still had power over him as much as over me, I had been wrong for years, living in a false, fool's paradise. A door came down that night, shutting us from the future I had planned, it was the end of all hopes, all dreams, all happiness.

I felt sick, my stomach churning with misery, I began to bite the side of my fingernail again, as I had done in the old, early, nervous days, I saw him notice it and turn irritably away.

He screwed the photograph up hard in his hand, twisted it around and around, but then kept hold of it; the rest of the magazine he threw across the room into the waste paper bin.

148

'You'd better get the cases out, and make a start in packing. It isn't late, I'll go and see if I can rouse them to have the bill ready.'

I turned round to him. 'Where are we going? What are we going to do?'

'Get out of here.'

'But when?'

'In the morning, as soon as we can – before breakfast if possible. We can stop and have something on the way if you're hungry.'

I dared not ask more. I supposed he meant to cut the trip short and go back down to Giles. But then, what then? I did not want to think of it.

He left me alone. The crushed up photograph had still been in his hand. I supposed that he would throw it into the fire downstairs and want to see it burned completely away, and I had a peculiar, superstitious impulse to go down and stop him, I felt afraid of what might happen to us, what she would do in revenge.

Don't be a fool, don't be a child, I said, dragging out the cases from the wardrobe, she is dead, it is just an old photograph, she can't hurt us now.

But she had, I thought miserably, folding dresses, pyjamas, socks, sorting out just the few things we would need for the morning; she had crushed my hopes, she had smashed my frail, transparent bubble of a future. We would not live at Cobbett's Brake, we would never come to this part of England, that too had become tainted, Maxim would never want to see any of these places again.

Where then? I pressed down a pile of handkerchiefs, to lie

149

flat. Back to Giles's house? But after that? Surely there would be somewhere, some corner in which we could hide. I began to think back furiously over the journey from Scotland, trying to remember some pretty, small, obscure place we might both have liked, but I could think of nowhere; I had seen the house I wanted, it had spoiled everywhere else, I thought, and would do so forever. It was more than a house, and now, because we would never go there, not see it again, it assumed an even greater perfection in my mind, it became a lost paradise, and I shut out forever beyond the locked gates, condemned to gaze down at its unattainable, rose red beauty, caught in a timeless present, in its green grassy bowl.

I slept a dreadful, restless, haunted sleep, that night, and woke, very early, when it was not yet light, and then lay, weak and sour with misery and disappointment. Maxim had scarcely spoken to me, only stood morosely at the window, as I finished packing our cases; the bill was paid, there was nothing to detain us.

'I loved it here,' I said once.

'Yes.'

'Maxim –'

'No.' He came and stood in front of me, looking into my face. His skin was grey, the lines that ran from nose to mouth etched more deeply, it seemed, as the last hour or so had passed. His eyes were far away, he had gone from me and I could not reach him.

'It makes no difference to anything,' I said.

'Whatever happens,' Maxim said in a low, hoarse voice, 'wherever we go, whatever we do, it will be the same. So long as we are here, there will be no rest – we can't take the chance, there will be something – like – like this, lying in wait, some trap waiting to spring, and after all, this has been nothing – trivial – other things could be – ' He did not go on. I took his hand and lifted it and held it against my face, desperate suddenly that we should salvage something from this, pleading with him.

'We are being weak,' I said. 'Maxim, it is so silly – we are grown people – we can't run away because of – you're right – of nothing – Some silly, trivial incident – we are together, it will be all right.'

'No.'

'Nothing can touch us.'

'But it can. You know that don't you?'

He took his hand gently away from mine. I could not look into his face, I was too near to tears. Everything, everything was lost then, we would never come back. And I was filled with a hideous, bitter hatred, against her for what she had been, but worse, against Maxim for what he had done, and it frightened me and changed me, I had never felt anything but love for him before. Love and fear.

We left soon after light, as the sun rose out of soft billows of mist. I sat staring ahead and could not bear to look back once at the little stone houses set around the square. There was no one about, we had only seen the plump, bleary waitress, setting out the breakfasts. I had glanced in at the lounge as we passed. The fireplace had been cleared, and fresh logs laid already in the cold grate. The pile of magazines had been

151

tidied away onto a window ledge. The dog was nowhere to be seen.

'Let me drive,' I said. I wanted to go slowly, to slip the journey through my fingers. Besides, if I drove, I would not find it so easy to think. But he would not, he gestured me to the passenger door, starting the engine impatiently before I had finished getting in, his fingers drumming on the rim of the wheel.

Then, I was unable to go on being silent, being patient, then, the pain of our leaving and my own disappointment and misery, rushed up within me and spilled out. I cried out, 'Oh, why, why does it have to be like this? Why must everything be spoiled? We can't go on running away, running away. I know you hated seeing it and so did I, it gave me the most dreadful shock. But Maxim, it was nothing – what was it? A photograph. No more, no worse, simply an old photograph in an old paper.'

He did not reply, only drove, with an awful concentration, very well, very fast. We were out of the gentle Cotswold hills already, going west.

'I did not want it to be over like this – and brushed away as if it had never been.'

'What?'

'This week. Scotland. This trip – '

'Well, it is over.'

'Does it have to be?'

There was a flock of sheep in the middle of the road, being driven from one field to another, a slow, heaving river. We had to stop behind them.

I thought, you never see real sheep abroad, only funny

little goats and scrawny, scraggy, jumping things. Not stout, creamy, satisfying English sheep.

There had been sheep scattered about the green bowl above Cobbett's Brake.

I felt tears prick behind my eyes.

'I telephoned to Giles to say what we were doing,' Maxim said, as we began to move slowly forwards again, 'but there was no reply. It doesn't matter, I can stop and telegraph from somewhere.'

I stared through my tears out of the window. A black and white dog was behind the sheep, rushing to and fro, crouched low, guiding them expertly in through the new gateway. I wound down the window a little. Shep – I thought he would be called. Shep or Lad. But when we passed the farmer and he raised his hand to us, I heard him call, 'Jess. Come on boy. Jess.'

I did not want to ask what he would tell Giles. Maxim had decided what we were doing, I had to go along.

He was driving fast again, looking steadily ahead, blinkered, grim.

'Cobbett's Brake,' I said, almost whispered.

'What?'

'The house.'

'What about the house?'

'I loved it. I wanted it. I've never wanted a place in that way before – never felt – felt as if I should belong there. Do you understand at all?' I waited, but there was no answer. I should have stayed silent then, if I had had sense and sensitivity, and any kindness, but I could not, I was feeling hurt and angry and not kind. 'You had Manderley.

You loved it more than anything, you loved it passionately, surely you know what I'm trying to say.'

'Do we have to talk about all this?'

'But it was never mine, I never belonged there, not really.'

'Well now no one does.'

'I want somewhere that will be mine – ours, where we can settle and belong – and – ours, mine.' I did not give words to the rest.

'I'm sorry. It's out of the question.'

'Why? Why must it be? Haven't you been happy this last week? Haven't you loved being at home – being in England? I think you have.'

'Yes,' he said very quietly. 'Yes. I have been happy, more happy than I can say or I can bear. But it is not a happiness that is possible or one that can continue.'

'But the house – '

'The house was a dream. A fancy. Nothing more – you must forget it.'

We had come into a town, and now, Maxim was parking the car.

'Come along, we'd better have some breakfast. There's a hotel over there, it looks perfectly decent. Go and sit down and order for us, I'll send that telegram to Giles.'

Dumbly, I got out and did as I was told. It was a rather cold dining room with a sideboard covered in dishes of food, and formal, pompous looking waiters. I sat down and ordered coffee, and toast, and cooked food for Maxim. I would not be able to eat anything, the toast was to give me something to do with my hands, and because I still had a lingering fear of waiters, still had to ingratiate myself with

154

them, try and please them. There were several men at tables, chomping stolidly, reading newspapers. The coffee, weak but hot, arrived as Maxim came back.

'I spoke to him,' he said, flipping out his napkin. 'He sounded in a frightful way still – can't seem to pull himself up at all.'

I drank my coffee, because I did not want to speak, stared miserably down at the tablecloth because I could not bear to look at him. I felt like someone at the end of a love affair, tidying up the last details before parting, all interest and life and colour had drained out of the world.

'He'll have to get back to work – I told him to go up to London for a week – start taking some sort of an interest.'

'I don't know you,' I said. And then I did look at him. He was buttering toast briskly, efficiently, cutting it into small squares, as I had seen him do every morning for eleven years.

'What?'

'I don't know you. Who are you? I don't understand what is happening to you.' It was no more than the truth. Something had changed him, brought out again a hard, off-hand style I had thought quite gone, only a defence against old unhappiness, for which there was no longer the remotest need. 'You sound unfeeling and uncaring, you are talking of Giles in that dismissive way as if you were contemptuous of him. And what about Beatrice? She was your sister. I thought that you loved her. I did. I loved her and I miss her and I understand what Giles is feeling. I hate it that you can't –'

'I'm sorry.' He laid down his knife, and reached for my hand. For a moment, for the first time, I hesitated before I gave it to him. 'I know, I simply can't take the way Giles is reacting, it isn't the way he feels I don't understand.'

'The way he shows it.'

'I suppose so, yes.'

'What are you afraid of Maxim?'

He went on with his breakfast. 'Nothing,' he said. 'Nothing at all. Eat your toast.'

'I'm not hungry.'

'I don't want to have to stop again.'

'Until we get down there?' I lifted the coffee pot. It was a long way still, I supposed that I had better drink.

'We're not going back,' Maxim said. 'I asked Giles to get what bits we left there packed up and sent on. I didn't see any point. It will be all right you see. I promise. Once we're away again, it will all be all right.'

'Away again,' I said, and the words came oddly out of my mouth, as if it were frozen and I could not move it properly.

'Yes.'

I looked out of the dining-room window, through the net half curtains, across the street. A small child in a blue hat was sitting down in the middle of the pavement howling, drumming its legs, beside a distraught, embarrassed mother. It was funny, or sad, it did not interest me, there was nothing of any interest left. I must not mind, I thought, I must not mind. I am with Maxim, I must take care of him, share what he feels. 'Where are we going?' I managed to ask, and a faint shaft of hope broke through, for perhaps it

156

would be all right, as he said, somehow it would come right.

He looked surprised, holding out his cup for more coffee.

'No,' I said quickly. 'Of course.'

I lifted the silver pot, and for a second, our reflections flared back at us from its surface, distorted, strange. 'How silly. Of course I know quite well that we are going back.'

'There is no other way. It isn't possible. You do see, my darling, you do understand, don't you?'

I looked into his face, and smiled, a sweet, false, dishonest smile. 'Yes,' I said. 'Yes, Maxim, of course.'

It was very fast, very easily accomplished, our running away, we simply drove and drove, down through the rest of England, and it paid out behind us like an unravelled ribbon and we discarded it. He was as good as his word, we did not stop, except once for petrol, so that we reached Dover by the late afternoon. He had arranged for the car to be left at a garage, and I supposed collected by someone later, I did not ask. He had telegraphed ahead for tickets, too, it was all done, all arranged.

We boarded the evening boat early. There were very few people about.

'We're catching the night sleeper from Calais,' Maxim said. 'I've booked our berths, you'll be able to go to bed straight after dinner.'

Sleep, I thought wonderingly, sleep. Dinner. Yes. All arranged, all will come about, as if it were any journey. And then, suddenly, I did not care any more, I simply

157

stopped feeling, stopped thinking at all, I was too tired. The past week had been a turmoil of discordant experiences, emotional, disturbing, I could not sort them out from one another, or discover which predominated, which mattered, the shocks, the fear, the pleasure, or the pain.

Maxim had walked very fast across the quay and up the gang plank of the boat, looking straight ahead, impatient with the porter for dragging the trolley with our bags. Now, he sat in the lounge reading the first edition of the evening paper the boy had brought round, and when I looked at him, I saw relief on his face again, and that the fine lines of anxiety and foreboding had smoothed already.

I turned away, walked out and up on to the deck, and stood at the rail, watching all the business of preparation for sailing, and then, I let myself turn to it for what I told myself would be the last time, and gazed upon it. Cobbett's Brake rode in my mind like another ship, at anchor in calm water, infinitely beautiful, and then another rode beside it, grander, more austere, but in its own grave way beautiful too, Manderley, silver grey and secret, under the moon.

I felt old then, and as if my life was more than half over, and all the important things past, not to come, old before I had ever been truly young.

I stayed there, resting my arms upon the rail, looking down, until the sirens sounded and we began to move, I stared at the gap widening between the ship and the quay, saw the water spread out in a broader and broader band, watched England drift away from me, out of reach, and soon enough, as darkness fell, out of sight.

Part Two

CHAPTER

Eleven

So it was all over, and quite soon I had accepted it and turned my back upon the dream of the house, so that it became fragmented and insubstantial, and when I tried to summon the picture of it to my mind, I found that I could not.

How quickly we can make the best of things.

We scarcely stayed a night in our old hotel, only long enough to pack up the rest of our belongings and pay what we owed to the manager – who behaved rudely, because he had lost good business he had been relying on for the winter.

We did not care.

'I want to show you so much,' Maxim said. 'Poor girl, you have been like a prisoner confined to one dingy cell, and very patient. Well, we shall make up for that. We shouldn't waste our lives in skulking.'

He seemed full of excitement and plans and I caught his mood, of course I did, it was a relief that our time was to be better filled, but more, to have him looking outward again, gay and high spirited. The small hotel by the lake seemed suddenly shabby and third rate, our room cramped and dingy. I closed the door on it for the last time without a pause, it had become as anonymous to me as all the others, in spite of the length of time we had spent here, nothing of moment had happened, nothing to remember. Yet I would remember it, some day, for no reason that I could discern, it would simply float to the surface and be there, in the middle of my doing something quite unrelated to it or to this time. Some part of my life had been spent here, a time which would never come back. I ought to be grateful to it, I thought, going on down the corridor, it was one of the rooms of my life in which there had been no fear, no distress, no dread. We had been perfectly, dully content.

We went away, travelling restlessly, always going on in search of a new sight, a fresh experience; we pored over maps and guides in cafés here and there, spreading them out, pointing, looking up routes and timetables. It was as though Maxim were hungry for other places, desperate to move on, to enjoy, not to miss, he would say, 'Let's go here . . . ' or 'Come on, I'll take you there . . . ' or 'I've never been to . . .' and we would be off. The succession of hotels, the small pensions, the neat little houses in which we took rooms, is a blur now, I will never remember any of those, just the pattern on a curtain, the random expression on a waiter's face, the sound of a window creaking as it closed.

We saw beautiful things, breathtaking, unforgettable; houses and mountains and gardens and palaces, seas and skies and churches and lakes, we went slowly down the River Rhine on an old fashioned boat fitted out entirely in gilt and mahogany, and stood at the rail or sat in the salon for hours on end, seeing the pale turrets and towers of fairy castles rise out of the dark green forests, along the opposite bank, Sleeping Beauty and Rumpelstiltskin palaces reflected in the wide water. I attached myself to them passionately, I think because they were so far from being what I had loved and wanted, so different in every respect from anything else I had seen or could long for. I did not want that gentle river journey to end.

Maxim was still wary of meeting anyone who might know of us, but all our companions were German or Dutch, we heard no English spoken apart from our own. We grew closer together again, interdependent, as we had not been during our brief time at home, we walked or were quiet together in perfect compatibility. Yet once, for no reason, as I leaned with him on the rail, gliding beside the enchanted forest, I looked at his hand, his long fingers curled loosely over the brass, and a voice in my head said 'That is a murderer's hand. The hand that held a gun. That man killed his wife. Rebecca,' and almost let out a cry, of shock, and distress, bewildered as to why, why it should have come, afraid of what, somewhere in the depths of my unconscious, clearly tormented me.

I must accept this too, it seemed, like all the rest. However far we fled, wherever we were, it would never be over, never forgotten, we would never finally be able to get away.

Once, in that time, there was a worse moment and a mistaken identity, a trick of vision echoing the past, played more terribly upon my dormant fears, quickening them to destructive life.

Sailing down the River Rhine, the weather had been quite cold, but from there, we went to Italy, and caught up with the very last of the summer. Here the sun shone again, in the middle of the day, and there was warmth in it, too. We turned ourselves to it, though early and late we wore warmer things, and here, too, the birds still lingered, the martins and the swallows, diving and swooping in the blue sky and in and out of the crevices of solemn buildings.

I will remember this, I told myself, and in order to do so, I must be happy here – this time will not come again. And I thought of how it might have been with me if Maxim had not rescued me, and that by now I would have been even better travelled, I would have spent the years of my young womanhood trailing wanly around the world as a paid companion to one awful, rich vulgar woman after another and, seeing lines at the corners of my eyes, felt the chill, first anxiety about the loneliness and bleakness of a genteel, impoverished old age. When these thoughts came, I despised myself for the faintest disloyalty I might ever, fleetingly have felt towards Maxim, the slightest, momentary boredom or dissatisfaction, and said my prayers fervently, in relief and gratitude.

On the morning of that day we had come out of the crowded streets and squares, out of the sun, into cool buildings, dark churches with domed and gilded ceilings in whose recesses flights of angels soared on pennant wings to heaven, and the quiet corridors of galleries where our footsteps echoed gravely, and we moved among pale, placid statues of men and gods, saints and virgins, ecstatic choirs, bland, marble fleshed cherubs. The images we saw refreshed me in some deep part of myself, so that my own small life and trivial concerns were, at least for those hours, set in a grander, more timeless perspective.

'I love it here,' I said, as we reached the end of a long cloister, that led out again into the world. 'I should like to stay – it makes me think of what matters and the rest is nothing but an irritation – like a fly buzzing about.'

'Then we should go.'

'Why?'

'So as not to spoil ourselves by having a surfeit – great art and solemnity and immortal longings are to be restricted to carefully measured doses, for best effect.'

He made me laugh, standing there so languid and English beside the marble pillar, speaking to me with all the offhand arrogance I had first loved, and so, out of an uprush of joy that he was more and more becoming that person again, I loved him, and took his arm as we strolled out of the shadow and into the full sun.

'If we are not to stay here, what shall we do?'

'Eat lunch, and go to a garden.'

The lunch was not, for once, in some small local café tucked away in a sidestreet, it was altogether grander.

'I'm tired of it,' he said. 'Come on.' And I knew that he meant hiding, turning our faces away out of habit when anyone passed and made to glance at us, tired of being afraid and ashamed, and relief made me giddy, and want to run about, laugh, dance in the street, not so much for myself – I was still happy enough to retreat and be anonymous, it was instinctive in me – but for him.

We ate at a hotel, under an awning on the terrace, and there were flowers on the table and a smooth, heavy

165

white cloth; the stems of the tall glasses were as fragile as twigs, and the shellfish tasted sweetly of the sea. Nothing could touch us. Once I said, 'I am so lucky. I had forgotten and now I have remembered,' and he laughed, and when I looked full into his face, I thought I saw only contentment there.

This will do, I said, if I cannot have the other, this will do, this sunshine and warmth and ease, these beautiful places; and I thought of how many, many would envy us. The secret is now, I said, looking down into my wine, tasting its faintly lemon freshness on my tongue. The secret is today; the past, tomorrow and the rest of our lives, are not to be thought of, we are simply not to contemplate them at all.

We lingered very happily for almost two hours over our lunch, eating more than was our habit now, and then took a bus, jostling with people, a little way out of the city, up into the gentle hills that surround it. But for the last mile, we walked, and it was wonderfully quiet, climbing up between the avenues of trees in the late afternoon sun.

The secret is now, I said over again, now, and thought that I could have stayed there, lived quietly in this beautiful place, and gone about the markets shopping, kept a small, white, neat house with shutters, and flowers in pots lining the steps.

'There,' Maxim said, stopping, catching my hand. 'Look.'

The villa was ahead of us, at the end of the last slope, rising above a broad avenue, surrounded by formal gardens. It was an austere house, elegant, graceful, approached by a double flight of stone steps that curved on either side and came together outside the porticoed entrance.

'I first saw it when I was seventeen,' Maxim said. 'I'll never forget it – never forget realising all at once about the *proportions* of things – it pleased my eye more than any building I'd ever seen – except my own.'

I stared up at it. I was not sure. It was too formal, too severe, I could not warm to it, it held me at arm's length and gazed at me severely.

As we walked up the smooth gravelled slopes, I saw the gardens on either side, and they were formal, too. There was water in long, stone channels, and fountains, their streams rising in fine arcs and plumes, carefully restrained. I saw lines of cypress trees and perfectly clipped little hedges, and the ilex and the poplars threw long, measured shadows.

Apart from some white geraniums, in great urns on either side of the steps, there seemed to be no flowers. But behind the house, the formal gardens led to rougher slopes, olives and orange trees, small, twisted, romantic things, in the long grass.

'You should see it in the spring,' Maxim said, 'it's carpeted with blue and cream flowers – and the blossom rises out of them – like snow – we'll come then.'

Spring. I would not think so far, would not think ahead at all, for fear I should remember what I had planned for that time.

After a while, I began to understand a little the seductiveness of the villa, the perfect, cool lines of it, its calmness and formality reached me, they were very certain of themselves, and so were restful. One let the house take control over oneself, it could not be altered or argued with. Perhaps, at last, I was changing, perhaps now, I was fully mature,

I thought, and it did not seem a foolish, laughable idea. I had never had a youth – though I had had a childhood, so long ago, it might have been in a story I had read – I had not been young, in any carefree, silly, frivolous way. I had married Maxim, I had lost myself in him, and in Manderley, and what happened to us there – yet I knew that in some deep, essential way I was not an adult, not mature, not a grown woman, though I often felt middle aged or even very elderly. It was a curious state. I was a wife to Maxim, and a child, too, and in our earlier exile, I had felt like a mother, leading him carefully by the hand.

We went on slowly, around the gardens, they encouraged a quiet, still way of walking, one could not imagine racing about, chattering, children's laughter. Like Manderley, I thought. That is why he is happy here, why the house gives him pleasure – it is like Manderley – it is grey, formidable, overpowering, ordered, harmonious, silent.

There were a few other people walking about as we did, solemn couples, scarcely speaking, and as we came back to the front of the villa again they began to come towards us, and a few others appeared, to gather in a group at the bottom of the steps. Maxim looked at his watch.

'Four o'clock. There is a tour of the house – the guide arrives here and waits – we may as well join. It's a bit ornate, but there are some wonderful things – pictures, too, I think. I don't remember it all.'

I was not sure that I wanted to go inside. I was happy to stay ambling about the gravelled paths, among the fountains, and not long ago it was the sort of thing that Maxim would have fled from, for the sort of people who went on such tours of public places were surely the sort who might see us, know us, stare and whisper. He did not seem to be concerned about any of that now.

A young woman was standing beside the flight of steps that led up to the entrance, tall, slender, dressed with impeccable Italian elegance, her hair pulled smoothly off her bony face into a black comb, the sort of woman who instantly made me feel scruffy, ill sorted, drab, aware of the buttons that had broken on my cardigan, the awkward way I held myself.

I did not fear women like that out of any insecurity with Maxim, no thought of his interest in anyone else had ever flickered within me. I had never for one moment been anxious that he might be unfaithful, though I sometimes wondered, as I always had, why he had married me, why he was apparently quite content, how love had come to us. I often stared at my own face in the glass and did not understand. There was only one woman I had been afraid of, one rival, but that was long over.

Yet the sight of this Italian, now, running lightly up the flight of steps, like a poised, self-assured bird, reminded me of it, and the photograph of Rebecca came into my mind, and I thought of how she would run up to the balustraded entrance of the villa, as if she were mistress of it.

We trooped obediently behind her, up the steps, a clump of a dozen or so, interested, polite, and because Maxim wanted to go inside, I followed, but I was sure, as we went into the great, shadowy hall, that I would not like any of it, it would be too forbidding, full of heavy, cold, impersonal things. And so it was, and the guide spoke Italian in a hard, high, fast voice. I could not follow anything at all and Maxim seemed distracted by her. When she pointed out this or that, he glanced away, studied some other part of the room. I wondered why he had come; perhaps simply to remember. He had said that he first came here when he was seventeen. I wondered what he had been like then, whether he had seemed boy-like, and clumsy. But I could not imagine.

We went in and out of the high ceilinged rooms. There were tiled floors, patterned formally, our footsteps rang on them, and painted ceilings, and carved swags of fruit and vines and ivy wreaths around the mouldings, above the doors. People would have listened to music here and stood in groups talking politely. They would have eaten beautifully arranged food, and never behaved impulsively, never been incorrectly dressed. They would not have done the normal everyday things, laughed and run about and argued and dropped things, and let the children shout.

The deeper we went into that impressive, perfect house, the more it repelled me. I disliked it, but I was not afraid of it, it did not intimidate me, and I was oddly proud of that.

I followed the guide, beside Maxim, faithfully for half an hour, but because I was growing too bored, too restless, and wanting a sight of the sunlit garden again, I gradually dropped back, dawdling unnoticed in a corridor, as they fluttered off towards a distant gallery, pretending to look more closely at some dull prints of amphitheatres and the colosseum, lining the walls. They were curiously soothing, a bland poultice to my restiveness.

The voice of the guide and the shuffling footsteps faded. No one had noticed me hanging back, though I supposed that before long Maxim would come to find me. A few yards ahead of me, at the end of the broad, empty corridor a staircase led up, and I followed it, feeling, as I climbed up past closed doors, like a child in a dream, wandering through a house alone, looking for someone or something without knowing what. No one else was about at all, and I supposed that the villa was deserted now, apart from the occasional influx of guides, and visitors, staring.

The staircase narrowed, and the last flight of all was quite steep. It was darker here, the windows were small and high, slits through which only fine arrows of dusty sunlight pierced, and there was nothing to see, no pictures, no furnishings. I meant to get to the top, in a superstitious way feeling that I must put my foot on the very last step before turning to descend again, but as I did so, I saw a rectangle of light ahead, falling onto the bare floor, and going towards it, I saw that two shutters stood half open, balanced together at the centre. I pushed them gently and as they swung, stepped forward into a small embrasure. There was no glass, it was an open space with a ledge around, like a balcony, and I realised that it formed part of a row of identical openings, that ran across the back of the villa.

What I saw took me by surprise, it seemed I had found the point of the house, after all. The orchard and the olive grove fell away, the formal gardens lay outspread like a carefully patterned carpet and beyond, dropping down to the drive and the great gates, the wooded slopes up which we had climbed to reach here. After that, in the distance, blue and grey and violet at the end of the day, were the roofs and domes, the turrets and campaniles of the city, with the river running through it, faintly visible.

It was beautiful. It was breathtaking, and mine, for that moment, a secret I had discovered and held to myself, pretending that no one else had ever been here, better beyond measure than the dull, pompous rooms and statues and cold corridors of the house below.

And then, leaning forward slightly, I looked not out and ahead, but directly down, and the stone terrace far below, with its urns and lions and tubs of clipped little trees, seemed to be lying in wait for me, beckoning, seductive. I began to tremble, my throat constricted, the palms of my hands were damp and slippery as I gripped the ledge.

The gardens were empty, quite empty, the shadows lay long and dark, like the shadows of tall women, standing there, stern, expectant. Then the voice came, whispering, I almost felt her breath on my neck, saw the black silk of her sleeve, her hand resting on the shutter beside me. If I glanced around, I would see her.

'It's no use is it? You'll never get the better of her . . . she's still the real Mrs de Winter, not you. And what about him? You know the truth, don't you, and so do I, and you can't forget it. We will never let you forget. She won't. She is still there, she is always there. You thought she had faded away into the past, that she would lie still and silent but she will never lie still, I will never let her. She wants me to help her, and I will. I never failed her, never, and I won't fail her now. I'll be here, I will speak for her when she cannot. He killed her, didn't he? We all know it. I know. She knows. You know. He murdered her. Maxim de Winter shot his wife and laid her body in the boat and put out to sea, and let it sink, so that it would look like an accident. But it wasn't an accident. It was murder. She didn't drown. I know the truth you see. I always suspected and now I know. So do you, and it is worse for you, isn't it? So hard. You have to live with it for the rest of your life and you can never *not* know, never escape, no matter where you run, to some other beautiful place, some quiet, private little town, it doesn't matter. You have to live with it and with him. When you wake each morning, you have to look at him and then you remember. That man is a murderer. That man shot his wife. He killed Rebecca. He is your husband now. When you go to sleep at night, you see him beside you, and it is your last waking thought, and it follows you into your dreams and curdles them so that they are dreadful, frightening things.'

The voice would not stop, would not go, it neither rose nor fell, but was monotonous, soft, the words pattered one after another, as seductive as music I could not choose but hear. The voice was in my head, yet it was outside of me, separate. I felt horribly faint, and yet I could not lose consciousness, there was no escape that way.

I opened my eyes, which had been half closed, and looked down. The light had changed, as the day drew in, it was a beautiful amber and rose, a perfumed, limpid sunlight that drew me towards itself.

'Yes,' the voice whispered. 'That is the way, isn't it? You know it now, you remember. Look down there, it's easy, isn't it? Why don't you jump? It wouldn't hurt, not to break your neck. It's a quick, kind way. Why don't you try it? Why don't you go? It would solve everything. You need never remember again, no one could reach you there. Don't be afraid. I won't push you. I didn't push you the last time did I? I won't stand by you. You can jump of your own accord. He will never know why, it will look like a terrible accident, and so it will be, won't it? He won't know I have been here. He thinks I am dead. So do you. They all do. Mrs Danvers, as dead as her mistress. Why don't you get away from us all for ever? You want to, don't you? You have never dared to tell him that you are afraid of him sometimes, because he is a murderer, you will never be happy with him, however far you run, or even if you go back and try to begin that new life you thought you wanted, you can never get away from us. Why don't you jump and let it be over?'

'No,' I whispered back. 'No. Get away from me, you're not real, neither of you, she can't hurt me, and nor can you. Get away from me, Mrs Danvers.' And then I cried out and stepped back, I heard my own voice coming after me like an echo sounding hollow from the depths of the sea, 'No, no, no,' as I fell.

Everyone was solicitous, everyone was helpful, and Maxim the most concerned of all. The memory of his tenderness warmed me. I kept on turning to it, during the next few days, as I sat in a little, sunny sitting room overlooking the courtyard and a sidestreet of our *pensione*. The signora had insisted on putting me there, I could not be in a bedroom all day, she said, that would be depressing and my spirits should be kept up, she would not have me mope. I was not ill, after all, I simply needed to rest, to be looked after, to have great care taken of me. And after a time, as she came and went discreetly, clucking and fussing, bringing up small tempting plates of fruit – fresh ripe figs, the last few peaches, or sparkling water and little almond biscuits I realised, with a flush of embarrassment, that she thought I must be expecting a child. There was an indulgence, a coyness mingled with sympathetic understanding, in her expression. It affected me. I wanted to be able to please her by confiding that yes, yes, it was so.

The courtyard had a gate in its far wall leading out into a lane, and at the end, stood what I learned was a convent, part of which housed a nursery. Several times a day I sat and listened to the voices of the children, high, bright, chattering little birds flocking to school, and laughing, calling, shouting at their play, over the high wall. Through an open window would come their chanting of rhymes, and their sweet, wavering singing.

I never saw them, I did not need to, I could imagine them well enough. I was unsure whether their presence made me happy or quickened my disappointment.

I was not ill, I had to protest that over and over again. I had felt horribly foolish, embarrassed, as I had been helped slowly down the flights of stone stairs and put on a great chair like a throne, in the entrance hall. Iced water was fetched, a car sent for, I was conscious of people peering discreetly, before glancing away.

I had only felt suddenly giddy, I said, it was the height, or the contrast with the light outside, as I had stepped forwards, perhaps I had drunk one glass of wine more than was sensible at lunch, when I so rarely did so. In the hallway, in the car, at the *pensione*, Maxim had looked at me with such love, such anxious tenderness, his face kept coming to my mind, and when it did so, guilt filled me, and shame, at what I had been thinking about him, what I had allowed the voice in my head to go on whispering; for it had only been in my head, I knew that. I had imagined it, hallucinated even, and done nothing to silence it. I had been transfixed, mesmerised, almost in some horrible way enjoying it.

I wished then that I had someone to talk to, and as I wished it, I realised that I had no friends, had never had them – not the sort of easy, cheerful confidantes other women always have, old school companions, sisters or cousins, the wives of their husband's colleagues – anyone. I had kept up with no one. I was an only child, there were no relatives, I had gone as a paid companion to Mrs van Hopper, but that had not been a friendship, I could never have talked of anything to her, and while I had been with her, I had been keeping a secret, concealing things from her. I had had Maxim. After that, there had been no need for anyone, or no place. There had been hordes of visitors, endless acquaintances, neighbours, all of them older than me, none of them remotely close to me, none of them, except in a prurient way, at all interested. There had only been Frank Crawley, loyal to Maxim, fiercely discreet, a rock when I had needed one to cling to, but not in the way I meant and needed now, a friend, and then Beatrice – I could have talked to her, she had been fond of me, I thought. But Frank had been Maxim's employee, Beatrice his sister, they were neither of them simply mine, on my side – though it ought not to be a question of 'sides', I knew, and that was something else to feel guilty about.

I began to feel sorry for myself, during those few days, and that sickened me. I caught myself indulging it one afternoon – how I had never had a youth, or friends of my own, how I had been forced to leave behind what I wanted, for Maxim's sake, how I wanted children and had not – perhaps could not – have them.

Maxim had left me, to go and walk again around one of his favourite galleries, whose formal, artificial paintings were not very much to my taste, though I had said that I would go with him, that I could not sit about here so much.

'I'm not ill,' I said. 'I'm perfectly all right, Maxim, I didn't want such a fuss made, I don't need to be treated like an invalid.'

He stood, looking down at me, generous, gentle, and I should have responded to it, I should have been loving, grateful, but it angered me, I felt irritated, patronised, pandered to like a child again. 'Go out,' I said. 'I'll meet you. We can have an ice in that café beside the old fountain.'

'Will you rest?'

'I'm not tired.' But then I felt guilty again, rejecting his concern. I said, 'I might, but I'm not ill – please believe me, it was really nothing – nothing at all.'

The afternoon was suspended, the autumn sunshine very still on the old walls of the courtyard. I heard the signora chatting at the front of the house, and then go out, closing the door. The children were quiet, having their afternoon rest, perhaps.

I wondered how long we would continue like this, being in this place or that for no particular reason, whether we would do it for the rest of our lives. I supposed so. I could not ask Maxim, I dared not talk to him about it. We were far apart, I thought suddenly, and yet I did not understand why or how it had happened. We had come through our trials into calm seas, and been as close as it is possible for two people to be. Now it had gone, that completeness, and I wondered if marriage was always like this, constantly moving and changing, bearing one this way and that, together and then apart, almost at random, as if we were floating in it, as in a sea. Or were we not powerless at all, did we will it, did we bring it upon ourselves by what we wanted and thought and said and did? Were those things as influential as out-side events, the chances of life? I spent an hour or more, questioning, puzzling, and only became more confused and bewildered, and did not even know why I had to go on, why I could not simply let it be, exist, without probing thoughts, and anxieties that disturbed and unsettled me, and so, Maxim, too.

Perhaps I was wrong, perhaps I was not well. I felt very tired, listless and uninterested, perhaps that was why I had heard the whispering voice, and fainted. Round and round went the thoughts and questions, round and round, and I with them, wearily, and so, after a while, slept a little, a strange, shifting, troubled sleep, in that silent house.

As I awoke, quite gently, in the late afternoon, I looked at the wall on the far side of the courtyard. I had been looking at it, I supposed, as I had gone to sleep, though without consciously registering what I saw there, but the image had done its work, and in some strange way, caused me to know the answer to something that must have been troubling me more than I knew, it came now clear and complete into my mind.

A creeper grew up the old wall – spreading itself to right and left, like arms outstretched – and clambering around the top of the gate; it was a pretty, pleasing thing, its leaves a bright, glossy green, and it was covered in hundreds of starry, pure white flowers whose sweet scent came to me faintly, on the air. I did not know what it was called, but I realised now that I had seen it growing over an arch at the villa.

The white flowers on the green reminded me of the others. And it was then that I was sure it had been teasing at me, puzzling me, somewhere deep down, the source of disquieting dreams and whispering voices, what had happened at the villa had been part of it.

Frank Crawley had tried to reassure me. He had brushed aside my concerns about the wreath left at Beatrice's graveside, tried to convince me that it was really of no importance, dismissed it, and the card, as nothing more than some trick, a sick, horrible joke. Jack Favell, he had said firmly, I've heard that he is still about – I saw him once. That is who must have planted it, of course, that is the sort of thing it would amuse him to do. Ignore it, forget about it. It means nothing.

But no, I thought now, No, it was not Jack Favell, that was not his style at all. Jack Favell was a weak, unpleasant, rotten character, a coward, a liar, and corrupt but not evil; Jack Favell was a sponger and a cheat, I remembered him now, big, loose fleshed, good looks running to seed, a soft, flabby sort of man, with a weak chin and whisky breath, leering, suggestive. Rebecca had despised him and so had Maxim. So had I, though I had been afraid of him too, but I had been afraid of everyone in those days. I would not fear Jack Favell now.

He had not left the wreath. He had not the taste, the subtlety, the finesse, he would make a mess of something like that, even supposing it had occurred to him to do it. He could never have chosen such impeccable flowers, with such care, and organised to have them left there by such stealth and exquisite cunning. He might have appeared at Beatrice's funeral – indeed, I realised now that in some shadowy way I had half expected it; I might not have been surprised if I had glanced around the church that afternoon and seen him at the back, looking at me with watering, fishy eyes, hair thin now, his neck creased with fat. But he had not come, probably he had not so much as known about Beatrice's death.

The wreath was not his doing. He could not have written the letter R, such a faithful replica of her hand, on the cream card. He did not have that delicacy, his ways were obvious, crass, blundering ways.

There was only one person in the world who could have planned the white wreath so meticulously, carried out such a clever, cruel hoax, forged the letter R upon the card.

The little children were coming out of the nursery, I heard their voices in a high silvery stream, over the wall, heard pattering footsteps die gradually away and then the courtyard was peaceful again. But she was there. She was in my head and before my eyes and shadowing even this innocent, private place.

I saw her dressed, as always, in silken black, with long bony hands sticking like claws out of the thin black sleeves, saw her skull face, parchment white, with its prominent cheek bones, and deep, hollow set eyes. I saw her hair scraped back from her face, flat, gleaming on her head, like the hair of the guide at the villa, and her hands folded together in front of her, saw her expression when she looked at me, scornful, superior, and then those other times, when it had flashed with hatred, and loathing, when she had despised me and mocked me and tried in so many subtle, malevolent ways, to undermine my fragile happiness and what little sense of peace and security I had clung to.

I saw her standing at the head of the staff arrayed on the steps of Manderley to greet me so formally there on my first arrival as a bride; at the top of the great staircase beside the minstrel's gallery, looking blankly, coldly down upon me; and in the doorway of the bedroom in the west wing, gloating, triumphant, catching me guilty and unawares. I saw her eyes, filled with satisfaction and exultation, the night of the Manderley ball, when I had fallen so easily into the trap she had set for me.

I heard her, too, her voice whispered again, intimate, unpleasant, soft as a snake.

I did not know where she was now. We had never seen her again, after we had driven down to Manderley from London, that last, terrible night. She had packed her things and left, they said, her room had been found empty that afternoon. And after that, the fire. I did not want to know about her, I wanted rid of her from our lives, and from my mind, I never thought of her, never let her shadow fall across my path or come between us.

181

Mrs Danvers had been Rebecca's, she had belonged with her and with Manderley. I wanted none of her. But Mrs Danvers had sent the wreath. I knew it. I knew.

I went out without taking my jacket or a bag, half ran, from the *pensione*, down through the narrow sidestreets, to the fountain. He was there already, sitting with his legs crossed and his glass of tea on the table before him.

'Maxim,' I called, out of breath, but trying to gather myself, trying to be as easy, as nonchalant, as he was.

He looked up.

'I'm better,' I said, brightly, 'isn't it lovely? It's still quite warm in the sun. I'm really perfectly all right.'

I saw a faint frown between his eyes, a look of puzzlement. Why was I so anxious to reassure him, why did I have to protest, at once and so urgently and lightly, that I was well?

I ordered tea, and a lemon ice. I was calm, very calm. I sipped my drink and ate tiny mouthfuls of the ice slowly, from the slender bone handled spoon, and in between them, I smiled at him. I did not blurt it out.

But at last, I said, 'Let's leave here soon. I'd like a change, wouldn't you? Surely we can enjoy somewhere else, before the winter comes.'

We had not discussed that. I supposed we must settle somewhere, when the weather changed, but it had not seemed to matter where. It still did not. I was only desperate to leave here, because it was tainted now, I could no longer be peaceful here, no longer walk about these streets and squares without feeling that I must glance behind me. We had to move on again, to find a place which was not yet spoiled. Now, I was the one who was restless, I was the one who needed to run and run away, even though it was futile, and what I ran from was in myself, I carried it with me no matter how far we went.

Maxim watched me. The cold ice made my throat ache as I swallowed it. I could not ask again, I thought, he would be suspicious and question me, and I could not have answered. I could never say her name, any of those names, out of that other world.

And then he smiled. 'Yes,' he said. 'I thought that we would go to Venice again.'

It was dark by the time we went back to the *pensione*, the air was cold. On a whim, I did not turn into the front entrance, but went a few yards on, and up the little alley way, leading to the courtyard gate.

'There's something I want to show you,' I said to Maxim. 'I hadn't noticed it properly before, but then, when I woke this afternoon, I saw it. It's lovely – it smells so sweetly – but I don't know what it is.'

Why did I want to see him standing there, beside the creeper? I was not going to tell him about the wreath, and yet, showing him this seemed to be a way of telling, a way of linking them together in my mind and the need to do that was so clear and so powerful that it frightened me.

'Look.' In the dusk, the foliage receded and the tiny flowers stood out, pale and ghostly against it. I reached out and touched a petal with my finger. Maxim's face was pale, too, in profile.

'Yes,' he said, 'pretty thing. You often see it in Mediterranean countries – a late flowering, before the winter.' He reached out, and broke off a twig of it, and held it out for me. 'It's called Maiden's Bower,' he said, and waited, so that in the end, I was forced to take the flowers and carry them with me, into the house.

By the time we reached Venice, riding at last across the open water of the lagoon towards that magic city at the end of the day, summer and autumn had withered away to winter, leaving no trace.

The wind was cold, it blew in our faces and whipped up the water, so that we retreated under cover inside the boat, and when we disembarked at the San Marco station, the stones of the streets and the square ahead gleamed with rain. It was quiet, too, only Venetians got off with us, men with briefcases, putting up their coat collars and striding quickly away, going home, a few old women in black, carrying raffia shopping bags, heads bent.

But it was still beautiful, I thought, it could never fail, I gazed across the water behind me at the dome of the Salute, and further across, to the island out of which the tower of S. Giorgio rose, so perfectly, and back as far as I could see, up the course of the Grand Canal, before it bent into the dusk, receding between the overlooking houses. I gazed not only in pleasure, but with a strange sense of unreality, as if I might close my eyes and blink the scene completely away. The last time we had come here it had been spring and the buildings had glittered in the thin, pale early sunlight, and I had had an even greater sense of disbelief, for then, I had been newly married to Maxim, and quite disorientated, shaken by the surprise and swiftness of it all, carried along by him, and by the event itself, unthinking, willing, bewildered, ecstatically happy.

I remembered so little of that time, I never had, it had been an interlude of uncharacteristic, carefree joy and irresponsibility, before we had returned to the real world, and its pains and cares and shocks had overtaken us again. Of all that followed, at Manderley, I recalled every detail, it was like a film that I could re-run on demand.

But of Venice, and the other places we had first visited together, it was only small, irrelevant things I could remember out of the vague, overall blur of optimism and light headed-ness.

Now, I saw it again as a very different place, with a sombre, darker expression; I admired it, I looked at it in awe, but, walking up the narrow alleyway beside a canal, following the porter who carried our bags, I shivered, not only because I was tired and chilled, but because I felt afraid of this ancient, hidden, secret city which seemed never to present a true face to us, but a series of masks, that changed, according to mood.

We had found yet another quiet, modest *pensione* – we had a genius for it, I thought, the places so suited us, and the way we always seemed to be in retreat, always carefully turning away our faces. I was used to it now, I did not mind; only, as I hung up clothes, folded things, slid open heavy drawers, I felt a spurt of raw longing, for my own rooms, my own furniture, home, and I indulged it, and Cobbett's Brake came, still and quiet and undisturbed, into my mind.

I measured out the time I allowed myself to spend on it most carefully, before going in search of Maxim.

We settled down quite quickly. We would stay, Maxim said, stay for the winter – why not? Indeed, we had had our share of sunshine. I was surprised how easily the routine of days together came back to us, how we fell into a pattern of fetching the newspaper, eating a late breakfast, walking, exploring, looking at pictures, at churches, at houses, at the faces of Venetians, at the boats gliding silently across the silky black water, at the sky, morning and evening, over the campanile. When we had last come here, we had looked at one another, so that I did not see the city, only Maxim's face.

The weather was mostly bleak, the wind bitter, snaking down alleyways and across the open squares, driving us indoors. But sometimes the clouds cleared, and then the reflections of the houses shone back from the face of the water and the gilding on the walls and the painted domes were sparkling. There was fog, too, when the footsteps that never cease in Venice and the bells and the stroke of the oars were muffled in it, and we did not leave the dark, red plush lounge, except for our private café, and then the time hung heavy, then I wanted open, wide skies, I thought of ploughed fields and bare trees and sometimes dreamed that I was standing on the cliffs above Kerrith, watching the breakers race in and crash up over the black rocks.

Maxim was at first quite unchanged, retreating into the old, familiar ways of our earlier years in exile, wanting my company, reading a great deal, interested in the dull, ordinary news from home, that came a couple of days late, not wanting to be reminded of painful, former things, so that I grew used again to being careful what I said, to sparing him, to concealing some of my own thoughts. We came to know Venice and a very great many of its works of art and ways of daily life as well as inhabitants, we were experts, we scarcely needed our guide books, we quizzed one another about dates and styles and history and doges and painters, and it was a pleasant and perhaps fruitful way of helping the time to pass.

Sometimes, I caught him looking at me, and his face darkened, I could not tell what he was thinking. Sometimes I sensed that he had closed himself off from me, and I retreated, and that was easy, I had dreams in which I could snatch ten minutes of nostalgia and fragile fulfilment, when it was necessary.

Letters came. We heard from Giles, Frank Crawley wrote once, there were business envelopes to be attended to some-times, but they seemed to be of little consequence, and to cause Maxim no distress. He only spent an hour or two dealing with them, at a table in the window of our room, and then I would go out alone, to wander about the streets of Venice, or ride up and down the Grand Canal, on the vaporetto, a cheap, harmless, hour of pleasure.

Christmas came, and it was as strange and alien as Christmas had been every year of our exile, and I was used to it, I thought, I would not feel any different. We would exchange our own presents and eat whatever it was the custom to eat and I would go to a foreign church and hear the service in a language I did not know, but otherwise, the day would pass much as any other.

I went not to one of the grand principal churches, with the dressed up crowds, St Mark's or the Salute, I felt no more inclined than ever for public display. Instead, I got up early, leaving Maxim barely awake, and walked through sidestreets and obscure, empty squares, over the Rialto Bridge to a church I had found one day in my solitary walks, and which had pleased me because it was quiet and plainer than was usual in Venice, not very gilded or full of precious paintings, but a more modest, a more *real* church, I thought. No one would come here to see and be seen, I would slip by unnoticed in my grey fur collared coat and hat.

Maxim never came. He did not believe, he said, except for 'some truths' and I had never questioned him further. I was not, indeed, very sure what I believed myself, I was uneducated in theology as in most other things, though I had been brought up with the usual teachings, the familiar stories, but I had prayed my desperate prayers these last years, and had had our reprieve, and our quietness and closeness together, as answers.

I made my way with the families and the old, black coated women who shuffled, arm in arm, nodding in response to an incurious smile, slipping in to the back of the church, to hear the Christmas Mass, and now, among the blaze of newly lit candles and the great urns of branches and waxen flowers, the rise and fall of the priest's voice and the murmured responses, I prayed again, to be scoured clean of the thoughts and memories, the reminders, the whispering voices, to forget, to forget. I meant to pray to be satisfied with what we had, too, to give thanks for it, to be modestly grateful; but as I knelt, I knew that I could not, I felt a tremendous, raw anger and desire well up in me, the house, Cobbett's Brake, was there, in front of me, and I longed for it and could not let it go.

I wanted Christmas, as it should be by now for us, Christmas in a house, our own house, with great green branches brought in and swathed around the mantelpieces and burning in the grate, scarlet and white translucent berries, the old words in English, the familiar carols, the hot, rich, comforting plates of food. I was bitter with longing, so that I could not pray, not decently, I only sat dumbly, enduring the chanting and the shuffling files of communicants and the clinking of the chain as the censer swung to and fro, waiting for it to be over, and I to be released.

The fog had come creeping off the lagoon and seeped into the slits between the gaunt old houses, it hung over the surface of the black water of the canal, sour and sulphurous, and I walked back very quickly, my head bent. Maxim was standing in the hall, talking in his fluent Italian, with great cheerfulness, to the hotel manager, holding a glass of wine.

'There you are,' he said, and put out his arm to me, his face full of pleasure that I had returned, and how could I not respond, and warm to it, how could I not go quickly to him, out of nothing but love?

I did, I did, and another glass was brought, and the proprietor kissed my hand and we wished one another a happy Christmas, in a foreign tongue, and I smiled, and it was not like Christmas at all.

But there was a rhythm with my moods, as with everything, and in any case, I kept them to myself, it had become the strictest point of honour with me not to let him know what I felt – and so, I supposed, also the ultimate deception. But I was used to it now, it was better that way.

And so the even tenor of our days resumed, and they were

companionable, undemanding, pleasant, and we quickly grew accustomed even to that bizarre, extraordinary city, and in the end scarcely noticed it and might have been anywhere.

That Maxim seemed to have secrets too now, that I caught him looking at me strangely, questioningly, that he seemed to need time to conduct matters of business did not trouble me, though I was surprised. I was glad of it, I thought it must mean that he had some interest elsewhere, outside of our enclosed, inward looking little world.

January passed in gloom and greyness, late dark and early dark, in bitter winds and rain that drove relentlessly across the lagoon. The water rose and flooded steps and landing stages, crept up the walls of the buildings, overspilled into the piazza, a foetid, damp smell curled into our nostrils whenever we went out, and the lamps were never switched off, day after day.

When relief came, it was not only with the sight of the sun, after the weeks of dark, not only with the faintest trace of something clean and new on the air that reminded us that there would be spring, it was with something quite other, and entirely unexpected. It came with high comedy and a reminder of that past in which I had very first known Maxim, which had nothing of sadness or unpleasantness about it, as so many of our memories had. It brought back the first flush of love, and my own innocence, and showed me again how well Maxim had rescued me.

It was my birthday, a happier day than Christmas, for Maxim always tried to give me not simply a present but some wonderful surprise, some pleasure I could not have anticipated. It was the sort of thing he was very good at, so that I woke, always, with that child-like sense of anticipation, the flutter of excitement, as I remembered the day.

The sun shone brilliantly and we went out very early. We were to breakfast not as usual, modestly in our *pensione*, but at Florian's, and as we walked over the bridge and down towards the piazza, among the Venetians hurrying to work, the women and toddlers, and babies, the small boys running to school, the sky was the enamel blue of the sky in a Renaissance painting, and indeed, that seemed the exact word for it. 'A new birth,' I said, as we strolled, 'a new beginning.'

Maxim smiled, and I suddenly saw his face as I had very first seen it, sitting on the sofa at the Hotel Côte d'Azur all those years ago. Then, it had seemed to me a medieval face, in some strange way, the face of a fifteenth-century portrait, a face that belonged to a walled city like this one, full of narrow cobbled streets, and it was so again, there was the same sharpness and elegance about it, so that he fitted in exactly here, though he was not at all like the jutting nosed, red haired Venetians.

The coffee tasted better than coffee had for years, real, rich Italian coffee, the taste belonged to the old years before the war and all the deprivations. Coffee had become thin, grey, gruel-like stuff, but this was fragrant, rich and dark, and the cups were large, with a delicate gold rim, and as we sat, not outside – it was still too chilly and too early for that – but on one of the plush banquettes beside the window, the pigeons rose in a cloud, and fluttered up and around and around the glittering domes of St Mark's, casually at home among the massive lions and the prancing horses, and then fell back again on to the pavement.

Maxim was leaning back, looking at me, his expression one of amusement. 'You have not very long left,' he said, 'you had better make the best of it.'

I knew what he meant at once. 'What shall you do?' I asked. 'We had better make plans. You will not like me then.'

'Of course. I shall disown you on the stroke of midnight, you will be cast into outer darkness.'

When I had first met Maxim, on one of those heady, unforgettable, first days, we had been driving back in his car to Monte Carlo, and something, some remark, had brought me back to myself and the reality of my situation, and I had blurted out in a moment of frustration and misery, 'I wish I was a woman of about thirty-six dressed in black satin and a string of pearls.'

For that had seemed to me the sort of age and type of worldly, sophisticated woman Maxim de Winter would prefer, and I had been so much younger, gauche and school-girlish, inexperienced, and stupid. But it had been me he had married, me he had wanted, astonishing, unbelievable as it had been – and still was, I thought, now, looking at him across the pink tablecloth of Florian's, still was. A woman of thirty-six in black satin and a string of pearls had been everything he had loathed and wanted to escape from, a woman like Rebecca. I had learned that.

But in a couple of years I would be thirty-six. Though I would never wear the black satin, I had once or twice secretly wished for the pearls, for they were flattering, gentle and softer than most jewels, which had always seemed to me hard, brittle, repellent things.

The age did not matter, I knew now that on some days I was older than my mother had been, as old as it was possible ever to be, and on others, a very few – today was one – I was the age I had been when I had met Maxim, and would never alter or grow older. Most of the time, if I thought of it at all, I was some dull, indeterminate middle age.

But this morning, my birthday, I was as new born as the day, and the sunshine, the air, the sparkling city, filled me with delight, I would never whine again, I said, I would never be discontented, never look back over my shoulder, pining for lost things. I had no need of that.

The day brought small pleasures but he waited until darkness to surprise me best, telling me to change into an evening frock, and wear a fur wrap, and then leaving me alone, to get ready. I had supposed that we would walk across to one of our favourite small restaurants near the Rialto Bridge, but we went only down the side street, as far as the landing stage, and there was a gondola, waiting like an elegant, dark swan on the gleaming water, with torches lit and glowing golden around its prow. We had ridden like this the last time we had been here, on our honeymoon, Maxim had made just such romantic gestures a dozen times a day, but I was not used to it now, our life was not like that, I had forgotten how good he had been at it.

I wanted time to stop, and the quiet journey down the canal to last forever. I did not look back or long for anything else, but only wanted the present, in this place – such times are the more precious for being rare. But it did not take very long, we were slipping up to a landing stage, and I saw the entrance doors of the hotel opened by attendants, the lights gleamed on the water and bobbed there.

I had never truly enjoyed smart places, we had both done with all that; and yet, once in a while, it was an excitement, a brief, fluttering episode of pleasure, to dress up and sit under chandeliers and be attended to, and perfectly harmless, for it was a game now, a treat, not a way of living, not essential to our self image, as I knew it was to very many of the people Maxim had once known – Maxim, and Rebecca.

He had been so wary of such places for so long, afraid of being seen and pointed out, as well as afraid of reviving memories he found painful, that I was quite used to our hiding away and did not mind it. I was surprised now, that he had wanted to dine at the oldest, smartest hotel in Venice.

'You deserve a special occasion,' he said, 'you've had so few of them. I've been too dull for you.'

'No. That's what is best – what I like. You know that.'

'Too wrapped up in myself then. I intend to take myself in hand.'

I stopped, just as we were about to go inside, between the uniformed, braided porters, holding open the glass doors. 'Don't change – I wouldn't want this often.'

'Certainly not, I'm far too old to change.'

'It will be lovely – I've walked by here so often and looked in – it always seems so beautiful – like a palazzo, not like a hotel.'

'That's what it was.' We went in, stepping on to the jewel coloured carpet. 'And we are very unlikely to meet anyone at all. If people still take notice of such things, it isn't yet the smart season to be in Venice.'

194

It may not have been, but there were smart people dining in the hotel that night nonetheless, mainly older people, clearly rich, in a dull, old fashioned sort of way, women in small fur wraps and emeralds, with balding men, couples who sat and stared ahead of them complacently, and scarcely spoke. We passed between them unremarked, and I wondered whether we seemed old too, whether any young people ever did come here.

And then I saw one. He came down the velvet carpet, between the brocaded sofas, the deep, ruby red chairs, and I could not help staring at him, because he was young, as young as any of the junior waiters, but of a style and type I did not recognise, could not place. He was very slim, with beautifully shaped, dark hair that looked as if it had been carefully recombed only moments before. He wore a dinner jacket with a black satin tie which Maxim would probably frown at as being slightly too wide; for that was the kind of thing he still noticed and counted as important, a small, innate snobbery, and it seemed that I had acquired it, I was judging the pretty young man with a critical as well as a curious eye. He paused for a second to let our waiter step back out of his path and I saw what a beautifully shaped mouth he had, how perfect a skin, but also, that he had a discontented, faintly supercilious expression. A younger son, or a grandson, I decided, enduring a holiday with older relatives and longing only to get away from them, but obliged to sit listening to talk about people in whom he was not interested, and play bridge and walk rather slowly about Venice, and to fetch and carry – for he held an envelope and a spectacle case that I was sure were not his own. I supposed that he had expectations and so must be dutiful, careful not to offend for fear of being cut from the will.

All speculation over in a moment, the young man summed up, pigeon holed and dismissed. I felt so ashamed of myself that, as he caught my eye, glancing across at us, I half smiled, before looking away again in embarrassment. His eyes flickered, there was perhaps a movement at the corners of his mouth, before he moved on. I saw Maxim raise an eyebrow at me, understanding at once everything I had thought and decided, and in complete agreement with me, I could tell without his having to speak. He looked amused.

Then, I heard a voice from the sofa in the corner just behind us, a loud voice, aggrieved, complaining, a voice that came ringing to me across the intervening years, and turned me into an awkward, ill dressed girl of twenty-one again. 'My goodness, you took your time, whatever were you doing? Why on earth you couldn't find them right away I just can't imagine.'

Maxim and I stared at each other, our eyes widening in disbelief.

'Now do sit down again, you're hovering, and you know I can't stand you to hover. No, not there, there. That's it. Now, just pass me the envelope, I'm sure the cutting I want is in it, there was a photograph, it was in *Paris Soir* – oh, I know it was an old one, from years before the war, and I daresay it may not be him, I daresay he is dead, like the rest of them – only there was something so familiar about the back of his head, I could swear it *was* the Comte – he had such style, you can't imagine – well, no, *you* couldn't;

so French, he kissed my hand every time we met with such wonderful panache – only French men know how to bring that off, they know exactly how to treat a woman. What ever is the matter with you now, why are you fidgeting like that? We'll go in to dinner in ten minutes.'

The last time I had seen Mrs van Hopper she had looked up at me, pausing in the act of powdering her nose in the mirror of her vanity case to tell me that in agreeing to marry Maxim de Winter, I was making a big mistake and one that I would bitterly regret. She had doubted my ability to function as mistress of Manderley, poured scorn on my hopes and dreams, eyed me with a prying, unpleasant expression. But I had not cared, I had been able to stand up to her and disregard all she said, for the first time since I had gone into her employment as a paid companion, because now I was loved, now I was to marry, I was to become Mrs Maxim de Winter, and could take on anyone, I thought, face anything. Her power over me had been loosened in an instant, I was no longer paid by her, and no longer made to feel inferior, stupid, inept, clumsy, a non person. The dreadful weeks of embarrassment and humiliation and tedium were over, the endless bridge parties and cocktails in her hotel rooms, the fetching and carrying, the meals at which I was treated with barely concealed contempt by waiters, having to put up with her snobberies and self-regarding conceits, all were over, and I was rescued, safe.

I had gone out of the room, and down to where Maxim was waiting for me, impatiently, in the foyer, and I never saw or heard from her again. Once only, having nothing better to do, I wrote her a brief letter. She did not reply, and after that

I was engulfed by all the terrible events that came one after another like storm waves, and broke over our lives. I don't think, in the quiet years that had followed, I had spared her more than a couple of passing thoughts, had never wondered where she was, or even if she were still alive. She had nothing to do with me, she had passed out of my life that day at the Hotel Côte d'Azur in Monte Carlo. Yet I should have thought of her, if we owe our thoughts to people who have been so important to us. If I had never become her companion, and if she had not been addicted to preying upon and mercilessly cornering anyone she considered smart and worth knowing, anyone who was anyone, I would not be here now, Mrs Maxim de Winter, my life would have been different in every possible respect.

I assumed that he would want to avoid her seeing us, that we would lurk here, hunched on our high backed sofas until she had gone into dinner, and then fled, gone on somewhere less public to eat; but something of the old confidence, even a faint arrogance, had returned to Maxim; perhaps he did not care, perhaps he felt less vulnerable – I could not tell. At any rate, he leaned forward, his lips still curled in amusement, and whispered to me, 'Finish your drink. I think we are ready to go in.'

I looked at him in surprise, but he smiled, and the smile was mischievous, I saw that he intended not merely to brave the moment, but to enjoy it, and I remembered how cruelly, subtly adept he had been before at dealing with her.

Now, he stood up. His face was a perfect mask. It was all I could do not to giggle. 'Don't look,' he said. The waiter came forward, to lead us towards the dining room.

Don't look. I did not. But of course, there was no need. As we passed her corner, looking straight ahead, our expressions bland, I heard her intake of breath, and the dreadful sound that carried me back to the past again, the snap of her lorgnette.

'Why it is – my God – quick, stop them, get up, move – stupid boy – it *is* – well, Maxim de Winter!'

What she wanted most, of course, was to be invited to dine with us. She had not changed, she was as transparent, as manipulative as ever. Her ploy was to ask us to join her at her table. 'So many years, such old, old friends, however could I not leap at the chance – I really can't take no for an answer.'

But she was obliged to. 'I am so sorry,' Maxim said, charmingly, impeccably polite, 'but it is a very special occasion, we are only in Venice a few days and it is my wife's birthday, we are having a particular table. I'm sure you will forgive us.'

She would not. I saw her mouth open and close as she fished about desperately for the right words to detain us, have us change our minds. Maxim was there before her. 'But we would be so pleased if you would have coffee with us after dinner – you,' his eyes flickered briefly, quizzically to the young man who had half risen to his feet as we stopped, but now was sitting again, looking sulky, '– and your friend,' and smoothly, without pausing, he put his hand under my elbow and steered me ahead and into the dining room. I longed to look back, to see the expression on her face, and dared not. But I knew that the young man was not gauche and shy and embarrassed by her, as I had been, I saw that he had a conceit and a superciliousness about him which I could not like, and so, I did not sympathise with him, did not feel for him at all. Instead, I felt an odd pang of pity, even of fondness, for Mrs van Hopper, for I did not think that he would last, nor that he would be very nice to her. She had bought his companionship, as once she had bought mine, but our arrangement had been businesslike, and quite usual, and if I had been exploited that had also been usual in such a situation. People like me were a particular sort of servant who ought to expect that. This time, I thought, it might be the other way around.

Mrs van Hopper was an old woman, over dressed, over made-up, her skull showing a little through the thin, white hair, her hands podgy, the flesh tight around her array of rings, her eyes oddly flat, sunken into the sockets. Otherwise, she was unchanged, as vulgar, inquisitive, insensitive, as before.

They were seated on the far side of the dining room, right away from us, which clearly annoyed and frustrated her, for I saw her call over the head waiter almost at once, and begin to gesture to other tables – but without success. He merely shook his head curtly, and they were left, she marooned with only her lorgnette, which she flicked up and down, throughout dinner, several times, and quite blatantly in our direction.

'I wonder how long our young man – man, just, I think, but certainly not a gentleman – has been in tow,' Maxim said at one point. 'Poor Mrs van Hopper – from you, a perfectly respectable little paid friend of the bosom, to that. By what steps did she make the descent do you suppose?'

'I don't like the look of him,' I said.

'I should hope not. She's a silly old snob but she doesn't deserve that.'

Out of the corner of my eye, I saw her turn to stare at an elderly couple who were coming into the room, but almost at once the lorgnette was lowered, dismissing them from her sphere of interest. But for some reason I went on looking at them, as they settled at a table quite near to us. He was frail, his skin paper thin and yellowing, stretched over his skull and long bony hands, his eyes rheumy, and she was solicitous with him, and loving, patiently helping him to sit, taking his stick and laying it down, saying something across the table to make him laugh. She was his wife, I could see that, she was much younger, but not young enough to be his daughter, and besides, there was a tenderness between them, a long familiarity of look and gesture, which was not filial. He would die soon, I thought, he had the curious transparency that comes to the very old a little while before death, the air of slight detachment and dreaminess, as though they have already half left the world. I looked from them, across to Maxim, and saw us, in thirty years time, close, loving, yet waiting as they were, for separation, saw us still in exile, belonging only in hotels, childless, too, for I somehow knew that they were. I looked out of the window quickly, at the lamp on a gondola, bobbing slowly past. I would not think of it, I would not mind. After all, I might have been here, at the other side of the room, with Mrs van Hopper.

Over our coffee, in the lounge, Maxim became gravely courteous to her, sitting beside her on the sofa, passing her cup, impeccably attentive, and she bridled and blushed in response, tapped him with her lorgnette, and I felt calm and strong and tolerant. He was very clever in making her talk of herself, of where she had been living, of her family, even her hapless nephew Billy, whom she had once used as a flimsy excuse for an introduction, and she prattled about her travels.

'Such a relief to be able to get back to Europe, I can't tell you, after all those dreary years stuck in America and never getting away. I so longed for everywhere, for Paris and Rome and London and Monte, for a bit of style and life again, and to read about you all in such dreariness and squalor was really too much to bear.'

'Yes, indeed,' Maxim said, 'it must have been dreadful.'

I looked away quickly, turned to the young man. He was American, and was, he said, 'a designer' but he would not elaborate, and made only the barest effort to be polite to me – I was of little interest, I realised, a plain, dull, early middle aged woman of no account. But I saw that he eyed Maxim slightly surreptitiously, glancing at him under his lashes, summing up his clothes, listening, and squirrelling the information carefully away.

Once, Mrs van Hopper sent him off for a photograph she wanted to show us, ordering him and yet with an ingratiating, unpleasant little plea, not exactly in the peremptory way she would have dismissed me. He went without a word, and yet made it clear that he might equally well have chosen not to, and I liked him even less, felt even sorrier to see her with him.

And then, suddenly, like a cat flashing out its claws swiftly and without warning to an unwary prey, she turned to Maxim, catching him quite off guard. 'You must have been devastated when Manderley went up in flames – we read of it, of course, it was the talk everywhere. Such a terrible, terrible tragedy.'

I saw his mouth set, his face flush very slightly. 'Yes,' he said.

'Tell me do. Whatever happened? Was it deliberate – no, surely not, whoever would have done such a dreadful thing? An accident I suppose, some careless stupid housemaid not putting up a firescreen – I hope they suffered. Your whole world gone up in flames like that – all those priceless treasures.'

'Yes.'

'And was anyone burned alive? I suppose there were people there at the time.'

'No, fortunately, no one was hurt.'

'But you were not there I understand, you were – where – in London was it? All sorts of stories went around, I can't begin to tell you.'

She glanced at the young man who sat, silent and sullen beside me. 'Now, just go quickly upstairs again and bring that crocodile wallet, the one with all my cuttings in, I know I've got them with me – go on, do –' She turned back to Maxim, ignoring me entirely. 'There was so much about it in the press and of course all the business of the inquest – and what a horrible thing that must have been and I have to say it, really quite bizarre. I don't suppose you've seen half that was written at the time, you dashed off goodness knows where, to get over the shock I suppose. Not that running away does any good, you take your troubles with you – but

I daresay you've found that out. Tell me, they brought in a verdict of suicide. Now why on earth would a beautiful, rich young woman with everything she could possibly desire, a great house, an attractive husband, the world at her feet you might say, *why* would she want to kill herself? It simply defies belief.'

I could not bear it then, I did not care whether she still despised me and wanted to pretend that I did not exist. I did. I said, 'Mrs van Hopper, please don't –' but Maxim interrupted, standing up as he did so and looking down on her with loathing barely concealed behind a cold politeness.

'Your world may think what it chooses,' he said, 'but really, opinion and gossip count for nothing at all against truth – I'm sure you agree. Now, I know you will excuse us, it has been quite extraordinary to meet you again.'

My last sight of her was an expression of helpless outrage, annoyance that she had been left abruptly, looking foolish, and that she could do nothing at all about it. She struggled to get to her feet and pursue us, but Maxim was too swift, and she was infirm and old and fat and, I saw, had a stick beside her. She had barely addressed a word to me. And I noticed that, far from jumping up to run her errand, as I had always, nervously, done, the young man had remained seated, ignoring her order with complete, insolent self possession.

But it happened that they could not find our coats and in the end, Maxim went impatiently to the cloakroom himself in search of them. I waited, looking idly at a copy of an old map of Venice, on the wall behind one of the thick marble pillars, so that Mrs van Hopper and the young man did not see me, as they came, she limping, holding on to his unwilling arm, out of the lounge.

'He used to be such a glamorous man in those days, quite a catch, but for some extraordinary reason I never understood he married that little mousey thing, and now look – my God, what a dull, dreary couple they've become – mind, if you ask me, there's a lot more to that business over his first wife than ever came out. Don't pull away like that, I need you to steady me.'

And so they passed on, her voice continuing, querulous and nasal, out of the foyer towards the lifts.

'I'm sorry,' I said at once to Maxim, as we were leaving. 'I'm so sorry.'

'What on earth do you mean?'

'Well, that awful woman – those things she said –'

'And that was your fault?'

'No, of course not, I know, but –'

I felt that I should have shut her up, protected him from her, I could not bear it if he had been hurt and would be forced to brood all over again.

Maxim held me firmly by the elbow, as we got into the gondola, a plain one this time, without the extra, celebratory lights. As we got out into the Grand Canal, a sudden wind cut coldly down, smelling of the sea. 'Forget it,' he said. 'She's a stupid old woman and they deserve one another.'

But I could not forget, I went on remembering that she had said she had a folder of newspaper cuttings, about the inquest and the fire, had kept them, talked about it all with her friends, heard her words of suspicion. 'A lot more to that business than ever came out. Why would she want to kill herself? It simply defies belief . . .'

Yes, I thought. Yes, of course it does, because it was not true. It was obvious to them, and I knew the truth of it. Rebecca had not killed herself. Maxim had murdered her.

And I looked at his profile, as the gondola swung and turned out of the Grand Canal and the wind caught it broadside and rocked it a little. His face was stony, I could not tell what he was thinking, or how he felt, I was shut out from him again. I glanced up at the black, shuttered buildings, and as I did so, the voices began again, whispering, whispering out of the darkness.

Perhaps it is not in human nature to be content with our lot, however good, in this world, perhaps, because life is a process of change and flux, growth and decay, we have to be restless, have to experience discontent, yearnings, hopes, desire to move on, and can do no other.

So I could not help standing at the narrow window of our room, looking across at the opposite buildings, or down into the canal, and wishing for something else, somewhere else, against all reason. But looking back now, I know that I did not revel in the present sufficiently, did not give thanks often enough, that I was not glad, as I should most earnestly have been, that we had become Mrs van Hopper's 'dull, dreary couple.' For it did not last, it could not, simply because nothing does, but more, because I willed that it should not and I got my way. I remember hearing someone once say to me, when I was a child, demanding this or that, 'Beware of wanting something too much – you may get it' and I did not understand. Now I do.

Is this all? I asked myself. Will there truly be nothing more than this perambulating, pointless life, trundling through our middle years down to old age and infirmity and separation and death. Is this all? No, it was not.

It is better that we cannot see into the future. We are spared that. The past we carry with us forever into the present and that is enough to contend with.

Maxim seemed to have a flurry of business to attend to again, he wrote letters, sent cables, became preoccupied. I did not ask about it but it troubled me that he did not tell me, not out of any real desire to know the details but because we had shared everything and now, there were secrets.

Winter gave way finally, wonderfully, to spring, and Venice came alive, it was the season again. We left, going east to Greece and to mountains covered in flowers and air that smelled of honey. I was happier again because we were moving on, I had no time to brood, there was too much that was new to divert me.

It was May when we left, to sail for Istanbul, and I did not think that I wanted to go there, for some reason I was afraid of the idea of a place so entirely foreign, so strange in every possible way, I wanted change and new sights, yet at the same time to remain within certain bounds. It would have been easier if Maxim had not been strange too, and far away from me, distracted by something, often staring ahead of him with a slight frown. I dared not ask him why, it seemed safest to be ignorant, but I speculated endlessly; that it had to do with what Mrs van Hopper had said, or that there were problems to do with the family's affairs, after Beatrice's death; even financial anxieties.

The last two days of our time in Greece were tense and miserable, the distance that Maxim seemed to be putting between us was greater than ever. We spoke calmly, coolly, talked of what we saw, what the next stage of our journey was to be, and I longed for the old closeness, the way he had been dependent upon me, but growing older takes the edge off impatience. This had happened before, I said, I would ride it out. He would come back.

I could not have dreamed how.

The weather was perfect, warm, scented, glorious spring, the world washed clean. The day had been held, poised between cold dawn and the chill of night, so that I had spent much of it on the deck of the steamer that was taking us down the Bosporus towards Istanbul. And now, we were almost there, I had seen the domes of the old city come riding towards us, seeming to float, insubstantial, glittering things haloed in the light of the setting sun which lay, gold leaf upon the surface of the quiet water.

Maxim was standing beside me in silence. The light changed, flushing rose red, the whole western sky was suffused with it, and the line of the buildings darkened and flattened, the domes and turrets and thin spires were paper on coloured cloth.

I had not expected to like this place, I had thought

everything about it would feel alien, and, when we finally reached the shore, perhaps it would, but now, looking, looking, I was caught up in it and moved as I had rarely been by the simple sight of anything. Except the house. The rose red house.

'And now look,' Maxim said, after a moment.

I followed his glance. Above the line of the city, above the colours of the sunset, the night sky began, miraculously dark, and against it, a crescent moon was set, the thinnest, most brilliant paring of silver.

If I close my eyes I can see it now, it comes back to me at moments with absolute clarity, a comfort as well as pain, and I rest on it and feed from it, and I hear Maxim's voice, again, the next words he spoke.

'Here,' he said. I saw that he was holding out an envelope. 'You had better read this now,' and then he turned his back and walked away to the other side of the ship.

The envelope might be between my fingers now, I can feel it, smooth, but torn at the top where it had been opened. I stood holding it, looking at the sky, but the sun had gone and the last stain of bright colour faded, the domes had been absorbed back into the darkness. Only the moon remained, the pure, bright wire.

My heart was beating too hard. I did not know what the envelope might contain, what words I would have to read. I did not want to, I wanted to stay unknowing, poised in this time when all was still safe and contained and I had nothing to be afraid of. But I was afraid.

Everything will change, I said. This will in some way put an end to things as they are. And so it did.

I sat down on an uncomfortable, slatted bench in the shelter of the bridge. There was a storm lantern with just enough light to read by, it threw a grubby orange glow down on to the paper. I wondered why Maxim had left me alone, what he feared. It must be some dreadful thing in this envelope, something he could not put into words, it could not be simple, ordinary, bad news, some death or illness or disaster, or surely, surely, he would have stayed with me, told me, we would have been together. But we were far apart. I could feel tears stinging at the back of my eyes, small, hard tears of some bitter substance, not tears that would spill easily and so be in some way a release and a comfort.

One of the crew went by, the band of his cap bone white against the darkness. He glanced at me curiously, but did not stop. From where I sat I could not see the moon, only a few distant, pricking lights from the shore. I smelled the oil from the engines, heard the noise they made, throbbing away at my back.

Please, I said, though I did not know for what I was so desperately asking. Please. A cry for help.

And then, I took the single sheet of paper out of the envelope, and held it to the light.

Inveralloch. Wednesday.

My dear Maxim,
In haste to let you know the final outcome. I am sending this by express, poste restante to Venice, in the hope that it will reach you before you leave.
I have this morning heard that my bid on your

behalf for the freehold purchase of Cobbett's Brake
has been successful. As soon as you receive this, will
you please telegraph final confirmation so that I may
see Archie Nicholson in London next week and have
him draw up the deeds and covenants ready for you to
sign as soon as you return.

I will be glad to know a final date. There are
some details to be gone over but once the documents
have been completed, the house will be yours to move
into as soon as you find convenient after returning to
England. I am as delighted by this as I hope you will
both be,

Yours ever,
Frank

My hand trembled, I had to clutch the paper, for fear
that it would fall from between my fingers and blow away.

I looked up. Maxim had come back. 'We're almost
there,' he said.

And so we went to stand at the rail of the steamer, and
rode slowly in, to where the old, mysterious city held out its
arms to greet us.

Part Three

CHAPTER

Twelve

We came home to Cobbett's Brake in May, just as we had to Manderley. But how different it was, how different in every way. A new beginning. And whenever I recall it, even though it is in the light of what happened, it *is* the light, there are no shadows, and my memories of that time are perfect and joyful, I do not regret anything, I would not have had it any other way.

Remembering Manderley, which I still do, I remember how inadequate I was, how out of place, I remember the awkwardnesses and the way the house overpowered me. I was tremulous with a nervous, disbelieving happiness when I first went there, and it changed, almost at once, merging into mere anxiety. But I came to Cobbett's Brake on a great surge of confidence and release, of re-kindled, intense love for Maxim, who had done this thing, with optimism and sureness of purpose. I felt that I had been waiting for years for life properly to begin, that everything else had been a preparation, but also something I had looked on at, a play in which everyone else had real parts, but I had been only pushed dumbly about the stage, not speaking, never belonging, never making any move to rush the action along. Everyone had stared at me, there had been peculiar, menacing silences sometimes when I had appeared under the lights, and yet I had been of no consequence. Now, it was not a play, it was life, and I plunged into the midst of it and was carried by it, with such eagerness.

All the time that had remained to us abroad we had lived on two planes. Letters and telegrams had flown in both directions between Frank Crawley, Maxim, the land agents and solicitors, Giles, the people at the farm. Maxim had spent hours on the end of a bad telephone line, shouting instructions, trying to discover whether this or that would be done, and all the time, we were plunged into the mysterious, exotic hubbub of life in Istanbul, and the countryside of Turkey, and I loved it; it did not frighten me at all, I adored everything about it and felt and saw and heard and remembered it with a piercing intensity because I knew I was leaving and these were the last days of our exile – only now, it was not exile, it was simply pleasure, and after it, we were going home, and life was about to begin. We wandered about the streets, choked with people and animals, buyers and sellers, beggars and babies, went into mosques full of bells and chanting voices, smelled heady, overpowering scents, cloying, odd, unpleasant, always unlike any I would ever smell again, so that now, they are locked away in a box somewhere forever and I have no key. If I had, if the box were to break open, that place, that time, those memories, that are packed so tightly together with the scents, would overwhelm me. There were tastes, too, sweet, spiced, smoky tastes always

216

in our mouths, and sometimes, I have caught a faint trace of those, eating some piece of meat, or a pastry, and after a bewildered moment, been catapulted back to those days and nights.

There were no misunderstandings or silences between us, there was only love and resolution, and exquisite happiness, in time and place, so that I wept to leave, the beauty of Istanbul was more than physical, it was personal and poignant, imbued with a sense of fragility and impermanence. When we left, and the glittering, painted city was finally out of sight, I believed that it might indeed have simply dissolved, and ceased to exist at all because we could no longer see it.

We travelled back in quite a leisurely way across Europe, paying out the time gently, making it last. Frank had seen to the final details of the purchase, but we would not know until we arrived back and could finally go over the house, how much work might have to be done, whether we would want to keep any of the furnishings that had been sold with it. The old couple had not wanted to go back, and their son, newly demobbed from the army, had only cleared out all the personal effects and things of value, much of the furniture remained, but Frank had had no time to take an inventory and seemed to think little of it would be of use. He had rented a small house for us nearby where we could stay for a shorter or longer time – though I knew that even if we were forced to clear the whole of Cobbett's Brake, and work upon it, I wanted to be there, I would not mind confining ourselves to a few temporarily furnished rooms. We belonged there, not in another place, discomfort and inconvenience would be of no consequence.

It was the warmest May for years, people said, it didn't really do to be as warm as this so early, no one knew what the weather was coming to; but 'let's make the most of it, we should enjoy it while we can.'

And we did, oh, we did. England smelled of spring and the flowers and the grass, the bluebells were almost over, but here and there, we passed a small wood or a quiet copse, and saw a flash of that incomparable blue, deep down below the first, fresh leaves, and stopped twice on the way, to climb over a fence. There was a latticework of sky between the branches over our heads, and at our feet the flowers were damp and cool. I bent down and plunged my arms into them, closed my eyes and let the smell overpower me.

'No use taking them,' Maxim said. 'They'll be dead within the hour.'

And I remembered then, armfuls of the pale, yellow-green, etiolated stalks flopping over in the basket of my bicycle, when I had not been able to resist picking them as a girl, and giving them to my mother to put in jars, certain that in some magic way she would have power to revive them.

'But she did not, of course,' I said, standing up now.

'And you learned your lesson.'

'Perhaps.'

I saw then, as he stood looking at me, how his face had changed, softened and lightened, how he seemed suddenly younger – years younger even than when I had met him – but of course, he had seemed gravely old, then, that had been part of the point.

The daffodils and the apple blossom were over, but the lilac was out, a tree of it in every cottage garden, white and pallid mauve, and the hedgerows on either side of us were ribbons of dusty white – hawthorn in full flower, whenever we stepped out of the car, we smelled its curious, bitter scent, baked in the heat of the afternoon sun and that, too, was another smell of childhood, I remembered vividly how I had sat beneath a great bush of it in some old woman's garden when I was five or six, picking off twigs of the little clumps of blossom and playing with them, spreading them on the earth, making patterns. It was as though my childhood, those happiest of early years that had been snapped off so sharply with my father's death, were being given back to me now, they were clearer and closer than they had ever been; the years between, the time before Maxim and then, of Maxim and Manderley and after, all of them until now, receded, blurred and shadowy. This time was linked across them like a strong bridge, with that time further back.

As we drove deeper into the heart of the country, I realised that everything was white; there were white lambs, and the high creamy white heads of the cow parsley springing up from every ditch, and lily of the valley in the shady corners of gardens, over low stone walls. I felt like a bride again, as I had been on our way home to Manderley, but glancing at Maxim across the car, I did not say it, I did not want any mention or reminder of that time to throw the faintest shadow over this day. We did not hurry, there was no reason to hurry. We lingered over every sight, every detail, having a slow, pleasant late lunch, then stopping a little later to visit a cathedral, where we wandered and gazed up at the windows and the roof, the glorious stone arches, like visitors who had never seen such things before. When we came out, the light had changed, it was pale lemon coloured against the buildings, the day had slipped down a little towards late afternoon.

For the last few miles I made Maxim go very slowly, I was committing everything to memory, learning the lanes by heart. We had made arrangements for the house to be opened by Mrs Peck from the farm. We would look round briefly now, and come back first thing the next morning to begin the process of deciding, planning, making arrangements. But there would be no one waiting, no rows of uniformed staff on the steps and in the drive, no staring, curious, eyes following me – no Mrs Danvers. This was mine only, mine and Maxim's.

We reached the lane in which we had first stopped, beneath the old wooden signpost.

'Stop here,' I said. I opened the door, and in the faint ticking silence after the engine had died, I heard the low coo of wood pigeons, high in the trees above our heads. The air was balmy, and damp smelling. 'You take the car.' I climbed out. 'I'd like to walk.'

I did not want to arrive, grandly, down the drive to the front door. I wanted to approach it by degrees, by accident almost, to see it again from the grassy bowl in which it lay and then slip quietly and alone down the slopes and in at some small side door. And quite suddenly, fiercely, I did not want to share that even with Maxim, the rush of desire for the house to be absolutely mine, for a short time, was intense within me.

He understood. He smiled, turned the car and let it slip away, back down the lane, and then I was alone. I stood, with my eyes closed, feeling my own heart beat, hearing the branches of the trees stir as some bird flew among them. And then I began to walk, clambering down the narrow track that was overgrown now with wild garlic and tall nettles, grass, and low overhanging branches which I had to push aside. The light was an undersea green, but there was nothing sinister here, everything was fresh and newly grown and innocent; there were no blood red rhododendrons towering over my head, nothing rare or strange, all was familiar and right. A rabbit ran across the path and into a hidden hole, I caught a glimpse of a single, startled, translucent eye as it glanced at me.

The last time I had come here, the light had sifted through the almost bare branches so that I had had a sight of the open space ahead, but now, the growth of the trees was so full and high that I was enclosed in my green tunnel until, abruptly, I shoved aside a last, sweeping branch, and was out into the evening sunlight. And there it lay, Cobbett's Brake, calm and quiet and beautiful.

I saw it and could look down on it all of a piece, it was not too big to contain within a single focus. I seemed to hold it still, the gates, the drive, the walls and chimneys, the windows and gables, the gardens surrounding it. It was like meeting someone with whom one has fallen in love after an absence and the doubt and anxiety which that has brought have been swept away by the first, new sight of them, and there is only certainty.

I began to climb carefully, half slipping, balancing with my hand outstretched, down the slope between the grazing sheep, to where I saw Maxim, at the entrance to the house.

There was a jug of country flowers in the hall, and a second, smaller one in the middle of the kitchen table, beside eggs and milk, and a fruit cake; fires had been laid, though not lit, the boiler was stoked. It was a strange house, we had never set foot inside it, the furnishings that had been left were old and unfamiliar, and yet it was home, and ours at once, we were not intruders.

'I could stay here,' I said, 'live here now, we've no need to go anywhere else.'

We went quietly from room to room. It had been cleaned, polished, and tidied, but there was more than that; it had been loved and cared for, for years past, I thought, even though some of the rooms were clearly long unused. There was nothing too formal or cold about them, nothing I did not like. I looked round and saw that a chair needed recovering, a door rehanging, some pictures chosen to fill blank pale spaces on a few of the walls, but nothing had to be done urgently, and there was nothing I greatly disliked.

'We will make it ours,' I said. 'There isn't any hurry.'

We had nothing, after all, the fire had burned our possessions; we would begin again. I was happy about that. Those beautiful, precious things, the china and portraits, the silver and rare furniture, had not been mine, I had never felt at home among them. They had belonged to Maxim's family – and to Rebecca. These things that furnished Cobbett's Brake were not mine either but I did not feel the same about them, I felt even now that we had not so much bought as inherited them, they were part of the fabric of the house and we were to look after them in the same way.

We went up into the attic rooms, dusty and empty now, with bare white walls, but I furnished them in my mind, for the children, and put linen in the cupboards and china and glass in the cabinets.

I turned and looked at Maxim, filled with my new found delight and pleasure. I said, '*Now* I am happy. Do you understand?'

But then at once regretted the words and would have taken them back, for perhaps he was not so sure, perhaps he had done this only for me and would never settle here – it was not Manderley.

'Come outside,' Maxim said.

It was still warm but the air smelled of evening now; a thrush was singing madly from a lilac bush. We began to walk through the garden, beneath an old pergola that ran along the south side. Roses and clematis had scrambled rampantly up and over, and cascaded down like wild, tangled, unkempt hair. They needed to be restrained, shaped and cut back, and yet for now, they were right, the starry white clematis flowers already out, the roses fatly in bud.

All around us, flowerbeds, shrubs, climbers, had been left to riot, but I was happy to see it like this and planned to bring it gradually, gently, to order. I did not want a neat, clipped, sterile garden, organised by a team of men I scarcely dared speak to for fear I would offend them, or reveal my own ignorance. I *was* ignorant, but my father had had a garden, and I remembered it still. I would learn quickly, I knew, it was in my blood.

'I thought,' Maxim said now, 'that this would be a place that you wanted, but it is what I want now. When I saw it again today and went inside the house – I realised that it would be mine too.'

He stopped, and looked slowly around – at the grassy slopes and the sheep grazing on them, the trees beyond. 'I never thought that I would be able to lay the ghost of Manderley – but I will. It will happen here. That is over and past. Manderley is dead to me.' He looked at me. 'It has taken over ten years. I'm sorry it has been so long,'

I went to him, but as I did so, a voice inside me said, 'But not only the house, not only the house.' I did not speak, we simply went on, walking, looking around us, and Maxim began to talk of buying more of the surrounding land, a farm perhaps.

'I shall try and tempt Frank down here again – we can manage it together.'

'He'll never want to leave Scotland.'

'We'll see.'

I thought that we might, because Frank's absolute loyalty and devotion had been not so much to Manderley as to Maxim, and perhaps he would want to work with him again.

And so we went on, making small, happy plans, as the light faded and night crept over the house and garden, and there was nothing but joy to look forward to.

Thirteen

I was like a child, playing at houses, Maxim said, and it was true that with such happiness, such daily pleasure, it did seem a little like a game, moving into Cobbett's Brake, going over each room carefully, deciding what to keep, what to replace. But beneath the play, I felt as if I were living real life for the first time ever. The present mattered more than any past, and the future was only important so long as it was a simple continuation.

Mrs Peck from the farm came in to help me at first, and after a few weeks, found a young woman, Dora, who bicycled from the next village, willing to do anything in the house. I felt at ease with her, I suppose because she was young, and there was nothing in the least difficult or intimidating about her, she was only friendly and anxious to suit. I did not feel that she was a servant. As we made lists and took down curtains and examined the insides of cupboards together, we giggled and she told me about her family, and only fell silent and seemed in awe if Maxim appeared. Once or twice, I caught her glancing at us, puzzled, perhaps, at the disparity in our ages or the difference between us – for every day, when I woke, I felt as if I were growing younger, retrieving years I had lost, shedding all the staid, depressing intimations of middle age. I sang about the place, I felt giddy and light hearted.

And gradually, the house began to come under my control, I got to know its ways, which door did not close properly, which windows let in a draught, where the morning and the evening sun fell, how uneven the boards were on the upper landing. Men came in to paint, room by room. Some of the wormy old kitchen furniture and a few ancient rugs were thrown away and I decided to have new chairs in the long, light drawing room that looked out on to the best part of the garden. Cobbett's Brake felt friendly, when I walked about it, early in the morning, from kitchen to dining room to hall, opening windows and doors, looking out at the grassy slopes rising around us, I felt that it welcomed me, almost that it had been waiting, expecting us.

Maxim had begun to go about the district, talking to farmers and landowners, finding out which land he might buy, what farm was to let. He would have sheep, he said, and plenty of woodland, a dairy herd, and good grass – but he meant to take advice, and move slowly. There were four cottages, as well as the Home Farm, belonging to Cobbett's Brake, and he began to look for help, too, to get to know men in the village: it was not a large estate, not after Manderley, but because we would not have anything like the number of staff, there would be more for Maxim to do. I watched him grow younger too, saw him stride out and down the drive, climb fast up the slopes, saw the colour come to his skin as the sun shone – for we had a warm, dry, perfect spring and early summer. He was well, he was entirely content, I thought, this was our happy ending.

Yet we lacked something, though we never spoke of it, and as that early summer moved on, and the roses opened and cascaded over every wall and pillar and fence, glorious ramblers, blush and shell and blowsy pink, and billowing, purest white, as everything flowered and flourished and the trees were thickly green, so that we were drunk on high summer, I began to be conscious of it more and more. There was a hollow place at the heart of things.

One morning at the end of June, I woke at five and could not sleep again, the night had been oppressively close, and I felt stale and heavy eyed. The scent of the rose that hung in great swags from the low roof below our open bedroom window was musky sweet, overpowering in the room.

I went downstairs quietly, and slipped out of the side door. The air was fresh and quite cool, the sun not yet up, the sheep rested, heavy and still, scattered about the slopes. I walked under the arbour, and out on to the path that led to the big, raised round pond. We had not had a chance to clear it or mend the fountain, and I looked down between the mesh of old flat water lilies to the still green water below, wondering if there were great fish somewhere, moving about in an ancient, slow, secret life. I sat on the flat stone rim. The sky was pearl grey, the grass dark with dew.

This is happiness, I thought, and I am held within it. Here. Now.

And I looked up and saw them, coming across the garden, from the glassy slopes, saw them quite as clearly as if they were there, three children, boys, as they had been boys when I had imagined them at Manderley – two older, strong, sturdy, vigorous, shouting and pushing one another, and the little one, quieter, more thoughtful, keeping more to himself. They ran across the grass, along the gravel path, one pulling at a flower head, another waving a stick in the air above his head. I saw their bright faces, that they were open and full of humour, saw their bodies and scruffy heads, the same beautiful shape as Maxim's. I saw them so clearly, that I might have opened my arms and they would have run into them, tumbling over one another to be first, to tell me this, make me laugh over that, I felt them against me, I knew what their hair felt like, thick, slightly dry, springy to my touch. I looked over to the little one, beckoned to him, and he smiled, very seriously, but would wait to be close to me until later, when the others had gone bounding away and we could be quiet together. Then perhaps we would sit and stare down into the dark, deep water of the stone pond, and wait to see the pale streak below, the gleam of a fish. He would not speak or startle, he would be very still, very patient, quite content just to be with me, waiting, and the shouts of his brothers would come back from the end of the drive, as they went racing off again.

I sat on there, dipping my hand into the water and letting it trickle between my fingers, as the sun came up, slanting pale gold across the grass and touching the petals of the rose Albertine that grew over the east wall. I had spent every evening of the past week sketching out new plans for the garden, making lists, drawing what it would be like here, and here, and over there, in a few years' time; and now, just as I had seen the children, I saw the garden as it would be, and longed for it, too. But that would be more easily accomplished, that was only a question of time and application. I heard a window open above, the faint sound of water running. In a few minutes, Maxim would come out to join me, we would go around the garden together, I would say, I think we shall take down this, prune back that, dig out a new border here, repair the trellis – I must see about the fountain – Mr Peck is sending a man who will do the vegetables – he may even come today.

All of this was easy, I could talk about it happily, feel confident, but the children – I could not talk about them. For some reason, I was terrified that if I spoke of it at all to Maxim, it would be bad luck and I would never succeed. Rebecca had not been able to have children, they had found that out at the end. I would not be like Rebecca, must not be.

I stood up, my mind quite clear all at once, the decision made. I could not speak to Maxim, not at this point anyway, but nor could I drift on through the months and years, hoping, trusting to luck, doing nothing else about it. I had always assumed – we both had – that we would have children, so far as I knew there was no reason why either of us should not, but I did not know – I knew very little about myself at all, I was never unwell, had rarely visited a doctor. Indeed, I realised, now that my mind was made up, that I did not know any doctors. The last one I had set eyes on had been the specialist in London to whose house we had all gone on that terrible, stifling afternoon when we had needed evidence about Rebecca. Dr Baker. I could see him now, coming into the room in flannels, interrupted in the middle of his game of tennis.

I could not go to him. Then who should I see? How would I find out? I knew no one to ask. If either of us were ill, I imagined we would easily find out the name of the local man, probably from Dora or Mrs Peck. But I shied away from the idea of seeing anyone I might have to meet socially some day – for we would get to know people, I wanted to be friendly, to fit in to our neighbourhood, and the doctor was such an obvious person to invite. I felt that I could not face someone I knew, or might come to know, if I had consulted them about this, it seemed too worrying, too intimately connected with our life here.

I wanted to go to London, just as Rebecca had done, I thought, in an impersonal way, to consult someone quite formally, who knew nothing about me. In the old days, I would have been able to ask Beatrice for advice. Now, I knew no one. How did one find a London doctor? I felt oddly panic stricken and helpless, isolated here for the first time, out of touch with the world.

Maxim came out of the door, stood for a few seconds looking around him, taking in the house, the garden, the slopes, I saw the pleasure lighting his face, the air of satisfaction. He was happy, as I was, he loved Cobbett's Brake. We could not moulder here by ourselves, there would be so little point in restoring everything, adding to the land, building it all up to something even better, if we were to slip down into old age as the previous owners had done, and leave it empty again, falling into neglect, because we could no longer manage and there was no one else to carry it on into the future. I must have the boys, I thought fiercely, I must, I will have them, for myself, because I have seen them,

I almost know them, but even more, for Maxim, and for Cobbett's Brake.

And I went up the path towards him, and the children were there, just out of sight, following me.

Fourteen

I had forgotten about calling, that dreadful custom in the old country society that had caused me so many agonies of embarrassment and awkwardness at Manderley. Everyone had come, there was a new visitor every afternoon, it seemed, inquisitive women and occasionally a husband, too, curious about the new bride. I had had to sit on the edge of a chair in the formal drawing room, making light conversation, trying to answer their questions, for half an hour or so, and even worse, return the calls, never knowing what to say, waiting for the clock to tick the heavy time away. But that was a lifetime ago. We had been away for so long, and then there had been the war, which had changed so much – I could tell that even in the course of those first few weeks at Cobbett's Brake; some of the old formalities and social barriers were breaking down and I was relieved, glad things were to be less rigid and pre-ordained. I had never felt at ease, never been confident of knowing the code, and Maxim had cared about it all so much in those days, I had been so anxious never to let him down.

I knew that he had introduced himself to a couple of neighbouring landowners and the local farmers, and was sure that Mrs Peck and Dora would have spoken about us, though I had tried to explain that we were very private people, liking each other's company and a quiet life – I did not want to risk news of our arrival spreading too widely – people here were not familiar with our story, perhaps, but someone might remember, dig out an old paper, talk to a relative, perhaps, from our old part of the world.

So that I was apprehensive at once, hearing the sound of a strange car, the crunch of tyres on the gravel at the front of the house. I had been talking to Ned Farraday, who was working in the garden now, about whether or not to try and rebuild an old, dilapidated wall that bounded the south side, or whether it was too far gone and should be replaced. In the Manderley days of course, Frith would have come to find me, in his solemn, stately way, bearing a white visiting card on the silver salver. Now, Ned looked over to the drive and said, 'Mrs Butterley – you'll have met her then?'

'No,' I said, and at once was aware of the nervous churning starting up in my stomach, and that I was clenching my fingers tightly into my palms. 'No, I don't believe I have. Is she a neighbour, Ned?'

'You might say,' he grinned. 'Lives over at Thixted – married to the old colonel – only everybody's neighbour to that Mrs Butterley, forty miles around.'

'I see.' I left him, full of apprehension, already forming the polite sentences, and the evasive answers, in my head, resenting her for disturbing us. I had such a selfish, greedy attitude to my days at Cobbett's Brake. I felt time slipping past and that we had lost too much of it already, I could not bear to waste any more on people I did not have to know, I wanted to arrange everything in the house, plan the garden, be with Maxim. And brood, dream, make my plans. I felt like an old, bad tempered recluse, jealous of our privacy. 'Good afternoon,' I said, and smiled what felt like a stiff, false smile. 'How very kind of you to call,' and walked up the drive to meet her. But even as I did so, even as I spoke, and before she did, I knew that I was wrong, quite wrong, and felt a barrier fall and my defences and reserves dissolve away. I looked into her broad, eager, open face and saw that of a friend, someone from whom could come no possible threat.

She was a tall woman, broad shouldered, with wildly straying, auburn hair going grey at the sides, and she was carrying an armful of roses bundled up into newspaper, and something else wrapped in a tea towel. 'Well,' she called, bursting into peals of laughter, 'coals to Newcastle I see, I might have known you'd have got all the old roses back – simply too much of a temptation and besides, really, they were so well established, they simply have a mind of their own and will flower where they will flower. Still, here are some of ours and you can never have too many, I like bowlfuls all over the house don't you?' She had grasped my hand firmly in hers. 'How do you do – I'm Bunty Butterley, neighbours more or less – of course, we knew the old Dennises well, poor things. They struggled on here for too long, I'm only glad it's got someone to give it lots of love and attention. That's all a house needs, isn't it? Love – like the young and the old, really –' She turned and stood, surveying Cobbett's Brake with pleasure.

'And my God, what a house – it's perfect really, isn't it, nothing wrong at all? You should see our Victorian monster – I love it in its way, of course, wouldn't be anywhere else, but we put up with its ugliness and discomforts. You've nothing to do here but admire and enjoy and keep it going in the old way.'

'Won't you come in – I was just going to have coffee. Dora would call me in five minutes.'

'Yes, you've got that angel, Dora Ruby. Salt of the earth.that family – '

She followed me in through the side door, calling out, going towards the kitchen. I knew that it was all right and I need not be concerned – this was a friend, not a 'caller', I could take her happily into whichever room I chose.

'I brought you a cake, because I suppose one feels one should, instinct to feed and so on, and what a joy to be able to give away food after we all had to be so greedy and secretive and squirrel it into our own little stores through those dreary years. Mind you, with Dora you don't need me and my offerings – hello Dora, my dear, you'd know I'd get here in the end. I don't suppose Mrs de Winter has been overburdened with visitors, we've rather given up on all that and a good thing too. We're all properly busy now, and call when we want to, not because we think we ought.'

She is like Beatrice, I thought as I stood, smiling, listening to her boom out so cheerfully, seeming to fill the kitchen full of herself, she has the same easy, open way with people, no side, no falsity, that's why I feel at ease with her. And I went forward and took the tray from Dora. 'I'm so glad you came,' I said. 'I've been wondering when I would have someone to chat to.' And I realised it was quite true, I found I wanted to talk, to ask questions, to enjoy her company.

'Bunty Butterley,' she said, following me to the small sitting room, which got the best sun at this time of day. 'Isn't it a hilarious name. I was born Barbara Mount, much more staid but somehow all Barbaras were Bunty to our mothers' generation and then I upped and married Bill and took Butterley on board. I'm used to it now of course.'

She plumped down in the armchair beside the window, and looked round the room immediately. 'Yes. You're loving it, I can see. Freshening it up, making it sprucer, but keeping its heart and soul intact. I approve of that.'

'It felt so right when we came in. I didn't want to make many changes. It was the outside of the house I fell in love with.'

'Who wouldn't? It had got rather bleak in here, you know – we came over one afternoon the winter before last and it was cold as a vault and everything was so shabby and to tell the truth, a bit grubby, too. You took a good look at your spoon before you stirred your tea with it and gave it a surreptitious wipe on your skirt! We all wondered who'd take it over once it was obvious Raymond wasn't interested – he's a career soldier, of course, can't wait for another war I daresay. Bill was never like that, for all he was a colonel. He's years older than me, I don't know if anybody's told you – married twice, first wife died after only a few months, poor little thing, and then he had the army and so forth – I was quite long in the tooth, well over thirty, when he took up with me, but we've managed four girls all the same – all left home now, of course, though they're back this weekend with boyfriends and whatnot in tow, such a sweat. Still, we wouldn't change it, so long as they leave us in peace in between. Yours are off at school I suppose?'

'No,' I said briskly, 'no, we don't have any children, it – '

'Oh, dear – is that a problem? My dear, do forgive me, how very tactless – it's nothing whatsoever to do with me, forget I said it.'

'No.' I got up quickly, and refilled my cup. The sun was brilliant, flooding the comfortable little room, and I felt a sudden urge to talk, to pour out feelings and worries I had kept locked tightly within myself for years. I had never met anyone with whom I felt so instantly at ease, and trusting. She was not a subtle or an oversensitive woman but she was kind, warm, generous of spirit, I did not feel that she would be dismissive or critical.

'Actually –' I said, 'to tell you the truth, it is a problem – it's very difficult. Perhaps you could tell me of a doctor I might see? We've been abroad – I don't know of anyone really, or how to go about finding the right one. Only – I wouldn't want it talked about.'

I felt my face flush. She looked at me squarely, her eyes quite serious. 'Absolutely understood. You may be surprised but I am very good at not blabbing – my father taught me. Tittle tattle about any old stuff, he'd say, but never betray what matters. I've tried to stick to it.'

'Yes,' I said. 'I believe that. Thank you.'

'And as to your doctor – I'll have to make a few very discreet enquiries. I'm afraid I had mine just like that, you see, and old Broadford, the local chap looked after me – he's retired now, of course, there's a sharp new young man I don't

237

much take to but he's fine for all the coughs and colds and Bill's arthritis. We're never ill much, though I suppose one has to look to old age. But I've a niece and a sister in London who'll be able to advise. I'll let you know and I won't keep you waiting. Shall we go out and look at the roses and I'll tell you what's been lost through neglect, if I can, you might want to put something back, though of course you'll have your own ideas and quite right too. Are you a very keen gardener? We are, frightfully.'

And she was off, striding out of the house, calling out to Ned. I wondered what Maxim would make of her, whether he would find her tiresome. But it did not matter. She was good for me just now, her forthrightness was what I needed. And she had asked no questions about us at all, only appeared to accept whatever we were at once and carry on from that point.

We went out, into the sunshine of the garden.

'His name is Lovelady.' She had telephoned me early that evening. 'Which you will have to agree is the most divine name for a gynaecologist, and my niece says he's the absolutely top man, she wouldn't look at anyone else, and very sympathetic and all that, which I'm sure you want, but no smarm either, tells you what's what.'

'I think I'd prefer that too.'

'Well, of course you would, you want to know where you are. He's not in Harley Street either, which is a blessing I should say, it's such a dreary street. He's in Kensington, a nice quiet square.' She gave me the address and telephone number. 'I'd offer to come with you, I wouldn't mind a day up in town, and of course you've only to ask, but I should think you'd rather go alone, wouldn't you?'

'Yes, actually I do think I would, Bunty. But thank you.'

'No bother at all – now don't worry, my dear – what will be will be – you might as well be philosophical – but of course it's stupidly easy for me to talk. Good luck.'

I had written the name and number on a piece of paper and now, hearing Maxim on the staircase, I stuffed it into my pocket, as if I were guilty of something. I felt guilty. I did not understand why, but I wanted to do all this in secret, never to tell him. If the doctor suggested that he wanted to see Maxim too, I would simply say it was impossible, and bury the whole matter, it seemed almost a matter of pride that I saw to it alone. We never spoke of children now.

I tried to plan out very carefully how I would broach the subject of a visit to London, turned phrases and reasons over in my mind, even mouthed them to myself. I thought that I would choose the right moment, say it as I went out of the room perhaps, casually, as if it were of no particular importance, an afterthought.

But now that Bunty had given me the doctor's name, I could think of nothing else, it seemed so urgent, I could not wait. In the middle of dinner, I said, 'Maxim, I want to go to London,' blurting it out, so that he glanced up in surprise.

'You never want to go to London. You hate London, especially in this weather.'

'Yes, I know – what I mean is, I need to go, I really must get some summer clothes, I don't have anything much, and then there are things for the house –'

239

I knew what someone must feel, lying in order to meet a lover. I was sure he would be suspicious. Please, I said, please.

'Do you want me to come with you?'

'Oh, no,' I said, too quickly. 'No, you'd be very bored.'

'Yes.'

'Just drive me over to the station – I'd like to go early – one day next week, I think.'

'Fine. I wish Frank would write – I do want to know whether he'll come down and go over that farm and the extra woodland with me, I need his advice.'

With relief, I plunged with him into a land discussion, eager to show interest, eager to leave the subject of London. It had been easy after all.

But not so easy to get what I wanted at once. Dr Lovelady's diary was very full, I heard when I telephoned early the following day, he had no appointment for almost a month.

'Oh, I hadn't realised,' I said. 'Of course, I understand – but is there nothing, nothing at all – I'm – I'm so anxious to see him.' To my shame, I heard the fears in my voice, my own distress and agitation. I had not known how desperately I wanted this, now that I had made my decision, I could not bear the idea of waiting several weeks.

'Would you wait a moment, please.' She went away. I heard her footsteps, voices in another room. I imagined her saying, 'She seems to be very distressed, there's obviously something very wrong, do you think you could manage to see her?' and felt foolish.

'Mrs de Winter – Dr Lovelady will see you after his

hospital rounds on Thursday – will you be here at three?'

'Yes. Yes, of course – oh, thank you so much.'

I wanted to weep, and dance, and run to Maxim – 'It's going to be all right, we shall have our children,' and I saw them again, darting across the lawn, going up to fetch the ponies. For I was far ahead, all the problems done away with, I was not anxious now, it would all work out perfectly, just as the house had done.

I heard Dora arrive, and begin to stack the crockery into the sink, singing cheerfully.

'I'm going up to London, Dora,' I said, 'on Thursday. I shan't be back until late. I wonder if you'd just prepare something light for Mr de Winter's supper?' And we went on to discuss trout or salmon, and whether the tomatoes were ripening up, and as we did so, I realised that I felt different in some way, confident – grown up, at last.

'You look quite excited,' Maxim said, amused. 'You look as if you were off for an assignation.'

I felt my face burn.

'And so you should – you need a day out – I'm sorry you haven't an old friend to go with.'

'I'm perfectly happy on my own, Maxim, I shall like it much better.'

'Well, make sure you treat yourself to a very nice lunch.'

'Oh no, I shall only have a sandwich somewhere, I'd feel wrong eating lunch alone.'

No, not for that reason, I thought, getting into the train, looking out after Maxim, waving as we pulled out, but because I could not eat, could not swallow even the sandwich, not until I have seen him, heard what he will tell me, not until I come out again into the street, knowing, knowing what will be.

London was beautiful to me that day, the streets sparkled, the windows of the buses and taxis were flashing mirrors reflecting the sun, and the trees were bowers under which I stood to refresh and cool myself. The buildings seemed more graceful, more stately than I had remembered, and the curve of Albert's back as he sat gravely in his memorial was described as elegantly as a bow. I saw it, as I saw everything, with new eyes. I walked through the park, I looked at skipping children and navy blue nannies clustered together with their prams, and watched the birds and the sailing boats with a heart as light as a feather, for they would be mine, my babies, my sturdy, sunlit children, flying their kites into the brilliant sky, their faces seemed so bright, their eyes danced, there was nothing but playfulness and laughter on the air.

Earlier, I had gone into shops, and had to buy a couple of skirts and blouses, take some samples of fabric, because otherwise, what would I have to show for my guilty visit? But I had hurried over them – choosing anyhow, and then gone to wander among nursery things, chests and cribs, and up, among the cricket bats and dolls' houses, seeing this or that in its place at Cobbett's Brake, smiling at the sales girls, as though sharing a secret.

I could not have relished it so much if I had not been alone. I spent the day hugging the pleasure close to myself, savouring it, making it last. I shall not forget this, I thought. I did not see the bomb sites, still strewn with rubble, cratered and ugly, only saw where the wild flowers grew up between the broken, blackened walls and heaps of stones.

It was very hot, but I was not aware of being tired, I walked an inch above the pavement and the journey was effortless.

The square was large, with tall, pale cream houses, and chestnut and plane trees throwing deep pools of shade. There was a garden behind railings in the centre, where children played among great green shrubs, I heard their voices, more children.

And then, the house, with the brass plate that seemed to me to be made of gold, magically lettered. I went up in an ancient lift that rose magisterially, through the shadowy, quiet house.

'Would you go into the waiting-room, Mrs de Winter? Dr Lovelady won't be very long.'

But I did not mind, I was happy to wait here, in this cool, high ceilinged room, full of a ticking clock and the distant shouts of the children in the square, a little antiseptic, a little lavender polished. I did not pick up any of the fan of magazines, or look at the newspaper, neatly folded, or even at the cartoons on the walls. I wanted to sit, holding myself and my awareness of where I was and why, like a precious object.

'Mrs de Winter?'

He was younger than I had expected, sandy haired, heavy. His eyes looked directly at me, so that I felt summed-up, pigeon-holed.

I sat down, and was suddenly weak, I felt myself twisting my fingers together in my lap.

I began to answer the questions.

CHAPTER

Fifteen

On a corner of the street, close to the underground station, an old woman was selling violets, sitting patiently on a small canvas stool, her face upturned to the sun; I bought a bunch from her, and gave her too much money, and walked away not taking the change. I pinned the flowers on the lapel of my coat with the brooch I was wearing. They would wilt and die before the end of the afternoon but I did not mind, for now they were damp and fresh and sweet smelling. They reminded me of the woods above the house, and the deep, cool banks on either side of the stream that ran down the hillside and along the bottom of the garden.

I was walking again, through the hot, bright early afternoon streets, walking but I wanted to dance, and run and spin around and around, to stop passers by and tell them, have them dance with me.

'Any worries about anything?' he had asked. I heard his voice now, friendly, at ease, almost matter of fact. 'Apart from your very understandable worry about not having conceived.'

'No,' I said. 'No worries at all.'

For there were not, were there, not real ones? The unpleasantness about the wreath, the whispering voices, those were over, I dismissed them as trivial, fantasies I had made too much of, the evening Maxim had handed me Frank's letter about Cobbett's Brake, it was as though I had watched them slip over the side of the ship into the black water of the Bosporus and drown, and I had given no thought to them since.

'No worries.'

'You eat well – sleep – have plenty of things you enjoy doing – that sort of thing?'

'Oh yes.' I had told him about the house, and the garden, and all the joy of it, and he had looked pleased, had nodded and made a note. I felt he approved, and somehow that mattered, as though, if he were pleased with me, he could pronounce a hopeful verdict, as though he had magical powers over me by his approval.

I had been nervous, not of the examination or the questions – I had always been perfectly easy about anything of that kind, I had had a sensible mother – but because of the significance of it. Everything seemed to be hanging by the finest thread in that dim, quiet room, with its moulded ceiling, its tall curtained windows, its important looking desk. He had not hurried, there had been silences while he thought about something I had told him, or made a note.

As I walked past the ornate façades of the museums and the Brompton Oratory, along the wide pavement, I went over and over the scene in my head, watched it, like the repeated re-reeling of a film. I could not get enough of it, I wanted to be sure that it was lodged in my memory forever. I knew where I was, but I went ahead unseeing, unaware.

He had leaned back in his chair, fingertips together. They were very clean fingertips, I had noticed, immaculately shaped nails, good hands, pleasing to look at. 'Of course,' he had said, 'there are no certainties. I'm sure that you understand that. These are very delicately balanced, very sensitive human mechanisms – I often wonder whether, all other things being equal, it is not as much a matter of pure luck as anything else. But you have to remember, nature is on your side, and that is a tremendously powerful force. She is on the side of life – she wants you to have children – it's in her interests. She wants us all to be fruitful and multiply – it's her *raison d'être*.'

I thought that he had probably made the speech before – perhaps he made it almost every day, but I listened to each word as if it were a divine pronouncement, and infallible.

'I want to reassure you at once. I have found nothing whatever wrong with you – no physical or, indeed, other reason why you should not conceive a child – children. Naturally there are things I cannot be sure about from this sort of consultation and in time, if things have not gone to plan, I can make further investigations; but I suspect they will not be necessary. I want to give you every possible encouragement to be optimistic. Simply don't *worry* about it. I have a feeling that now you are happy and settled in your life, everything will take its course – and that before too long, you will be coming to see me again and I shall be confirming the good news. I know it.'

So did I, oh, so did I; he had told me he was sure too, it must be true.

I began to be hot and tired, suddenly, and very thirsty. I had walked too far. I hailed a taxi, and asked for a street off Piccadilly where I knew there was a quiet hotel in which I could have tea, and sat in the back, and smelled the faint smell of the violets and knew that it would be bound up forever with this day, this feeling of confidence and new beginnings.

At the end of the street a brewer's dray was blocking the way, and the driver had to stop there. I could walk the few yards up to the hotel. It was very hot indeed now, the pavements baked, the tarmac was sticky and pungent as it melted here and there. I had thought that I might walk further, go along to the shops in Piccadilly, or to sit among the fountains of Trafalgar Square, but now, I wanted only to rest and have my tea, and then go to the railway station and home. I longed for the garden in the last rays of the evening sun, the smell of the roses, sitting talking to Maxim, my hand in the cool still water of the pool.

I walked around the brewer's dray, and the men rolling the great iron hooped barrels down planks and into the black cellars below the pavement made way for me, shouting cheerfully. Then, I heard another voice, a different sort of shouting.

There was a telephone kiosk, with the door propped ajar as the man inside leaned his back against it. He had a suitcase propped up on it too, and protruding from the open door, a collapsing, ancient, stained cardboard thing tied across the middle with a frayed brown leather strap. Things were bursting out of it, bits of dirty cloth and what looked like yellowing newspapers.

The man had hold of the telephone receiver as if it were a weapon, I thought, gripping and brandishing it, as he shouted violently. The words were incoherent, ravings, and I wondered, as I passed by, if he were one of the mad, war damaged who seemed to be about the London streets, frightening, odd figures, in their own, terrible, locked worlds, and I stepped back instinctively, afraid that he would burst out of the door and into me, but I could not help looking at him as I did so. He wore a raincoat, with hair long and unkempt over the collar, and shabby brown trousers.

He did not back out, but as I went past the half open kiosk door, he turned and looked straight at me. His eyes were wild and bloodshot, and I knew them.

I began to run, stumbling in my shoes that had suddenly begun to feel pinched and hard after so much walking, anxious only to get away before he recognised and came after me, pushing hard in my panic against the revolving doors into the foyer of the hotel.

But then it was safe, it was ordered and calm and dim, the receptionist looked up and smiled.

'Good afternoon, madam.'

I went up to her in relief, saying that I would like tea.

'Of course – the porter will show you into the blue lounge. You'll find it very cool and quiet in there, really pleasant after this heat.'

'Thank you. Oh – and may I use the telephone – I realise I've left something at my last appointment.' I had bought a silk scarf, on impulse, earlier in the day, meaning to give it to Bunty Butterley, to thank her, and I had realised in the doctor's rooms that I had left it behind on the shop counter – it was not among my other things.

It took some time to get through to the correct department and make myself understood, but in the end, the scarf was found, and I gave my name and address, for it to be sent on, annoyed that it meant there would be a delay – I wanted to see Bunty, I felt a great warmth towards her, because I had been able to talk to and confide in her, and it had been she who so promptly had found the doctor for me. 'I would be so grateful if you would put it in the post today – it is a present, I don't want it to be delayed,' I said, and repeated the address slowly. But it would be perfectly all right, she assured me, they would send the junior to pack and post it at once, I should receive the scarf the following morning.

'Thank you,' I said. 'Thank you so much,' and put down the receiver, and turned, to face Jack Favell, the man with the suitcase, who had come to stand very close to the telephone booth, so that as I stepped away from it, I had no escape, no means of avoiding him at all.

It was the eyes that I had recognised, the eyes I had first seen in the drawing room that afternoon at Manderley, but now they were insane, wild eyes, the whites yellowing and bloodshot, the pupils staring: they were unnerving, I could not help looking into them – he made me do so, standing up close to me, never looking away.

'Well,' he said. 'Well, well, well – Mrs de Winter,' and there was a sneer in his voice, but something else, too, something almost triumphant. 'How very strange to bump into you here.'

'Is it?' I heard my own voice, cracking with nervousness. 'Yes, I suppose it must be.'

I made to move past him, further out into the neutral open space of the foyer but he did not let me, his big, heavy body, in the shabby long raincoat, and the suitcase, continued to block the path. I felt pushed backwards, cornered and afraid.

'Odd – as you went by out there, I looked at you didn't I? You recognised me; I thought, good God almighty, that little lady – never expected such a stroke of luck.'

'Luck?'

'Oh yes.' He was leering, his mouth half open so that I could see how bad his teeth had become. His face had fallen in, the cheeks and jowls folded and crumpled, loose flesh with a blue tinge where the beard would grow. Once, he had been good looking, in an obvious way – never attractive to me, but now, he was not, he was repellent, much older, seedy. And mad, I thought, looking unwillingly at the eyes again. He had not been speaking to anyone in the telephone kiosk, I thought suddenly, he had been raving into a blank receiver, living out some paranoid fantasy.

'Would you excuse me,' I said now, in desperation, for he still had not moved. 'I must have a word with them at reception.'

He paused, then stepped slightly aside, but as I moved past him, followed me at once, so that when I reached the desk, he was at my elbow.

'Did you manage to sort everything out, madam?'

'Yes, yes thank you, it's all fine.'

'Then I'm sure you're ready for your tea. The porter will show you to the lounge.'

'Tea!' Favell said. 'I say, that's a damn good idea – I could eat a plate of decent toast and a few sandwiches –

yes, I'll escort you in to tea, we've got a lot to talk about.'

'Actually,' I said, reaching for my bag, 'I don't think I have time after all, I think I'll just ask for a taxi and get to the station – Maxim will be waiting.'

'No.' He picked up the dreadful suitcase. 'I insist. Of course you're having tea, don't you want to hear what your long lost friend has been up to?'

'Not particularly, if you want the truth.'

'Ah.' He stopped in the doorway to the lounge. 'The truth. Well, we all remember a thing or two about that, don't we?'

I felt my face flush.

'I think you will have tea,' he said, 'won't you?' and he went ahead, crossing to some chairs in the far corner of the room, where subdued couples, pairs of the elderly, ladies resting from the heat, sat before silver pots and jugs, and white plates of scones. I felt a dreadful shame at being with him. They looked up and stared at us, and looked hastily away. I wanted to turn and run, now, very fast out of the hotel and into the street. But he had a grip on my elbow, and the waiter had appeared, the chair was being pulled out for me, there was nothing at all I could do.

'Tea,' I said. 'China tea –'

'With sandwiches and cake, madam?'

'I – I'm not –'

'Oh, yes, the lot,' Favell said, laughing an unpleasant, loud, embarrassing laugh, so that I felt heads turn again. 'The works – muffins, scones – only I'll have a whisky and soda, not tea, and you can bring that first.'

'I'm sorry, sir, I'm afraid that the bar is not open at this time.'

'Not open? Bloody hell, what kind of service do you call that, on a hot day?'

'I'm very sorry, sir.'

'Yes, well – can't you – you know?' He winked at the man, and made a gesture, rubbing his palm, so that I wanted to dissolve with shame and embarrassment, and once, would have done. But I was older now, I knew better how to handle things, and I had remembered my news, that I was happy, that things would be all right and Jack Favell above all, could not touch me.

'Thank you,' I said to the waiter, very calmly. 'Just tea, that will be fine, and only a little to eat.'

'Here, give a man a chance, I haven't eaten all day.'

'Some sandwiches then, just for one.' I tried to smile charmingly at the waiter to win him round, but I could not, his face was frozen, barely masking his distaste and disapproval. I did not blame him. Favell looked like a tramp, his trousers were old and ill fitting, his shoes worn at the toecaps, and with the fronts of the soles flapping open. His collar was greasy, his hair uncut, unwashed. I thought with horror that he might indeed be living on the streets, or at least in some dingy, temporary hostel, out of the cardboard suitcase.

'Oh yes,' he said, his eyes hot and blue and wild, staring, staring into my face. 'Take a good look. While you and Maxim have been living cosily in your nice little hideouts abroad, some of us have fallen on hard times. He's got a lot to make up for, you can tell him that from me.'

'I'm afraid I don't know what you mean.'

'Oh yes you do, don't look at me in that baby-blue-eyes way.'

'How dare you be so offensive – ? What on earth are we supposed to have done to you?'

'You? Well I admit you didn't actually *do* anything – you weren't even there, didn't even know him then did you? You were an innocent as well, I agree you can see it like that. Clever, of course, and scheming – not such a little Miss Prim and Prissy and innocent as you've always liked to make out. But you found out the truth; he told you didn't he? So that makes you a guilty party, too, you're an accomplice.' His voice was raised.

'Mr Favell –'

'I've spent much of the last ten years – all of my time since the end of the bloody war, trying to get things moving. No luck. No joy. Nothing. Until today. And *what luck*, makes up for everything, just about.'

'Will you please lower your voice – people are looking.'

'Oh, we can't have that. Dear me, no.' He leaned forward, legs apart, hands on his knees. They were bloated hands, creased at the joints, the fingernails filthy.

'Do you have any cigarettes?'

'I'm afraid not, I don't smoke.'

'No, of course not, you never did anything, I remember. Never mind.' He turned in his chair and began to look around the room. 'I daresay I can cadge one off some old boy in here – I don't have any money of course.'

'Please don't, please – look,' I opened my bag, 'go and buy some – here – please don't go to anyone."

He grinned, showing the stained, misshapen teeth again, inside the loose, soft pink mouth, and reached for the pound note.

'Thanks,' he said casually, and then, as he stood up and began to go, paused and looked down at me.

'Don't go away,' he said. 'We've got things to talk about.'

I watched him amble across the lounge, in search of his cigarettes. He had left the suitcase beside his chair; it might have been taken off a rubbish tip, the hinges were rusted and snapped, the corners split, it contained nothing, I thought, old newspapers and rags, perhaps a few of his bits and pieces. He was half mad, he was destitute, and he was going to threaten me in some way.

I would give him money, I decided, I had a cheque book with me and a little cash. It would be easy, I would ask him how much he wanted to go away. He did not know where we lived, and when I left here later, I would make sure he did not follow me. He had begun to mutter things about the truth, but I remembered how he had been after the inquest into Rebecca's death and the verdict of suicide; all he had wanted then had been money.

The waiter came with the tray of tea. He set out two small tables and put the tray down carefully, and as he did so, I remembered Frith and Robert bringing the tea to us every afternoon at Manderley, the elaborate, formal little ritual, the silver pots, the plates, piled with triangular sandwiches, hot floury scones, toast thick with melting butter, crumpets, muffins, several sorts of cake. The tray was more modest now, but the smell of the hot water steaming out of the spout, and of the warm toast, brought the old scene back to me. The waiter had a superior expression, not unlike that Frith had always worn. I saw him glance at the empty chair opposite to me and the suitcase, his mouth curled in distaste, and I tried to catch his eye again to show that I hated it, too, and was helpless, that Favell was not a friend, I had rather anything than have to be here with him, but he did not look at me.

'Thank you,' I said. He bowed very slightly, and turned away.

I would not tell Maxim, I thought, pouring out my tea. It looked good, strong and hot. I needed it, drank it at once, scalding my mouth, not minding. I would simply give Favell what he asked for and get rid of him. Maxim should never know. Favell was finished, a pathetic, shambling, half mad man, I began to feel sorry for him.

When he came back, walking with a touch of his old cockiness across the long room, he had a cigarette in his mouth, and his hands in his pockets. He was unattractive, weak faced, but I was not afraid of him now, he could not touch us.

He sprawled in the chair again, smoking, letting me pour his tea. He said nothing, for quite some moments, until he had eaten greedy, messy mouthfuls of the food, drinking at the same time. Once or twice, he looked at me over his cup, the blue bloodshot eyes still staring, still mad. I waited, eating nothing at all, drinking my own tea, I did not look at him. How much would he ask for, I wondered, would I have enough in the bank to cover it, or have to make some hasty, furtive arrangements? I hoped not, I wanted this to be done with, I did not want to have anything more to do with Jack Favell.

Now, he put down his cup clumsily so that it did not sit properly in the saucer and I had to lean forward to right it. I felt his eyes on me, following my slightest movement. I tried not to look back at him. He had lit another cigarette and was lounging back.

'Decent tea,' he said insolently, 'no more than old Max owes me of course. No more.'

It was coming then, I was quite prepared. I waited.

He said, 'I expect you'd like to know what happened.'

'Happened?'

'That night – oh, don't tell me you haven't both speculated, been wondering this or that, all these years. No one knows, I can tell you. That old woman Frank Crawley came noseying around, for a bit, kept looking me up and quizzing me, and then Julyan – I sent them both packing . . . So did Danny.'

'Mrs Danvers?' I felt a stab of pain, under my heart. I recognised it, it was a familiar pain from that time.

'Where is she? I thought –'

'What? What did you think?'

I did not reply. I could not. Favell crossed his legs. 'Oh, Danny's still around somewhere. I don't know – haven't seen her for years.' His eyes flickered. 'Manderley,' he said. 'What a show. Frightful. I suppose you saw it?'

I swallowed, my tongue swollen in a dry throat.

'I didn't, of course. I was in London, well, you know that. You remember all right, seeing that bloody doctor.'

Then I knew that what I had always suspected was true after all, the complete simple facts. I heard Favell's voice that night, as he spoke to Maxim, smiling the old, unpleasant smile. 'You think you've won, don't you? The law can get you yet, and so can I, in a different way . . .'

That way had been immediate and easy. He had telephoned to Manderley and Mrs Danvers. She had taken a long distance call, Frith had remembered. Favell had told her, very quickly, what had happened, and they had arranged it together. I wondered if it had been his idea or hers. But she had done it. She had laid the fire and poured the paraffin trail, secretly, in some far part of the house. She had lit the match, where no one could see. I saw her gloating, satisfied face, white in some dark passageway. And then she had left, a taxi had come, her things had been packed into it and she had gone. From somewhere, she had rung Favell – told him. '. . . and so can I, in a different way.'

I looked at him, smirking, grubby, loathsome. At least he had not been there. He had never had the final pleasure of watching Manderley burn, his revenge upon Maxim had not been completely satisfying. I thought something else, as I drank the last of my lukewarm tea. I had not believed Favell capable of organising the white wreath at Beatrice's graveside. Now, looking at him, I was not so sure. There was something reptilian and cunning about him which was new. I imagined him laughing wildly. There was only the question of money. He had none, he was destitute, that much was obvious. The wreath had been very expensive.

'I shall have to go,' I said. 'I don't want to hear anything.'

'What a pity. I hoped we had such a lot to talk about – ten years' worth of gossip. Not that I've much to tell. I had a garage, I lost that of course, things went rotten as soon as the war came. But I do a bit of dealing here and there when

257

I can get hold of something. Not easy. You wouldn't know, would you? Never wanted for a thing. Lucky old you.' He leaned forward suddenly. 'He should have *hung*,' he whispered violently, spittle flecking his lips. 'You know it as well as I do.'

I felt myself shaking inside, but outwardly I was so calm, quite calm. I said, 'I imagine it is money you want, that is what you are working up to. You tried blackmail before didn't you? Well, I will give you money, because I want Maxim left undisturbed. He is happy, very happy, we both are. Nothing must disturb that.'

'Oh, of course not – of course.' He mocked me with his face, his eyes.

'Tell me how much you are expecting me to give you. I want to go home, I want this over with.'

'Ten pounds?'

I stared at him, repeated his words stupidly. 'Ten pounds? Is that all?'

'It's a lot to me, my dear. But all right, if it will make you any happier, let's say fifty.'

I did not understand. I had expected him to ask for hundreds, thousands perhaps, something to set himself up, buy a business. I reached for my bag, and began to count out some notes. 'I don't have as much as that. I can give you a cheque for the rest.'

'Make it to cash then.'

I did. It was hard to make my handwriting clear and normal. He took the cheque and the money and folded them carefully together. His cigarette had burned down to a stub that hung from the corner of his mouth.

'You'd better pay for the tea,' he said.

I hated him, I thought, I hated the way he spoke and how he was able to make me feel, embarrassed, ashamed, guilty somehow. I got up, not answering.

'They were good days,' he said, 'at Manderley. Good times, before it all went wrong. Those days won't come again. We had a lot going for us, Rebecca and I, good fun, tremendous larks. Poor old girl.'

'Goodbye.'

He got to his feet and his hand shot out, I felt him grip my arm. It made me shudder, the thought of his dirty nails digging into my coat. 'You think that's it, don't you?' he said. He spoke lightly, pleasantly almost, and as if he were greatly amused.

'I'm sorry?'

'Yes. Fifty pounds! My God!'

'Please let me go and please keep your voice down.'

'Tell Maxim.'

'No.'

'Tell him — money's the least of it.'

'I don't understand.'

'I won't say I can't do with it because I can and I won't say I shan't need any more because I will. But that can wait, that isn't the point at all.' He dropped my arm. 'I want more than money out of him.'

'You're talking nonsense,' I said, 'you're mad.'

'Oh no.' He laughed again, and his eyes were horrible, I wished I had not had to look into them, I knew I would not be able to forget them now.

'Oh no. You'd better get off to your train.'

But for a few seconds, somehow, I could not, I did not know how to do such a simple thing as walk away, out of that room, I felt confused, paralysed, as though my body would not work, my mind could not co-ordinate things.

'Thanks for the nice tea.' I had been expecting him to follow me but instead, he dropped down again heavily into the armchair. 'I think I'll stop on here until they deign to open up and then I'll have some whisky. You might pay that at the same time, don't you suppose?'

I went, angrily, in an awful, tearful muddle. I fled from the room, and, as soon as I could get the girl to take my money which she did so pleasantly with such unhurried politeness I thought I would scream, fled from the hotel and into the street, and the heat from the pavement came up and hit me in the face, and it was all I could do to hold on to myself and not to faint, as I waited to see an empty taxi.

Sixteen

Happiness or unhappiness, whether we love or are alone, safe or in danger, and the final outcome – that day, I still believed these came from outside, the result of chance, and the actions of others. I had not yet learned that we make our own destiny, it springs from within us. It is not the outward events but what we allow ourselves to make of them that count.

It was the blindest chance that I had met Jack Favell. He had spoiled the joy of the day, because I let him: so that now I sat in my seat on the train staring out of the window, thinking, thinking of him, and what our meeting might come to mean. I took no interest or pleasure in what I saw, I could not have said how the light lay over the fields, or whether the trees were yet losing their most intense, fresh green, for the dustier, darker tones of late summer. I had had too much time at the station. I had drunk a cup of stale tea that furred my mouth and left a bitter taste, and then sat dully on a bench, looking at the pigeons pecking around my feet, and cared nothing for them. I bought a magazine and a paper and they lay unopened beside me.

I felt dead and sick inside. I had not forgotten the morning and my sense of joy and strength, they were simply gone, I could remember but not feel them any more. From being sure, I was in doubt, for what, after all, had been said, what difference was there? He could find no reason – yet things might never be right, reason or no. Plenty of people were childless, and there seemed to be no reason. He had only examined me briefly, only talked. What did he know? What had he changed?

I had not told Maxim where I was going, but as I came out from Dr Lovelady's rooms, into that golden street, I had known that I would be able to say, at once, it would have been impossible to remain with my secret: 'We may have children.' I had planned to say it in the garden that evening, walking quietly among the roses – 'there is no reason why not and every reason, now we are settled and happy, why we will.'

I would not speak of it now. There would be dull talk of shops and the heat, I would make up this or that, drop the subject as quickly as I could. Above all, I could not tell him about Favell. There were still some things I had to protect him from whatever the cost. He was happy, he had said so, Manderley no longer mattered, and the past had no power over him – nothing must alter that.

I realised that I loathed and despised Jack Favell, that he disgusted me: I was angry with him for what he had done to this day, but I was not afraid of him. He was too weak, too pathetic. And gradually, as the miles increased between us, and London receded and I began to feel myself near to home, I felt that the worst was over, it had been a short unpleasantness, no more. He had not followed me, he did not know where we lived – even, I realised, that we had come back here for more than a short time. He had not asked – I was surprised that he had not, but it meant that we were not very important to him. Only a few phrases lingered in my mind. 'You found out the truth. He told you, didn't he? That makes you a guilty party too.' . . . 'He should have *hung*. You know it as well as I do.' 'Tell Maxim – money's the least of it. I want more than money out of him.' But he had always made hasty, empty threats, tried to impress me by insinuating things, dropping hints. He had not changed.

By the time the train slowed down, coming up to the village halt, I had put it into perspective, talked myself round, I thought, quite successfully, and dismissed Favell almost completely, so that I could go to Maxim, cheerful, smiling, ready to trot out all the little sentences I had composed for him, about my day.

But I dreamed of Favell. I had no power over my unconscious mind. He had come to Manderley bragging of the sports car he was driving – 'much faster than anything poor old Max ever has,' and today he had mentioned selling cars, until the war spoiled his luck, and so, it was of Jack Favell in a car that I dreamed. We were driving up a steep, narrow road, and I had thought that I was with Maxim, but then he had turned to grin at me and the face, the fleshy blue jowls and bloodshot eyes, was Favell's, and it was his podgy hands with their dirty fingernails, on the wheel. It was dark, as if there might be a rainstorm at any moment, and the road was lined with tall trees, their dark, gleaming trunks rising above us threateningly, crammed together like teeth in an overcrowded mouth, and leafless until the very top, when most of them spread out overhead, blocking what was left of the light. I knew that soon, we must reach the brow of the hill and come out into the open, but the car was grinding, too slowly, I felt desperate to urge it on, to get ahead, because I knew that when I did, Maxim would be waiting for me, with his own car. I could not understand why I was not with him now.

Favell went on glancing at me, leering in an awful sort of gloating triumph, I felt he had made a fool of me and yet I did not know how, and so, could do nothing about it.

Then, at last, I almost cried out with relief and joy, the trees were thinning out, and sky was clearer here, a bright, brittle blue, the air was not foetid as it had been as we climbed between the trunks and mould damp, earth banks. I saw the sunlight ahead, framed in an archway. The car began to speed up, it was smooth now, oiled, we went without noise, faster and faster, hardly seeming to touch the ground.

'Stop here!' I said – cried out, for we seemed to be racing towards the light, no power could make us brake or slow down. 'Stop, please – oh, stop! STOP!'

But we did not, we went faster, and I began to feel breathless, and to choke at the speed, and then, I realised, as I had realised once before, that the blazing light was not that of the sun, but of fire. Fire.

'It's fire!' I came to, sitting up and gasping for air, and trying to shield my face from the heat.

The window was open, the air was quite cold, and smelled of the night coming in from the garden. I had woken Maxim, he was there, leaning down to me.

'It's nothing. I got too hot and tired. London was so exhausting. You were right.' I got out of bed, to go for a glass of water. 'I do hate it.' And I made up a confused nightmare, of baking pavements and hooting, jarring traffic, and told it to him in elaborate, lying detail, and allowed myself to be comforted, while Favell's face went on smirking at me from the heart of the real dream.

It was over and done with, I said. Jack Favell could not touch us; but he did, because I let him, I could not forget. He was the past, and again and again, I turned to look at it over my shoulder, but he was the present, too, and I feared as well as despised him, because of the things he had said. He hated us, and he knew the truth, and I did not trust him. He was not quite sane either, and that frightened me. Every day I woke, I was aware of his existence, somewhere in London, and I let that awareness lodge like a thorn in my flesh, I could not pull it quickly and cleanly out.

We make our own destiny.

The weather changed; it turned cooler, the mornings were grey, and sometimes there was rain. Frank Crawley came down from Scotland for four days to go to a farm sale with Maxim, and then advise him about the future, and the plans for enlarging the estate. It was a pleasure to have him in the house, he brought his old, even tempered, steadying presence, his loyalty and cheerful common sense. Yet he, also, belonged

265

too much to the past, so that part of me wished that he was not here. Manderley had been his, as well as Maxim's; I realised that I did not want Cobbett's Brake to gain a place in his heart, it was to be a new life here, and ours, only ours.

But I wished that I could have talked to him more easily. If he had been a woman, I could perhaps have told him of my new hopes for children, as I had told Bunty Butterley, for there was enough I had to keep to myself, I needed one person to share things with. She had been as I would have expected, supportive, interested and pleased. 'Now, take my advice, my dear. I'm a good few years older, so I shall talk to you like a mother hen. Try and throw yourself into other things – cram your life absolutely full. Don't brood about it, don't watch and wait, it'll do no good at all.'

'No. I think you must be right.'

'You've had your reassurance – and if it's meant to be, it will be.'

I listened to her, and I was touched, and heartened too: she believed what she said, her own life had been guided by such simple, wholesome platitudes, they had not failed her. I should let her set me an example, I should not dread the worst, not brood, as she told me, not brood. More than ever, she reminded me of Beatrice, she gave me a little of what Beatrice had given. I welcomed and was grateful for it.

And gradually, over the next few weeks, as the summer drew out, I relaxed, and my fears lost their edge. We took a few days away, to walk in the Welsh Marches. Maxim and Frank bought a second farm, and a large tract of old woodland which needed rescue and restoration. We went to a drinks party at the Butterleys', though Maxim was reluctant. 'Someone will know,' he said that morning. 'Something will be said – or they will look in that way I can't bear.'

But they did not. Our name seemed to mean nothing at all to any of them, we felt welcomed, we were of interest because we were new. No more.

There was only one moment of terror, so unexpected and violent that I felt the room begin to spin crazily. I could not focus. I do not know when it came. No one said anything, no one looked. It sprang from within me, I caused it.

Maxim was beside the window, talking to someone I did not know, and for a moment, I was alone in a space at the other side of the room, in one of those sudden, odd islands of stillness that appear in the noisy, swirling sea at a party. It was as though I were immured, I could see out, but not reach or speak to anyone, and all the surrounding talk was meaningless, the chatter of a foreign language.

I looked towards Maxim. 'He is a murderer,' I thought. 'He shot Rebecca. That is the man who killed his wife.' And he was a complete stranger to me, I seemed not to know him or have anything to do with him. But then I remembered Favell. 'He told you, didn't he? That makes you a guilty party too. You're an accomplice.'

I believed it, at that moment. I carried guilty knowledge. I felt complete panic rise up in me, at the full realisation of this truth. I did not know what would happen because I did not feel strong enough to bear it in secret, to spend the rest of my life saying nothing, doing nothing, but knowing, knowing. 'That man is a murderer.'

But now, he turned, looked up and saw me. He smiled, the murderer, and made the faintest gesture, which meant he wanted me to go over to him, rescue him from some bore, perhaps. I did so, edging between the broad backs and gesticulating arms and booming voices. I was dutiful, and when I reached his side, I behaved quite normally, I spoke and acted as I always had; but I was afraid, standing there. I looked at him for reassurance, that the nightmare would recede, and the words, the truthful words that rang in my head would be silenced. He had not changed, and in one way, nor had anything. We stood together, here in this drawing room full of photographs and flowers and little, irritating tables, Mr and Mrs de Winter, of Cobbett's Brake. All that was still true. I loved him. I was his wife. We would have our children. We had bought a new farm and a wood, the garden would grow, the sheep grazed on the slopes around the house and the morning was cool and bright. I ran through it all, as the man with the wart at the side of his nose talked on and on, and it was fine, it was all true, nothing altered any of it. There was only this other fact, of the words in my head, and the seed of fear that had been sown, and taken root deep down inside me. Some days I would scarcely be aware of it, everything else would matter more, on others it would stab alarmingly like an unanticipated pain. But it would never go completely, never not have been, and the future was altered and shadowed because of it.

A few days later, a letter arrived by the afternoon post – Dora brought it out to me where I was cutting the overgrown edges of one of the borders. The envelope was a cheap brown one, addressed in an ugly, scrawling hand I did not recognise.

'Mrs de Winter' – no Christian name or initial.

I took off my gardening gloves and went and sat on the bench. It was cool still, the sun fitful – not July weather, but it had helped the last of the roses to linger, though the grass beneath them was thick every morning with fallen petals.

There was a tray of tea beside me. Dora had left it there. I remember I poured myself a cup, before I slit open the letter – I suppose, much later, someone must have found it, cold and stagnant as a pond, and taken it back into the house – I had not drunk a sip of it.

There was nothing in the envelope except an old clipping from a newspaper, yellow at the edges, but oddly flat, with precise creases, as if it had been pressed like a flower within the pages of a book.

There was a photograph, I recognised it as the one from which the old picture postcard I once bought had been made.

DISASTROUS FIRE AT MANDERLEY, the headline ran, and below that, DE WINTER FAMILY HOME GUTTED.

I did not read any more, only sat, holding the piece of newspaper. I had known, really, that it was just a matter of time. I had been waiting for the next thing to happen, and now it had, I was oddly calm, in a cold, numb way. I was not afraid.

I sat on and on, not thinking, leaden inside, but at last, growing too cold, I went back into the house. I should have destroyed the newspaper cutting, stuffed it inside the range and burned it then, at once. Instead, I folded it, took it upstairs and put it into the old brown writing case I had had as a schoolgirl, and now never used.

Maxim would not find it there.

CHAPTER

Seventeen

The next one came a week later. Maxim passed it to me across the table at breakfast, but I did not need to look at it, I knew as soon as I saw the blotted handwriting across the brown envelope.

He had not taken any notice. I had two other letters, and slipped it between those, but he was preoccupied with reading what Frank Crawley had to say.

I went upstairs.

This time it was longer, an account from the local newspaper of the inquest into Rebecca's death.

SUICIDE VERDICT.

INQUEST INTO THE DEATH OF MRS MAXIM DE WINTER.

It is strange, I thought. That is my name, it has been my name for more than ten years, and yet when I see it like this, it is her name only. Rebecca was Mrs de Winter, I do not think of myself in connection with it at all.

I wondered wildly if Favell's suitcase were crammed full of cuttings, and if he planned to send them to me one by one, for years and years. But sooner or later, surely, he must write and ask for money, he would not be satisfied with trying to torment me at such a distance, never seeing the effect he was having.

I seemed to be living my days and nights as two people, one secret, hidden person, who received the terrible envelopes and scurried to put them away out of sight, and waited for the next, dreading that it would be something I did not yet know about, some awful revelation: that person ran along a single groove of thought, about Rebecca and Manderley, Favell and the cuttings, what he wanted, how to get rid of him, how to conceal all of it from Maxim; but the other continued in the old way, doing the garden, talking to Dora and Ned, going around the new land with Maxim, having Bunty Butterley to lunch, and sometimes, very early in the morning, or at the quiet end of the day, alone outside, saw the children, heard their voices calling in the distance, caught sudden glimpses of their fresh, bright faces.

I was very good at it, I thought. Maxim had no suspicions, never once looked at me closely, did not ask any questions; he himself was the same, full of his new life, energetic, making decisions about the estate. He was usually out now for most of the day but every evening we sat together in the way I used to imagine, during our years abroad. We read books, sometimes we listened to the wireless, I made notes for the garden. I had begun to keep a diary of my plans for it and filled that in, sitting at the small desk in the corner of the room, beside the French windows. I thought ahead to next spring, which steadied me. Bulb catalogues arrived, and I ordered by the hundred, as if in a fever to see the lawns and beds and all the grassy slopes clotted thick with flowers, narcissi and daffodils yellow as the sun, and crocuses and scillas of a deep, heavenly blue that would run like rivers across the grass. But not white. I did not want any white flowers.

We played cards or backgammon, too, and each did a crossword, and the darkness drew in a little earlier; it rained softly in the night, releasing all the sweetness from the earth up through the open windows.

I had what I wanted. It was here, now, this present.

Beware of wanting something too badly, my father had once said, for you may get it. I had wanted this quite desperately, and now it was dust and ashes, I felt detached, and leaden; I had what I wanted and no power to enjoy it, it had been given and taken away at the same time.

A photograph came, a crumpled snapshot of a boat in the little cove. I did not mind that, but what made my heart stop, was Jasper, good, strong, eager, faithful Jasper, a puppy, standing on the sand beside it, looking so excitedly, devotedly up. I cried then, and tormented myself with the picture, taking it out and staring at it several times, as if willing Jasper alive.

I wanted to burn that too, but I could not.

'We must have a puppy,' I said to Maxim, going into the study where he was fingering some map.

'That old footpath has been completely buried – ploughed over, then left, it's all overgrown. We must get it back – ' He turned, smiling. 'A puppy will scrabble up your garden.'

'I don't mind, it won't be for long – I shall train it.'

I had meant to wait until the children were here, but now, I wanted it for myself.

'There's bound to be a litter somewhere or other – ask the Pecks. A good labrador or else a sharp little terrier. Whatever you want.'

Jasper, I thought. I want Jasper.

'Yes.'

'I'll keep my ears open. Come here and look at this.'

Maxim was pointing at the map, showing me the line of the old path, and as I went to stand beside him, I looked down at his hand, the forefinger outstretched. I had always loved his hands, they were long and beautifully shaped, the nails carefully trimmed. But now, I could only see them as the hands which had held a gun and shot Rebecca dead, and moved her body into the boat, wrenched open the seacocks, manoeuvred the whole thing out into open water so that it would sink. I had not read the newspaper cutting about the inquest and yet the words seemed to have permeated my consciousness and overlaid my brain. I knew what they said because I had been there, I could see the description, the record of the evidence, Maxim's words, and now, I looked at him all the time in this new and dreadful way. I was frightened of myself, I seemed to have no control over my thoughts and feelings, it was like a sort of madness, and I reached out to him to comfort me, I put my hand on his and stroked the fingers, so that he glanced at me, smiling, but questioningly.

'What's the matter?'

'Nothing.'

'You've been very strained – you seem tired.'

'It's the weather – the summer seems to be slipping away and we've had no warmth and sunshine – I find it a bit dispiriting, that's all.'

'It will change. We'll have an Indian summer, you see.'

'I expect so.'

He bent and kissed my forehead briefly, already pre-occupied with something else.

What has happened? I thought, wandering out into the garden, where the wind was tossing the heads of the trees and battering at the last of the climbing roses. What has changed? Why is it like this and not as I had dreamed and planned? Was it only that I met Jack Favell by blind chance, and now he is tormenting me, dragging the past up to the light, as Rebecca's body was dragged to the surface of the sea?

But I knew that was not so, that the voice in my head had whispered months before, on the railway station platform, during that melancholy journey home to Beatrice's funeral. 'That man is a murderer – that man killed his wife.'

The seeds had lain with me, and like weeds that will spring up here or there, without apparent reason, but quite inevitably, had come to life, at last. I had done this, the fault was mine.

We make our own destiny.

Nothing came by post for almost two weeks, but I did not believe that it was over. I was dully expectant, this was only a short reprieve, another part of the torment. I wondered sometimes whether he would send anything that would surprise or shock me. The cuttings and the photograph were locked in my writing case, and when I passed the drawer in which I had concealed it, it was as though it charged the air like electricity, I felt affected by it, unnerved, and tempted to take the case out and open it and look, look.

But when it came, it was a sheet of lined paper roughly torn out of an exercise book. On it was written £20,000 and a London post office address.

It was an odd relief, I was not disturbed by this, it was straightforward and I knew how to deal with it. The demand for money was so obvious, so crude. I tore it into pieces the moment I was alone in the house, and dropped them into the range, pressing them hard down with the poker. And as they burned, I willed this to be the end of it.

It grew warmer again, the sun rose high and early, and baked down upon the countryside all day, but there was a just perceptible change, during the days of greyness and rain the year had moved on, and now looked and smelled of late summer, there was a heavy dew on the lawn each morning, and once, a pale mist lingered between the trees. The roses were over, hollyhocks grew tall and flowered, the colours of old faded chintz, and the leaves were a dead, even green, quite still and dusty in the middle of the day.

Maxim went to Scotland for three days to consult Frank and, I thought, try to persuade him to move down to England again. I did not think he would succeed. There had been a restraint about Frank, when he had been here, as though he were distancing himself from Maxim's plans, interested, supportive, but not involved. His heart was in Scotland now, I thought, he was happy and loved it there, because of his family. He would never feel about Cobbett's Brake as we did, and as he and Maxim had felt about Manderley.

Maxim had worried about leaving me, tried to persuade

me to travel with him, but I wanted to be here, and alone. I had a longing to walk in the garden in the evening and very early, before the sun was up, quite by myself, to feel the house settle down around me at the end of the day, to absorb this place even more deeply into me as if I breathed it in with the air itself. A year ago, I could not have imagined wanting to be apart from Maxim, I would have been anxious, insecure, or only half a person, and afraid for him, too, he was so dependent upon me. But we had changed, moved on, that time was over, we did not need to cling so desperately to one another, like frightened, vulnerable children wanting constant reassurance.

It was a good sign surely, it seemed to me, in my best moments, it did not mean that we had grown apart, but that we were stronger, and the moments when I looked at him and was afraid became fewer, the whispering voice was so faint, and so soft, I could believe I did not hear it.

It grew hotter, the nights were sticky and airless. I slept with the windows wide, lying awake until the slight chill before dawn made it easier to sleep. I was quite without anxiety or alarm, I felt so safe in this house, every room, as I walked in and out of them all for sheer pleasure, was accepting and sheltering to me. I missed Maxim in a pleasant, untroubled way. The truth was that I was finding my deepest contentment and fulfilment, for this time, at least, in being here alone.

Two days after he left, I had walked down to the farm to collect some eggs and stayed to talk to Mrs Peck over tea, play with the baby, and watch the cows amble up the lane and into the yard to be milked. I was in no hurry, at all, it was an easy, gentle day, and still very warm, as I returned, the hedgerows and banks dusty and dry, the stream scarcely running.

I stood for several minutes, looking down at Cobbett's Brake as it lay below me, red gold in the late afternoon light, the shadows from the holly and chestnut and balsam poplars long upon the grass, and it still seemed to me an enchanted house, not built by men but somehow sprung up magically from the ground, whole and complete. Later I would come back here again, when I had switched the lamps on all over the house, even in the attic room, for then, it was beautiful in a different way, it rode like a great, glittering ship out of a dark sea. I loved it so powerfully that day. I felt at one with it, and part of its fabric, bound up with its past, as well as the present and future. I felt as I had the first time of seeing it, as if it had been here and only waiting for me all my life.

As I walked into it again, it seemed to draw me gently back into itself. I went into the cool larder to put the eggs on to the stone slab. And as I did so, from the far end of the long passage, I heard the doorbell ring.

I was surprised. I had heard no sound of a car, but it was true that I had been on the side of the house farthest away from the drive. Then it occurred to me, as I walked towards the door, that it would be Bunty, come to cheer me up, take me out of myself, as she had promised, 'It's good to have a breather from them, don't I know it,' she had said when I had told her Maxim was going away, 'but it won't do you any good to get glum and start to brood.'

I was not glum, I was perfectly happy, but it would be good to see her for an hour all the same. We would have a late cup of tea, in the garden – it was still warm enough.

I opened the door.

'Good afternoon, madam.'

I do not know if my face was drained of all colour, I do not know whether the absolute shock, followed at once by a great flood of fear, was visible at all. I can't believe that it was not, the emotion was so immediate and violent.

There was no car, no sign of anyone else. She stood quite alone, very close to the door. She looked a little older, and I was not used to seeing her in outdoor clothes – indeed, almost the first thing I realised was that I never had. She had always been indoors, dressed in deep black, the dull textured yet unpleasantly silken dress, long and with tight sleeves, and a high, buttoned neck.

She was in black now, a coat to her ankles in spite of the weather. She carried a handbag and gloves, but wore no hat. Her hair was scraped back in the old way, smooth and tightly drawn over the high, prominent forehead, and coiled at the nape of her neck. But now, it was grey hair. The face was narrower and more lined, there seemed even less flesh on the white skull, the eye sockets were deeper.

Outside, in the world that lay behind her, there was absolute silence, the dead silence of late summer, when the lambs that have bleated are grown and gone away, and no birds sing.

'Mrs Danvers.'

'I hope I have not startled you?'

She stretched out a white wrist and hand from the black coat, and I was forced to take it. It was hard and narrow and cold.

'Not at all – or rather, yes, of course, I'm surprised to see you, but –'

'I'm sorry, I was not able to give you any warning. If it is inconvenient, you have only to say.'

'No – please come in.'

'I had some unexpected free time, and hearing that you were now in the neighbourhood, naturally I wanted to call and wish you well here.'

I stood back. She had stepped into the hall, and was waiting, not looking around her but staring at me, her eyes steady on my face from the hollow sockets. It was too dark here, too shadowy, I wanted to be at the back of the house, where the late sun would be flooding the small sitting room, and the windows were open on to the garden. I needed to be able to move away from her, to have the open air around me, the wide sky above my head, I would choke if I were forced to stay in a closed room with her.

Her footsteps were hard and sharp on the flagged floor, I heard the slight rustle of her skirt and it was a dreadful reminder. I was terrified of it, I almost ran towards the light.

'Would you like some tea Mrs Danvers? I haven't had any myself, I was about to make it.'

'Thank you, madam, that would be very pleasant.'

She stood in the sitting room, her back to the windows and the garden, the outside world, but it was as though she had not seen them, they held no interest for her, and I realised that, just as I had never seen her in outdoor clothes, nor had I seen her anywhere else save inside the house at Manderley.

'Perhaps you would like to go and look at the garden – I'm afraid the roses are over but the borders still have some interest, though I'm really only beginning to bring the garden back – it was so neglected, it will take years.'

She did not glance around. Her eyes had not left my face. 'Yes, you have only been here since the spring I believe.'

'That's right, we came in May, we were abroad for – for some years.'

'Ah yes.'

There was a silence. I did not mean to feel guilty, I had no reason to do so but as she continued to look at me, I felt myself flush and glanced quickly away. The words lay between us and did not need to be spoken, the reason for our time abroad and all that had gone before it was laid out like a pattern on the rug, it was as though we could both stand and look at it.

'Please do sit down. I – I'll make the tea. It won't take long.'

Her eyes flickered away from me for a few seconds, her eyebrows were very faintly raised. She is despising me, I thought, she is sneering.

'I'm afraid that since the war it has been so very difficult to obtain the right help, young people do not seem interested in going into service now. But I'm sure when you settle you will find people to come.'

'Oh, I have help –' I said hurriedly, 'as much as I want, that is. It is really not like the old days –' The words 'at Manderley' hovered in the air. 'I have Dora every day – and Mrs Peck from the farm helps sometimes.'

'I see.' The disdain in her voice made me flush again, in spite of myself, and I was angry that she still had such power to humiliate me.

'I really do not want any grand array of servants, Mrs Danvers, it never suited me.'

'No.'

'Things are much less formal here.'

'Yes – and of course it is quite a small house to run by comparison.'

'Yes,' I said, 'yes, it is,' and I fled away from her, down to the kitchen.

My hands were trembling so much I was afraid that I would drop the china, and when I poured the water I splashed some of it and scalded the back of my hand. It made a long scarlet mark which was acutely painful.

The questions flitted about inside my head like bright, darting birds trapped in a cage, their voices sharp and urgent. How had she found us? Where had she come from? Did she live nearby? If so, was that chance? What did she know of our life before this, and now, since we had come here? I imagined her somewhere not very far away, knowing every detail of our movements, watching us, spying.

And how had she come here this afternoon? It seemed unlikely that she had walked.

The tray was heavy, and before I lifted it, I had to stand, holding on to the wall, steadying myself with deep breaths. I should not let her frighten me. I must not, there was no reason. She had no power.

But I knew that she had, in a way that Jack Favell did not, and never could have had. She had always had power over me, I feared and hated her and she despised me and thought me of no account. I withered to nothing in front of her. With Favell and in every other respect now, I had more strength, more confidence. But seeing Mrs Danvers, I had become the uncertain, awkward, self abasing creature who had first arrived as a bride at Manderley and dared to try and take Rebecca's place.

But I stepped out as briskly as I could along the passage, and only my burning hand was a reminder of what, in a few moments, she had done to me.

She seemed not to have moved at all, she still had her back to the garden. Her eyes found my face at once, and remained, large, gleaming, steady upon it. She watched as I set down the tray and took out two small tables, put down the stand and pot and cups. She did not make any gesture, did not offer to help. I felt foolish and clumsy, I should not be doing this, there should be a bell to ring, at least one servant to bring us tea. Her face was set in the old curl of contempt. I was nothing. She was effortlessly superior to me.

'This is such a nice house, madam. You and Mr de Winter will be very happy here, I know.'

'Yes – yes, thank you Mrs Danvers, we are – we love the house and we are buying more land about – it's exactly what we want.'

'Of course it is very different from Manderley. No one would ever compare it with that, would they?'

'I suppose they wouldn't.'

'But then, there was never anywhere to compare with that and never will be.' She sat, very erect, on the edge of her chair, holding her cup, I wished she would not stare at me and never move her eyes away. My hand was very painful.

I said, 'I'm afraid I don't think about Manderley much now.'

'Don't you? But then you were never very happy there, were you? It was never really yours. I'm sure Mr de Winter thinks of it all the time.'

'No – no I don't think so.'

'I know that I myself do. It is always there isn't it? It never leaves me.'

I had brought in a small plate of lemon biscuits and now I picked them up to offer to her and then realised that I had not brought side plates for them, and stood up to get them. As I did so, I knocked the biscuits to the floor. They lay in a crumbly pile on the carpet, poor, dry, stale little things. I stared at them and felt tears pricking my eyes, tears of anger and humiliation. I knelt down to scrabble about, picking them up, and she watched me pityingly, though when I sat back on my heels and glanced at her, the white skull of a face was masked, only the eyes glittered.

'Mrs Danvers –' I blurted then. 'How did you find out where we were?'

She did not hesitate, the voice came slipping softly, glibly out.

'I have a very pleasant situation not very far away, in the village of Fernwode. Perhaps you know it?'

'No, no, I don't think so.'

I scraped the remains of the biscuits on to the tray.

'I am housekeeper companion to an elderly lady. She is alone in the world, and really, my duties are quite light – it suits me very well indeed, though of course, nothing will ever be the same as it was, will it?'

'No, no, I expect it won't.'

284

'And Mr de Winter is well?'

I had meant to go on asking questions, wanted to know what she had been doing for these past years, where she had gone from Manderley, what had happened during the war, but I could not. The way she sat, so stiff, so menacingly still, the eyes never leaving my face, froze the words on my tongue, I dared not speak them.

'Yes,' I said. 'Maxim is fine. He's in Scotland at the moment, seeing Frank Crawley about some matters to do with the estate.'

'Ah yes.'

The moment I said it, I wished I had not told her. I did not want her to know I was here alone.

'Only for a couple of days. I think he may even be home tomorrow.' I heard the nervousness in my voice, and knew that she had easily seen through the lie.

It was not only frightening to be sitting here in this room opposite to her again, it was odd. She had always been standing, apparently deferential, awaiting instructions, or orders, and yet I had never felt her superior, she had always been in control. Now, I had served her tea, she was sitting in a chair in my house, and yet it felt wrong in a new way, I was not her employer nor her equal, I was as inferior to her as I had ever been.

The sun had shrunk gradually from the room, and there was a shadow over the garden. It was airless and still uncannily silent.

'I was so sorry to hear about Mrs Lacey, it must have been very distressing for you both.'

And then I knew. I saw it in her face, though it was

285

still expressionless, saw it in her eyes, that seemed to be two hard, bright points of light in the dark sockets. It was you. Of course, I had guessed it and I was right: it was you, who sent the white wreath. But my mouth was dry. She watched me, her face bone white in the gathering dusk.

Why, I wanted to cry out, for God's sake, what more do you want? Of me? Of Maxim? What are we expected to do? *What do you want?* Then I heard the soft crunch of the gravel on the drive. Mrs Danvers stirred.

'That will be the car.' She stood up, her skirt falling into place with a silken sound. 'I asked him to wait outside, in the lane. I am very fortunate in that my employer rarely needs it. I am at liberty to make use of it when it is available, with the driver.'

Dumbly, I led her towards the hall. On the drive the black car waited, the driver holding open the door. I ought to have been amused, I thought. Maxim would have laughed, to see me carrying the tea tray, serving Mrs Danvers, to witness her being handed in and driven away by a chauffeur. 'Trust Mrs Danvers,' he would say, 'she always had a sort of style, don't you think?' and then dismiss her, as of no more importance in our lives.

But I knew that was not true.

I had shaken hands with her and she had turned away and climbed into the car without a word, and it had driven off at once.

Awkwardly, making the wrong gesture as I had always done, I raised my hand to her. She did not wave back, only sat motionless, but looked out at me when they turned, her skull's face gleaming pale, against the window, her eyes steady upon me.

When I lowered my hand, I felt the scald upon the back of it burning, burning.

Eighteen

'Are you all right?'

'Yes, yes, of course I am. It's been rather hot that's all.'

'Yes.'

'I'm fine, Maxim.'

'It's glorious up here. You'd be very envious – they had a cold late spring, so everything was put back. Janet's roses are a marvellous show still.'

'Oh – oh, yes – I suppose they must be.'

'The only tiresome things are the midges – I was eaten alive up on the moors today.'

'Oh.'

'Are you sure you're all right?'

'Why do you keep asking me that?' I heard my own false little laugh.

'You just sound a bit odd.'

'Really, I'm perfectly all right. I like it – I'm quite happy. I went over to the farm to collect the eggs.'

I was in the study. I had had my back to the window,

but now I turned. I did not like to think of being seen by anyone outside.

But there was no one outside, I knew that perfectly well.

'Frank would like me to stay on a few more days to fish.'

'Oh.'

'But if you'd rather I come home as planned on Wednesday, I will.'

'No – no, Maxim, of course you must stay. You'll love it.' No, I thought, please no. Last night I would have urged him almost guiltily to stay on in Scotland, last night I was relishing being alone. Not now. But I said, 'Come back whenever you like.'

'Saturday then.'

'That's fine.'

'Don't be by yourself too much. Get Bunty Butterley or someone over.'

'Maxim, I shall be all right. Give them my love.'

'Yes. If you're sure.'

I wanted to scream.

When I had set the receiver down, the house seemed to creak around me, settling back into itself, and then was uncannily silent. I stood, for a few moments, not even able to draw the curtains, mesmerised by the darkness beyond the windows, like blank eyes, turned to me.

She had managed to destroy it all, to undermine my new found confidence and sense of peace, to make me uneasy, wary and afraid. She had made me nervous of the house and of being alone in it, of walking from room to room, and of the night outside, the deserted garden, the countryside that lay all around. I felt spied upon, as though something or someone lay in wait for me, breathing softly.

But I forced myself to go about swishing every curtain roughly across, turning on as many lights as I could. At first, I sang to myself but my own voice sounded odd and hollow, I let it peter out, and then there were only my footsteps.

I switched on the wireless but I did not want the crackle of voices disturbing the room, I could not hear any other sounds there might be. When it went off, there was only deathly silence again.

I felt safest upstairs. I went to bed very soon, with some toast and a boiled egg on a tray, and lay trying to read. The air was close and heavy. I had the window open, and several times, I got up and leaned out into the darkness, trying to make out the shapes in the garden, but it was a moonless night, and I saw nothing. There were none of the usual night rustlings, of small animals, no movement in the trees.

The words on the page made no sense to me, and after a time I put my book down and switched off the lamp and then, her face seemed to come floating up to me and hang suspended there. She was all I saw, all I could think of, the black figure, the white skull, the hollow eye sockets, the gleaming protuberant eyes, the hair smoothed back. Her voice spoke softly on in my head, whispered relentlessly, and after a while, what she had said to me here, in this house today, merged into my memory of things she had said at Manderley, and then into the whispers I had heard terrifyingly in the villa in Italy. I drifted in and out of a half sleep, but there was no way of escaping her, she kept pace with me quite easily, I knew she would not let me go now.

'This is such a nice house, madam. You and Mr de Winter will be very happy here, I know.'

'Of course it is very different from Manderley. No one would ever compare it with that, would they?'

'Do you think the dead come back and watch the living?'

'You come here and think you can take Mrs de Winter's place? You. You take my lady's place? Why, even the servants laughed at you when you came to Manderley.'

'Why don't you go? We none of us want you. Look down there. It's easy isn't it? Why don't you jump?'

'That is Mr de Winter. That is your husband. Her husband. That man is a murderer. That man killed his wife. He shot Rebecca. Have you ever thought that he might do it again?'

I struggled to wake, as I had surfaced crying out from my dream of driving fast in the car with Jack Favell, but this time I could not. A hand, a cold, bony hand was over my face trying to push me back and stop my mouth so that I could not breathe, could not call, I was pressed down, down into the suffocating depths of the dream again, where her face floated and her voice was whispering and whispering.

At last, I did not wake but slept for a time more deeply, plunged into a place below and beyond the dream, and that was the only relief, when eventually I came to, her face and her voice had receded and were farther away. I sat up and switched on my lamp and at once a moth came fluttering about, its soft, pale, furred body patting against the shade. There was still no air, no breeze, or coolness from the garden. It was a little past two o'clock. I was hungry and thirsty but I dared not get up and go downstairs alone through the house, as I had done quite easily before, I only lay, rigid and afraid – and angry, most of all bitterly angry at what she had done to me and to the house, how her poison had begun to spread through it like a gas, permeating everything that had been light and welcoming and full of love and acceptance, and souring and staining it.

I hated her, as I had never really hated Rebecca, for how could I hate someone who was dead, someone I had never seen, never spoken to, only been made aware of through others? She meant nothing to me at all, I felt neither fear of her nor jealousy nor the slightest resentment.

It was Mrs Danvers who had power over me, Mrs Danvers I feared and hated, in a wild, unfocussed, frustrated sort of way, that had no edge to it and, as she must surely know, caused me more hurt and distress than it might ever cause her.

I did not sleep again, only waited for the relief when the first thin colourless dawn light edged into the room and I could go downstairs to make myself tea.

I went out, taking the car early into the market town, and shopping for groceries. After that, the day hung heavily and I did not know what to do. It was hot again, stale, tired August heat, the streets were dusty, people behaved irritably. I spun out an hour over coffee, but I did not want any lunch, I only walked up as far as the bridge over the river and stood there, watching the water, and looking up now and again over the rooftops to where the handsome tower of the parish church soared out of the low land.

I tried to think of Cobbett's Brake as I had done, to long for it, to see it in my mind's eye; it is the same, I said, it is no different, she has gone, she can do nothing, but I knew that it was not true, and that the blow had fallen already.

I could not look ahead, I was miserably bound to the present, as on a wheel, going round and round our conversation, and how she had looked, what she had made me feel. I wanted to cry, bitter tears of frustration and rage, at the unfairness of things. *Why*, I wanted to shout to the sky and the water and the innocent passers by, why must this happen, why does this come back to us, are we never to be free of it, why?

But I knew why well enough.

In the end, I drove to Bunty Butterley's with some excuse about wanting the name of a dentist. She did not believe me, I could tell at once by the way she looked at me as I spoke. But she gave me tea, and we sat on an old, shady seat near the cedar tree, and chatted about nothing. I felt better for it, I was glad that I had come, but all the time, I was conscious of something, a physical sensation in the pit of my stomach, like a small clenched fist that bored and probed into me, and knew that it was fear.

'You need that husband of yours back, my dear,' she said, walking me to the car. I had a bundle of sweet peas she had cut for me in my hand.

'Yes.'

'You're melancholy.'

'No, really.' The easy lies again. 'I'm fine.'

'You need a night or two in London – see a show, get him to take you dancing. That always used to put me back in good spirits.'

I imagined her, foxtrotting cheerfully about some dance-floor, dressed rather unsuitably in shiny, bright material, perfectly happy, not caring for anyone. Like Beatrice. On an impulse, I leaned forward to embrace her, because of the way Bunty had reminded me of her.

'Now mind you do as I tell you – no good brooding.'

'No, I won't. Thank you, Bunty.'

She stood and waved, stout, beaming, and yet quick, I thought, perceptive, not one to be deceived. If it was cooler, I would weed and dead head the whole way along the south border, I would not let myself brood, I would not give in to fearfulness.

The brown envelope was on the top of the pile of letters Dora had put on the hallstand.

I ripped it open at once, I wanted it over and done with.

This cutting was not old and yellowing, it had come from a very recent paper. Indeed, I had already seen it, but I had turned over the page quickly. There were some things I could never bear to know about.

CLERK HANGED FOR LOVER'S MURDER.

EARLY MORNING EXECUTION AT PENTONVILLE PRISON.

There was a photograph, a mean, postage stamp thing, of a moustached, pathetic looking man with frightened eyes.

He had been a post office clerk who had killed the woman after some violent, jealous quarrel. But it was different, I remember noticing, quite different. He had not had a gun. He had stabbed her, after she had first attacked him with the same knife. There had been a plea of self defence, but it was no use. He had been hanged a couple of weeks ago.

I crumpled the paper up in a ball in my fist, crushed it so tightly my nails hurt my palm. This had nothing to do with us, this I would not keep. I burned it.

The hollow fist in my stomach had become a pain, another sort of burning.

But it was beautiful in the garden, the shadows violet coloured across the dry grass. I took my fork from the tool shed, and knelt to prise couch and groundsel from around the old pinks that edged the border. They had been heady with sweet, clove scent in June. I planned to divide them and put in more, so that next summer this whole bed would be crammed with flowers chosen for their smell. Gradually, working my way along, not allowing myself to think, I became steadier, the fist in my stomach unclenched a little.

A blackbird had come out of the syringa bush and was watching me, eye gleaming like a bead, waiting for me to leave the freshly turned soil so that he could pick for worms.

In winter, I hoped there would be a crowd of them, all manner of birds, coming in for the berries. I would never let the children take their eggs, I thought, for all I wanted them to be country boys. And I had for a few seconds the wonderful sense that they were here with me, laughing faces peeping out from the shrubbery, hiding in case I should look up and shoo them away to bed. Oh, you can have a few more minutes, I thought indulgently, because it is summer holidays after all and you don't sleep these hot nights. I shall pretend I have not seen you just yet. And I bent my head again to the border.

I heard nothing, no footsteps on the gravel, or the grass, nor the slightest rustle of clothing. She always used to do it, appear quite suddenly and silently, in a doorway, at the end of a corridor, just at my shoulder, it had been one of the things I had found most frightening about her.

Now, her shadow came across my patch of earth, shutting off the last, slanting rays of the sun. 'A garden in the evening is such a pleasant place, I find.'

I thought that my heart had stopped. I spun round, and almost overbalanced. To save myself I put out my hand and it went deep into the soft, newly turned soil. She glanced down at it, a barely discernible trace of amusement on her lips, as I tried to wipe the earth from under my nails and between my fingers on the side of my skirt.

'Did I startle you, madam? I am so sorry. I should have spoken to you from the path.'

'I – I didn't hear the doorbell.'

'I saw you as I came down towards the house, so of course I did not bother to ring. I knew you had no one to answer it to me.'

'Have you – have you come for tea again?' I heard my voice sounding unnaturally friendly and cheerful. 'It does seem rather later than yesterday but I could still make some – or a glass of sherry.'

The awful instinct to be polite, to offer hospitality was

ingrained in me, I had been very properly brought up, and yet she despised me still because I was uncertain, and did not know on what footing our new acquaintance ought to be. She was no longer a servant and I the mistress, and in any case, perhaps that order of things was dead everywhere now. I had heard Bunty and others talk ruefully about the war as 'the great leveller.'

'I happened to be passing nearby and I asked Purviss to stop. There is something I want to show you.'

'Oh, yes? Whatever is it Mrs Danvers?'

'Not here. At my present house.'

'Oh.'

'I thought you would like to visit me there. It is really a very pleasant place and my duties are quite light. If you are free tomorrow afternoon, I shall have the car come across for you.'

'Oh, no –' I should have said at once, 'No – I do not want to come. No, it will not be possible, Mrs Danvers. I had much better say so at once, for fear there is any misunderstanding. Mr de Winter and I would prefer not to have any reminders of the old life. I know you will understand.' Or simply, 'No, my husband will be home tomorrow.'

It was not true but she must not know it. But I said nothing and the chance was lost. I dithered, nervous and awkward and uncertain of myself, she reduced me to the old, inferior, stupid creature she had known previously. I am not like that now, a voice within me was struggling desperately to say, I am older, I am confident, I am secure here. I am not afraid of you.

'Shall we say three o'clock, madam? Purviss is always free in the afternoons, my employer rests then.'

She stood, tall and gaunt and black, a few steps away from me. The garden at her back and the slope that rose behind that lay golden and tranquil in the still evening sunlight, but I could not reach them. I was frozen before her, and in the brief silence, as I looked at her chalk white, impassive face, she seemed to grow taller, to tower above me, higher and higher, menacing me, and I shrank back, I was a poor, small thing of no account, and she might step forward and trample me.

'I shall look forward to tomorrow,' she said softly, her eyes steady on my face. 'It is such a pleasure to me to know you and Mr de Winter are nearby.'

I heard my own voice, though I did not know how I spoke for my tongue seemed to have swollen and stiffened, I was not sure I could make any sound come. 'Thank you, Mrs Danvers.' But it was not my own, natural voice and I do not think that she heard it. She had turned and moved away, and I did not go with her, I could not move, but only stayed in the quietness, looking up weak with relief at the sky and the rising slopes that were no longer shadowed by her. But it seemed to me that where she had stood, the patch of grass was scorched and blackened.

I would not go, of course I would not, why ever should I? I did not have to do what she said. Whatever she had to show me could not be anything I wanted to see.

I sat in the kitchen huddled at the table. I would not go, and then Maxim would be back, I had only to endure another three days. She would never dare to come when Maxim was here.

But she would watch, the voice inside me said, she would spy and know, and when he went out, as he did for a good part of every day, she would see and come then. I could not tell him. He had never understood why I feared her, to him she had always been merely the housekeeper. He had neither liked nor disliked her, that was not what you did with servants -- though I think he had always admired her efficiency. Well, so had I, she had run Manderley impeccably. We had shared everything, Maxim and I, in the years away, but I had never been able to tell him what had passed between Mrs Danvers and myself, what things she had said, gloatingly, about Rebecca, hatefully about him, and derisively about me. There would have been no point, even had I found the words. It was over, I had told myself, she had gone. I would never think of her again.

But deep down, there had always been the whispered doubt, the small nag of fear. And it had been right, of course, and just as I had always known.

I would not go. I need not.

I would go out. Not be here. I would drive over to the Butterleys'.

But the next morning, Bunty telephoned to say that they were off to Paris for a week.

'The dear old boy decided I needed a bit of a treat. God knows what it'll be like at the fag-end of the summer – *fermeture annuelle* and all that but if it's dead as a doornail we'll drive on down to the coast – Biarritz I should suppose.

You ought to join us – can't you get Maxim to drop everything and come?'

I had not thought I would want to run away abroad ever again, I had thought I would want to spend every day for the rest of my life here at Cobbett's Brake. But as she spoke, I had a wild urge to agree, and to persuade Maxim, the thought of getting away, to be free, to sit on a terrace in the sun and drink pastis idly under an awning, of going where she could not follow, was quite desperate.

And of no use. Maxim would not dream of going away, and I could not possibly explain why I wanted to so badly.

I could not run, I must not, it was a feeble, childish, cowardly thing. What are you afraid of? I began to ask myself over and over again, what can happen, what can she do?

Nothing, I said. Nothing. Nothing.

And I realised that when the car came for me, I would go, because I must confront her, there were things I would say, questions I wanted to ask. I must show her that I was different now, and quite in command, and I would tell her never to come to Cobbett's Brake again, that it would anger and upset Maxim.

I practised the sentences, mouthing them to myself as I went about the house and garden, I heard my voice sounding calm and reasonable, cool but not unfriendly. I would act, pretend, and the pretence would become real.

I dressed with a great deal of care that afternoon, choosing a smarter frock and jacket than I would normally bother to wear in the country, brushing my hair so that it hung well. She had known that I had no clothes sense, dressed timidly in the wrong cuts and colours for my age, compared me, whenever she looked me up and down, with Rebecca, who had such taste and style.

I was pleased, looking in the mirror, the blue I had chosen suited me, I felt confident.

'Oh, London clothes, London clothes, Mummy,' the boys would say, dancing gleefully around me; but the little one would turn away quietly, not wanting me to go.

The car came slowly over the gravel, scarcely making a sound. I was waiting, so that as soon as I heard it I opened the front door, and of course that was not correct, I should have been a few moments in coming, I could see that he knew it. He was a dour, thickset, silent man.

'Thank you,' I said, as he opened the car door, and bit back some friendly remark I almost made about the hot weather, for he would tell her, I was sure, they were two of a kind, Purviss and Mrs Danvers.

As we slipped up the drive and through the gates, I looked back to where the house rested, in the sun, all of a piece and contained within its green slopes, beautiful. But I thought that it had somehow become impervious to us, and to our doings there, it simply existed as it had always done and we came and went about it like ants on the surface of some ancient hill, scarcely making any mark with our presence.

It will be all right, I said fiercely, it will be as it was, I shall not feel like this after today, it is only the shock and the effect her coming has had upon the house. It will not be like this for very long.

Must not.

If I had not been so tense, anxiously rehearsing what I

must say, I suppose I would have found my situation that afternoon quite funny. That Mrs Danvers should have the use of a car with a chauffeur to take her out when she chose, and that she should so grandly have ordered it to come for me, was bizarre, laughable, and yet I could not laugh. I was struggling too hard not to feel powerless and inferior to her again, she had such effortless, sinister control over not only my actions but over almost every corner of my consciousness, the nooks and crannies of my feeling and thinking. I tried to fix my mind on the return home after it was all over, and on Maxim's coming back but all there seemed to be was a cloud of concealment and deceit, through which I could not penetrate.

We did not drive very far – four or five miles perhaps, going east to a village I had not seen before. It was dull, a long straggle of uninteresting houses along the main street, and the fields around were flat. We turned up a lane beside the church, which had a spire not a tower, as was usual here, and seemed oddly out of keeping, in a rather suburban way, with grey slates and an ugly brown painted lychgate. To one side was the rectory, and beyond it, a single further house, not country looking but like some Victorian villa taken from a town. It was quite large, with tall narrow windows. The curtains seemed to be half drawn.

I did not want to be here, I would have given anything not to have to get out, this was a strange place, it might have been in another country, I wanted to go back home.

He had opened the car door and was waiting and when I looked up, I saw that she was waiting too, standing on the top step, her hands folded in front of her black dress, it was the same as it had been that first day, nothing had changed, nothing would. And though I stepped out of the car and across the path towards her boldly enough, she was not fooled, I could see that perfectly.

'Good afternoon, madam.'

I had gone very cold.

'Do please come in.'

No, I wanted to say, no. Let me stay out here, in the light, in the outside world, whatever it is we have to say can be said here, and then I can go. We need not meet again. She had taken a step inside and paused, waiting for me. The car had slid away, the drive was quite empty.

I turned and followed her into the house.

It was not pleasant, it was dark and stuffy and over-furnished. When the front door closed I wanted to run out and down the drive, and as far away as I could.

Doors opened on to dim rooms with heavy, half drawn curtains, tables and chairs covered in plush, huge, sombre portraits in gilded frames, cases of butterflies and stuffed fish and dead birds. The countryside might not have been outside, I thought, no one ever opened a window here, no fresh, sweet smelling air ever drifted into these dreadful, oppressive rooms.

But we were not lingering, I was following Mrs Danvers as she climbed up and up the turkey red carpet, to the next floor, and around again, and up. Here, the doors were all closed. There was no sound except our footsteps. No one else might have been in the house at all.

Her dress swished softly. She did not glance round to see if I was behind her. She had no need.

'Please come in, madam. These are my own rooms, overlooking the garden.'

She held open a door at the end of a corridor and stood back in it, so that I was forced to pass close to her as I went inside.

'I am very fortunate, my employer has made over quite a good portion of this top floor to me. I have a sitting room and bedroom – and then another room at my disposal.'

I was filled with relief; it was a plainly, comfortably furnished room with two tall windows that let in plenty of light, slightly anonymous but not unattractive, not threatening. There seemed nothing at all of Mrs Danvers impressed upon it, it was a neat, ordinary room that might have belonged to anyone or no one, a room in some private hotel.

'Do sit down, madam. I will ring for tea in a while.' She stood over me, smiling in an open, perfectly pleasant way, but the irony of her invitation, and her sense of position here was not lost on me.

'How long have you been here, Mrs Danvers?'

'Not very long, madam, a few months. Why do you ask?'

'Oh – it seems – it seems such an extraordinary coincidence.'

She said nothing at all, and when I looked at her, she was still half smiling but in an odd, expressionless way.

'I mean – that you should be so near to us.'

She walked to the window and stood looking out.

'It is very quiet here, very peaceful and there are few visitors.'

'Your – your employer is rather old?'

'Oh yes ... I often stand here for a long time, looking

out at the fields. I miss the sea of course. Do you ever miss the sea, madam? The sound of it drawing up the shingle so softly, and the crash of the waves when it was stormy, I often lie awake and think I hear it. Don't you?'

I felt my lips go dry. Her voice was low and monotonous. 'Mrs Danvers –'

'Please sit down, madam.'

'No – no thank you.'

There was a silence. She had her back to the light and she did not move, only looked steadily, expressionlessly at me. I realised that I did not know exactly where I was – I had not noticed the name of the house – and that the car and driver, my only means of getting home, had disappeared.

She was waiting and so as not to appear harried or in any way alarmed by her, I did sit down then and placed my handbag on the floor beside me.

'This is such a pleasant room,' I said. 'You must be very comfortable here.'

'Oh, yes, and I have such light duties. I am not young now, I would not feel up to the challenge of running a great house again.'

She did not sit herself. 'Have you ever thought of it?'

I did not answer.

'I think of it all the time. Every day. Surely you must too. Have you been back?'

'No,' I said. My voice came oddly out of my dry throat. 'No.'

'No. It is better not to go back. I went, once only. I had to see it. It was terrible. Quite terrible. And yet in a way right, don't you think? Manderley was never happy after she

305

had gone. You know that of course. You felt it too. Fire is such a cleansing thing. There was no other way.'

I stared at her, and her eyes bored back, two bright pinpoints, and I saw a flicker of triumph and excitement there. She was telling me now, and yet she had said nothing. If anyone accused her she would be easily able to deny it.

'I found another place, in the north. I did not want to stay anywhere near, and then during the war, I was a governess and a nurse companion. Nothing was ever the same, of course. Nothing ever will be, but I never expected that. And it did not matter.'

'I'm sure – I know we would like to think that you had – had settled happily.'

'Did you, madam? Did you speak of it?'

'Well – no, no – we – Mr de Winter did not want to talk of that time.'

'Of course. Yet he could never forget it could he? However would he be able to do so?'

'Time – helps things to fade.'

'Does it? I have not found so.'

'We are very happy now.'

'Are you?'

'Yes.' I burst out angrily, and I heard the tears rise into my voice and was powerless to control them.

'Yes – we love Cobbett's Brake, it is all we ever wanted. It is beautiful and we will make it even more so.'

'But it is not Manderley.'

'That is why we love it,' I whispered.

I could not look at her, but I was dreadfully conscious of her dark presence, silhouetted against the window. I struggled to summon up all my courage and self possession, my fingers gripping the edge of the chair.

'Mrs Danvers, there is something I must say.'

She did not reply.

'I find it – I find it such a strange coincidence that you should be here – so near to us. And of course, it has been very pleasant to find you – well, and so – so comfortably settled, but Mr de Winter must never be reminded of – of the past. I very much hope that you will not come to the house again – in case he should see you and –' I paused, and then I stood and confronted her, my courage strengthening as I spoke. Why should I fear her, why? What could she possibly do to me? I was contemptuous of my own feebleness. 'Mrs Danvers, have you been – been writing to me? Sending me – things?'

Her face remained quite blank.

'Certainly not, madam. I have never addressed you at your house.'

'Then it must have been Mr Favell. I met him in London. He – he has been sending things through the post – newspaper cuttings and – other things. He has been trying to blackmail me. But you knew that, didn't you? You have been in touch with him. You found out our address because he told you.'

I waited. Surely I was right. I must be right, and why would she bother to deny it?

She went on standing, without moving, without speaking, her eyes on my face. It was all she had to do, she knew that. My hands were trembling.

And then she stepped forward, and walked past me to

307

a door at the far side of the room. She opened it wide, and then turned to me.

'I told you that I had something to show you,' she said. 'Come in here.'

She did not ask me pleasantly, I heard a note in her voice I could not disobey. I went slowly across the room and through the door she was holding open. 'I've tried to make it a pretty room,' she said softly.

Oh, it was . . . it was. There were delicately printed curtains and drapes to the bed and the dressing table, a rose patterned needlepoint rug, beautifully stitched. For a split second, I thought it was surprising that Mrs Danvers should have such an airy, light room to sleep in, with the things so immaculately placed and chosen with such care. But almost before I had thought it, I looked at the dressing table top, at the brushes that were set out there, their silver backs gleaming.

'Yes, of course, you recognise them. You touched them once, do you remember? You picked them up, thinking that you were alone and that no one in the house knew where you were. I had so few things of my own and they did not matter, they were of no account at all – easily replaceable. All I packed and took with me that day were her things – everything I could carry. I've had them with me all these years. I have never been parted from them. I was waiting, you see, for a home where I could place them as I wished – as perhaps she would have wished. Of course it is not the same – it could never come up to her standards of taste and luxury. She would not like the house. It is an ugly house, so dark and unappealing. I'm sure you agree with me. But that does not matter at all, because it suits me so well – I have been able to do exactly as I wish – I have been given a free hand to decorate and furnish as I choose, my employer takes no interest in it but she is glad that I want to stay. She had difficulty finding anyone prepared to stay, but the moment I was shown up here to these rooms and told that I was welcome to use any of them, I knew I had found what I wanted.'

I thought that she must be mad. Yet her voice did not sound so, it was soft and monotonous as always but quite reasonable, quite plausible. Her face was pure white, the eyes burning. Was that a sign of madness? I remembered Jack Favell's wild, bloodshot eyes. They had seemed mad.

'Look,' she said. She was holding open the wardrobe door. I did not want to look, I knew what would be there well enough.

'I could not bring dresses and furs and so on. I left almost everything. It did not matter. Only this one dress. It was always her favourite and so naturally it was mine. Look at it.'

And so I must. It was green, a slim, silken sheath of dark emerald, with a single halter strap to be worn around her neck. I remembered the magazine photograph, it was before me now in every detail, the head thrown back, the arrogant gaze, hand outstretched to the rail, the beauty. I thought this had been the dress she wore then.

'She had such light, delicate things, they were so easy to pack into my cases.' She was opening drawers now, as she had done that other time, pulling out underwear, nightdresses, stockings, a fur trimmed wrap, a pair of gold slippers. The dressing case embroidered with her initials. R. de W. 'Look,' she said, and her voice was greedy, 'such beautiful, lovely things for my lady.'

You are mad, I wanted to cry out, you are quite insane, you are obsessed, and she drove you to it. I was terrified, fascinated.

Now, she had closed the cupboard and the drawers. 'Come and look out of the window,' she said. I did not move.

'Don't be afraid.'

'No.' I swallowed. 'No.'

'Oh, I wouldn't harm you now. I don't want you to harm yourself either. I used to hate you. You are not my concern now. You are of no account at all. Less than none.'

'What are you trying to say to me? What is the point of all this? What do you want, Mrs Danvers? Is it money? Are you in league with Jack Favell?'

She gave a hiss of derision, but as I had spoken, I knew that I was wildly wrong.

'He had a use,' she said, 'and I used him.'

'He told you where we were.'

'Let him beg for money, stupid fool. Let him get what he can. Why shouldn't he? It has nothing to do with me – why should money mean anything?'

'Then what do you want? What use is all this?' I sat down suddenly on the satin quilt covering the bed, my legs would no longer hold me. I felt that I might cry, I was like a child who is a victim, I was in a trap and knew of no way out. I did not understand and I felt helpless, but she was not a monster, she was a human being, why could she not have some spark of feeling for me, and sympathy. I felt snivelling and pathetic before her. 'Mrs Danvers, please tell me what you want and why you have brought me here. I don't understand.'

'Don't you?'

'I know you hated me for marrying Maxim.'

'Oh, no, I never cared a jot about that. Let him marry whoever he wanted. It was no interest to me. I only despised you for daring to try and take her place at Manderley.'

'I'm sorry – but that is over, over long, long ago. Can't you forget it? Can't you let the past lie buried?'

'The past is all I have, all I have ever had or will have. The past is everything to me.'

'Surely that need not be – you should make another life for yourself. As we have done.'

'Have you? Do you really believe that?'

'Yes,' I almost shouted. 'Yes, if you will only let us. If you will leave us alone.'

'Never.'

I looked up, startled by the venom that spat out of her mouth in the single word. There were two small blazing scarlet patches, hardly more than spots, on her cheekbones, and her eyes were horribly bright.

'How does it feel to be married to a murderer? That is what he is and you know it and I know it and he knows it, and I wonder how many others know it? He killed her. He shot her. Suicide? Kill herself? My lady? Never. No matter what was wrong, what that doctor had found. She was the bravest one that ever lived. She would never have taken the coward's way. Would she? Would she?'

'I – I don't know. I never knew her. And there was the verdict – the inquest. You were there.'

'Fools!'

'You heard the evidence.'

'But not the truth. Never mind. It will come out, one way or other . . . It's what I live for, you understand that don't you? It is what I have been living for for more than ten years, biding my time, quite sure it would come right. She is guiding me, you see. She is with me, leading me, telling me. She knows. My lady never leaves me. She never did. Of all the people in this world who claimed to love her, thought they loved her, from her own mother and father on, she knew only one who truly did. She knew I worshipped her and would have died for her, any time she crooked her little finger. She still knows it. Revenge, Danny, she says. Every night she comes to me. I wake and she is there, smiling, whispering to me. Make him pay, Danny, only you can. Make the truth come out. Don't let me down. But she is teasing me. Let her down? Does she need to ask me?'

At the inquest, I had fainted, and in the turret at the Italian villa, I had fainted too. Now, I willed myself to faint, I wanted to be unconscious, it was the only way I knew I could escape her, the black figure, the white skull of a face with its burning cheeks and eyes, the terrible, relentless, insane voice.

But I could not faint. I only sat, trembling, on the edge of the bed.

In the end, she released me.

It was as though she had been in some kind of hypnotic trance, thinking and talking of Rebecca, and that, within a few seconds, she had come out of it. She said, in a perfectly normal

312

voice, 'When you are ready, please come into the sitting room. I shall ring for tea,' and she went quietly out.

I did not want to stay there, in that cold, prettily decorated shrine, a room dedicated to the memory, not only of someone long dead, but who had never been there, a morbid fantasy of a place, peopled by the shadowy figures of one woman's imagination. But I did not get up at once to follow her, I felt too shaken and unsteady.

She had left one drawer slightly open and a piece of flimsy pale apricot silken stuff trailed out of it like breath. I wondered if she had ever worn it, but I was not troubled by it, I felt no fear of Rebecca's ghost, she was not the one who threatened me.

I heard a knock on the far door, voices. I stood up and went, without glancing back, into the outer room where a young maid was setting out tea on a small table, watched sharply, critically by Mrs Danvers, and where there was an air of everyday reality from which I could draw some relief and courage.

'Please sit down, madam.'

I saw the girl glance at me. It sounded odd to her too, that she should call me that, but what else was there? I knew that 'Mrs de Winter' would never cross her lips in relation to me.

The tea was well made and hot and I drank it greedily, but we sat in silence for some while, for how could I begin to make normal, light conversation with her after what had happened? She sipped tea, watching me, neither of us ate, the cake was uncut, the scones left to go cold.

I wanted to ask her if she had sought this position out

deliberately, as soon as Favell had told her our whereabouts, I wanted to say I saw the wreath you sent, I have the card you wrote. You sent it to frighten me, didn't you? Why? Why? You say that she whispers to you and that you will never let go, never leave us alone until – until what? What will you do? What will satisfy you? Haven't you done enough in destroying Manderley? You did do that, it was you, wasn't it?

All of those questions hung in the air between us, the silence was electric with them, and they could never be asked, some words would never be spoken.

All I managed to ask, blurt out, and without preparation, so that the question surprised me, I had not known that I was going to put it, was, 'Are you happy here, Mrs Danvers?'

She looked at me pityingly, as one would look at a very stupid person, or a young, silly child. 'Happy? I have never been happy since my lady died, surely you must know that, and I never expect to be so.'

'Surely you should try and make some sort of new life now – I know –'

'You? What do you know? That she meant everything to me in life, from the first day I set eyes on her and will do until the day I die. If you do not know anything else, know that.'

'Yes,' I said. 'Yes, I suppose I do.' I felt suddenly, desperately tired. I thought I could have laid down then on the floor and slept.

'I count myself blessed to have had her, to have loved her and known her. Nothing else could possibly be of significance.'

There was nothing to say. I finished my tea.

'Purviss will bring the car round for you whenever you are ready, madam.'

Could this be all then? Had she simply wanted me to see the room, to remind me of the past? To have afternoon tea and go home again? It seemed unreal. I wanted to laugh, hysterically, sipping the last of my tea opposite to her, as she sat stiff backed and motionless, black, gaunt, staring. You are an old woman, I thought, alone and pathetic, you live in and for the past, while we have a future. And I saw the children running down the slope, saw Maxim come into the house, smiling his familiar, languid smile.

How could she touch that, how could this one old woman take any of it away? And then, I felt a great surge of new strength and resolve rise up within me; I was no longer a timid, shy, uncertain little thing, I was a woman, I had confidence and some experience, I was not afraid of Mrs Danvers. I was angry with her, angry not only with what she was trying to do now but with what she had previously done and been, the way she had tried to belittle and humiliate me, drive me from Manderley, part me from Maxim. For a moment, we looked at one another across the anonymous sitting room. She does not know me now, I thought, she is remembering the girl I was and playing upon my old fears.

I stood up. 'Mrs Danvers, I don't think you understand how very different things are now. You are living in another world – another time. Everything has changed.'

She stared at me, her eyes were hard, very bright. I could not tell what was going on in her mind.

'Please listen to me. I find it very strange and very

sad, too, that you are living like this – that you dwell on the past – talk about Mrs de Winter – Rebecca – keep that – that shrine to her; doesn't it seem strange to you? A morbid thing? What can you hope to gain from it? You will only make yourself more unhappy – you cannot live like this – don't you see that?'

'How dare you tell me what I can do? You? What do you know? You know nothing. You never knew her.'

'No, though I feel as if I do – I have lived in her shadow – lived with other people's memories of her for what feels like half my adult life. It seems odd that I never knew her.'

'She would have despised you – laughed at you.'

'Probably. Yes. As you do.'

'Yes.'

'But you see, that doesn't hurt me – doesn't affect me. I don't care about that. I have Maxim – we have a new home – a new life. A future. The past cannot touch us now.'

The laugh she spat out then was a harsh, bitter, dreadful thing.

'Leave us alone. Leave us. There is nothing you can do, no possible harm. Don't you see that? That I cannot be afraid of you.' It was the truth. I meant it. It would not be Mrs Danvers who could hurt us. It was not pleasant to be in the room with her, the black figure and gaunt, white, impassive face still made me shudder. But I had drawn her sting, I felt superior to her, standing there now, something had happened and I drew courage from it, courage and resolve. I wanted to laugh in her face. 'Goodbye, Mrs Danvers,' I said, and held out my hand to her. She did not take it, only went on staring at me, but I did not feel embarrassed or awkward, I simply withdrew my hand, and met her gaze without flinching.

As she crossed the room towards the bell and the outer door, and I followed her, she paused and without looking at me now, said, 'He should confess. That will be the best way of all. It is what she wants you know, to have it out in the open and dealt with at last. Then it will be over. She will not let me rest until then, you see. It is what I am for now, all I live for. But you know that don't you? You understand.'

And she went ahead of me, down through the silent, cold house, without another word, and once I was in the car and it was moving slowly away, stood watching me intently, her white face quite stiff, quite expressionless, until we had rounded the bend between the great, spreading laurel bushes that lined the drive, and I lost sight of her.

CHAPTER

Nineteen

I could not eat that night, and I had not expected to sleep, but the afternoon had drained me, and I slept the instant, heavy sleep of extreme exhaustion, lying on my bed with the covers thrown back, which helped me to be cooler. There were no dreams of any kind, no voices, and I awoke quite peacefully, into silence.

Moonlight flooded the room. I got out of bed, went to the window to look at the garden, and as I did so, remembered Manderley on a summer night, and the garden after Beatrice's funeral, and it seemed that I had never been easy and peaceful for long, that some dreadful thing had always threatened, or else I was in the midst of turmoil. And so it was now, and I wondered if it would ever be different. There seemed every reason why it should not.

I did not want to be there for hours, brooding, going over and over the previous afternoon. I thought I might as well be outside, sit in the garden that had come to mean so much to me and where I had, for a few weeks, been so happy.

It was hot and still but as I went through the side door and on to the terrace, what I was most aware of, apart from the silver-white moonlight that overlay everything, was the night scent of the flowers, the honeysuckle that hung in thick overgrown swags on the brick side wall, and the white stocks in the border, the trough full of pinks beside the gate. I stood still and breathed them in and could not get enough of them, the scent filled me and calmed me, and brought the recent past back to me too, and the sweet smelling climber whose starry flowers were pricked out against their green foliage on the wall in Italy.

And at once, the memory was spoilt, as my pleasure in the flowers had been spoilt there, by those other, perfect white flowers, lying on the churchyard grass. But I was used to it now, and I thought that I must simply accept and carry on. One thought led always to another and the thoughts danced in a ring around and around me, and I was coiled up in and snared by them.

I wandered along the paths, across the dry grass, to where an old, comfortable bench stood, under an apple tree – the fruit was heavy and silver and before long it would ripen and fall. Already, in the afternoons, I had heard the grind of the threshing machines in the fields and the heavy wagons going along the lane at the end of the day. Harvest. Autumn. The turning of the year. I wondered how much it would matter, and whether I would mind the winter when it came.

I sat down, and for a few moments, there under the beautiful tree, I seemed to float, to detach myself from my own body and look down upon the garden. I was very tired still, and the afternoon seemed like some odd hallucination, thinking back to that dark house, and to Mrs Danvers, in the pretty, nightmarish bedroom, I wondered if it had ever happened or whether I had made it up, as a child weaves a vivid fantasy that runs through its everyday life so convincingly that it cannot tell where reality begins and ends.

And at that moment, as I sat alone in the night garden, I began to tremble with absolute, cold fear, that I was somehow mad, that at last everything that had happened, and that I had lived with and kept to myself for so long, had come together to turn my mind. Perhaps I was like Favell and Mrs Danvers, perhaps my eyes looked wild and strange, perhaps the craziness had begun to show in my own face. I put my hand out and touched the back of the other, ran it up my arm. It is all right, I said, it is perfectly all right. Maxim will be here the day after tomorrow. Everything will be better then.

Maxim. I tried to picture him and could not. Every face I had ever seen in my life, it seemed, and which had never meant anything to me, was there, the faces of hotel porters and waiters in foreign cafés, of Clarice the maid and Jack Favell and the priest at Beatrice's funeral, my father's face, the young man who had been with Mrs van Hopper. Frith. Colonel Julyan. And then Mrs Danvers' white bony skull, and hollow eye sockets and bright, mad, staring eyes. But not Maxim. Whenever I turned to him, there was nothing, a blur, a name, I could not see him, I had no idea what my husband looked like.

There was a sudden rustle, a faint movement in the long

grass close to the hedge behind me. The garden was a cold, unfamiliar, haunted place. I did not recognise anything. It was as though I had never been here before. Something moved again. It might have been some night bird or tiny, hidden creature but it was not, I knew that it was not. I waited for her to emerge, for her shadow to fall across the grass in front of me, curdling the moonlight, but it did not, and I supposed that she preferred to stay out of sight, and torment me more subtly and surreptitiously.

I saw nothing, only the voice was there, the whispering voice, cool and soft and limpid as water flowing into me. 'You are of no account at all. Less than none. He is the one who must confess. It is what I have been living for, that the truth will come out. She is guiding me, you see. She knows, and she tells me. He is a murderer. How does that feel? Surely you think of it. Yes – I know you do, I see it in your face, your eyes. When you look at him, catch sight of him in an unguarded moment. When you are together. When his hands touch you. His hands held the gun, his hands were covered in her blood, his hands lifted her body into the boat. His hands. I have waited such a long time. I am so tired. She is not. She will never tire. 'I'll wait forever, Danny,' she says, 'but you have to help me.' I do. I am helping her now. It will come out, of course you know that it must. Did you really expect to come back, and live your lives out here quite happy and undisturbed, like innocent people? To enjoy this lovely house. So lovely, but not like Manderley. To have children here, and bring them up without their knowing the truth, pretending that the past did not exist. Of course you did not. I shall never rest. I shall never leave you alone until I have done what she wants. Make it easy for us. Then it will be over for you too.'

On and on the voice whispered and I sat and heard it in the cold moonlight and could neither stop my ears nor move away. She went, in the end, she released me as she had done before. There was silence in my head and the garden was empty. I went back to bed and slept like a dead thing until after sunrise.

It was still early, I was heavy eyed and numb with sleep when the telephone rang.

'Maxim has taken the first train,' Frank Crawley said. 'He thought he would get off once he'd decided, rather than wait to ring you himself.' His voice sounded so matter of fact and cheerful, the old, dependable Frank, I almost wept to hear it.

'Oh – Frank, thank you. I thought perhaps – no, well it doesn't matter.'

'Is everything all right?'

'Yes – yes, of course.'

'You sound anxious. Has something happened?'

Why did I not tell him? I had no one I could confide in, knew no one else who would have understood at once every nuance and shade of meaning involved in the story, I needed desperately to talk to him, my head seemed to burn with the fears and thoughts and whisperings and memories that flickered about inside it, telling Frank would ease them, he would say the right, reassuring thing, know at once what I ought to do. Frank was a rock of steadfastness and sanity.

He had been a friend to me at Manderley when I had been bewildered and afraid, he had told me about Rebecca, he had been my supporter, always on my side. I had had no one else to turn to and I still had not. I knew I must tell him.

But I did not.

'I've been by myself long enough,' I said. 'I'm glad Maxim will be home tonight. There's nothing else, nothing wrong at all.'

I spent the whole of that day alone. Dora sent a message up by Ned to say she had an abscessed tooth and must go into Harburgh, and he worked at the farthest end of the garden, I scarcely caught sight of him. No one telephoned, the post was thin and none of it for me, no one came to the house. I could not settle, I wandered from room to room, fiddling with this or that, unhappy, accomplishing nothing. It was still hot, but there was no sun now, heavy, close, copper coloured cloud pressed in from the hills and hung down over the house. Gnats jazzed in little clouds above the pond, under the trees. I felt suspended, restless, oddly afraid, but there were no voices, no whispers, no shadow or footfall came over the grass.

It is all nonsense, I said to myself quite suddenly, she is mad, what harm can she do? and went upstairs to change, riffling through my wardrobe of plain, pleasant, serviceable things to find something I thought Maxim liked. I remembered the flimsy silks and chiffons, the rows of expensive, beautiful clothes, but not with envy, for what good had they done her, how had they made her loved and happy, what meaning did they have now, except for a furtive, obsessed old woman?

I stood, and looked slowly around the room, it was

calm, I thought, a pleasant, unobtrusive room, a refuge, as steadying as the house itself, and it seemed that it had been waiting quietly for me to come to out of some feverish nightmare in which I had behaved wildly but was not to blame, and the house knew that and accepted me back like some wayward, passionate child who has had a tantrum of rejection.

I had put on a cream linen frock and tied my hair off my face, and as I did so, looking in the mirror on my dressing table, I saw some streaks of grey at my temples, and began to push them out of sight, but they would not be concealed, and then I thought that they did not matter. There was something else, too. I was still quite a young woman, but I was older by some years than Rebecca had ever been, and it occurred to me as a sort of triumph. She had no grey hairs, I said, and for a second, the image of her in the picture came into my mind and I felt nothing but a mild, detached kind of pity.

Where was Rebecca? Dead. Nowhere. I did not know, it was a line of thought I had never followed. I was not deep and questioning in that way, but now I remembered the child I myself had been, and the growing girl, and then the gauche young woman who had met Maxim, the bride arriving at Manderley, the passionate, loving, bewildered wife in awe and dread of it all, places, people, memories, I saw them all standing in a line, one fading and giving way to the other. They led here, to this woman with the beginnings of grey hair, staring out of the mirror. They were that person. Me. And yet they were not, they were ghosts, and they had vanished. Where to? Where? They were not dead, as she was dead, but they no more existed than the newborn baby or toddling child I had also once been. How many selves do we contain, like Russian dolls concealed within one another?

For a moment, I became dreadfully frightened, for I had lost touch with the person I had known so well for so many years, the calm, dull, steady, loving wife, who had been so content to live in exile, unquestioningly loyal, having no secrets, knowing no shadows, hearing no whispering voices. I needed her, I needed her strength and calmness, I needed to lean on her and confide in her. I had changed, and gone on changing, but I did not fully remember how it had begun, or understand why.

But then, I heard a blackbird pink in alarm, scurrying low into the bushes on the far side of the garden, and the sound of car wheels on the drive, and after a moment, Maxim's quick footstep, and his voice, calling to me, and the sounds seemed to recall me, so that I was quite myself, running along the passage and down the stairs, to where he stood in the hall, looking up to me.

CHAPTER

Twenty

Cobbett's Brake was almost completely enclosed in its bowl, with the trees rising beyond, but at just one point there was a spot where the eye was led out, through a gap in the fold of the hill. It was on the west side, at the far end of the kitchen garden, and when we had first come there was only rather an overgrown and scruffy track, leading to an old beech hedge. I had stood several times for the pleasure of the unexpected sight of a distant, silver church spire which at certain times of the day caught the sun, and best of all, in the evening, seemed to recede in a violet blue haze merging with the darkening countryside and sky, and over the past months, I had become especially attached to this quiet corner of the garden. By looking through old books and magazines in the evenings – for I was trying hard to learn as much as I could – I had put together a design, sketching it out several times, before eventually taking it to Ned. He had cleared the ground, and we had planted a little glade of trees, beyond a door in the wall of the kitchen garden, and at the bottom of the glade, we had set a walk of nut trees, tying the tops loosely together to form an arch. The beech hedge had been cut down and a small wicket gate set in the gap; eventually, perhaps next summer, I would put a seat, so that I could walk down through the glade and under the nut trees, and then sit, to look out and ahead to the gap in the hills and the silver spire, but for now, a couple of old tree stumps with a plank across served.

I was proud of my piece of garden, I loved it because it was all mine and particular to me, a vision achieved, not inherited or got back from any previous person. I had never felt such a sense of pleasure and ownership before, though I knew it was not much, set beside the other, grander parts of the garden. In the autumn, Ned and I would plant hundreds of bulbs under the trees; he had even investigated an old spring that came up from the ground under some stones, wondering whether we might somehow bring it to the surface again and make a channel for it to flow through.

It was the most beautiful evening, the ends of the days were always best just now, when the staleness and closeness of the late summer air dispersed, and there was a sweetness and the faintest smell of mist beneath the trees. We took our drinks down through the garden, towards the nut walk and the bench, Maxim talking about Scotland, his fishing with Frank, the boys, how the future plans looked now, and I listened to him, and I felt very still and calm and detached, as though he were a person I scarcely knew.

The Maxim I had first met all those years ago had seemed such an urbane man, a man of hotels and London and suits and society, even when we had been at Manderley, he had seemed like it. He had cared very much for the cut of his shirt and where his shaving cream was bought, and whether the post arrived precisely on time. I had been afraid of him then, alarmed by his routine and his standards, and although he had never made impossible demands of me, I had always gone in fear and trembling that at any moment they would be made and I would not live up to his expectations.

But then, everything had changed, and he had crumbled in front of me, and become wholly broken and lost, during our years of exile, dependent on me, on my strength and devotion, and closeness. I had grown familiar with that, loved and felt happy with this new Maxim, and been able to relax and be untroubled, so long as we stuck to our safe little measured routine.

Now, looking at him as he sat beside me, I realised how greatly he had changed again; Cobbett's Brake had been my need, I had first seen and loved and passionately desired it, it had been altogether my dream to come here.

So it had seemed, so I had believed, yet it was Maxim who had been transformed by it. He was a countryman now, in a different way, he was coming to know and love this place, these acres, this particular part of England, in a deeply satisfied, intimate way, to walk the fields and look at the woods and hedgerows, to understand the crops and animals, know the farming tenants, to be the estate landlord in a wholly absorbed and committed way, rather than in the more aloof, feudal manner that had been his with Manderley.

He looked younger, his skin had darkened because he was so much outdoors, he had lost his old, city veneer almost entirely, though he was still well dressed, by an innate instinct for the best cloth and cut and style, he looked right without effort, in a way I never had and now never would.

I sat and drank my sherry and listened, and looked at him, and after a while, we were silent, and I could just hear, very faintly, the tinny little bell from the far away church, striking the hour. I smiled and nodded agreement, too, as I had welcomed him, and what had happened while he had been away, I buried deep, deep, and turned from. He would never know from me that she had been here and cast her black shadow across the grass and tainted the air and terrified me with her madness, so that I could never feel the same about the house again, but only about this corner, beyond the glade, at the end of the little nut walk. This was mine, she had not been here, not seen or known of it. This she could never spoil.

'Something is wrong,' Maxim said.

The air was suddenly chilly, and I had no jacket. We were walking slowly back towards the house. 'Do you think Frank really may come?' For that had been the talk. The Crawleys were to come down for a few days in September, to see how they felt, and look at Tinutt's Farm, which was empty, and which Maxim planned to make over to them. He needed Frank, the estate was far too big for him to run in the way he wanted, on his own. 'I should love to have them nearby – I'd feel we were somehow extending the family.'

He had stopped in front of me, and now, he looked down at me, his eyes steady on my face, his hands on my shoulders. 'You can't deceive me or hide it from me or lie to me, you know that we have no secrets.'

I could not speak, only thought of the little layers of secrets that had begun to pile up since we had come home. And before, before.

'What has happened? Look at me.'

He spoke in the old, curt, clipped way I had first known. 'I know you too well. Do you think I have forgotten? I know there have been shadows – anxieties – fears even. I've lain awake at night beside you and known it and seen that troubled expression in your eyes. You are very dear and good and try to be bright and to conceal it from me. You tried very hard when we were abroad and I always noticed, always knew.'

I felt tears begin to sting at the back of my eyes, I wanted to lean on him and cry and tell him everything then, every detail, every past small fear, to pour out what had happened since I had found the wreath, about Jack Favell and Mrs Danvers and most of all, about the terrible, whispering voices. I felt his hands touch me, and knew them so well, the hands I had looked and looked at, holding the wheel of the car, and peeling a tangerine and using a nail file and resting on the rail of the ship, hands whose exact shape I could trace in my mind's eye and which I loved so well, which meant Maxim to me more than even his eyes or his mouth, his voice or the shape of his head.

But I could not quiet the voice, evil, insidious, disturbing, that whispered to me of the same hands. 'I'm tired,' I said. 'It's been so hot. And I've hated you being away.'

I turned and went in through the door.

Why did I not tell him then? I know now that it was what I should have done, without any question, he would not have been angry, he was strong enough now, he was no longer afraid of the past, did not need me to protect him. He had come through. Yet I said nothing. I was afraid and confused and far from him, and when he

330

came behind me into the house, I began to question him more about the Crawleys. He replied briefly, before going down to his study and closing the door. The moment had gone. I carried my secrets still with me, and they were hard, heavy, bitter things.

When I went up to bed later, Maxim was standing at the open window. On the slopes above the house, the little owls were flying between the trees, making their short, harsh cries.

'I wish it would rain,' I said.

He did not speak. I went to stand beside him, looking out, but he did not touch me, or turn to me. I was puzzled, sensing a new, different kind of withdrawal. I did not know how to deal with it. I was to blame, I had shut things away from him, and sensing it, he was hurt.

No. There was something else. I felt as if we were being caught and held tighter and tighter in a web of intricately tangled, invisible threads, and whatever movement I made to break or smooth them simply wound them fast.

I lay beside Maxim for a long time, miserable, frightened, hearing the owls, far from sleep.

But at breakfast, he glanced up from the newspaper and said, 'The weather is set to hold. Perhaps we should give a party.'

'A party? Who for? What kind of a party? Why?'

'My dear girl, there's no need to look so panic-stricken. You'll be able to show off the garden.'

'There isn't anything to show off, it's past its best now, and besides, I've hardly begun to do things to it.'

'Does it matter? It looks fine to me, it's tidy, there are flowers. People will admire it.'

'What people?'

'Neighbours – people from about – we can't be hermits and as we're buying land and enlarging the place, everyone will be interested and quite simply, it's important to get on well with people locally. The Butterleys seem to know everyone, ask her who to invite. I've already met some of course. And spread the net a bit, there are a lot of surrounding villages.'

Yes. I knew, I knew. I did not want to think of it.

At Manderley, there had been endless visits to and by neighbours, half the county had come to call, and parties were expected, Rebecca had given parties, she was famous for them. I remembered my only party as mistress there, the fancy dress ball when I had made such an appalling mistake.

'I thought we would be quiet here,' I said. 'You never much liked all the social round. You said you wanted us to come back and – ' I bit my lip. Hide? I could not say that. But he was changing so much, changing back, I thought, becoming in so many ways the old, confident, Maxim, in charge of things, knowing precisely what he wanted and how it all should be, the time between when he had been lost and withdrawn, had gone forever. I realised that I wanted it back, because only that Maxim, in the years of exile, had been close enough to me.

He stood up. 'I don't mean a grand affair – just a garden thing. Drinks – you can see to that can't you? It's what you need.'

'What do you mean? Something to occupy me? Something to pass the time?'

'No, I do not mean that.'

'I'm perfectly happy.'

'Are you?'

'Yes, Maxim, yes, yes – what is happening? Why are we quarrelling? We never argue, never quarrel.'

He went to the door. 'Sometimes being perfectly happy is not quite enough,' he said, and went out.

I stood, looking down at his empty cup and the apple peel, neatly coiled on his plate. I did not understand what he meant. Everything was strange and different and I did not know why, or what to do about it.

Miserably, I went to telephone Bunty Butterley, about our neighbours.

Twenty One

But it would be my party. I would plan it and arrange and prepare for it, no one else would take it over. It was going to be a wonderful day, because I would make it so. Once I had realised that, I felt quite differently, I began to look forward, and at once, the shadows retreated and there were no more whisperings.

When Maxim had first spoken of it, I had thought at once of the Manderley ball, and been terrified, the evening had returned in a series of tableaux, frozen in my mind, I gazed upon them, and upon myself in the midst of them, and it was as if my heart stopped.

But that had had nothing to do with me, it had been a lavish, ostentatious affair, of the sort I had never liked nor would ever want, and it had been so God knew why – for no good, stated reason. Not, certainly, because any of us wanted it. It was a tradition, and a duty, it was the sort of thing Manderley was for; the county had expected it. 'It used to make the summer for all of us in this part of the world,' a tiresome woman had said, 'we all miss the Manderley gaiety.'

Rebecca's, she had meant, balls and parties were how she had showed off, and got people to adore her. They were what she was best at. The party had been her creation, hers and Mrs Danvers', and the staff's, and in Rebecca's absence, things had been no different, I had had no part or say in it at all. Perhaps, I saw now, if I had wanted to, had insisted in hearing every detail of the form and plans, had decided on this or that change or innovation, I would have enjoyed it more – at least before the horrible business of my own costume, the trap into which Mrs Danvers had malevolently led me. But I had been too nervous of them all, even of the men bringing in the chairs, and so it had swept by me like a river in full spate and I had stood hopelessly on the bank, watching.

We could never have that sort of affair now, in the years so soon after the war it would have seemed indecently out of place, Maxim had not suggested it, there would be no lobster or champagne, no band or fairy lights strung by the yard through the trees, no especially laid dance floor, no fireworks or fancy dress. Teams of estate workers had left their normal jobs for weeks and given themselves over to it, the servants had talked and thought of nothing else.

But there were no estate workers here, apart from real farmers and their men who were gradually becoming our tenants, and we did not have teams of servants, I had Dora and Ned, and the chance of a girl from the village or Mrs Peck, if I really needed them. Cobbett's Brake was not Manderley, it was not grand at all, it was loved and shabby, and old and beautiful, it did not belong to half the county.

I went out and climbed the slope and sat on the grass, looking down at it. Mrs Danvers had only darkened it briefly, and now it lay in the light again, given wholly back to me.

I began to make plans for the party reluctantly, because I could not think of any more reasons to resist Maxim's idea. But as the days passed, and I went several times to see Bunty and twice, she came to me, I began to take pleasure in it, it became fun, a challenge. It would be my party after all.

It was to be a garden party, in the later part of an afternoon. There would be tables, as many as I could find or borrow, set out under the trees, on the terrace, on the lawn, and the drawing room and the small sitting room in the house would be open too, older people could take their tea and sit comfortably in the coolness – for it would be hot, I was sure of that – the long, hot, golden days went drifting on and no end to them seemed in sight. But I would not only ask older people, I said to Bunty. 'I want the young – will you ask your girls and ask them to bring friends – I'll get Ned to look at the old tennis court, he can mow it and see if he can mend the net, and they can play croquet, too, I found an old set in the cellar – I'll clean it up. I want there to be young people laughing and enjoying it all too.'

There would be tea laid out in the kitchen and under the sunshade at the side of the house, a good, old fashioned, proper tea, which people expected, sandwiches and cakes and scones and fruit bread, and raspberries and cream. Later, for the people who lingered, enjoying the last of the late sunshine, there would be drinks.

The only decorations I planned were as many flowers as I could put in jugs and vases and bowls on all the tables, and everywhere in the house. Bunty promised to bring what she could, and so did Dora and Ned, and they would be simple,

336

country flowers, not stiff, false, florists' arrangements.

'I must say, I think it's tremendous of you,' Bunty said. Her face was beaming and she was adding names to a list, as they occurred to her – I was relying on her almost totally, to provide us with the right guests.

'We haven't had a party hereabouts since, oh, before the war, if you don't count all the usual harvest homes and that sort of country thing. It was when the Kirkley girl got married, the last big do, and there was a dance in the old tithe barn, and they rang the bells at midnight! I should think there'll be great excitement – you are good.'

So no one thought it was only our duty, then, they would be grateful and happy to come, but it was not that we were going to a huge amount of expense and trouble because the county said it was no more than was expected of us, Cobbett's Brake was not Manderley and no one thought anything about the de Winters here.

'You were right,' I said to Maxim later. 'I'm glad you thought of a party.'

'Good.' He did not look up from his book.

'I'm still surprised, that's all. You were so worried – people would ask questions – bring – bring things up –'

'Yes.'

'No one has.'

'No.'

I wandered away. I could not reach him, it was a pointless conversation.

But I would enjoy the party, I must. It would be the beginning of things, I said.

And so it seemed. The weather held, we worked the whole of the day in the sun, Dora and her sister, Mrs Peck, Ned. We carried out tables and chairs borrowed from the village hall, and set them up, and spread freshly laundered cloths, flowers stood in buckets and bowls in every sink, huge sheaves of chrysanthemums, grasses, beech leaves, the last of the roses. Everyone was cheerful, laughing and making silly jokes, everyone wanted it to be a success, and I was in the midst of them, asking for this, suggesting that, doing things with them, they came to me to ask what was wanted, how something should be done. I saw the point of it all, as I had never done with anything at Manderley.

Maxim spent part of the morning away from the house, but just before lunch, which would be cold, a salad, he came to find me in the garden. 'You look pleased.'

I pushed the hair out of my eyes. 'It's fun,' I said, 'I'm enjoying it so much. Do you mind?'

I looked up at him. 'What is it?' I said. 'What's wrong?'

It was there, in his eyes, but I could not tell what.

'It will be all right,' I said. 'Everyone will be kind.'

'Of course.'

'Maxim.'

He touched the back of his hand lightly against my face. What was it? What? I took his hand and held it there. I did not want the shadows falling between us.

'Should I put another trestle up on the terrace there, Mrs de Winter? Dora says the kitchen is spilling over, just about.'

We were caught up in the party again, the day had

338

its own momentum.

And after all, it was worth it, it was the most beautiful day, I thought, walking round just before it all began, it would be perfect. The sun was still warm, but there was a gentleness about it now, the midday glare was softened, when I went across the garden under the trees, beneath the rose arch, the grass sprang to the touch of my feet where Ned had mowed it lightly, releasing a faint, sweet, nostalgic smell.

Everything was expectant, as though a play were about to begin. Everything was untouched, undisturbed. The cloths hung in folds, the chairs against them, the croquet mallets and tennis balls were set out, waiting for games to start. I went through the kitchen garden gate and out under the trees of the nut walk where the shadows were dappled and when I lifted up my hand to move aside a branch, the light played like water to and fro on the leafy ground. Ahead of me, I saw the green countryside and the church spire, framed in the last arch, and I rested in it, I felt myself let go of some last nervousness and worry inside myself as I let out a breath. I realised that I was excited, like a child. Nothing would go wrong, there would be no dreadful mistakes, they would all come and we would welcome them, and so would the house and the garden. We would give them all such pleasure.

In a moment, I must go back, in a moment, the first of the cars, voices, people. It would begin. But just now, I waited, in the quietness under the nut trees, and no one came to find me, no one was concerned that I was there. If I ran away now, I thought suddenly, no one would notice, it would all take place as planned, without me. But that was not true, as it had been so true of the ball at Manderley. There, I had been incidental to everything, there, I had had no place, I had not mattered. Here, I was at the centre.

This was mine.

From far away, I heard a voice, calling, the chink of plates, but even then, I waited, I did not move, only stood, holding the still moment closely to myself, wanting the world to stop here, just exactly here. But then, glancing round, I saw the children, coming quietly under the nut trees towards me, holding out their hands, faces shining with expectation. 'Come with us,' they said. 'Come on now.'

And so I went, turning my back upon the distant countryside and the silver spire, under the nut trees and through the gate, into the garden, where the people had begun to arrive.

Whenever I have remembered it, during all the years since, I remember a day of delight, perfect in every way, until the end came. So many people, so much laughter and talk in the sun, so many faces turned happily to one another, and to us; and the young people who had come with the Butterleys hit the tennis balls anywhere, and ran to rescue them, after they had gone sailing through the gaps in the old wire. I remember the toc of ball on racquet, and the heavier clunk of the croquet strikes, and little ripples of applause. The sun shone, and moved, and a violet shadow crept over the slopes, but we were all in the light and would be so for hours yet.

And suddenly, easily, Maxim and I came together and I thought that nothing had been wrong, nothing, it had all been my worry and fantasy. We moved among them separately, welcoming, talking, laughing, being introduced, but every now and again, were pulled together, and walked across the grass with linked hands or arms, for a moment, and there were no shadows, nothing but love and easiness lay between us.

There was a moment I can look at now, whenever I choose, it is as clear as a picture in a frame in front of me, a moment when we stood together and I saw them all around us, poised, frozen in time. Dora coming out of the kitchen carrying a tray loaded with white china, Ned following, carrying a heavy, steaming jug of hot water, a woman setting down a cup, a man lifting his hand to pick a dead head off the climbing rose, Bunty Butterley standing at the back of the tennis court, holding a racquet, threatening to play, her head thrown back in laughter. Maxim is smiling, holding a lighter to someone's cigarette, I can see the exact curve of his neck.

The grass is pale on the surface, hay coloured where it is so dry, and the house rises up behind us all, and the chimneys, the buttress on the far side, the tables and windows and rose red walls, all of a piece, setting off the play which is being acted in the garden.

The boys are somewhere, too, playing hide and seek, chasing balls, the little one under a table, not far away from me. They are only just out of sight. But what I see most clearly when I look at it now, is myself, at the heart of it, in my cream linen dress, what I remember most vividly of all is the feeling I had, of enjoyment and love and pride and deep, contented pleasure. I feel it again, from far away, like an old scent caught in a bottle, and opened again. When I catch the feeling faintly, I am back in that place, on that last, perfect day, before it was all, all so quickly over.

Someone moved, the kaleidoscope was shaken, and the bright pieces fell out in a different pattern. The sun caught one of the windows and the glass flared and flamed incandescent coppery red.

Bunty was a few paces from me, so that I heard her voice quite clearly. 'Good heavens! Old Lady Beddow's just arriving. Now that was a long shot on my part. She almost never goes anywhere nowadays but she likes to be kept in touch. You really can count it a successful party!'

I suppose that I knew, even in the split second before I looked up and across to where they were coming very slowly under the archway into the garden, though I had not known her name and the address had been unfamiliar when I copied it from Bunty's list – but then, most of them were.

I knew, yet for a split second, to see her shocked me, I was no longer afraid, and yet the sight of the tall, black figure moving slowly nearer gave me the old shudder, the old hollow, helpless sensation, it would never finally leave me. But I knew also quite surely that what I had said to her in her sitting room that afternoon had been true. I saw her for what she was, a peculiar, old, sad, crazy woman who had lost touch with reality, and had no final power over me in any way.

But Maxim did not know that. Maxim did not know that I had seen her, it was how her presence here would affect him, what he would think and feel, that was my only anxiety now, and it preoccupied me completely.

I saw her black shadow fall across the sunlit grass.

Maxim was coming from the opposite side. I dared not look at his face, I knew what it would be like, a tight, white lipped mask, polite, controlled, showing nothing. One or two people were glancing around, and where she stood, with the old, old woman clinging to her arm, there seemed to be a space, a circle within which it was silent and still and cold.

I rushed to pull out a chair, to clear things from a table. 'Good afternoon, Mr de Winter. I have come with Lady Beddow – she was very anxious to meet you. She knew the house long ago. Perhaps you could speak up, she does not hear very clearly.' She glanced around, and I felt her eyes on my face, staring, gleaming from the hollow sockets in the skull. I saw amusement in them.

'Good afternoon, madam. How very pleasant and how nice the garden is looking, though of course, a lot of the flowers have gone over since I was last here.'

I felt Maxim stiffen, but he would not look at me. He had taken the old woman's arm and was settling her into the chair, saying this or that polite thing, while Mrs Danvers stood, poised and black as a crow, hands together in front of her. I fled to the kitchen, to get hot water, fresh tea, threw food on to a plate anyhow, my hands trembling so violently that I dropped it and had to begin again. I was not afraid of anything except Maxim's reaction.

'Are you all right Mrs de Winter? You look so white – has anything happened? Here, let me do that, don't you worry.' Dora was bending, clearing the mess cheerfully.

'Thank you – I'm sorry, Dora – sorry – I was – it's nothing –'

'You are honoured, if that Lady Beddow has come.'

'Yes – yes, so I've been told.'

'Never goes out much at all, hasn't for years. There, that's all clear. Let me do that, you'll scald yourself on the boiling water. Sit down a minute, you've tired yourself, that's what it is, all that work, getting ready and then the excitement, and the sun. Let me pour you a hot cup of tea and you just stay here a minute. They're getting on fine, they won't miss you.'

I sat down, as she said, grateful for her easy, friendly concern, letting her chatter on as she passed out tea and rearranged fresh food on plates, and after a moment, put my head down on my arms and rested it there. She was right, I was tired, but the exhausted, weak sensation in my limbs and the odd light headedness had nothing to do with tiredness, they came through shock and dread and foreboding. I wondered vaguely what Maxim was doing, saying, most of all, what he was thinking. Nothing else mattered.

'You drink this while it's hot – and I daresay you haven't eaten anything yourself have you? Been too busy seeing to everyone else. Well, it's always the way at parties. Have these egg sandwiches, I've cut them fresh.'

'Thank you Dora. I'm fine. Just a bit tired suddenly, as you say.' I stared at the white bread with its crumbs of damp egg oozing from the sides and felt suddenly very sick, and would have got up and gone upstairs, except that I heard Maxim speak from the doorway.

'You'd better come out again, hadn't you?' he said coldly.

I dared not look at him. I could imagine his face, I had seen it before, the last time we had had a party and she had spoiled it, in a different way, but just as deliberately, just as thoroughly. There was no delight left in the day now, no pleasure, it was broken and the pieces thrown about anyhow. We had to get through it, that was all. It wouldn't be for long. They would go, she would go. Then I would be alone with him, then I would have to explain. What should I say? What did I have to tell him?

Dora was watching me, I could see alarm and concern in her face. She had never heard Maxim speak to me in that way, never seen anything but love and easiness between us. I tried to smile, to reassure her. I said, 'I'll ask Maxim when we should serve the drinks – I'm sure a lot of people will want to stay, they all seem quite happy.'

And so they did, I saw it as I went out again. The sun had slipped down a little further, late afternoon was merging into evening, the smell of it was in the air. The tennis game seemed to be over, and only a couple of people were playing croquet. Everyone else was sitting at the tables, or in deck chairs, talking quietly, strolling along the paths, some going towards the kitchen garden and the nut walk. They seemed so at home, I thought, as if it were a hotel and they had paid to be staying here, the grounds belonged, for the time being, to them. I minded that, hated it passionately, and there was nothing at all that I could do.

I went over to where Maxim stood, to the side of a group of people. He was talking politely about something to do with the farms, bringing back some land to good heart. From his face and his voice, they would know nothing, it was all so pleasant, all so normal. I recognised faces, could not put names to them, smiled vaguely, generally round. I was the hostess, I was on view, there were certain ways to behave, and that helped me a little.

'I was wondering if we should serve the drinks. Dora and Gwen are clearing the last of the tea things now.'

'I'll see to it. You will all have something, of course?' He smiled, as I was smiling, and they smiled back, I saw their mouths move, heard the appreciative little murmurs. I wanted them to go. I did not. I wanted to touch Maxim, for reassurance, say something to him, that would explain everything. Be alone in the garden with him. I did not. I wanted none of it ever to have happened.

'You must be so very proud of everything,' I heard her say in the sweetest of soft voices. She had come silently across the grass and was standing very close to us, I could smell the faintly musty smell of her clothes. She was motionless, eyes not leaving our faces, hands bone white on the black dress. Why always black, I wanted to scream out at her, why? 'It will be such a lovely home for you in time.'

She turned slightly. The people around us, half a dozen or so, seemed to be mesmerised by her, and puzzled too. No one seemed to find anything to say, they merely waited, silent, polite, listening. 'Of course, nothing will ever take the place of Manderley. Mr and Mrs de Winter came from a magnificent house – it is some years ago now – I was privileged to be there then. I'm sure you will have heard of it.'

'Mrs Danvers –'

'And the tragedy there. Everyone heard about it, didn't they?'

'I say, now you mention the name – Manderley – Manderley – I seem to remember something – ' Some fat, gobbling man with yellow whites to his blue eyes. I wanted to put my hands around his throat.

'Yes, it was famous – in that part of the world, I suppose it was the most famous place of all, for every reason – I'm sure Mr and Mrs de Winter would agree with me.'

She turned slightly to look at Maxim, I saw their two faces in profile, the skin stretched taut over their bones, eyes full of loathing. I felt soft and weak, like some helpless, amorphous thing trapped between rocks. I was not there, they did not see me or take any note of me, I was of no relevance now.

'Under the circumstances, I feel you are so very fortunate to have found happiness here. I hope it can continue.'

There was a strange little silence. No one moved. I looked at the face of some woman in a red frock, and saw her eyes flick away from Mrs Danvers, saw that she was uneasy, but did not know quite why.

Maxim might have been turned to stone. I stood between them, knowing quite certainly now that in some way she would eventually succeed as she intended, and as she believed that Rebecca intended. She would destroy us.

I know now that the moment when I should have summoned up my strength and defiance and courage to stand up to her for the last time came then, in the garden on that late afternoon. But I did not take it, I did not confront her and defy her, did not tell her that she had no power over us, could not touch us, that we were impregnable and she a deranged, deluded, vengeful old woman. I let the moment slip away and did not make use of it. It would not come back.

Strangely enough, the end of the party was not spoiled, my memory of it is not unhappy. Some left early, Lady Beddow and Mrs Danvers did not stay to drink. I watched the black car slide away up the drive and through the gates and it was as if the air had lightened after an oppressive storm. I turned back into the garden and wanted to laugh and dance on the grass and hold out my arms to embrace everyone who was left. I smiled at people, they seemed old, dear, good friends. I did not look for Maxim.

The young ones were playing tennis again, a rather silly game in which people kept swopping racquets and places and partners and the balls went anywhere, there were shrieks of delight, shouts, jokes. I stood for quite a long time watching them, and then went around the croquet course with nice, amiable Bill Butterley, who flirted with me and flattered me and made me smile. The drinks came out, trays of glasses chinking gently, and people exclaimed and raised them and drank and were pleased. There was a light heartedness, they began to regroup, old friends came together, I saw people strolling under the rose arch, up towards the nut walk, pulling the tables forward into the last patch of sun. But it was cooler now, there were violet shadows over the grass. I went into the house and switched on the lamps, and the house seemed to sparkle and glow, and sail like a ship out on the darkening evening.

I did not look for Maxim.

Some of the young people left the court and scrambled up the grassy slopes, pulling each other, laughing and calling; but once there, they grew quiet and sat together in small, still, contented groups, enjoying the gentle drift of the party down to its close. I became strangely contented and calm myself, suspended in a sort of bubble, immune from feeling, not anxious, not looking ahead, and I had an odd sense that this was the end of more than a garden party, and that I must remember it, hold on to it now, now, before it slipped away.

I had fetched my jacket from the house, and now I climbed the slope myself, but away from everyone else, on the far side, and leaned on a tree trunk and looked down over it all and was happy that they were there, and would talk on the way home about what pleasure they had had, remember it as a good day.

I went through the gate out of the darkening kitchen garden and up the nut walk. No one else was here now. I touched my hand to the slim trunks of the young trees, on either side, reached up and touched the cold, soft leaves overhead. I could not see through the arch at the end, it was too dark, and there was no moon, no stars, clouds had begun to come over, but I knew it was there and looked ahead to the open country and the distant silver spire and saw them in my mind. As I see them now, whenever I choose.

But at last, because I heard voices calling goodnight and the closing of a car door, I had to go back, and say goodbye and thank you, thank you for coming, yes, it's been lovely, hasn't it been a beautiful day, we've been so lucky, yes, they say the weather is going to break, we couldn't have picked a better day.

It was as the very last people were leaving that I saw the car come too fast, crazily down the drive, headlights glaring at us, so that the others had to swerve and brake to avoid a collision. Maxim started forward, but by then, they had driven away.

I knew who it was even before I saw his face, before he got out of the awful, battered, foreign-looking car. So it was to be this then; I did not yet understand quite how, I simply saw that she – or the two of them together, had arranged it this way.

'Bloody breakdown on the way,' Jack Favell said, standing swaying slightly in front of us, 'missed your party, blast you, Max, the whole idea was to queer your pitch at the party, plenty of people here, you see, plenty of witnesses. Bloody breakdown. Never mind, I've got the two of you, you're the most important aren't you?'

Maxim was a foot away from me. I reached out and touched his arm, but I could not look at him and he did not turn to me.

From the house, I heard the sound of Dora's voice, then the glasses being loaded on to a tray.

'Get out of here,' Maxim said. He had stepped forwards.

Favell looked bloated and dirty, in the lights from the house, his eyes went from Maxim to me and back, but he stood his ground, and began to reach in his pockets for cigarettes.

'You are not wanted here, we have nothing to say to one another. You are unwelcome. Get out.'

'Oh no. No, I'm going to come in Max, into your nice home, unless you want a scene in the drive that will bring out all the servants. Do you have servants? Run to those? I bet you do. You've feathered your nest all right, we always knew you would. I need a drink.'

I heard footsteps along the side of the house, and when I glanced round, saw Dora hesitating, uncertain whether to speak to me. 'It's all right,' I said to Maxim. 'I'll see to it. You'd better go in.'

Somehow or other, I dealt with things in the kitchen, spoke to them in what seemed a surprisingly normal voice. They were doing the last of the clearing up, in the garden Ned was stacking the tables, Dora and Gwen were washing glasses. Dora glanced at me once or twice. They were subdued, not singing and joking as I knew they had been. It must show on my face then.

'Leave it, Dora – do the rest in the morning.'

'I'll get things straight if it's all the same to you, Mrs de Winter. I like to see it clear.'

'All right.'

'I've left some soup and a plate of cold meats and there's potatoes in the oven, and fruit. Ned wants to get the chairs in, I know, they say the weather will break tonight.'

'Yes. Someone told me.'

'You go and sit down – it's taken it out of you, I can see that.'

No, I thought. Oh no. It isn't that. The party was happiness, the party didn't make me tired. I loved the party. 'Thank you Dora. You've been such a help – you've all been a wonderful help.' I found that when I said it, I was close to tears.

Then I heard raised voices. Maxim's. Favell's. Dora glanced at me.

'Thank you Dora,' I said. 'I'd better go and see if Maxim needs me.'

'Goodnight then, Mrs de Winter, we'll slip out when we're done and I'll be here first thing in the morning.'

I closed the kitchen door and the door from the hall into the passage. I didn't want them to hear.

They were standing in the drawing room. The windows were wide open on to the garden and I went across and closed them. A breeze had got up, and was blowing the curtains inwards.

Maxim had given Favell a tumbler of whisky but he had nothing himself.

'Maxim –'

'She'll tell you. Ask her, she won't lie to you. Not a liar, are you?' Favell leered at me. He looked worse than when I had seen him in the hotel, his collar was frayed and filthy, his hair greasy, flattened on to his head. The hand that held the whisky tumbler shook slightly. 'I was telling Max about our nice tea in London.'

Maxim did not look at me.

'Why have you come here?' I said. 'I told you – we don't have anything to say to you now – there is no reason why we should meet. I heard Maxim tell you to go. Please drink your whisky and do as he asks, please.'

'He told me to get out the last time. I remember that. I bet you do too.'

I did not answer. Neither of us did – we stood opposite Favell and yet we were not together, there were continents between us. I think Favell knew that.

'I've come with these.' I saw now that he had a thick envelope in his other hand. He waved it, flicked it insolently into my face. 'Evidence.'

'What on earth do you mean? What evidence? What about?'

'Don't give him a lead,' Maxim said curtly. 'Don't ask him. That's what he wants. He's drunk and deranged.'

Favell laughed, opening his mouth wide and showing broken, decayed teeth, a yellow furred tongue. It was the most unpleasant laugh I think I have ever heard, if I listen, I can hear it now. 'Danny told me about the party. House warming, meet the neighbours. Bloody breakdown. Not a patch on old Manderley here, come down a bit in the world haven't you? But nice enough, nice enough. You couldn't keep up a bloody palace like that now. Anyway, you needed Rebecca for that and she isn't here, is she, or there; we all know where she is.'

He flapped the envelope again. 'I haven't been idle. Nor has Danny, though she's gone a bit – ' he screwed a forefinger to his head and laughed again. 'Gone over the edge, I'd say. Can't blame her can you? It's all she lived for – Rebecca. She never cared that much for anyone or anything in her life – except Manderley, and that was because of her, that was the only reason. Nothing to do with you Max. She knows the truth. We all do. Plenty of us did. Well, of course we did, and you know we know it. But I've had to delve and burrow and ask questions, and get evidence very, very patiently these last few years. The war got in the way. But I knew I'd get there and I did and here I am.'

'Maxim –'

'He is bluffing and lying, he is drunk and crazy.' Maxim spoke very quietly, very calmly. 'He's done all this before. You remember it perfectly well.'

'You killed her.'

'When he finishes his drink he will leave.'

'You shot her, and I'm bloody going to see you hang for it. I've got evidence.'

He flapped the envelope again. 'You don't know what I've got here.'

'Maxim, take it from him, you don't know what he might have, you –'

'I have no intention of touching it or him.'

'We've worked bloody hard at this, Danny and I. She's on my side you know.'

'I doubt it.'

'I'll have some more of this.'

Maxim took two paces forward, and held out his hand. Favell gave him the tumbler, leering again. I wondered if Maxim was going to hit him, as he had the last time – I remembered the sickening sound of his fist cracking against Jack Favell's jaw. But he simply put the tumbler down on the tray and turned back. 'Get out, Favell. Get out now and don't dare to come back. If you do not go, I shall call the police and they will no doubt arrest you for being drunk in charge of a car. I suggest you park up somewhere for a few hours and sleep it off, or you'll kill someone.'

There was a single moment when everything was held still like a photograph. It was silent, too, except for a slight rattle of the windows in the rising wind.

I thought that Favell might laugh, or hit Maxim, or take some dreadful paper that told the truth out of the envelope, or even, as I saw his swerving, wild, bloodshot eyes look in my direction, make a lurch for me. I did not know, I felt sick and faint, but I would not faint, that was all I was sure of, I was never allowed that way out.

The photograph stayed, and we were frozen within it.

Then, without a word, as if he had collapsed somehow within, Favell swayed, turned and walked out of the drawing room. I expected threats, sneers, more ravings about evidence, but there were none.

I realise now that he knew, even in his muddled, blundering, crude state, knew quite surely that he had done the harm he had come here to do, caused the damage, set the final careering downhill cart in motion. He and Mrs Danvers – they were together, though only Favell was here now. They had planned it, it had all been started long ago. This was only the end. It had been easy, too.

We make our own destiny.

No one said anything else. Maxim went to the door. I stayed, I waited in the drawing room. There was nothing I could do.

I heard the starter grind. Grate. Go dead. Grind again, and then the wheels, the gravel, the slam of the gears. I hoped he would do what Maxim had said and park somewhere, to sleep. What happened to him did not matter but he must not harm anyone else. Anyone innocent. He had done enough harm to us.

I sat down suddenly in the chair beside the empty grate. I was shivering, it was cold in the room. The curtains shifted slightly in the wind that came through the gaps around the doors. The end of summer, I thought. There ought to be a fire. I could have brought in paper and sticks, there were a few dry logs in the shed, but I was too tired. I just went on sitting, leaning on my knees, staring into the black hole of the hearth.

I was frightened, I remember that, and now I realised that I had been frightened for a long time. I was weary of it, weary of everything. It seemed so long since I had had any rest that was without anxiety, untroubled by the whispering voices and the shadows.

And then Maxim came back. I heard the door close gently. I thought, perhaps he will kill me, too, and it will be the best thing, what I deserve, perhaps that is the way out.

I looked up at him then. He was very still, and the expression on his face was infinitely tired, infinitely tender, infinitely sad. I loved him in that moment in a way I think I had never done, not in the early, youthful days when love had made me hold my breath, nor in the desperate way when, during the last, worst days at Manderley, we had clung to one another in terror and relief. This love was whole and entire of itself, untainted, uncompromising, it was not a feeling, it was a state of being. I loved him absolutely and transcendentally, without dependence or even need.

But I did not speak or make any gesture towards him, I only looked, and loved, and then looked away.

He said, 'When did they begin?'

'They?'

'The secrets.'

I stumbled to find words and could not.

'With this?'

I saw that he had taken something from his pocket and was holding it out, to me.

'Yes, I suppose so. I'm not sure. Yes.'

The card was pale but it seemed to be burning in his hand.

'Where did it come from?'

'It was on a wreath. She sent it. She didn't say that she had, but I know. It was beautiful, perfect white flowers on dark green leaves, it was lying on the path beside Beatrice's grave when I went there early in the morning.'

'How did you know?'

'I didn't. I – I wanted to go to be there by myself quietly and I found it. She meant me to find it; or you. Either of us would have done.'

'Why didn't you tell me?'

'I didn't want you to be hurt. Maxim, you must believe that.'

'Hiding it – secrets – they are much more hurtful, when they are found out.'

'You might not have found out. I didn't mean you to.'

'You dropped it in the wardrobe,' he said. He went to the tray and poured himself whisky, offering the bottle to me, but I shook my head.

'All that time,' he said quietly, 'all those months.'

'Yes, I'm sorry.'

'I thought she was dead.'

'Yes.'

'And then?'

'I don't remember.'

'Favell?'

'I suppose so. Yes.'

'Was it true that you met him in London?'

357

'By chance. Maxim, you don't think I would have gone deliberately to see him.'

'I don't know. He might have been trying to get something out of you. Money – that's his line.'

'He did. But that was afterwards.'

'I wondered, you see. You never go to London. You hate London.'

'Yes.'

'Where were you?'

'Going to tea – in – in a hotel. It was so hot. He was – I think he is insane.'

'Yes.'

'He was in a telephone kiosk with a suitcase. I don't think he was making a call – he – he was raving down the receiver, but I don't think anyone was there. And I went past and he saw me and followed me. And I had to ring a shop – I'd left a parcel behind and – I suppose he overheard me giving this address.'

'But you never go to London. Why in heaven's name did you suddenly decide to go there? It isn't the way you behave.'

'I went to see a doctor,' I said miserably. And I heard the words and what they must mean to him, what they would remind him of and I could not look at him, only said, 'No – not – there is nothing wrong. There never was – it –'

'*What* doctor?'

'I so wanted to have a child. When we came here it was all I wanted – I needed to find out –'

'And did you?' I scarcely heard him.

'Yes – oh, yes – he said – we would – we could – he saw no reason why we would not.'

'And you could not even tell me that?'

'No – yes – Maxim I was going to, of course I was – as soon as I got home. I was practising what I would say – but then I met him – Favell.'

'And?'

'And I couldn't. It seemed to – spoil everything, and – I couldn't talk to you.'

'When did she come here?'

'After that. A few weeks ago.'

'A few weeks.'

'I'm sorry, I didn't want you to worry about what they might do.'

'What could they do? She's mad – they are both mad. Obsessed – crazy – jealous. Two sad, insane people. What possible harm can they do to us? Either of them?'

'There are things I can't tell you.'

'More secrets.'

'No, I won't hurt you.'

'You do.'

'She is evil, she hates you – us – she wants to hurt us. Both of us. It's twisted and warped and mad, yes – but she means it. They use each other – he wants – oh, I don't know – money, I suppose or revenge of a different kind.'

'Justice,' Maxim said.

I looked up in alarm. He had spoken so calmly. 'What do you mean?' I heard my own voice but it was not mine. I stared at him.

'I thought the one certain thing,' Maxim said now,

'through everything that happened and all the years since – the one certain thing was that we were together and that there were no secrets – nothing – nothing except love and trust between us. No deception, no anxiety, no fear – and so it was for me. I carried the knowledge that I was guilty of murder and had been reprieved – but you knew that.'

'It didn't matter – it has never mattered.'

'Hasn't it?'

I could not reply. I owed him the truth now, I thought, he had had so little of it lately. I remembered the voice whispering. That man is a murderer, that man shot his wife. He killed Rebecca. I looked at his hands now and loved them.

'It is all my fault,' I said, 'for wanting to come back. Beware of wanting anything too much, you may get it.'

'Yes.'

'But it's all right.' I stood up and went to stand in front of him. 'Favell has gone – she has gone – they can't hurt us. You said so. Maxim, it's all right. It means nothing. They can do us no harm.'

'They have.'

'It won't matter.'

'Is there anything else?'

'Else?'

'Any other secrets?'

I thought of the newspaper cuttings and the photographs in the brown envelopes upstairs in my writing case. 'No,' I said. 'No – no other secrets.'

He looked into my face. 'Why?' he asked then. 'Why? In God's name, why?'

I could not answer.

'We should never have come back. You are right, of course, as we should not have gone back to Manderley. And yet I knew that we would – we had to. There is no point in running away. They want – justice.'

'Revenge – wicked, pointless, cruel revenge. They are *mad*.'

'Yes, but it will still be justice.'

'Will be?'

'If I say nothing – do nothing – if we try to stay here, it will be like this forever. We may never get away. You will not trust me. You will go on being afraid of them and of me.'

'I'm not afraid of you.'

'No?'

I looked away.

'Thank you for that,' Maxim said.

'I love you,' I said. 'I love you. I love you.'

'Yes.'

'Maxim, it will be all right, please, *please*.' I took his hands then and held them, lifted them to my face. I saw him look at me, so full of gentleness and regret and pity and love.

'*Please*. They won't win, they can't – you must not let them win.'

'No,' he said gently, 'no, not them, they are incidental. It is her.'

I felt horribly still and cold, cold.

'What will you do?'

'I must tell the truth.'

'*No.*'

He did not answer, only let me hold his hands to my face.

The wind whipped suddenly hard against the window, rattling the panes, and I realised then that we had been hearing it for some time, getting stronger, whining in the dark empty chimney, blowing a thin draught at us under the door.

'I'm tired,' Maxim said. 'I'm so tired.'

'Yes.'

'You go up to bed. You were already worn out without all this.'

'Was I?'

'After the party.'

The party. I had forgotten. I wanted to smile. The party – it was a thousand years ago.

'What will you do?'

'Stay up a bit. There are some letters.'

'Maxim, are you very angry?'

'No,' he said wearily, 'no.' But he took his hands away from me, and moved back.

'I didn't want those secrets. They gave me no – no satisfaction, no pleasure.'

'I know.'

'I couldn't help it. One led to another, but I wanted to protect you – to keep things from hurting you.'

He bent and kissed me, very lightly and chastely, like a father kissing a child, and I could not make any move to draw him closer to me. Tomorrow, I thought. We are both tired, we don't know what we are doing or saying.

'Tomorrow.'

He looked at me. 'Go to bed now.'

Tomorrow, we would begin all over again. The secrets were over, there would be no more of them. And no fears, I told myself. No fears.

As I went towards the door, unsteady, dizzy, with exhaustion, I said suddenly, 'Will Frank leave Scotland and come here? Have they decided? Did he tell you?'

He paused, looking at me as if my voice came from far away and he had difficulty in focusing on what I said or even recalling who I was. Then he said, 'Oh – yes, yes, I think perhaps they may.'

Then it would be all right. That was my last thought, as I left the room. Frank would come and there would be a new beginning. It would be all right.

As I got ready for bed, I heard the storm rising, tossing the trees, rushing down the slopes and across the garden, to beat and beat at all the walls and doors of the house. But I pulled the covers high over my head and then there was only a sound like the sea, racing up the shingle and over me, pulling me back and down, down into itself.

All that night, I was tossed about by my dreams, and by the sound of the storm. Several times I struggled to the surface, and did not know whether I slept or woke, and each time, I was dragged under again. There was never wind like it, crashing through the trees, hurling itself again and again about the house, the whole world seemed to have gone mad and run loose, I heard myself call out to Maxim and thought that he replied quietly, soothing me, but then his voice seemed to be sucked into the eye of the storm and swirl about within it, receding further and further away. My dreams were dreadful, crazed, confused, full of whisperings and sudden wild gusts of wind, and moving, menacing shadows, but more than anything else, they were dreams in which my feelings were most vivid of all, fear and bewilderment, and a terrible hollow yearning, a searching after someone, something, and flying after my own voice which kept escaping from me as if it had a separate life. But then, there was only sinking down into a heavy, bottomless depth of sleep, where no sound or light could penetrate.

I woke in a panic, not only because of the ravenous, angry, tearing sound of the wind outside, but because of a dreadful sense of unease with myself. I switched on the lamp. Maxim's bed was in disarray, but it was empty, and the wardrobe door was hanging open.

In my sleep, in some place below my dreams, I had been talking to him, arguing passionately with him, and now, the same strength and anger I had felt at Mrs Danvers, was like the storm, battering at me, urgently, and I knew it would not let me rest until I had found him, said what I must, made him understand.

Ten years of guiding him, protecting him against the truth and the past, shielding him from reminders, preventing him from brooding, of deciding and building up my own frail confidence, ten years of growing up, seemed to have come to a head. I knew what I thought, could see sense from nonsense, I would fight for what we had achieved, how we had won. I knew what I wanted, what must be, I was not prepared to throw any of it away, or to let Maxim fly off on a whim, in confusion and distress.

I ran down through the house, pulling the belt of my dressing gown into a tight knot as I went, not stopping to put slippers on my feet. The wind kept dropping, and there would be a minute of absolute quiet, before it gathered its strength and hurled itself at the windows and around the chimneys again.

There was a line of light under the study door.

'Maxim.' He looked up. I saw that he had been writing something. 'Maxim, why are you dressed? Where are you going? You can't go out, it's the most terrible storm.'

'Go back to bed. I'm sorry I woke you, I didn't mean you to wake.' He spoke very gently again, with extreme care and concern.

'Maxim – I need to talk to you. There are things I have never said and I must say them.'

'It would be better not, don't you think?'

'Why? To create misunderstanding? What use is that?'

'There's no misunderstanding between us. None.'

'Yes. You haven't understood me. Maxim, we have everything here, we have come through to this.'

'Have we?'

'Yes, yes, I was right to come – you know it. Nothing can change that. Are you telling me you are afraid? Of what? I'm not afraid.'

'No,' he said. 'No, you're not are you? Not now. I see that.'

'And I'm not wrong. I won't be made to feel that coming back was foolish. I've watched you – I know. It is what was right for you – what you wanted.'

'Yes. Perhaps you're right.'

'You were tired and shocked and upset. You talked under strain – but you have nothing to fear, nothing to hide.'

'Yes I have. You know that I have.'

'What can they do?'

'I don't know, but they will do it. And I can't live with it – or live under that shadow, not any longer.'

'And I?'

'You?' He looked distant for a second, then he came to me, and touched my face gently.

'I think of you,' he said, 'believe me. All the time.'

'No, you don't, you can't.' But he did not reply, only made to go past me, out of the room. I went after him.

'Maxim, come upstairs and sleep. We can talk about it tomorrow, if we must.'

He did not seem to hurry and yet he moved quickly, walking across the hall, taking down his coat, picking up the keys to the car from their peg.

'Where are you going?'

But he would not answer. I ran and put myself between him and the door, and he stopped then and kissed me, as if he were leaving for an hour, and I took hold of his hand hard, but he was stronger than me, and had no trouble in pulling away.

When he opened the door, the wind raced into the hall like a demented, howling thing, I could not hear what Maxim said, if he did say anything. I wondered if he were planning to go to Frank, or to London – I could not think. The wind was driving any coherent thoughts from my head,

I wanted to slam the door and retreat, to protect myself from it.

'Maxim – Maxim, come back! Wait – wherever you are going, don't go now. Please wait!'

But he was walking very fast across the drive in the teeth of the wind, and it was pitch black, I could not see him. I tried to follow him but the wind was tearing at my hair and my clothes and I cut my feet on the gravel. The headlamps of the car went on, and then I did run, not caring about the storm, I ran almost into the path of the car but he swerved easily around me, I saw his face, set and white, staring ahead, and not looking, deliberately not looking at me, and then he had gone, out of sight up the slope and into the raging wind and rain and blackness.

When I returned to the house – because there was nothing else that I could do, I went at once to the telephone, although I knew that it was in the middle of the night – waking them did not matter, it would be what they would want. I did not think about it twice. I knew that he could not have thought for a moment of driving up to Scotland, but somehow, I believed he would contact Frank, somehow he might get there.

There was no sound. The lines were down in the storm, the telephone was dead.

After that, I could do nothing, only sit alone in dread, listening to the battering of the gale and the rending and crashing sounds as trees were uprooted and torn down. It was terrifying, and I dared not imagine what it would be like to drive the car through such a wind, could not let myself think of that. I prayed, desperate, bargaining, blackmailing prayers.

In the end, I went and lay on my bed, and heard the wind and begged for Maxim to be safe, as if willing it with all my new found confidence and strength.

I must have slept at last, more disturbed, haunted sleep, rent by dreams and terror and the sounds from outside.

I awoke to an unnaturally quiet morning. The light coming into the room was curiously pale. I went to the window and looked out, and saw a world washed clean and clear and a scene of devastation. The garden lay on its side. The slopes were strewn with branches and half trees where the storm had hurled them, and above the grassy bowl, there were jagged gaps, and daylight and sky where no sky had been before.

I went downstairs. Maxim was not back. I could see from the window that the car was still out of the garage. I tried the telephone again but it was still dead, and so because there was nothing else that I could do, I dressed quickly, and went outside, fearfully, to look at the damage the storm had done, and my fear about Maxim, and all the memories of the previous night stood a little way off, watching, waiting, and I was able to hold them there and not turn to them, simply because of the horror of what the wind had done. I picked my way over this or that uprooted, felled, broken thing, not touching, only looking, looking. I did not cry. Tears were poor, irrelevant things, no sort of a response to this.

I went into the kitchen garden. I thought that the walls would have sheltered it but the whole of the far one had fallen into a heap of rubble, so that the wind had been given a way in and roared about like an insane thing, tearing, uprooting, flinging about. The gate was off its hinges, I had to push and push to get through. And when I did, half stumbling over, I wished that I had not.

The nut walk had gone. Where the beautiful, slender young trees had arched up and over, where I had walked up to the view of the open countryside in the distance and the shining silver spire, was a tangled mess of broken branches and poor, pale, raw stumps.

I wept then, as I stood there, but they seemed pointless tears and were soon over.

It was quite cold. The sky was an even wash of grey, the light watery. My shoes were soaking wet and the hem of my coat clung to my legs.

And then fiercely, desperately, I wanted Maxim and nothing else. I could not bear to be alone here. I did not remember what we had last said to one another, how much misunderstanding there was between us. I knew that I had not explained everything properly, I had not made him understand why, why, the reasons for everything going back over this past year or even further. I had not said that I was sorry.

I half ran over the grass and up the terrace to the house. I must somehow try to find out where he had gone, and get him to come home.

But as I crossed the hall, I saw the door of the study standing open, and that there was a letter propped up on the inkstand. I went in. It was in a plain, white envelope, not addressed. But I knew that it was for me, and sat down on the chair, and opened it, and read what was there.

Though I knew. I had no need to read it. I knew what

had been in his mind and in his heart, what had come to obsess him, knew about his guilt and how he perceived the truth of it all to be.

We are not punished for our sins, we are punished by them. We cannot live with guilt for the whole of our lives.

And as I finished reading, I heard voices, Dora calling my name.

They had come to find out if we were all right, what damage there was, they were concerned. I wept then, at their kindness and gentleness, and in weeping, told them what I could about Maxim, and then it was all taken out of my hands, messages were sent, people came and went and after that, for hours, all I could do was wait, wait for news, and for the telephone to be repaired, as in the end it was, so that when it rang for me, I could answer it, and listen to what they were telling me, about Maxim.

CHAPTER

Twenty Two

He was almost there. They had found the car off the road, crushed against a tree, down on one of the narrow, twisting lanes not far from Manderley. I had driven along it myself the year before, we had both driven there so many times.

I did not want to go. I asked them to send for Frank Crawley. He was an old friend, I said, he would identify Maxim, surely, what difference would it make? But that could not be, they did not allow it. I was his next of kin. His wife. Mrs de Winter. I must go.

He was strangely undamaged, there seemed to be only some faint bruising on his forehead. I could not understand why he was dead.

But I do not think of that. I do not see him there. I see him in every other place we were together, driving up the road at Monte Carlo, striding down through the Happy Valley with Jasper jumping at his heels, standing beside me with his hands resting on the rail of the old steamer, as we sailed into Istanbul between the sunset and the crescent moon, looking down from the grassy slopes on to Cobbett's Brake, cupped below.

No, I do not see him there.

At first I did not want a funeral at all, not of any kind; but there has to be something, and others wanted it, Giles and Roger, Frank Crawley, old Colonel Julyan. But it must not be in the chapel at Kerrith, or even in the village church near Cobbett's Brake. I wanted none of that, I was surprised how determined I was; and that there should be no grave.

He should not be buried in the vault, beside her. I could not have borne that, and there was nowhere else, and so he would not be buried at all, there should be no body left to bury. What there was I would look after in another way.

We went to a small, bland, new place, twenty miles from where the car had run into the tree, and I had never seen it before, and would never see it again, it was too anonymous for me even to remember. That was why I chose it, with Frank to help me. He found it, he made the arrangements.

There were seven of us, and the clergyman, it was soon over. I had made quite sure that no one else should know about it. But afterwards, when the curtains had parted and closed again, and he had gone, and we were walking out into the grey, damp air that smelled of autumn and the sea, I saw a figure in an overcoat, tall, thin, vaguely familiar, but he turned away out of respect, and when I looked back again he had gone. It was only a long time later that Frank said that it had been young Robert, the footman from Manderley, who had heard some rumour, and come from Kerrith, where he lived still, but had only hovered, not liking to intrude.

Robert. I put his name aside somewhere in my mind, to think of him later. Remember.

There was nothing else, no tea, no gathering. She did not come. Nor Jack Favell. But I had known that they would not, there would have been no need, they had what they wanted. Revenge, I would have said. But Maxim called it justice.

There was only one thing left to do and that was for me alone. Frank, dear Frank was desperate with concern, he would have come, thought he should be there, for me and for himself. But when I insisted, he did not press, only understood.

A car I had hired took me there and I collected the wooden box which bore his name, and then we drove to the harbour, where the boat waited, and I saw that it belonged to Tabb's son, and although I had not wanted anyone I knew to be involved, I did not really know him, and somehow, it was right, and I was glad of him.

It was still damp and grey and misty. I felt the spray on my face as I stood in the boat and we crossed the bay, going towards the cove. The water was not rough. I suppose because he thought it was the right thing to do, he did not go fast, the motor was quiet, it seemed to take a long time. We said nothing at all to one another, until, suddenly, I saw the trees rearing up from the banks, the undergrowth climbing like a jungle, and beyond them, within them, completely hidden, whatever there was of Manderley.

'Here,' I said. 'Stop here.'

He switched off the boat's engine and then it was perfectly silent, except for the crying of the gulls. I saw the cove ahead, and the beach, but I did not want to go any nearer. I went to the side and waited a moment, and then I opened the small box, and overturned it gently, tipping its fine pale powder out, and as I did so, the ashes lifted, and blew away from me, carried towards Manderley with the salt wind from the sea.

THE MIST IN THE MIRROR

The tale that Sir James Monmouth has to tell is a strange and sinister one. On the surface he seems normal enough, but he is troubled by memories of a time, in the autumn of his fortieth year, when he returned to London from Penang. His first night back in England, a country he had not seen since the age of nine, was not auspicious. The Cross Keys Inn near the docks might provide shelter from the rain and the chill wind, but it offered few comforts to body or soul. The boy with the pale face . . . the old woman behind the curtain . . . the terrible scream . . . the mist in the mirror . . . did they have any reality beyond his fevered imagination?

'Not just a completely absorbing and thoroughly frightening read, but a tremendously intelligent one . . . With or without that leather armchair, this is a book well worth losing a foggy night's sleep over'

Literary Review

'Reader beware. When you turn the last page of Susan Hill's ghost story, you do not just close the book but emerge with an icy shiver from a Victorian age that seems for quite a few moments more real than the here and now . . . *The Mist in the Mirror* has all the ingredients of a classic ghost story'

Daily Mail

'Thoroughly frightening'

Daily Telegraph

AIR & ANGELS

Celibate, irreproachable and distinguished, Thomas Cavendish is in his mid-fifties and the obvious man to become Master of his college. But, walking by the river, Thomas sees a young girl standing on the bridge. It is an apocalyptic vision, one that alters Thomas's life irrevocably and tragically, but with the beauty and joy of a love never previously imagined.

'Subtle and profoundly moving, this novel is rich in the qualities for which Hill has won such high praise in the past. She returns to the eerie landscape of the East Anglian marshes, which was used to such magnificent effect in her classic ghost story *The Woman in Black* . . . One of our finest novelists'

Sunday Times

'It is a novel that Colette might have been proud to have written. It contains some of the most beautiful and evocative writing you could wish for . . . It is a novel to treasure. It has been worth waiting for'

Scotsman

'Susan Hill's first novel in sixteen years is as light as a feather but as powerful as flight'

Observer

THE WOMAN IN BLACK
A Ghost Story

Proud and solitary, Eel Marsh House surveys the windswept reaches of the salt marshes beyond Nine Lives Causeway. Arthur Kipps, summoned to attend a funeral, can have no inkling of the tragic secret it withholds – nor can he guess, until too late, the terrible purpose of the mysterious black-robed woman who haunts its shuttered rooms.

'Authentically chilling'

Sunday Times

'She writes with great power'

Daily Telegraph

'A rattling good yarn, the sort that chills the mind as well as the spine'

Guardian